THE SOUTHERN CROSS

PAMELA ZDENEK

Aboriginal, Torres Strait Islanders and Māori viewers are advised that this book may contain images of and/or references to deceased persons.

I wish to pay respect to the Aboriginal, Torres Strait Islander and Māori peoples of the Australian and New Zealand island nations. I acknowledge them as traditional custodians of Australia and New Zealand (Aotearoa) and surrounding islands, and they are admired for their continuing connection to the land, the sea, the culture, and the communities in which they have resided and continue to reside.

They have made important contributions culturally, spiritually, artistically and historically, and continue to do so in the societies of both countries. The continuance of educational efforts and community endeavors to recognize this key contribution is of critical importance to me.

Author's Note:

A historical fiction novel is often premised upon existing and past places, as well as actions during recognizable events in time. As with any historically-based novel, creative license is taken with businesses, places, and scenes in this book to convey their prominence during the war. Although many actual facts surrounding them are interwoven into the story and are intentional in this novel, references to historical events, real people or real places are used fictitiously.

For prominent historical and central figures during the war, the dialog and the scenes conveying their actions are purely fictional and intended for entertainment and loosely-based historical context only.

For characters who are not historical in base, any resemblance to actual persons, living or dead, is purely coincidental.

Any mistakes on the part of the author are mine alone to claim. Every effort has been made to accurately reflect actual battles, documented decisions, and historical events to the extent possible in creating this storyline.

Photo and Illustrative Credits:

Cover design, back cover schematics, and title page illustrations: GaryZDesign.com.

*The cover photo is of Hamilton Island, Queensland, Australia, by Pamela C. Zdenek

*First Nations acknowledgment page photo by jcomp@Freepik

the SOUTHERN CROSS

TRAGEDY, LOVE, AND TRIUMPH AMIDST THE WINDS OF WAR

Americans and Australians
Fight the Axis Powers
Down Under

My lovely family tree…

To my fantastic hubby Mark- *the inspiration behind the best parts of Sean, Patrick, and Tim*

The first love is always the deepest. You are the heart and soul of me— my partner and sidekick, my best friend, and my soulmate. Every dream I ever had became a reality because of you, including this novel. You are, and always will be the wind behind my sails on the open seas of life.

~

To Kathleen, Christopher, Meredith, and Michael

My incredible children… you have totally rocked my world since the day I first held each perfect, tiny offspring in my arms. You will never quite know how much you have given both of us in return for the small sacrifices we made to raise you in the best way we possibly knew how. My heart forever…
~ the "favorite" mom

~

To Emmett Stone and Ada Taylor

I cannot imagine <u>not</u> having my beautiful grandkids in my life. Every moment with you breathes new life into my soul, and you fill every room you enter with energy and joy! Unfaltering love always…
~ your very smitten Ami

~

Special thanks to Karen, Judy, Belinda, Mary, Diana, Jacky and Erica … My "Rocks" on both sides of the ocean
(in the order of when you first came into my life!)

and to John… the sibling with all the musical genius! My musical talents failed me… hence, I write!

TABLE OF CONTENTS

ABOUT THE AUTHOR

ACKNOWLEDGEMENTS

USS Decker, DE Evarts Class-dad's ship in WWII (US Navy Bureau of Ships photo)

"The first casualty when war comes is truth."
-Hiram Johnson; U.S. Senator; State of California: 1917—1945

The first soldier's death marks the place where war begins, but the first deaths are often not found on the battlefield. They are civilians caught up in the mire of human strife and angst created by the insatiable drive for man to conquer man; and, in some cases, by simple unfortunate casualties, for good to outlive evil. They are the unsung heroes.

This novel is a story of five young codebreakers, doctors, and spies whose lives were dramatically changed by war...

It is a coming-of-age tale of two sisters... their innocence swept away as they faced horrific tragedy, and rose to the call to serve their countries.

It is the heartfelt story of families separated forever by the unimaginable losses, and of those left behind to pick up the pieces of their shattered lives and learn to live again.

Red Beach: Leyte, Philippines ~24th Division Landing
Left Sector, 24th Infantry "Taro" Division…

THE
RETURN
OF
MacARTHUR

October 20, 1944
Leyte, Philippines

PROLOGUE

BOOTS OF OUR FATHERS' BLOOD

The ominous smoke suspending from the aftermath of the battles momentarily obscured critical landmarks from view. When a sudden shift of the wind rolled back the smoke, the shoreline was finally visible. With the ocean roiling from the landing craft activity, the skipper abruptly changed course and increased his speed to break through the turbid waters.

Inside the landing craft, Lt. Commander Kate Lawrence twisted her long blonde hair up into her combat helmet, fastening it tightly onto her head. She moved a pistol from her waistband to a shoulder holster, readying herself to exit the boat. At one time considered contraband for medical teams, if anyone disapproved, no one voiced any complaints about the weapon to her now. It was firmly ingrained into the navy medics that carrying a weapon voids their protection under the Geneva Convention, especially if they commit any acts outside of their humanitarian function. But this was war with the Japanese. If the Japanese could refuse to follow the protocols of the Geneva Convention, Kate could too.

At precisely 1330 hours, the Australian Coxswain made the foreboding announcement:

"Two minutes to landing. Just a reminder, mates! Assault landings began at 1000 hours. You should be safe from enemy fire by now, but be on the lookout for snipers. Good luck and Godspeed to the lot of you!"

After days of concerted efforts by the navy minesweepers to deactivate mines in Leyte Gulf, the assault teams prospered from the lessons learned during D-Day, over four months prior. The medical landings followed four hours of heavy bombardment from naval ships to the shore, and the first assault waves of the infantry. Luckily, on this day the 24th Division had been on the only landing sector to pick up enough enemy fire to force the diversion of subsequent landings. Unfortunately, that was Kate's division.

By the afternoon, enemy resistance was contained enough that the medical corps could revert to their initial landing zones. Kate looked across at the team as the landing craft slowed. Some were looking far out at the distant horizon. Others stared vacantly as they awaited their fate when the ramp opened. She met the glance of one young, frightened medic and noted for his benefit, "The beach is secure. We'll be looking for casualties that need medical attention. No worries, mate," using an Aussie phrase and a slight smile to break the tension.

The changing tidal currents had caused the vessel to veer farther left than intended. A sandbar 100 meters from the shoreline halted its path in several feet of water, forcing the occupants of this outermost vehicle to jump off the ramp and tread water toward the beach. Kate was the first to exit the landing craft, calling out as she jumped in the water, "Rucksacks up! Keep 'em dry!"

She sloshed through waist-deep water to the shoreline, the waves lapping gently at her feet as the last few yards were navigated to dry sand. Her fatigues soaked, she thought fleetingly about blisters forming soon with the waterlogged boots.

Flashes of hundreds of trench foot cases the young nurse had treated crossed her mind as she made her way across the long stretch of beach. *It's funny what thoughts enter your mind at a time like this*, Kate observed as she sank into the soft sand. Glancing to her right toward the curved shoreline, she saw that the nearest landing crafts were able to drop their occupants closer to the beach. They exited the prescribed way, by charging down the lowered ramp into a foot or so of water.

At least thirty crafts with medical provisions, corpsmen, and supplies were landing simultaneously with her division.

The *USS Nashville* was two miles offshore, carrying General Douglas MacArthur and his military entourage. Kate's team was given strict orders to ensure proper medical attention to casualties before General MacArthur's beach landing. The nearby temporary hospital was already under its planned construction, with equipment being unloaded onto the beach close to that site.

In due course, Kate and a command unit of medical officers were to supervise the installation of a permanent medical facility to support the allied troops. In the meantime, it would not do to have MacArthur and the media corps stepping amongst the blood and gore of any wounded or dead soldiers.

Having gained valuable insight from the landings in the Normandy Beaches, some 7,081 miles— and over 10,000 casualties away, the medical landing teams were now supplied with assault team support. Soldiers were moving across the dunes toward the interior, scouting for potential snipers.

The Red Cross brassard usually worn on Kate's left arm was gone. People identified as "medical support" were entitled to complete protection and deference, but the Japanese didn't see it that way. The corpsmen were targeted more than the soldiers, to break morale and cause chaos on the battlefields. In preparation for the Leyte invasion, such lessons from previous amphibious assaults were in full use now. As a part of MacArthur's elite Forward Medical Division, she knew that the most extensive naval engagement in history was already in play. Under Vice Admiral Thomas Kinkaid, the nearby 7th Fleet was preparing the line of battle, with the 3rd Fleet, under Admiral Bull Halsey, flanking the Allied battleships on two sides. U.S.-led and Australian-backed forces of over 200,000 personnel were assaulting the Japanese on the islands of Leyte and Samar, and fighting on toward Luzon.

The redeeming moment had finally arrived. MacArthur had triumphantly returned to the Philippines.

Kate's sharp eyes scanned the wide shoreline, noting a few patches of tall palms, and the tropical landscape just beyond the endless stretch of pristine white sand. Her blue eyes were tense and penetrating as she reached the dunes and searched beyond them for movement.

At 24, she was not the youngest of the military personnel on the beach. Still, she was the only female in the first wave of their forward medical positions. She was determined that her performance would not be distinguished by her age, her physical strength, or her sex. Kate had more experience in the jungles of the Philippines than almost all of the medical landing personnel combined. As such, she was more than qualified to lead this first team in the medical support patrols.

Beyond the beaches stood acres of lowland swamps, then vast expanses of dense, forested woods stretching for miles into the interior of the lush Leyte Valley. Sean was out there somewhere, she hoped in her path, where she could protect him— if her husband was still alive. This was one of the primary reasons she had insisted on landing with the advanced teams to set up field operations. MacArthur himself had granted her that request.

Notwithstanding the extensive experience from her hospital work in the Philippines, Kate's long connection with MacArthur had afforded her the honor of being one of the commanding medical officers on the beach. Some would call them privileged, witnessing the invasion firsthand. Some would call Kate foolhardy for requesting to lead them. She considered herself lucky to be among the selected medical elite.

As the teams scattered across the broad beach, she passed the second dunes cautiously, eyes searching for any sign of movement. She spotted a fallen soldier on a nearby dune about 50 yards to the left. He was moaning softly, and as she approached, she saw that his right leg was mangled. She knelt in the sand to assess his wounds. The combat boot that held the lower half of the leg steady was caked with dried blood from a wound still oozing from his knee and thigh.

She threw her medical rucksack down and reached for a pressure bandage to staunch the wound.

As she bent over the soldier, she remembered a censored military photo from World War 1— an empty boot filled with blood and gore. The ragged stump of a leg was standing upright in the boot. "Boots of our fathers, filled with the blood of war…" she recalled the stark caption.

Reaching into an interior pocket for a morphine syrette, Kate was again thankful for the meticulously organized medical supplies. In the days before the assault, she had conducted the training drills for the medical units. Each corpsman knew with precision where all critical medical provisions were packed, from the first-needed pressure bandage to the morphine vials, scalpels, and tourniquets.

Under the stress of a fast triage, the rucksack drills she had commanded with mock casualties would be valuable. Under any panic, such as bullets whizzing by, it would allow medics to work even when their minds were frozen with fear. Practice makes perfect. It also saves lives, as Kate had long discovered. She placed a tourniquet above the knee, calling for the stretcher-bearers again as she administered the morphine.

The young man had managed to pull out a photo, a cross, and a letter, whispering that he wanted them sent to his wife. Bending low, Kate responded with a slight smile, "You can give them to her yourself. You'll be just fine after we get you down to the medical tents." She patted his face soothingly as she spoke, looking directly into his eyes. "It was critical that the wounded see confidence in your face as you treat them…" That handy recitation came from a D-Day medic during her initial combat training.

The corpsmen arrived, and she settled the young man onto the stretcher board. Kate turned, moving well beyond the beach to manage treatment for two more wounded soldiers. She stepped over two dead Japanese as she swept further away from the landing zones.

"The first wave of hand-to-hand combat," she mumbled as she spotted two nearby dead marines. She moved toward them, noting names and wound details in her medical diary. She said a quick prayer over the fallen men. Kate's mind was focused, intent on her work. Her heart was another story. These were sons, perhaps even fathers and husbands. They deserved some form of peace where they fell— and died— for their country. She vowed to write to their families later that they had been given the utmost respect in their final repose.

As the corpsmen began moving around her, she turned to the lead medic and said, "Pass the word on to make sure your teams pick up all Japanese weaponry. We have a medical team studying advancements in their combat technology, for our surgical and wound techniques."

Standing under a palm for shade, Kate turned toward the vast jungle and stared out into the distance, wondering where the nearest enemy position was… wishing she could protect those now in harm's way as they advanced toward it. Her husband was among them.

Sean, where are you? Please, please God, be alive and safe.

From the far recesses of her mind, her thoughts flashed back to the years of code breaking with Sean in Australia, the months of tedious preparation with MacArthur for this key invasion, their long-ago, dangerous voyage from Corregidor, and last, back to the start of their lives together… their first propitious meeting in Maine..

USS *Squalus*
Photo courtesy of the Boston Public Library, Leslie Jones Collection

THE GATHERING STORM

May 1939
Kittery Point, Maine

CHAPTER ONE

THE SKY'S THE LIMIT

The two sisters pedaled their bikes down to Pepperrell Cove to watch the sunset. The late afternoon sun cast a radiant palette onto the shimmering waters of the quiet bay. Heading out onto a small dirt road toward their favorite viewing spot, the girls meandered down a path on the tiny peninsula to view the waning sun. There was a hint of the Maine spring chill remaining in the air, causing both to pull their sweaters out as they searched for a place to sit. It was their first day of summer freedom after their early graduation from high school. The elation over the occasion was in the air, and their spirits were high.

The twins were all but inseparable, and had been since birth. Katriana, or Kate as she was known since babyhood, was the youngest of the two by a scant 11 minutes. Tomboyish in nature, her long blonde hair was braided loosely down her back in an unceremonious fashion. Rolling up her jeans, Kate ventured to a nearby tidal pool to look for starfish. She balanced effortlessly on the slippery seaweed as her hand glanced across the chilly waters to stir up the sea creatures below the surface.

Kerri opted to stroll along the sandy cove, searching for sand dollars left behind by the waning tide. The wavy curls of her long mane were fastened into a loose chignon. Her cropped khakis matched her shirt and hair ties. Despite the differences in their attire and personalities, they were identical in every other manner. In the way peculiar to the strong bonds of twins, they could, and often did, finish each other's sentences, a trait they both enjoyed. As tiny girls, they even had their own language.

Settling a blanket on a smooth rock plateau, the two turned to watch the last of the sun's rays. Arms intertwined contentedly, Kate opened the conversation as she leaned against her sister's shoulder.

"So, sis, what shall we do with the rest of our lives?" she asked, as if the subject had never arisen between them.

"The sky's the limit, Kate! Knowing that Wellesley is on the table for both of us scholarship-wise, why don't we talk more about the career choices there?" Kerri offered. "I want to study minds. You want to study bodies. We'll both be healing people, and it doesn't get more noble than that. So how can we go wrong?"

"Unless mom and dad prefer to have us closer to home, career choices aside," Kate said somewhat impetuously. Kerri responded with, "Bates might be their only choice. It's their money…and Wellesley is expensive, even with scholarships. So, I guess it should be their decision."

"We'll see. They set the rules. But *we* made the grades they requested. We should have something to say about where we study!" Kate, the bolder of the two, indicated that she planned to make a strong appeal for Wellesley.

Silenced for the moment by the perfect sunset, they watched, mesmerized as the pinkish rays cast their light across the iridescent orange glow of the crystal waters. It was a magnificent evening sky, and each reflected upon their private thoughts at that moment.

With the sun settling below the rustic trees along the shoreline, they reluctantly packed up and started the bike trek home. A celebratory dinner would be waiting. Their parents, Cary and Catherine, were hosting this dinner along with their Aunt Maggie and Uncle Frank. The following day, the girls would head to Boothbay Harbor for their requisite month-long holiday with their maternal grandmother.

⸻ ele ⸻

THE DRIVE TO BOOTHBAY the next day was a pleasant one. Situated on a quiet cove on the innermost part of the harbor, the Girard family homestead was a spectacular cliffside mansion. Surrounded by tall, majestic trees and other expansive homes on the craggy bluffs, it was cool and inviting in the summer, and was afforded protection in the winter by the surrounding thick, impenetrable forest. The girls settled in, looking forward to their summer freedom. They cherished their time there.

The following sunrise found them sitting with their Grama Helene, enjoying the crisp air on the upstairs deck. The view from the third-floor balcony overlooked the entire harbor and town, heralding panoramic vistas of the tree-lined shores peculiar to Maine and the upper Northeast. The fragrant pink and white Summersweet Clethra bushes that bordered the home were just sprouting their leaves for the season. Their Grama's Pocahontas Lilacs from the greenhouse added to the pleasant aromas from the evergreens.

The sprawling house once held seven lively, rambunctious children. Several untimely deaths left Helene alone in the homestead, so she welcomed the arrival of the two vivacious granddaughters. The first of these family tragedies was the loss of a twin daughter Marie, who died at the age of eight during a typhoid outbreak in the winter of 1910. The three Girard sons— Henri, Samuel, and Michel— perished in the Second Battle of the Marne during the Great War. At dawn on a steamy summer morning, the Germans advanced across the Marne and overran their position. There were no survivors in their unit.

In 1926, when the youngest daughter Caroline died in childbirth at the age of 20, Marie's twin sister Maggie and her older sister Catherine were the only surviving offspring in the Girard family. The family seemed cursed with the ravages of the greatest tragedies of these times— war, disease, and the rudimentary rural childbirth practices of the day. Helene bore the pain of these losses with all the stoicism of a typical New Englander. She taught both girls much about showing dignity and fortitude in their sorrow… valuable lessons for both Kate and Kerri.

Years before his recent passing, their grandfather Jacques had constructed a large greenhouse and a glass apothecary and aromatic oils shop beside the home's ground floor. His furniture shop was on the top floor of the greenhouse. The front area was a storefront to sell healing salves and oils, aromatics, and cooking herbs. Kate spent much of her time apprenticing in the back of the shop during her summer visits. Kerri worked the storefront. Grama Helene's medicinal store was thus a small but lucrative family-owned business.

❧

INVITED TO SOME OF the late spring soirees in nearby Bowdoin College, the sisters were excited at the prospect of freedom from their required studies… eager for the relaxing summer days to begin. Nevertheless, Kate declined this first party, stating for Helene's benefit, "I'd love to take a drive and see the harbor lights. Besides, I'm looking forward to enjoying a good book that is not required reading." Kerri left soon after supper, buoyed by the prospect of far more stimulating socialization than their tiny hometown of Kittery Point could offer.

That evening, Kerri entered one of the campus fraternity houses with her chaperones, summer friends from her grandmother's community. Wearing a white satin cocktail dress cinched tightly at the waist, her cheeks were flushed with the excitement of her first college party. A tall young man chatting with friends near the fireplace turned to observe her as she walked into the room. His wavy blonde hair and expressive hazel eyes held her attention for a brief moment as she passed by. He stared as she joined a small group, mesmerized by her striking looks. Her dress was stylish, intricately tied with a white ribbon woven into the neck of a loose white chiffon overlay. Underneath the overlay was a tight, satin bodice. He noted the details because he could not stop staring at the slim young beauty. Timothy Custis Taylor IV worked his way across the crowded room. Using all of the charm and wit his handsome, 6'2" frame could muster, he introduced himself. Practiced at using these features to his advantage, Tim soon took over her group's conversation with polite but stimulating banter directed her way. He soon sensed that Kerri was intrigued by his obvious interest in her.

Studying her features as she chatted, he noted that there was a hint of ample cleavage under the satin curves. When his eyes moved swiftly upward, as polite young men are bred to do, the two eventually locked eyes. Kerri gave him an impish smile as he acknowledged one of her remarks on a political debate the group was engaged in discussing. He discovered throughout the evening that she was as well-read as he, if not better. But when he offered cautious innuendo while flirting, he found that certain banter designed to provoke the opportunity of a more private evening together went right over her head.

"Hmmm…beautiful, but inexperienced," he decided. He watched her cross the room to join in a fraternity game. She checked out nicely. Long, wavy blonde hair, gorgeous backside, soft curves… and he saw that other guys were watching these attributes as well. For the first time, Tim found himself wondering what it would be like to be with the same girl for a lifetime.

Sometime during the rush of the evening activities, they made their way to the back veranda to talk. After she capped one or two of his humorous remarks with a quick quip of her own, he decided this was a girl who would challenge him. There was a hint of fire and ice, and the thrill of a promising awakening.

The night was getting chilly. As Kerri placed a white cashmere sweater over her shoulders, Tim offered to assist. She started to thank him— face upturned to speak, and he moved in for a kiss. Startled, she hesitated as his hand moved to her neck, pulling her closer. His lips touched hers first softly, then more insistently.

Watching her innocent reaction, Tim smiled at the beautiful young girl before him. At the end of the evening, Kerri allowed him to walk her to her chaperone's house nearby. Smitten, the young man made it clear he was in her life to stay, one way or another. Their parents had never allowed Kate and Kerri to date during school, so this was a new state of affairs to navigate when the sisters left the bounds of a far more restrictive home environment. Their dating and social life were just beginning. And the future seemed refreshingly bright for the two Yeager sisters.

Photo Courtesy of Portsmouth Naval Shipyard Library

Portsmouth Naval Shipyard… Seavey's Island— Kittery, Maine

Bless those who serve beneath the deep,
Through lonely hours their vigil keep.
May peace their mission ever be,
Protect each one we ask of thee.
Bless those at home who wait and pray,
For their return by night or day.

(Submariner's verse of the Navy Hymn by Rev. Gale Williamson)

CHAPTER TWO

39 HOURS UNTIL DAWN

Submarine sea trials…May 23, 1939 ~ Isles of Shoals, Maine

Catherine Yeager turned onto the small bridge leading to Seavey's Island to report for work at her usual 0700 hours. The sun was already rising over the tree-lined, rocky shore as she headed across the bridge toward her destination: the offices of the Command Post of the Portsmouth Naval Shipyard. It was May 1939, and the signs of war were already ominous in Europe. The naval base was signing new construction contracts at a high rate. Thus, the work at PNS had taken on a new and critical pre-war role: the development of more modern class submarines, and the overhaul and repair of older ones.

In 1939, "The Yard," as the locals called it, was proudly hailed as the United States' shipbuilding leader in naval submarine design and technical maneuvering. Competing capably against three other immense U.S. naval shipyards, it also bested a competitive private contract sector as well.

Sitting at the mouth of the majestic Piscataqua River, the main building docks were protected against rough winter seas and gale-force Nor'easters by aligning the principal shipbuilding areas on the inside part of the harbor. There, they faced the tiny town of Kittery, Maine, and the larger one of Portsmouth, New Hampshire. Growing in size and in naval reputation, the base was the principal source of income for many locals. Fishing and scenic coast tourism employed much of the rest of the town. Thus, the bountiful North Atlantic— infinitely wild and untamable— nurtured all those invested in the lifeblood of its shores, as it had for centuries before.

Catherine was waved on by the guards at the gate. She pulled into the base and turned toward the naval headquarters. Twisting her light brown hair into her uniform cap, she parked and opened the car door, providing a brief glimpse of her long, slim legs as she exited.

At 41, Catherine worked in the highest-ranking civilian position in the Officers' Communication Quarters. With the advantage of two years of college, she performed as the superintendent of transport services for naval contractors. Her husband, Cary, was under contract to coordinate the dive team repairs for the submarine builds. In short, all underwater submarine inspections were in his purview.

It had been a productive month at the naval base. Two new Sargo class submarines, the *USS Sculpin* (SS-191) and the *USS Squalus* (SS-192) had just been commissioned at the shipyard this month. The *Sculpin* had completed her sea trials and was due to depart for her inaugural voyage near South America on May 23rd. The *Squalus* too was ready to set sail, once the last of 19 crash-dive tests was undertaken— a critical evasive wartime maneuver to submerge a submarine as quickly as possible in battle. This final exercise took her on that morning to the bone-chilling backwaters off the Isles of Shoals.

Catherine's job was to supervise radiomen and manage the security checkpoints for equipment and supplies entering the naval station. As part of that function, she also had access to radio dispatches during the testing phase of the submarine build outs. She was keenly interested in this particular dive test. Cary's diving team had performed the bulk of the underwater hull inspections for the two sister subs.

The rear compartments of the submarine housed the engines. On this cold, blustery morning, twenty-five submariners and a civilian from the naval base were in the aft area of the new sub, completing this test dive to ensure *Squalus*'s seaworthiness. Catherine listened to the radio chatter between *Squalus* and the surface command. Her boss, Commander James Keighen, left his desk to stand behind her.

"Plenty of chatter out there. Is the weather a problem today?" he asked.

Catherine responded, "Not too bad. These subs are always more unstable on the surface, and today we've got fairly gusty winds clashing with a rather nasty sea," she turned with a small smile.

"You know the Shoals, James. The seas today are more turbulent than usual, but the engineers said they'll be okay. They've got 18 good men in that engine room and Naquin is the best at keeping them on their toes," speaking of the captain fondly.

South and east of the base, aboard the *Squalus*, the men were scrambling to complete their surface maneuvers under the pressure of the massive waves. Once under the surface, the sub promised far calmer working conditions for the crew. The *Squalus* moved into position and the longitude and latitude were relayed back to PNS. At precisely 0840, Naquin gave the order to dive. The first klaxon sounded. Like clockwork, the hatch closed and the main ballast tanks were opened to the sea. All requisite vent and buoyancy tank checks were performed. Minutes later, the second klaxon sounded, and *Squalus* went into a steep dive…set to level off at a projected 60 feet. Just then, a slight agitation was felt in the forward compartments.

All of the equipment checklights registered green, failing to show that the main induction valve in the engine room still remained in the open position. This valve, which supplied air to the diesel engines on the surface, flooded the rear compartments instantly once she submerged below the 50-foot mark. Frantic voices from the engine room screamed out, "Take her up! Take her up!"

The desperate screams came across the Battle Phone. The seconds passed, with horrific cries of chaos as the water flooded the engine room compartments.

The *Squalus* pitched violently at a sharp angle, plunging rapidly to the seafloor in 243 feet of water, just off the tidal ledges of the Isles of Shoals. She settled on the bottom of the seafloor, first the stern and then her bow, at an 11-degree angle. The twenty-five men and lone civilian performing dive checks in the engine and aft torpedo rooms almost immediately drowned. Thirty-three other submariners in the stricken sub managed to find refuge in the forward torpedo compartment. There, the men faced the grim inevitability of death as oxygen began running out. Time suddenly became their greatest enemy.

When two hours passed without a "surface report" message, the base commanders knew something was amiss. The ominous dread deepened as the hours stretched further. The increasing concern caused the base to request that the *Squalus'* sister sub, the *Sculpin,* delay her departure to a patrol in the Panama Canal Zone. She initiated a search for any sign of the missing vessel from the original dive point. Through a stroke of sheer luck for the ill-fated crew, the submarine's communication marker buoy was discovered, and the two submarine commanders managed to convey that there were indeed survivors.

"*Squalus? Squalus?* This is the *USS Sculpin.* Do you read me? What is your condition?"

"Ollie Naquin here. Good to hear your voice!" came the voice from the commander. The sheer relief was palpable in his tone.

"Good to hear you, Ollie! How are you? How are the men?" came the welcome voice from the *Sculpin.*

"We're alive," Naquin called out to the sister sub. "We don't know what happened. We think the main induction valve failed to close – "

Then heavy seas cut the marker cables, and all communication was lost.

~ele~

PREPARATIONS FOR A rescue were mounted by the navy. The survivors of that fateful dive thus began the most terrifying night of their lives, with chlorine gas leaks adding to the ill effects and the fear after their tragic dive. By order of their commander, few words were spoken among the crew during that prolonged, horrific night. The precious air was needed for breathing.

The entire nation was soon gripped by the desperate plight of these men. Radio dispatches and telegraphs provided sensationalized reports worldwide. With modern telephonic speed and capability, people were soon glued to their radios. At dinner tables, fireplaces, and neighboring porches, America and parts of the world listened intently as the first dive bell rescue attempt in the history of submarine seafaring was planned.

The following morning, the rescue ship *USS Falcon* sped to the scene and began preparing to lower a new device called the Momsen-McCann Chamber- a modified diving bell rescue device. This dive bell had never been attempted at any depth except for practice runs around a shallow 20 feet. If the rescue succeeded, this would be the most incredible submarine rescue in history. If unsuccessful, the sensational news of the catastrophe would reach audiences worldwide. The Navy had no intention of failing. From Washington came the strict orders: this operation *must* succeed. The world was watching.

Catherine stayed throughout the exhausting night at the Comms center, knowing that her husband would be working with the navy to initiate the rescue. She heard Cary's authoritative voice over the radio:

"Water temperature is -30 C. Dive conditions are dangerous. No one knows if their oxygen levels will be enough to sustain the crew members during the rescue attempts. We need to move faster if this rescue is to be successful," Cary conveyed to the officers on the ship's bridge.

The fate of the submariners depended on the skill and courage of the rescue crews and the commanders who refused to give up on these valiant men. For 39 agonizing hours, with precious little oxygen, faltering lights, and frayed nerves, 33 men anxiously awaited their fates.

More familiar with the intricacies of diving the hazardous Isles of Shoals, the primary dive team was led by Catherine's husband Cary. A fearless Kittery Pointer who grew up diving off of the craggy rocks and harsh currents of the Maine Coast, locals at *The Yard* bragged that the 42-year-old man was far more at home under the water than above it. The toughest of a stalwart breed of Kittery men, he volunteered first, determined to see this rescue through successfully.

By noon on May 24th, the rescue chamber was painstakingly lowered by a wench and securely attached to the submarine hatch on the forward torpedo room, 240 feet below the surface. Both hatches opened without incident, and warm coffee and food were provided by the divers to hearten the spirits of the exhausted, strained men. Fresh air was blown into the sub, and the hatches closed once again. The first six survivors finally surfaced almost two hours later, cheered by everyone on board the *Falcon*. Each of the next painstaking trips evacuated nine other submariners.

On the fourth dive, Cary was required to take a break from the deep dives. Rotating the most experienced divers between his team and the *USS Falcon's*, he called out, "Badders and Mihalowski… take over the next dives!" At this time, the luck of the previously smooth rescue operations ran out. Cary's booming voice came across the airwaves as Catherine and James listened intently.

"The downhaul wire jammed at 150 feet. We need to dive down now to untangle it or cut it. Most likely, the latter!"

With the fate of the last eight survivors and the commander at hand, the divers entered the frigid, murky currents from the rescue vessel to cut the downhaul wire, which would, in turn, allow the chamber to admit water ballast to achieve negative buoyancy. The rescue chamber was hauled up by hand, under a slow ascent of four hours. In all, four rescue trips rescued thirty-three men, just as oxygen levels on the sub started to deteriorate drastically.

On his last rescue dive, Cary began to exhibit minor signs of decompression sickness. Waiving off his companions' concerns, he remained where he was, working with his team. The divers again made the last trip to the crippled sub, to determine if there were any survivors where the fatal valve malfunction occurred. They confirmed what was sadly suspected— and they began their slow ascent to the surface. When the team reached the naval base, Cary was dizzy and short of breath. The commander on board the *Falcon* ordered him to report to the base hospital for observation. Catherine was at her post when the news was radioed in about her husband's illness.

A cursory checkup from the medical team was all Cary would allow. He returned to the salvage site, acting as an advisor on the shoal currents and topographical concerns threatening to hamper the operation. Later that night, he began exhibiting further signs of illness. Catherine persisted and he was admitted to a hospital in Portsmouth, New Hampshire. With decompression sickness apparent, treatment was now critical.

Catherine stayed by his side for two days, requesting that their twin daughters in Boothbay not be notified unless necessary. At 2:15 am on the third day, his condition deteriorated rapidly and Cary went into full cardiac arrest. Half an hour later, despite the heroic efforts of the doctors, he was pronounced dead. His heart, strained by the exertions of the now-famous rescue and extensive dives, had failed him. Catherine rocked her husband of 21 years, whispering comforting words as he eased out of this world and into the next.

As the staff prepared the body for transport to a mortuary, the distraught widow left the hospital in no condition to drive, yet she had to be moving… anything to keep her heart from exploding from the pain of the loss. In this state of shock, she gave no thought to calling her sister to request help, or to drive her home.

As she weaved through the streets in the darkness of a moonless night under a dense fog, Catherine missed the fork at Pepperrell Road that marked the left veer onto the Haley turnoff. The car swerved and slammed into a corner pole signaling the curve, killing her instantly. Two vibrant lives were cut short in a scant one-hour period, and two teenage daughters were tragically orphaned.

IN THE AFTERMATH, their parents' funerals were a blur. In the first heartrending days of the long, difficult months that followed their deaths, Kerri and Kate clung to each other as ballasts in a sea of sorrow. The two were among the first of a great many American families who were catapulted by the tragedy of wartime accidents.

Like the millions already displaced worldwide, their lives would never be the same.

~ *the fate of the Squalus is set...*

The decision to raise and salvage the *Squalus* was made immediately by commanders at the Portsmouth base. The rescue operations soon morphed into an extensive salvage plan. Roosevelt himself was inherently interested in the process, and for reasons he knew would be apparent later, he was keen to establish a permanent salvage organization for the complex operation. This was an extraordinary procedure that would demonstrate to the world the U.S. Navy's expertise in submarine seamanship. And a feat of our engineering marvel and expertise, as well.

During the summer, Kate and Kerri remained in Boothbay under their grandmother's watchful eyes. The girls were as far away from the commotion and fanfare of the salvage operations as they could get. The naval base's recovery from the disaster was critical; the sensational news continued to grip the nation, and the small harbor towns of Kittery and Kittery Point. Uncle Frank relayed as many details to the young girls as he was allowed to reveal from his command post at PNS. It gave them both great comfort to know that the sub was to be raised and repaired.

From the sidelines of the White House, Roosevelt pronounced that the *Squalus* was to be the last submarine salvage maneuver before a naval command center could be formed for this task. His vision was to devise a program for sophisticated salvage technology. A massive and complex process, it had taken the entire summer to raise the stubborn hull of the stricken sub.

Upon return to Portsmouth, she was to be repaired and recommissioned, to be christened the *USS Sailfish*. President Roosevelt himself ostensibly proclaimed her new moniker after seeing photos of the first moments of the bow rushing to the surface, like a sailfish breaching the water.

Coincidentally, Catherine and Cary Yeager had honeymooned on a tiny yacht called the *Sailfish* 21 years earlier. To their twin daughters, it was a positive omen, especially with a christening by the likes of the President.

As the summer waned, the girls returned to Kittery, homesick for the beloved town that held cherished memories of their lives with their parents. Their aunt and uncle taxed themselves to the utmost to find some sense of normalcy as they all worked to heal their grieving hearts.

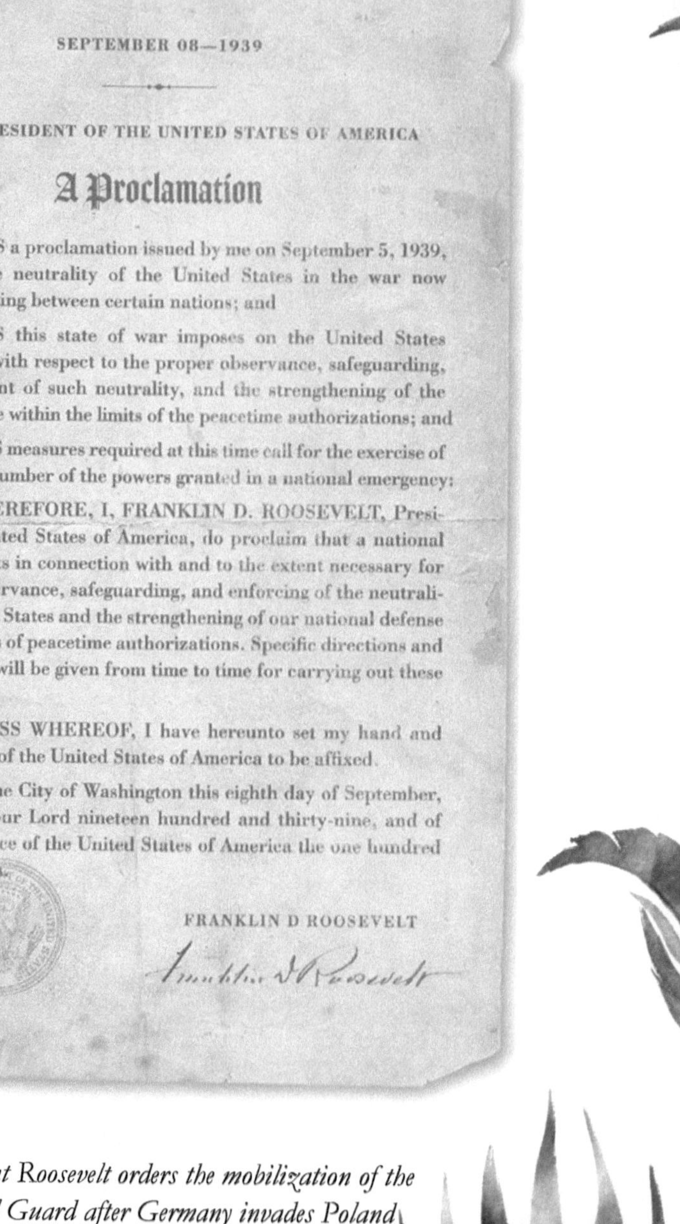

...President Roosevelt orders the mobilization of the National Guard after Germany invades Poland

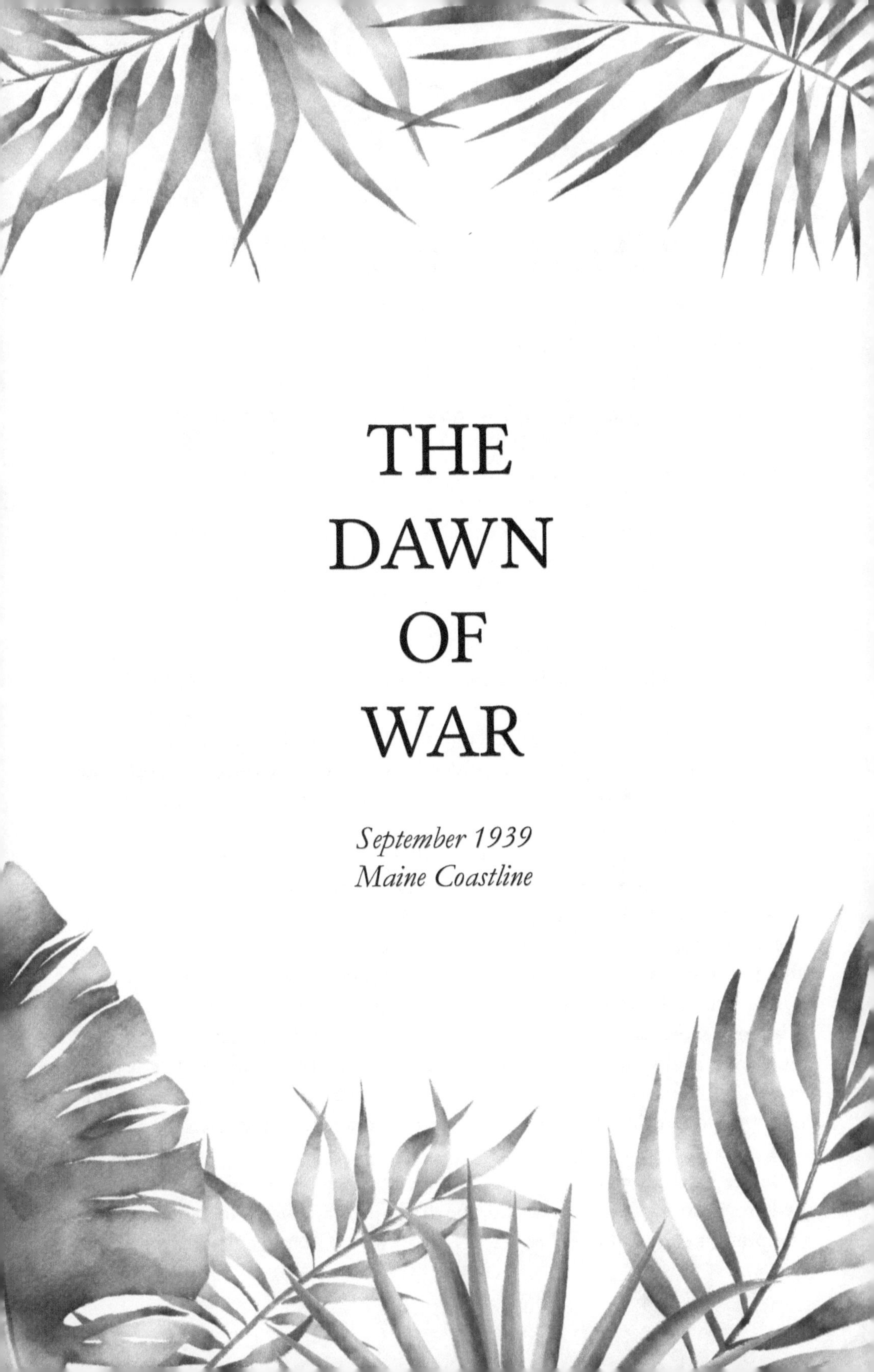

THE
DAWN
OF
WAR

September 1939
Maine Coastline

CHAPTER THREE

NEW BEGINNINGS

Portsmouth Naval Shipyard, Kittery Point, Maine September 15, 1939

The day dawned early on the eastern seaboard, with a heavy fog blanketing the horizon on this September morning. As was its usual fall pattern in this northern coastal town, dense, smoke-like tendrils crept over craggy hills and lush, green meadows. On this cool morning, they permeated the entire countryside and the quaint Maine harbors like a dark, symbolic shroud.

The twins awoke just before the light of the rising sun could brighten their room. They headed for the back door, passing by their parents' old bedroom where their Aunt Maggie now slept. They could hear no hint of stirring to indicate that their aunt was awake. Together they slipped out the back door and into the gloom. The trees near the driveway were still enveloped in an ominous nighttime veil of darkness, their trunks silhouetted only by a ray of soft moonlight that lit the path toward the side of the house.

The two mounted their bikes at the end of the drive. From there, they would take the winding road to Crockett Neck, then down to the second gate at the Portsmouth Naval Shipyard, over four miles away.

This unusually thick veil of impenetrable haze threatened any early morning outings planned by late season Kittery vacationers. The girls were used to it, though. Once the fog lifted, this route always heralded verdure coastal hills, with small streams and ponds marking their way along its narrow confines. Stone walls and split rail fences bounded most of the properties they passed, keeping farm animals, pets, and hapless kids from darting out onto the winding country road. During the daylight, the picturesque landscapes were marked by manicured lawns and homes.

Before dawn though, the girls had to watch for the oncoming headlights of any rare morning travelers along the foggy, dark-paved lane. Despite the omnipresent early fall cloud cover, the trip through this scenic area was most often their favorite part of the day. Against the backdrop of a rapidly brightening sky, the delicate flower beds and small family fruit orchards made an exquisite picture.

The guards at the naval gate knew them well. The two always stopped to provide them with bits of food from whatever they packed for breakfast from their aunt's bakery. After the death of both parents in May, the girls had become the unofficial adoptees of the naval base. They had the freedom to come and go on the tiny island, precisely as they pleased.

Today was an important day. It had been 113 arduous salvage days since the loss of the *Squalus* and 110 tragic days since the death of their parents. After months of mishaps, *Squalus* was returned to port. She was dry-docked, with the deceased submariners being respectfully removed throughout the previous night. The sub was under cover of tarps the day prior, to keep curious onlookers and reporters at bay during the macabre task.

Kate and Kerri pedaled toward the area where the work was being undertaken on the crippled sub. Once the first mournful death task was completed, they felt an inordinate sense of pride as they watched the colleagues of their parents initiate the tedious work on the overhaul. This held significant meaning to them. Their father had died after saving the lives of the survivors. Their mother was also a victim of the *Squalus* tragedy. The girls would forever be tied to this vessel.

There were some maritimers who felt that the submarine should have remained where it sank. Kate and Kerri were not of that mind. As long as the *Squalus* sailed, the girls felt their parents' deaths were not in vain. This gave them a considerable deal of comfort as they worked to heal from their grief.

The sisters parked their bikes close by, to take a better look at the sub without the protective cover of the massive canvas tarps. As they did, they noticed several officers occupying a small platform erected to oversee the work. They were used to the uniforms of the U.S. naval personnel. One uniform, though, had different markings from the others. The two with familiar U.S. naval insignias watched the girls approach, then immediately strode over to the young ladies. The third man stayed on the platform, turning to watch the conversation. Kate noted he had an air of command and confidence. For reasons she could not comprehend, she was compelled to observe him surreptitiously from the relative protection of the short distance, under cover of dark sunglasses.

As she was distracted, the two officers focused their conversation on Kerri, explaining politely that the girls did not have clearance to be there. Just as the sisters felt they were about to be chastised for their uninvited surveillance, the men were interrupted by a higher-ranking officer. Kate and Kerri recognized their mother's former boss, James Keighan. Hugging both girls affectionately, he turned to the two naval ensigns and stated that Kerri and Kate would remain there as his guests. His tone brooked no rebuttal, so the girls were somewhat hastily invited to join them on the reviewing stand. James climbed the platform and spoke a few words to the young officer in the unfamiliar uniform, who turned to study them again, with more intent this time. Chatting with Commander Keighan's two subordinates, Kerri did not catch the exchange. Kate did. She held her breath. For the life of her, she could not determine why she suddenly was anxious for this young man to take notice of her.

She smoothed the fitted orange shirt she wore, assuming an unconcerned pose that women instinctively manage when pretending not to notice they are being watched. Pulling out matching sandals from her tote bag, Kate put them on in a smooth, unpretentious manner. After a brief moment, the young man turned once more toward the sub. She relaxed, breathing a distinct sigh of relief.

The girls were beckoned onto chairs placed a few feet from the officers. The men were polite and conversational, but also intent on observing the work. The young man who had studied Kate had a different accent— somewhat clipped like the British locals, but with a vaguely unique twang. He was tall. Well over 6'3", he towered above Kate's height of 5'6". He was introduced by Commander Keighan as Lieutenant Sean Stuart-Lawrence, from Australia. As Sean turned to face them, Kate was taken aback, startled by a rare blue-green eye color that caught her attention. She was mesmerized by his intense gaze.

"G'day Miss Kate. Lovely to meet you," Sean smiled politely, offering a handshake, His smile showed a mix of kindness blended with an emotion she couldn't place. *Sympathy? Curiosity?* she wondered. His face was tanned. The high cheekbones gave his features a chiseled, intense look that might have been deemed harsh without the brilliant eyes. His smile displayed a mouth full of remarkably straight, white teeth.

A bit too handsome for his own good, Kate thought, somewhat grudgingly. He had an air about him that showed he was at ease around the opposite sex, but with no hint of cockiness in his demeanor. In fact, just the opposite. This conflicting air unconsciously repelled her at first— a protective action— then drew her toward him like a magnet. For the first time in her life the girl was compelled to know this intriguing man. Somewhat disconcerted by that reaction, she became aware that her long hair was windblown and unkempt, and to her, looking like she could not afford the luxury of a decent hairbrush. Thankfully, he was distracted from this unpardonable flaw by the introduction to Kerri, who had thought to put her hair up in a loose, twisted braid. It somehow looked effortlessly put together, like Kerri always did.

"It's a mite difficult to tell the two of you apart. Were it not for the differing hair, I'd be spending much of my time trying to figure it all out. Lovely to meet you, Miss Kerri," he responded with a slight bow of his head. His impeccable manners impressed Kerri. "If you'll pardon me, what part of Australia are you from, sir?" she asked.

"Southern Australia. Melbourne, specifically," Sean stated politely.

"Well, you have a lovely accent. I couldn't entirely place it!" Kerri responded.

She could tell he enjoyed the banter and appreciated the comment. "I'd say that's because my accent's muddled," he quipped. "Quite like my Aussie tan these days!" Laughing, he pulled up his sleeve to show the tan lines. "Raised in Australia, educated as a Brit. Half-breed. Half-accent. With some American colloquial phrases mixed in for good measure. I'd have a go at repairing those flaws, but it somehow gets attention from beautiful young ladies, so I don't rightly mind." The girls were charmed by the accent and Australian lingo.

Kerri, devoted to a serious romance with her boyfriend Tim, was not as entranced with him as Kate. She whispered to her twin, "Well, sister. He's all yours. Go for it!"

Kate sat down on the chair nearest him, fingering through her hair to restore some order. As he was intent on watching the work on the submarine hatch, she had an excellent opportunity to study him. The young Australian moved to the front rail. She studied his broad shoulders, which tapered down to a slim waist and hips. He pulled off his cap to wipe perspiration from his forehead, raking jet-black hair sideways. Picking up a pair of binoculars on the rail beside him, Sean honed in on the area of the sub near the hatch door. She had no idea what he might be searching for, but it was evident that *he* did.

"James, have a look at the white stress marks on the side of the hatch. Right. It's from being opened at the depth of 240 feet. You can see the indentations from where the Momsen was attached." Sean handed the binoculars to James, pulling out a set of plans that were rolled up on a nearby table.

Pointing to a particular layout with intricate drawings and labeling, he continued: "See right there. The hatch'll need to be double sealed, with a set of duplicate emergency indicator switches inside, one near the hatch, and one inside the engine room. All of the levers for the valves need to be separated further. They are too close together currently and in quick maneuvers mistakes are made. We'll have a go at the dive angles and the timing to see if anything else was amiss during the dive. It looks as if the bloody welding has held up well on the pressure hull."

Without a word, his long frame cleared the platform rail and he sprinted toward the side of the sub. Crossing a makeshift bridge from shore to sub, he climbed to the open hatch. Using a pocket knife, he scraped off some metal shavings where the hatch was welded. Observing them, he retraced his steps to the platform. He headed straight for a table behind his seat and turned to the plans, saying, "The British subs that are partially welded in that area are not as quick on the dive. Your fully-welded construction process improves the strength of the pressure hull. It also increases the diving depth and consumes less petrol."

Sean paged over to a close-up drawing of the same design. "Your precision on the construction is impressive. Even a one-inch deviation from cross-sectional roundness can give us an over 30 percent decrease in the hydrostatic load capacity. That can be disastrous on a sharp, evasive dive."

Turning to James, he stated, "This shipyard manages its construction jobs admirably. These are the improvements we're looking to see in order to pull off the depth dives in the waters near the Philippines. These subs are built for the Pacific, mate. That's where they should bloody well be deployed, too."

Kate remembered that their dad had told them that the new *S* class sub was indeed the best patrol sub for quick changes in direction and depth. They were also able to carry a heavy armament of long-range torpedoes. Kate was proud of her dad's dive work to inspect the subs.

"Direction change and fast dives," she interjected in Sean's direction. "That was the focus for these new builds. Our father managed much of the dive inspections on these sister subs. And my father also said they would perform better in warmer waters of the Pacific."

She was exceedingly glad her dad had taken her on dives to view the effects of stress tests. Her air of confidence in adding to the discussions was evident, and the Australian didn't seem to mind the interruption. He also appeared impressed that she was familiar with the "S" class subs.

Kerri exchanged looks with her sister, both pleasantly surprised when James agreed with the Australian and offered points of his own to the discussion.

After an hour, the girls reluctantly stood to leave. Kate and Sean exchanged a few words as Kerri removed a small cross from her pocket. In a wistful voice, she turned to him and said, "If you wouldn't mind, sir, could you find a way to place this inside the engine room when she sets sail again? It was our father's, and it would have great meaning to us to have it sail with her."

Sean smiled, saying, "I'll do better than that. When she's right to sail, you two can do the honors yourself." Kerri returned the smile as Kate watched the pleasant exchange.

Today was the girls' 19th birthday. Having planned a picnic, they had to end this addition to their usual morning routine. After a few minutes of final banter, they left for their planned birthday events.

CHAPTER FOUR

LIFE AFTER DEATH

Thankfully, the afternoon picnic and errands kept the girls gainfully occupied on this first birthday without their parents. Kerri focused on managing the upcoming weekend celebration and her planned activities after her boyfriend Tim's arrival. But for various reasons, Kate's thoughts remained fixated on Lieutenant Lawrence. When Tim arrived and the young couple left together for a scenic fall drive, Kate had a chance to speak with Uncle Frank alone about the Australian, whom Frank had met on several occasions.

"Sean has been here for about three weeks… flown in from England to help determine why *Squalus* was so damned stubborn about being raised from the ocean floor. He's about as smart as they come and apparently, even more likable than he is smart!" Uncle Frank offered.

"He's only about 24 or 25, if that. I led the interviews for his position and was more than a mite impressed with his credentials… a Master's degree in— I think it was marine engineering and naval architecture, and he has a double undergraduate in math and civil engineering. A dual citizen… British-educated for the upper education, but born and raised in Australia. He had been in London for months working on their submarine designs before heading here."

Uncle Frank continued, propping his tired feet up on a nearby footstool. "Sean is respected on both sides of the ocean. They're clamoring for him on both sides too. The navy officers here are damned impressed with the chap. He'll lead a charmed life, that one."

Frank paused once again to take a swig of hot tea, laced with his liquor of choice. Chewing on a warm chocolate cookie that Aunt Maggie baked for them on their return from Portsmouth, he teased, "So, little lady. Why the sudden interest in this young whippersnapper?" Her handsome uncle winked, staring at length into her expressive eyes to study her reaction.

"Well, they're using him to help with the design plans for *Squalus*. And I have a vested interest in wanting all of that to work."

An evasive answer, but solid enough to keep him from delving further into any ulterior motives on her part. Kate paused reflectively, then continued:

"Aside from you inviting him to dinner tomorrow night, which Kerri told me about, he has asked me to show him Nubble Light on Sunday. And maybe Ogunquit too. I asked him to tell me more about the design plans. Knowing his background will help keep the conversation running smoothly. "After all," she teased back, "by agreeing to be his guide for the day, I am acting as an ambassador for the U.S. Navy, you know. Don't want to disappoint our navy boys, Uncle."

"Be careful, please," her uncle responded. "He rented a place above the grocer's store near the shipyard entrance. He chose not to have a free place on the base. Some say that was so his visitors could come and go as they pleased. There may be few ladies in town clamoring to see the inside, and it might be for more than decorating tips." Uncle Frank offered suggestively.

"I might venture to say that was just idle gossip. Sean seems like a right nice chap. But I wouldn't want to take any chances with my darling niece."

Kate was still digesting his proffered advice as she climbed the stairs to her bedroom. "Well, Uncle Frank," she said out loud as she reached her room, "I have no decorating tips to offer him, and he can make his bed without me being there to offer advice." But for once, she was curious about what it would be like to see a man's bachelor apartment and learn how he lived without a woman's touch.

Her mom had always said, "The way a bachelor keeps house says a great deal about how he was raised."

For their 19th birthday party, Kerri's boyfriend Tim had taken time from his studies at Bowdoin to drive down and make the celebration as bright and cheery as possible. The young man looked forward to the weekend with much more anticipation than Kerri could know. He promptly charmed all of them by bringing champagne, flowers for both girls, and a bottle of wine for Maggie and Frank. He found that he and Kate got along well, once her protective eyes ensured that he kept his hands to himself while she was watching. The conversation at breakfast the next morning was entertaining, with Tim's easy humor and college stories adding to the tales of the twins in their younger days.

For Tim's entertainment, Aunt Maggie regaled them with the story of 13-year-old Kerri playing dress-up as a society belle. As Maggie explained, "the new local minister, Pastor Elroy, happened to be over with his wife Myrna for tea. Catherine and I had made painstaking efforts to make a nice spread to impress the minister and his wife. The idea was to keep them busy eating. They were a prudish sort and somewhat short on the virtues of humor, or stimulating conversation!"

As Uncle Frank offered for clarity, "They were short on humor, short on height, and long on everything else, including morality and rotundness," he added bluntly, receiving a frown from Maggie for his candid remarks. All three of the young folks laughed at his bluntness. Maggie continued, "At that point, we were discussing the church lecture and marquee for the next week:

You Can't Enter Heaven Unless Jesus Enters You!

Catherine was of the mind that the title needed a few strategic edits, as Cary had immediately found the title leaning toward a different tone than the good minister intended. We were getting nowhere on explaining why the church sign was all wrong when in the middle of this delicate discussion, Kerri made her appearance, waltzing grandly down the stairs, with red lipstick and rouge, and sporting flashy red heels like Dorothy on the Wizard of Oz!" Maggie said, laughing.

Uncle Frank interrupted, "Unfortunately for Catherine, the evening gown Kerri chose was a somewhat suggestive one purchased in a Boston wedding store on a dare from Cary. I might add that I recommended that Catherine take Maggie shopping there the following week," he winked over at Tim. Maggie said impishly, "My apologies, Tim. My husband is incorrigible at times!"

Tim replied, "He's quite entertaining! Something tells me Kerri and Kate were raised in an open-minded environment, so there's the promise of adding valuable humor to our relationship. I like that!" he offered playfully. Pouring some coffee, Maggie said, "At any rate, when Myrna's opinion slipped out regarding Catherine's wardrobe that young Kerri was modeling, I thought the second Great War was coming!" Maggie smiled ruefully at the memory of her sister Catherine's face at that moment. "Needless to say, Catherine and Maggie elected not to attend Myrna's free marriage seminars! And thank God for that!" Frank interjected, laughing.

As the conversation wound down, Kerri and Tim excused themselves to spend time alone. Driving along the charming coastal highway toward York Beach, they made their way to Cape Neddick. Tim produced a bottle of wine and two glasses to celebrate the pleasant early fall evening. There, sitting on a bench with the nearby picturesque Nubble Light as a scenic backdrop, he gave Kerri her birthday present. He went down on one knee and proposed, with a carefully rehearsed, somewhat shaky speech. He slipped a ring on Kerri's finger as he knelt before her.

"Since the day I met you, my plans for med school and a medical practice have all circled around you. We're all but inseparable now. I want us to be inseparable forever, Kerri. Will you marry me?"

Kerri accepted without hesitation, and they stood under the moonlight with the waves crashing onto the famous rocks behind them. Kerri's mauve silk dress billowed gently in the whipping winds, completing a propitious picture of a young couple in love. Onlookers smiled and a few tourists snapped photos, all of which were lost on the two lovers.

Eventually, they made their way back to the Yeager homestead to share the news. It was a shock to Kate, losing her most treasured family member to what would come in due time, but in this case, far too soon for her. With her parents not here to raise any objections, an early marriage was now in the plans.

Kate's tears of happiness for her sister were genuine as she joined in the champagne toasts. But the emptiness she felt marked the first estrangement of the bonds the twins had shared since babyhood. Their lives, she sensed, would never again be what they once were.

CHAPTER FIVE

LEARNING TO BREATHE AGAIN

The next morning, Kate awoke with a slight headache from the champagne celebration the night before.

She was somewhat subdued during the day after the events of the previous night, so orchestrating the evening dinner was a welcome distraction for her.

Sean arrived a few minutes before scheduled for their birthday celebration. Wearing a casual pair of dark slacks with a white shirt and a matching sports coat, he looked even more attractive than he did in his naval uniform. Tim had changed into khaki pants and a dinner jacket, with a black shirt that showed off a tan, lithe body from his sculling competitions.

The girls wore twin dresses of a deep blue hue. Most of their wardrobe was designed in duplicate by their mother but they rarely dressed alike. An accomplished seamstress, their mother insisted that her girls learn this skill, and they were grateful for the lessons now. Both wore pearls— gifts from their parents for their 18th birthday the year prior.

Their aunt and uncle outdid themselves with the traditional Maine seafood boil for the girls' first birthday without their parents. Uncle Frank initiated the story of Kate's first diving experience as he was passing around the steaming lobster and spiced vegetables. Both young men had their jackets off by now, relaxed in the casual atmosphere.

"Kate was just learning how to dive, so she and Cary moved away from a more crowded spot near the beach on Long Sands," Frank stated. "Her dad was already in the water preparing for them to make a shore walk into the ocean. Our stubborn little Kate wanted to dress in the car. Not a smart move, I'd say, with flippers on. As she shuffled over a dune she passed a little hut nearby, with nests built with twigs and mud scattered around the roof's surface. That was enough for her wise dad to note that it was a nesting ground and skirt the area. But Kate didn't hear his warning as she was working to put on her gear," Frank said, laughing.

"I did hear, Uncle Frank," Kate warned him, laughing herself. "I just didn't understand that I needed to be a half-mile away from their nesting spot!" she riposted. Sean laughed at her caustic retort, saying, "As my dad used to say, 'you never mess near a nest or the head of the roost will cook your goose!'"

They all enjoyed his Aussie humor and accent as Aunt Maggie interrupted Uncle Frank's narrative with, "Well, Kate certainly learned that lesson the hard way, Sean. She had on this garish-looking black and pink and green wetsuit that virtually glowed. As she passed the nesting ground, the birds attacked and her arms were flailing out against the frenzied mob. And those flippers! She couldn't run, so she was flapping around like some creature from outer space. People were watching her by now, and my protective sister Catherine was running at breakneck speed to save her little girl."

Uncle Frank picked up the story here, saying, "Anyhow, Cary arrives with a little starter pistol he carries for emergencies, firing it several times for good measure. He's having a little fun with this, we were guessing. Kate was carrying on, and the entire beach was watching this hilarious scene."

The exchange of laughter at the table was infectious. Winding Kerri's hair playfully, Tim asked where she was in all this commotion. Maggie responded, "Sitting calmly on the beach in her new blue bathing suit, reading a book. Paying absolutely no attention to the frantic scene!"

An observant Sean had noted the ring on Kerri's finger and asked politely, "How long have the two of you been engaged?" Tim and Kerri glanced at each other and answered simultaneously, "About 24 hours!" This segued into the sweet tale of the romantic proposal. As the conversation waned, Sean said goodnight, confirming a planned Sunday sightseeing trip with Kate.

THE FOLLOWING MORNING, Sean pulled into the driveway to pick Kate up for their outing. He wore khaki shorts and a casual blue and white pinstripe shirt that accentuated his lean body and his penetrating, sharp eyes. Today, they were a mesmerizing blue. To Kate, the piercing gaze was almost as though he could see through to the deepest part of her soul.

Kate wore a white shorts-skirt with a shoulderless blue top and elbow-length sleeves. A competent seamstress, she designed the flattering pattern herself. She had never been vain, but if there was anything to be especially proud of, it was her long, glossy curls and a toned, muscled backside, defined by years of swimming and biking. Her large blue eyes were highlighted that morning for the first time in her life. She had never worn makeup before, as her mother did not permit it. She was pleased when she noted that Sean's eyes skimmed over her figure as she turned in his direction. He loaded the picnic basket into the car and then opened the door to seat her. Retracing his steps to the front door, he shook hands with Maggie and Frank.

They headed up the coastal highway toward Ogunquit, making several stops at scenic points along the way, pausing to watch sailboats meander along the coastline. The Australian was impressed with the vast beauty of the rocky shoreline, and the imposing trees along the cliffs. They stopped at a nearby tidal pool to view the many vibrantly colored, delicate sea creatures scampering in between the rocks. Kate picked up an orange starfish to show him, and they both delighted in its slow, ticklish creep across her hands. Making their way around the slippery seaweed covering the rocks, Kate was proud of her ability to balance over the stones, straddling effortlessly between the pools of seawater.

The animated conversation continued, with Sean comparing some of the scenery to the coastal areas of Australia. He was captivated by the charming Maine coastline. They reached their destination in Ogunquit and headed up "Marginal Way" for their picnic. He located a shaded spot near some small cliffs and they sat down to watch the placid sea before them.

"I never tire of this type of scene," he said. "The ocean holds so many mysteries that I will never satisfy my desire to learn more about all the vast creatures in its depths. I reckon it's like the Outback in Australia."

Kate took a bite of her chicken salad sandwich and asked inquisitively, "What's it like living on the other side of the world, Sean?"

"What's it like eating all this amazing cooking all the time? Our fish and chips seem a mite plain in comparison," he retorted lightly, pointing at the mustard potato salad and a tangy cider vinegar slaw. His fingers dashed across the frosting on a chocolate cream cake that had been under protective cover from wayward flies. This drew a pretend grimace from her as she watched him destroy the painstaking decorations of her masterpiece. "I would *really* like to know what your country is like," she responded with more force.

He hesitated, looking silently out at the ocean. For a moment, they were both pensive as they watched the waves rolling their way in gently toward the shore, starting their journey inward from far out in the distant blue shimmering depths. She noticed an almost pained expression pass over his eyes for a second. *Homesickness?* she pondered.

"Well," Sean finally spoke in a softened tone, "Most everything is wild. And often dangerous. You learn to live with the danger and enjoy nature in its most untamable, awe-inspiring state. The tropics in the southern hemisphere are a vast mystery, holding all of their secrets, above and below the ocean, for literally centuries." He turned to look at Kate, drawing an encouraging smile from her as she listened, entranced by the vibrancy in his voice.

"For starters," he continued, "there is a rare blossom on an island off of New Caledonia where the bright yellow flowers turn a deep scarlet color after they fall and hit the ground. I call it color-morphing. It's absolutely stunning to see!" His face softened as he explained the vast beauty of the vibrant Australian flaming Poinciana trees and the exotic purple Jacarandas in their spring.

"And when one does a walkabout in the rainforests, it's a completely heady feeling. The cacophony of cicadas, the animal calls, the songbirds… they're like nothing I've bloody experienced in my life. You have vast canopies of tropical trees and the smell of the dampness, and creatures under almost every leaf."

Kate breathed in exhilaration of his words as Sean's descriptive narrative kept her captivated, wanting to hear more. "Go on," she requested with a smile.

"The trees there gnarl and twist and have life growing within the bellies of their trunks, like a mother with a new baby growing in her womb. It's amazing. And the mountain ranges— the brumbies, the koalas and the kangaroos. I can't begin to describe them. The people are marvelous too. Happiest I have ever known. You would love it there, Kate," he offered.

He hesitated, realizing that he felt he was droning on with his vivid descriptions. He turned to observe her reactions. Kate listened, absent-mindedly twisting her hair, as she often did when deep in thought. Absorbed in his words and saddened by the enormity of the distance between her home and his, she yearned to see these sights he spoke so fondly about. He described them well enough for her to find her mind right there with him.

"Such a beautiful home. Would you mind being my guide if I ever traveled there?" she asked as she reluctantly began packing up the picnic food.

"I'd be right honored to do so. And you must be our guest if you ever travel there. My mum and sisters would be so thrilled to have such a beautiful young lady visit us. Mum thinks I'm daft to be so focused on my work and career. Perhaps I am. Or…was," he chuckled, staring with bold intent at Kate. A tad disconcerted by the meaning behind that look, Kate changed the subject abruptly. "And your father?" She asked curiously. "What does he think about your work?"

Sean hesitated again, with a pang of sadness casting a pall on his former playfulness. "He died a few years ago. War wounds from the Great War. Shrapnel from the Battle of Gallipoli pained him so, and surgery just wasn't able to repair things as it does today. He was a talented man and a dedicated professor. He served as a military attaché in Japan when I was a young boy. During the Great War, he was an army liaison between the British and the Aussies. He performed his job extraordinarily well."

Sean became quiet once more and the silence was almost too painful to bear. Kate leaned over toward the chocolate cake, cutting a piece that was still decorated to display her talents as a baker. She was conscious that she had made an effort to impress him with her cooking. Noting her attempt to give him the side he hadn't destroyed, he promptly coated one finger with frosting, smearing it on her small, upturned nose. His eyes sparkled with mischief. Her eyes matched his look. She was on her knees in an instant and then sprung to her feet. To prevent her from gaining access to the cake to return the favor, he jumped up, captured her in his arms, and twirled her around, threatening to maneuver her closer to the imposing cliffs nearby. Her peal of laughter caused errant seagulls nearby to slow in their flight and peer at the couple as they fell to the ground, laughing. His lips brushed hers briefly as they untangled limbs and broke apart. She held her breath, knowing instinctively that he sensed this type of intimacy was new to her.

The moment passed, and Kate sat down again on the blanket, changing the subject to ask about his work at PNS. He began by mentioning that they were managing some torpedo studies to correct design defects.

"Why worry so much about torpedoes when we're not at war?" she asked. Sean backtracked, saying, "Well, *you're* not, but as of September 3rd, England and Australia *are*. At any rate, this is merely a protective measure to safeguard against any potential future enemy activity. Better to be prepared now than sorry later!" he added with a nonchalant air.

"And doesn't this sort of talk bore the feminine mind somewhat?" he teased. The quick flash in her eyes was challenging, showing considerable spirit on her part. "Don't you dare turn 'male chauvinist' on me, Sean Lawrence!" she retorted.

He smiled. "Wherever did you hear such a term? One of your feminist books, perhaps?" he asked, smiling. Once again, he noted that she was likely as well-read as he. His eyes were dancing as they studied her reaction to his comment.

"New York City. 1935. My mom took us to see a play called *Till the Day I Die*. I thought Lee J. Cobb was the handsomest man in the world, so I remember the play well!" She laughed as she detailed her mom's explanation of a 'male chauvinist.' She continued with, "Seriously, what sort of defects do you worry about? My father was involved in safety reviews, so I know a *little* something about this kind of work," she announced with confidence.

"Well, for starters, the primary torpedo in use is the Mark 14. They tend to run about three meters deeper than they should, so your aim is often off target from the start. The magnetic exploder sometimes misfires. We believe at least some of these misfires could be due to disturbances in the geomagnetic fields… like your Aurora Borealis. At any rate, they often tend to run in a circular spin. The idea is for them to straighten the run just before they hit their target. I've seen them return to the firing ship due to a failure on the gyro-angle setting. We are aiming to correct these errors."

He paused, wondering if this sort of conversation was heading down a path he didn't care to take at this point. A reminder of a vast European war he already knew was inevitable for many countries made him infinitely sad, so he abruptly changed the topic.

"Are we still heading to Nubble?" he asked, to break the small tension.

"Yes, of course," she answered. "But I'd love to know how you ended up in Kittery at this time, please." Her smile was both engaging and curious, so he obliged as they headed toward the parking lot.

"Well, it appears that your naval shipyard is years ahead of the game in submarine builds and design. Some brilliant strategist here in the upper echelons apparently decided decades ago that while other shipyards were cutting back on the experienced management teams, Portsmouth should retain its naval engineers and architects. So PNS upgraded its production capabilities in spades. I'm here to study torpedo designs and your firing techniques on the subs," he offered.

Packing up the car, Kate was thankful that she had listened to dinner conversations between her uncle and her dad many times. As they headed out to Nubble Light, Kate added her own knowledge to the discussion.

"Uncle Frank heads the Contracts Appropriations Committee. He's mentioned several times that there were numerous disarmament treaties—obviously a requirement of many countries after the Great War. So most naval budgets on other bases during the Depression curtailed submarine construction. But Uncle Frank opened up the review of the National Industrial Recovery Act. The NIRA kick-started a naval shipbuilding program here in 1933. Our navy yard has been setting records on our production for years."

"And how do you know so much about this, Kate?" Sean asked, curious about her sources on the information.

"Well, my mom secured a job for me in the naval base library. Our parents felt that Kerri and I needed some separation, so now I categorize the contract documents at the base. Kerri helps manage the bakery for our Aunt Maggie. The base pays me reasonably well and it gives me college credits. There are millions of government dollars at stake in these contracts, not to mention the jobs for half of the town."

Sean was impressed by her knowledge, but again recognized that much of their conversation would be deemed classified in the near future— the armament contracts in particular. Kate noted that his changing eyes were now intense, looking off into the distance again. She ached to know what he was thinking at that moment.

Noting the position of the afternoon sun, they decided to hasten the short drive toward the lighthouse and find a nearby dinner spot along the way.

CHAPTER SIX

THE FAULT IN OUR STARS

Kate directed Sean along the shore road to the lighthouse, stopping by to see the imposing Bald Head Cliffs and taking the picturesque, short York Cliffs walk. They explored for a while and then found a charming lobster house. Feasting on a delectable seafood salad, the two watched the rhythmic waves roll in from their vantage point at the sunny café. The conversation at dinner was light and airy. It was as if they had known each other for years.

As the last of the sun's rays were setting, they meandered onto the peninsula to the Cape Neddick area, known as Nubble Light to the locals. They parked and made their way out onto the rocks. The moon was rising over the water, and the sky was almost ethereal with its mystical deep blue color. She told him the history of this 1879 congressional icon, and he countered with some eerie folklore about the lighthouses on the Australian Southern Ocean. He had an intense interest in all things historical, like her.

Her eyes moved pensively toward the sky, remembering long evenings with her parents, enjoying the starry country nights on their little hill in the front yard. Kate spoke in a low tone, "Ever since I was a little girl, I always adored hearing my parents talk about the navigation principles with sailing."

She glanced over at him. Encouraged by his interested smile, she continued, "Our parents used to throw a blanket onto the lawn at night and teach us about the phenomenon of the Northern Lights, and of the constellations. I never grew tired of hearing them share the mythology behind the configurations and how they moved across the sky with the seasons. Did you know that at this moment, every single heavenly body is vertically positioned above a precise spot on this earth, like a beam of light?" She drew in the sand to demonstrate beside the rock they were perched on.

"So, if we could draw a straight line from the center of the planet, through us, to a spot on a star, we would be standing in the precise geographical position of that star. My dad had such a fascination with your constellations in the southern hemisphere that we cannot see here. I have always longed to view your brilliant 'Southern Cross.' One day I will."

"Then I shall have to take you there and be your guide. The Outback has the most brilliant sky in the universe— not to be outdone anywhere else in this world."

Standing there under the massive display of twinkling stars, they both looked upward. They relished the peace of the moment, with the waves breaking rhythmically against the protective rocks surrounding the lighthouse.

"The fault in our stars…" Sean said, his eyes still peering upward toward the night sky.

"Cassius and Brutus…" she countered, remembering a long-ago literature lecture at school. "And what does that saying mean to you, Sean?" she asked in a lilting tone.

"Well, it depends on your perspective, darling girl," pronouncing it 'daahling,' in true Aussie fashion. He moved behind her, leaning her back against him to ward off the chill of the night air. His tone was almost reverent.

"To me, Cassius is *saying* that it's not our actual fate that dooms men, but their own failings that make the mistakes that seal their doom." He glanced down at Kate as he spoke. "And you?" he asked curiously.

"Mine is a wee more sentimental than your definition, I would say," Kate observed. "The fault is not in our stars but in our hearts. We must endeavor deep in our souls to improve each day or we'll succumb to our own weaknesses.

And it takes someone with an eye for the good in our hearts to help us rise to that ever-infinite quest for improvement." "Are you always looking to improve daily, Kate?" he asked, with a wistful expression.

"Every— single— day." She responded with a smile. "I never want to forget what it's like to gain more insight into life," she said, almost in a whisper, as if afraid to reveal that there was much she didn't know that she felt he could teach her.

He turned her toward him and with one deliberate movement took her in his arms. *He must have read my mind,* Kate thought wildly. Lifting her chin up with two fingers, he responded with, "That's lovely, Kate. We Aussies love to teach. In that case, we'd make a wonderful pair, you and me."

With that, he bent down to find her soft, upturned lips and kissed her— a sweet, tender kiss. The giant passions… the surrounding awe and beauty of the iconic lighthouse, the waves splashing their foam up against the impermeable rocks, the perfect moment under the stars… for Kate, all of this came swirling down into the awakenings of first love.

It was a long moment before they parted. He drew away gradually and looked down at her upturned face. Her expressive eyes were a misty, penetrating, deep blue shade. She knew instinctively that he also felt the fire that moved in her veins. Kate inexplicably turned her head upward again to meet a second kiss. At the same time, an errant wave crashed nearby, spraying them with tendrils of white foam. It was followed by a giant wave of water that broke directly behind them. Both were soaked, and amused by the complete dousing of their passion.

"That would be my mom and dad," she offered jokingly. "They took their jobs as our protectorates seriously, as you can see," she said with a soft laugh. She worked to untangle one of the stray tendrils of her hair from a button on his shirt, realizing their bodies were still somewhat entwined together. Looking down at her wet, now clingy shirt, he said, "Let's get you home and dry Kate. Wouldn't want you catching cold and me missing any further tours of your imposing shoreline," he announced with a smile.

The drive home was quiet, but pleasantly so. Somehow the silence was natural, with occasional glances and a few comments about the night scenes along the way. He reached out to touch her hand, letting his hand rest gently on top of her petite, soft one. "Just checking to see if you are still cold," he said. Then he moved boldly to entwine their fingers together.

There they stayed, as if they had been intimate for months. His car pulled up to his apartment in town atop a small grocer's store near the base entrance. "Would you like to come up for a glass of wine? I don't bite, and I'm actually pretty harmless in such situations," he said, with a disarming smile.

"Yes, I think that's ok," she said, somewhat hesitant, but reluctant to end the evening. They climbed the enclosed stairs and walked into a neat room with enough decor to make it homey, but not so that she worried about that "feminine touch" Uncle Frank had mentioned.

"It was a fully furnished rental," he casually mentioned. "I'm paying dearly for it, but truth be told, there's no decent food on the base. We Aussies are used to having everything right and proper at our fingertips— the fruteria, the market, the bottle shop, a solid pub within walking distance— you name it! We're a fair bit spoiled, you might say," he laughed.

The table was clean, and a small lamp illuminated several drawings and scribbled notes. He added, "I admit it. I'm a confessed workaholic. I pretty much have no recognizable social life whatever," he added with a laugh. Satisfied that his reasons for taking the apartment weren't for the sheer enjoyment of the opposite sex, she smiled at the last vestige of fear about him being too social with the women in Kittery.

As Kate looked around, she realized that he did, indeed, appear to cook and enjoy the "fruits" of the nearby shops. There was a small curved bowl of fresh fruit arranged neatly on the kitchen counter. A frying pan on the drain next to the sink was clean and recently used. Baked croissants and muffins were sitting near a wine rack filled with four bottles of wine. Close by, a slender white vase held a solitary red rose.

Kate turned toward an open door, noting that it was his bedroom and the bed was unmade, but the comforter was spread neatly. A handmade quilt was folded across the foot of the bed. Seeing her interested look, he felt compelled to tell the story behind it.

"My charming mum and sisters made that doona for me. It has all manner of baby clothes I used to wear sewn into it. A sentimental lady, my mum. I'd not be surprised if my first nappy isn't lurking in there somewhere!" Kate laughed when he explained what a nappy was.

"About the rose," he said, noting the direction she was now staring toward. "It was my grandmother's birthday yesterday. She died last year. It's a fair tribute to have her favorite flower bloom nearby. She always said that life was meant to be like a perfect blossom that closes and fades with dignity along with the sunset. The good lady took her leave in the evening hours, just as the sun was dipping below the horizon. Quite apropos, that."

As if slightly embarrassed by this display of sentiment, he turned toward the wine and reached for two clean glasses, opening it for a generous pour. He headed into the bedroom to pull out a clean shirt to loan her while she was allowing her own shirt to dry. "You can remove anything else that needs drying as well." He continued as he left the room.

"Don't worry. I have four sisters. I have seen every feminine garment you could display. All part and parcel of being virtually surrounded by the female species." And there was the explanation for him being so comfortable with the opposite sex: a host of sisters.

Sean reached into his closet and grabbed a long heavier shirt for her use. "Here. Put this on, please, I won't have you catching a cold because you sat around in wet clothing." He walked to the small bathroom, allowing her to pass by and shut the door. She locked it, drawing a hearty laugh from him as he exited the room. "Force of habit!" she called out, somewhat ashamed about her action of locking him out.

"As I said. I won't bite, Kate," he retorted, amused at her overt platitudes. It was patently obvious that she *was*, indeed, nervous about being alone with him. She was certain he would shy away from her if he knew that she was inexperienced with men. The thought saddened her, thinking it too much of a challenge for him to attempt something more substantial than friendship with her.

The wine was sitting on a small coffee table and he, too, had changed into a clean shirt— one that fit his physique well. His loaned shirt was long, and the first button was so low that she was self-conscious about showing such cleavage. He walked back into the bathroom and returned with a safety pin for her use. "Ah… thoughtful, you!" she smiled pleasantly.

Leaning against the sofa on a soft rag rug, the conversation flowed smoothly. A second glass of wine was soon poured. Sean began to discuss the plans for *Squalus*, mentioning again that they would be shoring her up for trips to the far Pacific. Kate found herself fascinated with his expertise in naval warfare, and particularly, underwater battles.

He soon found himself stopping, recognizing that this conversation would again be deemed "classified" in the coming months. He knew without a doubt that Europe was a veritable tsunami thundering in toward a vulnerable American shoreline. Changing the subject abruptly, Sean faced her, asking in a compassionate tone if she minded discussing her parents. He knew much of the story, having learned it at the base. But he wanted to hear it from her.

At first, she recounted stories of her childhood, painting a picture of two adoring, but somewhat restrictive parents, and two willful, somewhat spoiled daughters, adding several funny anecdotes about their childhood mishaps. When she began reciting the events surrounding the loss of her parents, though, the effort became too painful to go further. The tears started flowing.

On instinct, he reached over and hugged her gently as she cried. Grateful for the comforting shoulder, she gained a measure of control. Sean looked down at her face, her dark lashes still spiked with tears. *God, she is so amazingly lovely*, he said to himself, kissing her forehead gently. It was a natural reaction—something he often did with his sisters. But Kate stood to find some emotional distance from their inevitable momentum toward intimacy.

She turned to reach out for her refilled glass. Unsteady from the rarely-imbibed alcohol, she slipped onto his lap, her hand falling onto his upper thigh. In her haste to right herself, the small safety pin popped. Gathering her shirt, and hopefully some of her dignity, she stood, wobbly under the unfamiliar effects of the wine.

Sean pulled himself up to help steady her balance. Her shirt was askew and his hand moved to her collar in a gallant effort to help hold the gaping garment together. But Kate was so taken aback that she struggled, causing his hand to slip precariously close to a full, naked breast. Pushing his hand away, she made a hasty exit for the door, toward the safety of the car.

Standing on the lower porch, her chest heaving from the exertion, she hesitated. "Take me home please!" Kate said emphatically. Sean searched her young face vainly for any relenting. Seeing none, he moved to the driver's seat. Turning toward her, he opened with, "Kate, I reckon you misunderstood-" She interrupted him in a forceful tone. "Just take me home please, Sean!"

It was an interminably long drive, with neither speaking after that exchange. When they arrived at her home, Kate exited the car quickly. At the front steps, she hesitated. With a sharp pang of regret, she stepped back toward the driveway, but the car was already in motion. *Had he noticed that she had turned back toward the car? And did he even care, or would he just seek a warm body from a nearby bar?*

She was still angry. But deep inside, her heart ached at what might have been the most perfect day of her life. She reached her room and undressed in silence, grateful that Kerri was still out with Tim. The tears flowed as Kate succumbed to a deep, sorrowful slumber.

Sean returned to the apartment. Pouring another glass of wine, he moved to the front window, watching the moon settle over the harbor as he recounted the eventful day.

Damn it. You took everything wrong, Kate!

He had blown a perfect chance to get to know her better.

He sat down at the kitchen table for a while, occupying himself with the sub plans, finishing the second bottle of wine. Sleep came at a high cost for him. Much later, he fell across his bed, exhausted. He would be nursing a massive headache in the morning.

CHAPTER SEVEN

MENDING SOULS

Kate slipped down the stairs the next day, thankful that her sister had already departed for a sunrise beach social with Tim. Noting her disheveled look and swollen face, Aunt Maggie poured two generous cups of coffee, set out some warm buttermilk biscuits, and sat down beside her niece.

Seeing Kate's downcast face after she relayed the last evening's events, Maggie opened with, "There was a time when I was going to break up with your uncle. He had an old flame, you see, and her brother was killed in a boating accident shortly after he and I started seeing each other. I was worried that the tragedy would bring them back together. And I felt ashamed of my reactions and tried to compensate by taking a casserole to the wake. As I drove up, out they walked— Frank and Louise…down the steps. I learned later that Louise had apparently turned her foot somehow. But all I saw was the two of them in a *mighty* close embrace! Well, I took off and wrote him a scathing note, which your wise mother promptly tore up. Catherine forced me to go and hear his side. I will never forget her words to me, and you shouldn't either:

'Communication between two lovers is as important to love as blood is to the body. Without it being in a constant, steady flow, that love, just as the body, will surely wither and die.'

Continuing, she added, "That was Catherine's personal pet phrase. It means, if we let wounds fester, it becomes more difficult by the day for us to forgive and forget."

Kate digested the proffered advice as Aunt Maggie continued.

"Never forget, there are two sides to every story. So go and hear his side."

Kate drove to the base, and seeking out Commander Keighan, casually asked where Sean was working that morning. Keighan responded with, "Sean has been sent to Washington. I'll let him know you came by, little missy." Her heart sank with the news. She found out from her uncle that Sean was flown abruptly to England. In the days following, he never contacted her to explain the quick departure, which only served to harden her heart against him. Her uncle staunchly defended Sean's top-secret work, and this heightened her awareness that their lives were moving in sharply different directions.

For the first time in her life, Kate hid her emotions from the keen eyes of her sister. The unspoken words between her and Sean lent a further shadow to the healing process. Everyone but Kerri assumed that she was adjusting to the loss of her twin to marriage. Kerri tried to gently pry the sorrow out of her, but Kate found that she could not talk with her soulmate about the handsome Australian. Explanations were impossible and denials even more frustrating for her, so she let them think as they pleased and her life gradually moved on. Both sisters soon found focus on the impending wedding plans.

A WEEK AFTER THE engagement, Kerri's fiancé Tim drove to Cumberland, Maine to visit his parents. He found a chilly reception from his mother, and a more congenial, but cautious one by his father. His parents had no intention of seeing their carefully-laid plans for him thwarted. An early marriage was not in the cards.

He walked onto the veranda, joining them in late night cocktails. Sitting in the large white leather chair near his father, he looked around at the well-placed crystal decanters and the expensive white damask sofa his mother was sitting on. *A sterile environment for sterile people*, he thought.

It was a stable marriage, but not an affectionate one by any means. His mother could manage a society gala of any size in their mansion. But her thoughts on love and life were a complete mystery to him, and to his father as well. She was that cold and reserved.

"Well, Tim. We knew you'd been spending a lot of time with this young lady, but we were unprepared for this sudden engagement," his father offered, in a carefully-initiated conversation. Usually congenial with his son, Custis Taylor was gearing up for an internal battle. His son could guess who instigated it.

Tim rushed in, "You needn't have been. As I have said, Kerri is the most incredible girl I have ever met. She is everything I ever imagined a wife could be, and I plan to have her by my side. That's all there is to it."

Hands locked behind his head casually, he deliberately adopted a semi-slouching position his mother detested. Her son was to be correctly postured, and adept at all the social graces at all times. Tim dared her to complain. Never one to kowtow, his mother upheld her disapproving tone.

"We thought that you were going to settle down *after* medical school. And now you've decided to orchestrate your entire life without asking us!" his mother observed.

"I am getting tired of how *you* are planning my life, including the likes of Kitty, the perfect, but infinitely boring 'girl next door'. The right girl for me, so you've said for years. I'm going to marry Kerri, and on my own time schedule. Not yours!" Tim faced them both with resolute determination, "These decisions are not yours to make!" he added in a deliberate tone.

"If you persist in making the wrong decisions, we can withdraw your funding for Harvard. At least until you come to your senses," his mother icily threatened. His father started to interrupt her, but Tim stood up, announcing his departure back to school in the morning. He slammed the French doors to the veranda, taking the stairs two steps at a time to his room. Soon after, he heard his father's footsteps on the landing near his door. *Right on schedule!* he thought bitterly.

Custis knocked and then entered, sitting down in a chair near Tim's study desk. Fiddling awkwardly with Tim's small human biology model, he said, "That was an unfair remark about Kitty. She is a charming young lady and her parents have always been so supportive of you."

"Dad, she can't put two words together in a sentence. Pretty, yes. But she's just another stiff, boring co-ed. We'd be 'Mr. and Mrs. Tweed suit and satin dress'. Antiseptic and sterile like you two, but perfect to outsiders looking in. Is *that* what you want for me?"

His father softened at the tone in his son's voice. *Another bitter remark*, he thought, *brought on by years of his mother's orders to escort Kitty to every society and college function*. In that moment he felt sorrow for his young son, working to gain a measure of control in his life. Susannah gave him little room to do so.

"OK, so let's be blunt here. Man to man. Is it about sex? Are you taking precautions to make sure you aren't getting bamboozled into a marriage?" his father asked cautiously. Tim stood quickly, hovering menacingly over his father. "Do not EVER discuss Kerri in that manner again, or you'll find my fist in your face, father!" using the stilted title to emphasize his anger. "She's not like that. She's guarded her virtue better than the Pope could. And I'm not pushing that aspect of our relationship. I respect her that much."

Tim softened his vitriolic tone, adding further words for his father to digest.

"She's an honors student and already has managed over a year of college credits. She plans on having a career herself. She is intelligent, well-bred, and we can talk for hours without ever stopping for breath. I have never felt so alive around any young woman. She's everything Kitty is not." He added in his most persuasive tone, "Let me manage my life. I do not want to be like you.

Or *her*," he said, pointing down to the veranda, where he knew his mother was waiting for his father to report the conversation.

His father stood to leave. Custis thought as he turned to look at his son's resolute face, *yes, he is a grown man now.*

And we no longer have any control over the way he manages his life. Surprisingly, he realized he felt an odd measure of respect for his tall, handsome son. *You'll have a much better marriage than me*, he thought bitterly, *without the requisite 'girl next door' that I ended up marrying.*

Custis watched Tim leave the next morning, wondering what this new rebellion would do to the family. A week later, the first salvo was fired by the son, now accepted by Harvard Medical School. Tim used the leverage of *their* notable future as the parents of a prestigious heart surgeon, knowing damn well that they would never withdraw his funds.

Kerri was still reeling in the sorrow of her parent's deaths, and her intuitive fiancé perceived that his father would be sympathetic to her parentless plight. So, Tim set the wedding date for Christmas, after his graduation. His mother, he found, surprisingly enjoyed the notoriety of Tim being engaged to the daughter of a hero of the *Squalus* tragedy. A young man to take advantage of all propitious situations, he formally announced the wedding in the Cumberland Society page. He decisively won the battle and started a war with his mother in the process.

❧

SEVERAL DAYS AFTER the wedding plans were set, Kate entered her room to find Kerri sitting in front of the vanity, absently brushing the soft blonde curls of her long hair. Kate sat on the bed, sensing that one of their sister talks was needed. Kerri turned and smiled at her twin, and the myriad shades of her own large blue eyes stared back at her. Sorrow still lent a mournful, expressive look to Kate's thin face, and the smile Kerri directed at her twin was forced. The strain of missing their parents was still obvious on both.

Kerri opened the conversation, her soft voice quivering slightly with the emotion of the words. "Today is… *was* their anniversary. It's hard not to reflect on how our lives would be if they were still here. They both wanted us to be educated. Mom was determined for us to have career opportunities. We've always known we didn't have much choice in that. Those plans aren't working for me now, though. No judging. Just listen, please."

She paused, expecting comments from her sister. When no words came, she continued:

"When we were little, you were the independent one, going with dad on his dive trips. I was the one who wanted to cook and sew with mom! They encouraged us to be different and made it *easy* to be so. And we're going in such different directions right now." Kerri bit her lip pensively as she continued. "I feel so motherless right now. And I just want to be loved. I know you're hurting now with the wedding coming up. And I don't know how to help you work this out."

Kate stood, moving around the bedroom, tidying up as her mother used to do. The familiarity of these gestures comforted them both.

Kerri continued the discussion.

"Kate, mom and dad didn't have to work hard at loving each other, so they had time to focus on loving us. I want what they had… the measure of respect, and the family unit they nurtured together… *that* will help to make me whole again. And I am often so empty now my heart aches. So, I'm letting Tim set the fast pace he wants for our future together. I need to know your thoughts about the separation," Kerri searched her twin's eyes for the answer.

Kate turned thoughtfully to her sister. "Let's go down and talk to Aunt Maggie as we used to do with mom. She'll be able to talk us through all of this."

Sensing that their morning routine had been longer than usual, Aunt Maggie set a pleasant breakfast table of fresh lemon scones and crème puffs. All three sat down, and Maggie let the girls talk freely about their future plans. She missed little, from the strength in Kate's voice about her desire for a college career, to Kerri's sadness as she determined that for her, moving on meant expediting part of her life that included marriage and all that entailed.

"Life moves on when such tragedies occur, as it must. But thankfully, the love travels with us wherever we go, so that love is never lost. It's forever tucked away in a special corner of our hearts."

Maggie let the words sink in.

"You both graduated with honors… co-valedictorians of your class, which I have to say is much your parents' doing. There were times when your uncle and I disagreed with the strict discipline on the studies, the piano and sewing lessons, and summer college classes. But all of that now is a solid foundation your parents gave to you — one that none of us expected you would need at this early point in your lives."

"Kerri, you want to see where your life will go with Tim in the picture. Marriage will be a healing factor for you. I approve, as long as you remember your educational goals in the process." She added further advice. "This will sound harsh, but I advise you *both* to always have an income, or at least the *ability* to have a solid income. You should be able to earn enough to be confident in telling your husbands to go straight to hell if need be. It puts the marriage on level ground!"

Both girls laughed at the statement. Aunt Maggie stated further, "That is the ONLY true ambition Catherine and Cary had for both of you: a college education, and an income safety net. It is my wish now, as well!"

She moved to the windowsill to water plants as she spoke. "Kate, you are ambitious and driven. As a young girl you had trouble focusing, but that is an asset now. Your mind wanders in many exciting directions! Let's see where all of this takes you. Sound like a decent plan?" Aunt Maggie asked. The twins both agreed on these goals.

Kerri made a permanent move to Boothbay to be closer to Tim for the wedding planning. Kate stayed for a short stint in Kittery to help her aunt with expansion plans for the family bakery. The Yeager home was sold to Aunt Maggie and Uncle Frank, to be willed back to the girls later. Soon after, Kate moved north as well, and began apprenticing in earnest at Helene's Apothecary Shoppe in Boothbay. Once again, she found herself completely immersed in her studies, learning medicinal herbal remedies, therapeutic healing oils, and the science of nature's best curatives.

Thanksgiving rolled around. Tim spent the long weekend in Kittery with them, and the mood was convivial, with the celebrants enjoying the champagne that he brought for the occasion.

Kate decided to help her aunt and uncle with the bakery's Thanksgiving preparation. It was a longtime tradition at the café to serve a festive meal for the naval personnel away from home. As she headed for bed, Kate gave her sister's future husband a look that said, "Be careful with my precious sister, big guy. I'm watching you."

CHAPTER EIGHT

AWAKENINGS

Sleep was elusive for both Tim and Kerri that night. Kerri sat on the window seat in her room, watching the moon rise gradually across the night sky. This was a view she would miss… one that heralded many childhood memories of her parents. She watched the night shadows play against the gnarled branches of the trees and onto the ground below, thinking of the plans Cary and Catherine had made for their daughters. Their untimely loss had accelerated her own rise to adulthood— to marriage, and to a family life of her own.

Sometime after 4 am, the front door opened and shut. Kate was leaving for her work at the café. As if compelled inexorably by some force, Tim rose from his bed, crossed the room, and slipped down the dark hall toward Kerri's room. He opened the door, thinking to just take a quick look at the sleeping girl who would soon become his wife. As the door opened, Kerri turned, half-expectantly waiting for him to join her. She was bathed in the moonlight from the window, in a sheer peach silk gown. Her face was pensive, lost in some emotion he couldn't quite capture. She turned her head back toward the window.

Tim stood still, studying her profile. After a minute, he crossed the room. The light from the moon cast its rays on a small upturned nose, a smooth, creamy complexion, and long lashes lining her expressive eyes. He reached the window seat and lifted her into his arms, moving her onto the bed. She was somewhat shaky, but offered no resistance.

The attraction between them was at full peak, and Kerri's inexperience was no contest against the awakening urges of her young body. She melted under the same sensual kisses he had offered so expectantly many times before. This time, there was no holding back.

Watching his eyes but offering no resistance, Kerri's heart was beating so quickly that she was afraid of passing out. "I love you so much, Tim. These emotions— they're— well it's like my body is betraying everything I have been taught to repress. I can't think— I can't breathe… but I know I want to be in your arms."

Tim smiled. "That's natural. You're looking at millions of years of pure evolution. There's a whole lot of puritanical B.S. out there, and it's crammed down the throats of nice girls like you!"

He kissed her tenderly on the forehead, saying, "And honey, I know plenty of couples who didn't wait. But again, it's up to you. I'll respect you and love you, either way. If you tell me to stop, I will. I promise. But I'm confident that at some point, once you get adjusted, you'll likely want it far more than me!"

"Hmmm… so that's what's supposed to happen?" He watched as she smiled up at him impishly. She was loosening up with the added confidence of his assurances. Her head leaned a little against his chest and he softly caressed her hair, massaging her tense shoulders. His hands moved smoothly down her arms, then easing around her waist and traveling upward. He touched one breast, and she caught her breath, hesitating for just a second.

Cupping it gently, he tipped her head toward him for a slow kiss. The gown she wore was tied loosely at one shoulder, with her long curling mass of blonde hair flowing down the other shoulder. He untied the gown, letting it fall to her waist. Turning, he laid her onto the bed, removing the rest of the gown as well. His robe followed the gown, and he was completely naked underneath.

Tim braced himself above her. One hand moved against the curves of her body, at first gently, then more insistently, as he let the sensations build between them.

She closed her eyes as each experience made her aware that her body was reacting in every way he had said she would. Tim focused on her expressions, watching her respond. Opening her eyes and breathing evenly, she let him explore. Even if she had wanted to, she couldn't stop the incredible wave of arousal.

His hands moved up again to trace the crest between her breasts. "You ok, honey?" he asked, his voice strained by the deliberate physical restraint.

"Yes," she whispered, with a surprising measure of confidence. She sighed, enjoying his sure knowledge of her own body. Her lips parted, and her mind whirled as she felt an incredible urge deep inside that was completely foreign. The magic of this intensity was blissful.

He kissed her, moving down her throat, between her breasts and all the way down to her navel, then inching back up. She was breathless, her cheeks flushed with the raw sensuality of his tongue. She felt herself responding, letting herself go as she relaxed further, reacting instinctively to his lovemaking. His hand guided her to explore him.

He touched her again, letting his fingers ensure she was ready. Sensing that the moment was right, he moved between her thighs. Poised above her, his heart beating insistently against his chest, he entered her, shifting against the slight resistance and working to keep his full passion at bay. She cried out in pain, and he stopped for a moment, allowing her time to adjust to the foreign intrusion. After a brief time, he began moving again, this time more urgently, kissing her as he gradually penetrated deeper. To Kerri, the budding sensations were incredible. The quicksilver pain hit sharply and then faded away somewhat. The buildup between them became more intense as he moved against her, and for Tim, the wave of languid pleasure was dizzying in its intensity. Moments later, he collapsed against her smooth, supple body, fully satiated. After a minute or so, he pulled out gradually, cradling her against him. It was perfect for him— such languorous ecstasy with this wonderful girl. He sat up and drew her onto his lap.

Curled up against him, she pulled the sheet up to the curve of her breasts, still somewhat shy about letting him see her body. For her, everything up to the actual act was an awakening. The sharp pain had halted the heady emotions of that awakening, and she wondered curiously if that was always to happen. Tim used his thumb to smooth out a small troubled wrinkle between her brows.

"If you'll trust me, you'll learn to enjoy it as well as I do. That I can promise, and this is one subject I will absolutely love to teach."

He fell back onto the soft pillow, taking her with him, and for a time, they slept together. He awoke again just before dawn. At that point, the loud, incessant ticking of the small clock on the dresser had become a clanging noise that he wished fervently he could stop, as it meant he would have to leave her side soon. For now, though, Kerri was in his arms. He was the happiest man in the world having her by his side.

She slept beside him, curled up nearby, her breasts rising and falling rhythmically with every breath.

A brief time later, he reached over to caress her cheek and kiss her, not wanting to wake her up but unable to resist the temptation to touch soft, full lips with his. Her eyes opened, and she stirred sleepily, pulling the sheet up again over her exposed body to stave off the cool morning air. He smiled and gently tugged it away, playfully retracing the curves of her breasts. His hand touched her belly, then moved lower. He began exploring her body, and the fires between them were once again flamed. Tim watched as Kerri arched her back and held her breath. The newness of these sensations was dizzying for her.

He entered her again. This time, she found that there was more magic to being aroused and taken with such dizzying passion. The pain was still there, but her body somehow adjusted to accommodate the intrusion, just as he said it would.

If this is what marriage is like, she thought, *I think I'll enjoy it very, very much!*

Tim traced one soft brow, moving her hair from her forehead as if he wanted full access to read her thoughts. "If this is what marriage is like with you," he said aloud, "I know I'll enjoy it very much!"

They laughed and finally fell asleep together again, just as an insistent sun rose in the distant eastern sky. The day would be a tiring one for both, but worth the loss of sleep, knowing that they had much intimacy to anticipate during their marriage.

THE DECEMBER CHRISTMAS nuptials were rather extravagant for Kittery, with Tim's father gallantly offering to pay for the ceremony and reception. Uncle Frank gave the bride away, and Aunt Maggie held the place of honor in the front pew, holding back tears as she reflected on this moment her sister would have cherished.

Kerri, dressed in the lace sleeved, tightly cinched silk ball gown that her mother wore 23 years earlier, looked ethereal, and much in love. She wore her mother's pearls as her only ornament…a mute reminder that everything was not perfect on this special day. Cary had long ago promised a tiny blonde girl he would place them around her neck on the day he hoped would be a long time coming.

Kate wore her hair in the same style, and the twins looked remarkably alike. The tea-length mauve dress she wore tapered down to a curved train in the back. The dress had been worn by her mother for a naval ball years ago and it was her favorite of her mom's party clothes. The entire town had gone to incredible lengths to ensure the Christmas wedding was as festive as possible for the young couple. After an elegant reception and dance at the Hotel Pepperrell, the young couple headed to Boston for their honeymoon.

The Honeymoon Suite of the Boston Ritz-Carlton overlooked the glimmering lights of the Boston Harbor. It was late when they arrived, but Tim carried her into the lobby, smiling. Twirling her around, he announced, "Meet my beautiful bride! I'm the luckiest guy in the world!" The hotel guests cheered for the young newlyweds.

Inside the suite, Tim poured champagne while Kerri unpacked her suitcase and found a cream-colored negligee her sister had sewn for the occasion— a silk and satin backless halter. The silk gown was as revealing as Kate had meant it to be, flaring down to Kerri's shapely calves.

Tim's shirt was unbuttoned as he uncovered a silver tray of chocolate covered strawberries. The young groom watched as Kerri exited the bathroom. She was somewhat shy again— a quality he loved about his young bride. He suspected that would fade in time, but all this was so new.

In fact, since that first time at her house, they had not shared any time alone except for brief intervals until the wedding day. That only served to make the honeymoon night even more memorable.

He approached Kerri with a glass of champagne in each hand. The slit up the side of her negligee that went to mid-thigh showed a smooth, shapely leg, the ambient light behind her leaving nothing to his imagination. He handed her a glass, downing his in one long drink. Wordlessly, he kissed the nape of her neck. Circling behind her, he removed one strap of her gown and kissed her shoulder. She reached up to stroke one cheek, finding the hint of stubble on his chiseled face alluring. Turning, they both faced each other. He unbuttoned the pearl fastener to her negligee and it slipped to the floor, the satin shimmering as it moved. Tim picked her up and carried her over to the bed. His fingers traced across her lips and then down between her breasts. A small bottle of scented oil soon followed where his hands touched her body.

Dripping oil onto her skin, he began rubbing it into her shoulders and neck to relax her body from the tensions of the long day. She melted as he caressed her body with the heady scent. Tim was intent on giving his wife a long, slow massage. It was Kerri who halted the process, initiating the next moves. The ensuing night of lovemaking segued into the remembrances of a first night as a married couple.

Sometime toward morning, Kerri entered the bathroom shower, letting the warmth of the water relax her exhausted body. Minutes later, Tim opened the shower door to join her. Fully aroused again, he said huskily, "Need some assistance, honey?"

She smiled as he closed the door and pulled her toward him, letting the foaming suds drip where they may, with his hands soon following. Gliding them down her curvaceous body, he said, "I have a few more things to teach you, my darling wife!"

He took his time arousing her again. Kerri's head tipped back as he entered her once more, the different sensations making her aware that there were many facets to the art of lovemaking. As promised, she proved to be an apt and willing pupil for her new husband.

CHAPTER NINE

LEÇONS EN MÉDECINE

For the first time in their lives, the sisters' paths were separated by vastly accelerated future plans. Kerri was managing the move to Boston, which left Kate to spend much of her time with her Grama. Much like Helene, the use of natural herbs fascinated her. They had always been the premise behind Helene's medicinal remedies, garnering a distinct following of loyal users.

Helene knew that losing her sister to marriage was more difficult than her youngest granddaughter cared to admit. One morning, Kate awoke to find a book bound with a beautiful red ribbon on her nightstand. Called *Aromathérapie: Les Huiles Essentielles Hormones Végétales*, it was written by a French chemist and scholar, René-Maurice Gattefossé. The note that accompanied it was penned in French. It translated thus:

Darling Kate,

This book will help to continue your French lessons and also help you navigate the world of antiseptic essences, antibacterial oils, and mineral agents. It has been hard for you and your sister during these last months to focus on your own healing when the direction of your former lives has changed so drastically. With Kerri managing the new marriage, you need to keep moving in the direction you wish to take, enhancing your education and a potential career in medicine. I hope you enjoy this work as much as I love having my beautiful granddaughter share my life here in Boothbay, and my love of healing.

~ Yours affectionately, Grama Helene

Accompanying the book was an old withered clipping that her Grama had extracted from an old article, abstract, or newspaper she had come across. In Gattefosse's words, translated, it read,

"The external application of small quantities of essences rapidly stops the spread of gangrenous sores. In my personal experience, after a laboratory explosion covered me with burning substances, which I extinguished by rolling on a grassy lawn, both my hands were covered with a rapidly developing gas gangrene. Just one rinse with lavender essence stopped "the gasification of the tissue." This treatment was followed by profuse sweating, and my healing began the next day (July 1910)."

The clipping clarified why her grandmother was so fascinated by the sterilizing power of essential oils. "That article lured me into the world of therapeutic herbs and antiseptic reagents!" Helene stated animatedly over tea one afternoon. Sitting on the veranda overlooking the beautiful cove and bay beyond, she added, "There will be a time when these studies will save a life, and you'll be responsible for averting that kind of loss with your knowledge,"

She explained some of the concepts after pointing out a few notes in Kate's new book.

Kate was intrigued by the discussions of gas gangrene. She researched all she could find regarding the processes that contributed to its spread, particularly during the Great War, which was now being deemed World War I.

This beautifully-bound book was soon to become her "healing bible," and she studied into the wee hours, soaking up her grandmother's knowledge, if not her vast years of practical applications. Kate absorbed information as fast as her mind could process the words. She found that when she did so, she had less time to focus on the urge to locate Sean on an annoyingly persistent basis, wherever he was managing the war efforts with England.

—ele—

AS KATE MOVED further into her studies, Kerri was still settling in Boston. She was encouraged by Tim's desire to carve out a career for her as well. Interested in the study of grief after her recent losses, Kerri wanted to complete studies in clinical psychology to help others move forward from such anguish.

Soon after the wedding, a large package arrived, with scrapbooks of their parents' keepsakes. A crystal decanter set was accompanied by silver service ware once belonging to her parents. There was a note inside:

Dearest Kerri,

When someone you love dies, you often forget that amongst the sadness and the pain, there is a precious gift of "second beginnings" for those who are left behind. The best lessons are gentle reminders that the living can turn their lives around at any point as they move forward. They can learn from their own trials, and gain insight from the goodness and also the faults and foibles of those they loved most dearly and lost. In short, you are never bound by any past mistakes— yours or others. Learn from these. And trust in God to find happiness in your heart once again. He has a plan that is greater than the infinite sorrow you left behind. But only you hold the key to your heart and a new trust in the unseen yet to come that will put that plan into fruition.

Go forward in your dreams of an education and career. Find your aspirations again, and let this beautiful marriage be a new beginning for both of you. Honoring you, your devoted parent's upbringing, and your future married life together— always,

With all our hearts ~ your loving Grama Helene
and your "other mom"— Aunt Maggie

Ambitious to prove to his parents that Kerri was a formidable asset to the family, Tim urged her to apply to Radcliffe College. In the meantime, he steered her toward part-time work at Massachusetts General Hospital in the psychiatry department. German-American psychiatrist Erich Lindemann was garnering great interest in his specialization of bereavement studies. Lindemann, also a psychiatry professor at Harvard, focused primarily on the effects of trauma on survivors after critical life events. His studies included patients with amputated legs, loss of eyesight or hearing, and organs that had been surgically removed.

Tim was confident that with Kerri's German background and her French language skills, she would be a favored candidate for an undergraduate internship under Lindemann. Kerri applied, winning the distinguished professor over after her arrival in his office with a stack of translations of post-World War I French military psychiatric studies. French neuropsychiatrists employed by the armed forces had instigated long-term experiments on the treatment of shell shock. Lindemann was aware that the French work was premised on managing the traumatic neurosis of prolonged battle fatigue and shock. Thus, the translations proved to be an astute approach. The notes enhanced the professor's trauma experiments tenfold.

The workload in his office picked up with Kerri's translations, and the appreciative professor moved mountains to ensure that her educational goals could be met with his support and academic connections.

With the war raging in Europe, interest in these studies was growing with rapid speed. The job was intensive, focused, and highly intriguing for her.

*U.S. Congressional Opening, Jan 1940, discussion on the
'Neutrality zone policy'*

A
SLOW
JOURNEY TOWARD
HELL'S GATES

1940-1941
Washington, D.C

CHAPTER TEN

NAVAL INTELLIGENCE

In Boothbay, Kate was restless after her sister's wedding, fighting the continued loneliness that ensued after their separation. She applied to summer school for June of 1940 at Wellesley and was accepted. In the meantime, early in the winter of 1940, Kerri and Tim encouraged her to take some math aptitude tests given by a group of Bowdoin professors.

Purportedly to initiate joint projects between Bowdoin and Wellesley, the professors were recruiting students adept at complex problem-solving. Anyone with a propensity for foreign languages was raised higher on their list. Kate fit the qualifications and passed the tests with ease. As this would enhance her Wellesley resume, she was happy to accept the credits offered and the role in the new projects.

Her French was almost flawless, having grown up as the granddaughter of two Acadian, French-speaking maternal grandparents. Her German from the Yeager side was also extensive; thus, she scored high on both language tests. Her aptitude for managing intricate problems came to the attention of a group of math professors at the college called the *Mensa Club*. Kate was proving to be a perfect recruit.

Her weakness…a propensity for going off in different directions at once…was not a source of concern for this large team of acadamiens. They were, in fact, *searching* for such quick minds, grooming them to contribute by learning the art of cryptology. During Kate's first induction discussions with one Professor Eric Jardine, she soon found that he had other academic tasks in mind for her as well. Two other men were waiting for her in his office when she entered the room to sign the academic papers. Professor Jardine opened the conversation.

"Kate, you've been brought here for some work we think will be challenging and rewarding. In the U.S., the intelligence field is only in its infancy. Still, with the war in Europe, agencies such as ours are working to recruit potential codebreakers and intelligence officers to support the war efforts. We also need linguistics experts and translators who can translate and decode the documents. It's called the 'field of cryptology.' So, in short, we are interested in your skills."

Kate interrupted him bluntly. "I must say, in most cases, you look for men. Not women…so why me, and why the change from just the 'Mensa' Club and some college credits for Wellesley?"

One of the other men, a Dr. James McDaniels, stepped in to answer her questions. "First, we like the female recruits. They are quiet about their work, focused, and often skilled in diverse areas. *And* extremely efficient." He studied her, sizing up Kate's inquisitiveness. Abruptly, Professor Jardine changed the course of the discussions by asking some pressing background questions.

"We've reviewed your school and employment records. We understand you worked in the local naval base library, cataloging, shall we say— interesting classified reading material. Kate raised her eyebrows, wondering who they had interviewed for that tidbit of information. He continued: "We're aware that you completed high school early, but your curriculum was expanded to include collegiate credits in English Literature, Latin, and Mathematics. Also, you were co-valedictorian of your class, with impressive marks. However, we want to learn where you picked up your German language skills."

The question sounded somewhat ominous, so Kate responded with caution. "My paternal grandparents on the Yeager side were both full-blooded Germans, born in Berlin. They came from the old country before 1890 and settled in Belfast, Maine. They spoke only German in their household, and my sister and I were required to speak and read German to communicate with them." With the professors appearing somewhat unconvinced about her explanation, she continued:

"My father was an only child, born here in 1897. Only my Grossmama is alive now. She is 88 and harmless, except for a mean backhand whenever you misbehaved."

Satisfied with her answer, Professor Jardine responded. "What I am about to say now is deemed *classified,* and it does not leave this room. Is that abundantly clear?" Kate nodded, tipping her head back to listen more intently.

He continued, "There are a growing number of men in Washington who anticipate that the U.S. will be brought into this war in Europe. To put it bluntly, men will be recruited for the armed forces, and in some cases, the men *we* want to recruit believe it is beneath them to take desk jobs when there's a war to be fought. These men want to rise to become commanders, generals, and political leaders. And frankly, we need them there as well."

The quieter of the men, Dr. Russell Tipley, elaborated further: "Women are proficient in handling what men often find the more mundane aspects of desk jobs— stenographer positions, document readers, catalogers of key intelligence reviews. So, Kate, we are recruiting you to monitor documents, translate them, and scan decoded papers for secondary meanings or encrypted phrases. Are you interested in the work?"

Kate processed her thoughts for a moment, then answered, "Yes, I'm definitely interested. But I will caveat that response with the request that I will be trained in this 'cryptology' you mentioned. And the code breaking— if they are not one and the same. I don't want 'just another desk job' either. So, when can I start?" The men smiled at the bold response. And thus, Kate was formally inducted into their secret "Mensa" group.

As Kate was soon to discover, most of the American cryptanalysis work was performed in Washington, D.C., and their focus was on the Pacific, as the English had the upper hand on the German cryptanalytic work. Kate was asked to remain at Bowdoin for a short period to initiate her employment with a small team of math professors and navy document readers. As their work was governmental in nature, they were sworn to absolute secrecy. The word "code breaking" was just beginning to be utilized.

The professors found suitable off-campus housing nearby for the few young ladies recruited there, and Kate immersed herself in her new work at the university. Weekends were spent studying medicinal remedies, anatomy, and a new subject… aromatic respiratory tract applications. The months passed quickly. In March, 1940, Kate was asked to move to Washington to study numerical codes with the Pacific team. She was soon assigned to a code breaking team focusing on ciphers and cryptanalysis. Less than 30 members were initially located in the small Virginia office, each with multiple assignments.

She also translated messages between the Germans and their Embassy in Washington. Rather mundane work by some standards, Kate studied them rapaciously for patterns and cryptic codes. The fledgling cryptanalysis office was in disarray, with crucial papers and documents in piles of messy stacks. Kate found it distracting to work in such a disorganized state. Within the first couple of weeks, her commanding officer, Dr. David Kell, wandered in as she was categorizing a stack of documents late one evening. She was coerced into adding this to her responsibilities.

"Miss Yeager, as you can see, we are in some need of organization here. I'd like your opinion, please, on the best way to work these into identifiable categories."

Kate replied with a smile and a slightly impish acknowledgment of the apparent disorder. "I would suggest categorizing them into date and key subject first, and color-coding by origin and their level of importance in the far right corner. Embassy messages need to be labeled as critical and separated from other documents. For example, take this telegram from the German Embassy dated June 9th: *'The Bayreuth Festival Begins Tomorrow.'* Now, looking back to a telegram from August 31, 1939, the same German Embassy message appears again from Berlin to Washington, which, after a cursory translation, reads as: *'The Cannes Film Festival Begins Tomorrow.'*

She paused to allow him to review the German telegrams and the previously translated notes by the American Embassy. Continuing, she said, "These two telegram dates are key. Poland was invaded on September 1, 1939, and Italy declared war on France and Great Britain on June 10th, just last week. These are patterns that could easily be missed. I believe them to be a code regarding these key invasions. I would think the War Department must have noticed this pattern, but if so, it appears that the pattern was not conveyed to our office when we received the copies."

"An interesting observation, but I'd like to know more. At first glance, these are merely festival announcements for traditional German holidays, Kate," said Dr. Kell.

"Well," Kate responded, "Take the word morgen in the telegram. In their written language, the German word *'morgen'* spelled with a small letter is an adverb meaning *tomorrow*. When capitalized, as it is in the telegram, it has a different meaning. Germans capitalize all of their nouns, and thus, this would typically be translated as *'morning,'* which is a noun. To further distinguish between the adverb and the noun, they would often add the word *"am"* before the capitalized word *Morgen*, as in *'Das Festival beginnt am Morgen.'* In each message, they omitted the **am** but capitalized **Morgen**. Since both festivals were to commence on the following day after each telegram, it would appear to be just a simple omission to the average American. But actually, it's not. Germans don't make this mistake, especially not in formal writing.

It sounds confusing, and yes, I could be misinterpreting this. But to me, the German Embassy is conveying that something is happening *tomorrow* <u>and</u> *in the morning*. Both invasions occurred the day after each telegram and early in the morning. That's it, but it's still pretty compelling to me. It was a signal to their intelligence officers in Washington about the impending invasions."

Dr. Kell was impressed with her language skills, and assessment of this translation. After this discussion, her secondary assignment was to categorize the disorganized mess and to focus on studying embassy message patterns. This had the added effect of allowing Kate to peruse all documents instead of having one piece of the many sectors of their work. Kate also reviewed German dispatches discovered and transmitted by Allied coastwatchers, as her skills as a translator for French and German communiqués became more widely known. Recognizing the increasing interest in her translation work, she exploited her persuasive negotiating skills, receiving a commitment that she would obtain more transferable college credits to Wellesley for foreign languages studies. She was determined to expedite her collegiate degree, and passing the class exams was not a difficult task for her.

Each of the few young ladies assigned to the office had extensive covers to keep even their closest family members in the dark about their work. Kate's cover was legitimately built around her interest in nursing. She was accepted at Mt. Vernon Seminary. As her credits continued adding up, she would enter Wellesley as a junior whenever she initiated classes there.

In a magnificently kind gesture spearheaded by her mother's former boss, James Keighan, her nursing tuition was paid for by the navy. Once she was ensconced in the nursing academy, Kate's thirst for medical knowledge was almost insatiable. She happened upon a classroom of nurses studying the science of antiviral agents called *Alternative Medicine*. She joined this Saturday evening class under a French teacher named Claudette. Claudette also used Gattefossé's training, incorporating staples such as oils of lavender, thyme, and lemon for antiseptic properties. These oils were free from the disadvantages of other antitoxic agents in use at that time.

One morning a few weeks later, Kate was called into the Dean's Office for a meeting. The Superintendent of Nursing attended, along with two naval officers Kate had never met. Dean Constantine opened the discussions. "Miss Yeager, the navy is interested in pursuing a position for you upon completion of your degree here. It will most likely be in a foreign setting, so we need to assess your interest." As Kate digested the proffered information, he continued:

"At this time, the Army Nurse Corps has about 5,000 members, while the Navy Nurse Corps has only a little shy of 700 nurses. So, you're slated to move into the Navy Nurses Corps after graduation. A notable coalition of naval officers and surgeons have come to value your aptitude. If you are willing to accept this path, there is an employment contract we would like for you to review and sign. There is additional scholarship money as well as room and board attached to the contract as well."

Kate fired up a list of questions regarding her future goals, which were duly answered by the next day. Satisfied with the responses, she became an official naval nursing recruit. She was moved into a small apartment house and allotted a vehicle for transport to Mr. Vernon Seminary. It would have been impossible to fast-track into advanced promotions during peacetime, but the government was accelerating many individuals like Kate.

To that end, Kate was enrolled in an upper-level program in operating room technique and management at the navy's expense. The additional year-long course for two mornings a week was in exchange for a two-year stint as a naval surgical nurse serving outposts. Since the assignment was far off in the future, the possibility of a remote assignment was not a concern to be reckoned with at the time.

As the months passed, mornings were filled with nursing classes and practicals, with afternoons at the code breaking center until 7 pm. Studying consumed Kate's late evenings. As Kate required little sleep, she was free to stay late at the nursing library and her office as well. She was lucky to enjoy considerable freedom in a town governed by strict curfews for young unmarried ladies. Her Saturdays were spent at the cryptology center, and her Sundays were often utilized to expand her medical knowledge base and training.

Kate made fast friends at the cryptology center with two dedicated young men named Connor and John. As well as decoding, both of them taught her how to review their work— categorizing numerical codes into more critical translations. Life for Kate was at a relatively breakneck pace, but it was exciting and all-consuming for a young lady in the fast-paced world of Washington. The time passed by quickly for her.

CHAPTER ELEVEN

A DISEASE CALLED HOMESICKNESS

In Boston, Kerri immersed herself in the role of a devoted wife. After the industriousness of the honeymoon phase passed and she found far too much time to herself, a short period of depression hit. Tim was studying voraciously, and college in Boston had not yet commenced for Kerri. She was employed part-time in the psychiatric clinic but spent many hours alone in the tiny apartment. In the homesickness that ensued after their move from Maine, she took to letter writing to communicate what was once at least a daily face-to-face conversation with her twin. As the months of correspondence passed, the sisters clung to each letter. The musings were a poor substitute for the physical bond they both relied on as young girls.

Nonetheless, the letters continued with great regularity.

Early on a cool spring morning, watching a glorious sunrise edge its way across the Boston horizon, Kerri sat down next to their kitchen window with pen in hand to write her twin.

Mar 26, 1940

Dearest Sister Kate,

I miss you today. Marriage with Tim is absolutely divine, but I miss our conversations more than you can know. In case you're wondering, my gorgeous Tim is attentive when he is home, which, unfortunately, is not often enough to suit his lonely wife! I'm striving to be content with part-time work and making his dinners and evening hours as pleasant as possible. I've been accepted at Radcliffe and am excited about school... Education was the plan all along for you and me. My goals have been thwarted somewhat, but this is the path I have willingly chosen, so I won't complain. His career comes first right now.

And yes, I'm happy with being a supportive wife. You'll laugh, but we still have yet to have our first fight. He often says, "It takes two flints to make a fire, and I'm as even-tempered as a wife can be, so that fight's not happening any time soon!" You know me! I was always the contemplative one, and you made your opinions known about as quickly as they occurred. I don't see a need to rock the proverbial boat. So, I won't.

That said, we have the most stimulating conversations on politics, our collective goals as a couple, and virtually all aspects of married life. He's pretty vocal about his opinions on sex and babies and love in general, and I often cap one or more of his enchanting comments with some candid ones of my own. So, we have great fun together— the two of us against the world. Who knows as we grow older? Our battles may be epic ones! We shall see...

I ache for our daily sisterly interactions. But the reunions will be that much more special! Perhaps that is what God intends. He wants us to appreciate and value what we have; thus, He teaches us these daily life lessons to strengthen that value. Nevertheless, I remain your most devoted sister, and the heartstrings attached to us both at birth will always remain steadfast and strong.

All my heart ~ Your loving sister Kerri

An equally homesick Kate read this heartwarming letter on a park bench in Washington, during a brief lunch break from her code work. She removed a pen and notepad from her work satchel and began a return letter of her own:

April 15, 1940

My Darling Kerri,

Your letter reached me on a day when I needed it most. I am most decidedly homesick today and wishing with all my heart we were sitting on the front porch swing together, waiting for one of mom's pies to cool as we watched for dad's truck to amble up the driveway. Our sisterhood is entirely one-sided with this separation and I admit that I am struggling with that too. Phone calls are cost-prohibitive, as are trips between Boston and Washington. So, I often find myself stopping to wonder what you are doing, where you are, and if you're happy in your wifely endeavors. This separation happened much faster than either of us was ready to accept. But life comes at you quickly, and you must learn to adapt.

And yes, I am a bit envious of your fulfillment through your new marriage and your exciting work with Dr. Lindemann! Just as you might be about how working life in Washington suits an independent girl like me. The two of us have never been separated like this. So from now on, most aspects of our lives are simply one-sided conversations. I'm sure every sibling has these pangs as their lives move on.

I am enjoying the nurse's training, and, like we did in school, I am studying voraciously to be at the top of my class. What competitive souls we both are! My work at the employment center in Washington is often relatively mundane. Still, it pays my bills and allows me some spending money for the rare occasions when I socialize.

As we grow older, we will value what we had even more and appreciate the deep love and commitment to each other as well. Tell Tim to kiss you on "my cheek", as I always ask, and tell him how much I value his dedication to my charming sister. He's a keeper, for sure!

Your favorite (and unfortunately only!) sister ~
Kate

Kate detested the deliberate omissions about her clandestine work. She had never lied to Kerri, and the lies twisted like a knife in her stomach. But she took the threat of a court-martial seriously. She leaned back on the bench, looking around somewhat morosely at her surroundings. The air was chilly, but not with the fresh crispness of the salty air in Kittery. She missed Maine, and the pain of their separation was etched into her still-healing heart.

She turned her head to observe a young mother strolling with a baby carriage nearby, twisting her hair as she often did when in deep thought. Smiling, Kate stood, facing the woman to comment on the tiny infant in the stroller. They engaged in a light conversation that broke Kate out of her short depression. The moment of friendly banter soon passed, and she finally repacked her satchel and headed back to her pressing work at the office.

THE YOUNG MAN STOOD at the window, watching the cars pass on the street below. His eyes settled on a nearby park bench, where a girl was engaged in reading. She finally looked up, absently twisting a few strands of her hair. Something about the gesture seemed oddly familiar to him, and he was intrigued. The slender blonde stood, moving toward a mother strolling nearby with a baby carriage. Startled, he studied her movements. When she turned in his direction, the familiarity struck him even more strongly. His eyes lit up, and he grabbed his jacket to head out toward her, as if he was compelled by some inner force to speak to this young woman.

A sharp, staccato knock on the door interrupted his determined foray into the park.

"Sean, the President's staff will see you now. After the briefing you will return to the hotel to pack. There is a military transport bound for London. You're to be on that flight at midnight tonight. You're to be working with Commander Charles Lockwood as a military advisor there, for advancements in submarine technology." The aide ushered the tall Australian out of the room, and Sean's pressing thoughts of his time in Maine with Kate were once again subdued. His focus returned again to Roosevelt's staff and the military briefing at hand.

DURING THE LAST DAYS of April, Kate asked to be transferred to a small team of submarine trackers in their building complex, using her navy connections in Portsmouth to raise the request to the appropriate decision-makers. She was still reviewing the sporadic messages from the respective embassies received from the State Department. To her dismay, though, the document readers from the State Department were increasingly hoarding these, which greatly hindered her work. Thanks to Dr. Kell, who held meetings with state department officials to promote Kate's notations on the German "festival" date patterns, these same officials organized their own translators. Paranoia, control battles, and personality clashes contributed to this massive setback for Kate. It was a common theme in the government, she was discovering.

Her new assignment picked up rapidly for two reasons. First, in subsequent team meetings, an enterprising naval supervisor, Commander Andrew

McHenry, provided daily afternoon briefings to expedite their work. Second, in her first week of work, his briefing inspired her. He knew exactly how to motivate his team.

"We are retrieving messages from the German U-boat fleet at an alarmingly high rate. Our spies have indicated that German Admiral Karl Dönitz is currently operating at maximum fleet capacity. He is known to be obsessively controlling over his ships. Fortunately for us, all vessel commanders are ordered to send continual position and fuel status reports for Dönitz's battle orders to be as accurate as possible. These messages are transmitted from the entire fleet, sent under high-frequency transmissions throughout long distances. Translation: Easier to decode, track and pinpoint."

"Let's get to work and find the patterns. The department is providing food and safe transport for those who wish to stay past their shift and continue their work. We need all available hands on deck!"

Kate readily took him up on those offers. Encouraged by his daily interactions with the group, she set up a chart reflecting the frequency of messages and the location of the Axis fleet. She picked up through careful statistical analysis where the fleet was moving, and calculated the approximate speeds. When it was noticed through this analysis and charting that the German subs were moving rapidly from the mid-Atlantic into the waters of Norway, she began to see another pattern regarding the words encrypted in the messages. The repeated patterns depicted "U-Bootwaffe", "Torpedokrise", and "Zonenkarte".

Excitedly, she spoke to Commander McHenry about what she felt this meant to their work. Dr. Kell asked to be present.

Kate booked a small conference room for a private discussion. After a brief introduction to her theory, she added, "These German words translate to 'submarine force', 'torpedo crisis', and 'zone map.' They're repeated throughout a number of messages, and the commanders are breaking radio silence to convey these. So, they must be significant.

I'm unfamiliar with German torpedoes, but I know a little about our *Mark 14*'s failures. At least some of these torpedo misfires were determined to be due to differences in the earth's magnetic fields at varying latitudes… obviously strongest at the poles and weakest at the equator. The torpedoes need a steady magnetic balance to perform properly."

Dr. Kell nodded for her to continue. Elated with his interest, she added, "I studied the phenomenon of the Aurora Borealis in my Astronomy classes, more specifically, its interference with the electromagnetism of the Earth's poles. It's purportedly strongest in Norway, and again, the magnetic fields are much stronger at these higher latitudes.

The Aurora also creates a plethora of geomagnetic storms, which have, on occasion, interfered with the firing mechanisms in the Mark 14 as well. The U.S. is working to correct those misfires now. So… in essence, the Germans are obviously having either these same issues, or remarkably similar ones. One more thing: the high mineral deposits of iron ore in Norway would also appear to contribute to these disturbances and misfires.

"A thorough analysis, and one that bears repeating to management, but I have to ask: where did you pick up your submarine knowledge?" Andrew asked.

First, my family works at Portsmouth Naval Shipyard on naval submarine designs. Second, my parents were amateur astronomers. So, I lived and breathed these interesting electromagnetism discussions when I was a young teen. Also, I have a friend leading projects both here in the states and in England. His work revolves around correcting torpedo defects.

"And your friend is…?" Dr. Kell asked curiously.

Kate hesitated, not wanting to cause any problems for Sean.

"Sean Stuart-Lawrence. From Australia. He goes by Sean Lawrence."

The professor responded, "Ahhh… Sean is well-known here in D.C. He is an acknowledged submarine expert, and we are quite lucky to have him on our side of the ocean when we can get him."

Kate was thrilled at the knowledge that he was acquainted with Sean. The mention of his name caused her heart to skip a beat, and she was aware that her emotions were undeniably still strong for the Australian.

"Do you happen to know where he is now?" she asked as innocently as possible, hoping for news that he was still in Washington.

"Last I heard Sean was headed for the Pacific. Australia is clamoring for him to return there, in his original naval position."

The disappointment must have shown on her face, and Andrew McHenry's sharp eyes were now watching her features more carefully. Before either had a chance to ask further questions about the brief friendship, Kate abruptly added, "At any rate, I'm happy to help analyze these messages. I hope to continue my work in this area." After a few minutes of banter, she dismissed herself and went back to her work regarding what was now called the "Norway Project."

Dr. Kell and Commander McHenry conveyed the details of her work to their superiors. Kate was not the only analyst who came to these conclusions, and once again, she noted that once a woman picked up the interesting patterns, the work was handed over to the men, who were deemed more adept with the difficulty on the analytics. For now, she would have to live with the frustration of this "male superiority" complex. But she was content knowing she at least contributed to the rising levels of "intelligence" on the German naval movements.

The Axis campaign against Norway ended with the full occupation of Norway by Germany. As "neutral Norway" fell to the Germans in June, the Battle of France was already underway. The Germans were well on their way to conquering all of Europe.

SEVERAL DAYS AFTER these conquests in Europe, both sisters wrote letters to their aunt about their rising separation anxiety, noting again that 1940 started in a starkly different manner than 1939 had. Neither sister felt it fair to burden the other with the pain of the transformations they had both endured at such a young age. They were comfortable confiding in their aunt, though.

As Kate wrote in a card to Aunt Maggie,

...The saddest aspect of my billet in Washington is knowing what it is like to be truly alone for the first time in my life. It has founded fears of us being separated permanently. I strive to remember the thousands of children in Europe who have been separated from parents they deeply love at a much younger age. It somehow makes my pain seem less burdensome. We mustn't forget that Europe is at war, and war is absolute HELL for these families. I'm blessed that we're only separated by earlier-than-expected events, and normal lifetime events at that— marriage and careers...

The loss of the *Squalus* and the subsequent death of their parents accelerated aspects of their lives that were supposed to be well into the distant future. Aunt Maggie was painfully aware that a happy marriage and a promising career had done little to soften the trauma of the separations and life changes the sisters had endured. Kerri freely confessed as much during the following week in a letter to her aunt:

...The changes in our lives and the world are so significant now, and it's like this change is lingering in the air. Marriage is a lifetime obligation I committed to at the age of 19. It boggles my mind to think how fast such things have happened! My work with the Professor has been a saving grace for me and a reminder of goals I have yet to manage. Still, studying the psychological effects of war on soldiers and veterans is a frequent reminder that war could be around the corner for our country as well! The ongoing European battles are at the forefront of our daily work. "

Their Aunt lent her support through cheery care packages and correspondence. Unfortunately, the posts were sent far too infrequently, as Maggie and the entire town of Kittery were preoccupied with the increasing demands at the naval base. They knew what the average American wasn't aware of… that there was an ominous threat to the rising orders for armaments, weaponry, and top-secret contracts. With the European continent at war, even the most complacent anti-war advocates were aware that the war was getting ever closer to our American back door. Such thoughts occupied a great many minds these days.

CHAPTER TWELVE

IN ENEMY HANDS

With Kate's frenetic schedule, the summer of 1940 passed by with great speed. The September sun was waning in the evening sky late on a Sunday afternoon. Kate was working at the downtown Cryptology Center in an area near where the German cipher device *Enigma* was under decoding. In addition to her translations and the review of embassy messages, she had been promoted to categorizing intercepted "traffic" on the French borders for the upper echelon to review. The work was often tedious and unrewarding.

Part of her job, though, consisted of analyzing circuits on German hand ciphers that appeared to revolve around the first seven digits of the mathematical constant *pi*— 3.141592. The use of these sequences by the Third Reich had already been discovered in early 1940, but the Germans were known for recirculating old code patterns. Whether from laziness or a cocky attitude negating the Americans' skills in cipher decoding, no one in D.C. cared. It was a lucky break for the American codebreakers. They were increasingly supporting the English in this endeavor. And in some ways, they were competing with them to break the German communication lines. Either way, significant progress was being made.

Kate's methodology was to stack multiple sequenced messages on top of each other by date, reviewing them to identify consistencies better. The stacks were checked for any nuances before and after translations that may be patterned. Kate always perused them again to determine if any easy, low-frequency codes were missed. She had a near-photographic memory for configurations that had been reviewed months before.

Taking a short break, she was at her desk working to peruse another recently received stack of encrypted German messages when a hand touched her shoulder, startling her and causing the tea she had been sipping to spill onto her papers. Annoyed, she looked up to find a man, perhaps in his early forties, just inches from her chair. Discomfited by the close proximity, she stood, trembling under the awareness that she was uncomfortable with his casual use of her intimate space.

"Can I help you, sir?" she asked, standing indignantly at her full height, but backing up slightly to obtain distance between them.

"I'm Dr. Mackinerary. Mack for short. Professor of Math at William and Mary. I have been assigned to your unit. And you would be?" he asked congenially enough, but in a tone that somehow seemed possessive over her, and marginally arrogant. She paused.

"Kate Yeager."

She wasn't sure why, but she didn't offer further conversation or volunteer to discuss her work, which she might be inclined to do under normal conditions. Kate excused herself abruptly to return to her translations.

He took a desk close by, moving papers around to study the contents of the occupant's work, which immediately annoyed her, although she again was puzzled as to why. After an hour passed, she decided to head home, distracted by the additional presence and the almost certain knowledge that he was staring at her from behind. Although it wasn't chilly outside, she donned the sweater that she kept on her chair, uncomfortable that she instinctively felt his eyes lingering on her. *You're being silly, Kate*, she admonished herself sharply. She left posthaste after locking all of her sequenced documents in her desk. There was no chill in the afternoon air, but Kate shivered as she exited the building.

The next afternoon, the arrogant newcomer had claimed that nearby desk for himself, moving a young junior cryptographer to the back of the room. She barely nodded as she sat down. Minutes later, she turned to find him staring at her, leaning back in his chair, arms casually behind his head. The smug look on his face told her he was used to doing exactly as he pleased and he wasn't the least intimidated by her slight glare. Mack was not ingratiating himself in any way, and at that moment Kate decided she didn't like him one bit. She liked it even less when she found he had asked to manage the female cryptographers. He was her new boss.

At the end of that harrowing first week, Mack informed her that he intended to supervise her work. Finding the need for a bit of fresh air after that conversation, Kate walked across the small office campus, heading for a coffee shop. Returning some moments later, she found him leaning against a tree watching her intently, his eyes penetrating and sinister. After the third time this occurred during the week, Kate abruptly decided to confront him.

Walking over to him with deliberate strides, she asked hotly, "Do you mind telling me why you are staring at me and why in God's name you appear to be following me?" Her body language showed she intended to halt whatever shenanigans he was up to, but inside she was quaking, terrified at what lay behind his cold, flat eyes.

"It's a free world. The office campus is beautiful, and I'm definitely one to enjoy *all* the views that are offered to me," he said as he leaned closer to her, once again invading her space.

"I'm most certainly *not* offering, and you need to know that if this continues, I'll report you to the authorities in our unit," she retorted between clenched teeth.

"And look outright ridiculous in the process, Kate," Mack responded. "I'm sure you're acquainted with my work. My recent papers on the cryptanalysis work managed in England?" His smile was sinister. "No one will believe you. Of that, you can be assured."

He had obviously anticipated her reactions and showed practiced proficiency at countering her protests. What's more, he knew she was terrified inside. With a swift motion, he took her wrist, caressing her hand with his thumb before she could jerk it away. She shivered, finding his touch repulsive.

"Touch me again, and you'll find yourself minus a few inconspicuous body parts. Emphasis on inconspicuous." His laughter showed he enjoyed her distress. His eyes gleamed, flashing something she didn't understand— a dark side she had never experienced in her sheltered life. She turned and made a quick retreat, anxious to move from his sight, and feeling objectified by his weird behavior.

Mack soon began requiring Kate to work longer hours after dark, alone with him. He assigned her projects that others had coveted, all in an attempt to isolate her from her team. For weeks, the stalking incidents near her apartment and on the office campus continued, terrifying her to the point where she was hyper-vigilant about shadows around corners…often perusing short distances to search for his location. He seemed to know most of her movements and her regular activities, and he showed up in many of these places, waiting for her.

She found that the fear sparked by this persecution significantly limited her trust of her male colleagues, on the few occasions she had time to socialize with them. With so little experience regarding the male sex, she began to suspect that this harassment could be the norm in a working environment, instead of the exception. Unsure of who she could confide in, she was almost as frustrated at this inability to rationally process her fears as she was over the harassment.

All of this had the unfortunate effect of making the brief encounter with Sean more prominent, and the infrequent encounters at local bars and gatherings in this hustling city did nothing to alleviate this negative opinion of men. The poignant example of her father's respectful treatment of her mother was becoming a distant recollection. She was troubled by the abundance of negative examples in D.C.

Kate began to lose sleep, wondering what lengths her new boss would go to while harassing her into forced intimacy. She didn't have long to wait for the answers.

Mack began scheduling supervisory discussions in the form of secluded one-on-one conversations. These were never about work, and Kate dreaded them more than the stalking. One Sunday morning, she arose from a fitful sleep and dressed, heading to the center. She arrived at 7 am to attempt to complete her translations and sequencing. Entering a back room where an early conference was to occur that day, Kate began placing documents around the table for the morning meeting. As she rounded the long corner of the table far from the door, she looked up to see Mack standing there, blocking the door from an easy exit. His eyes told her the moment was ripe for whatever approach he had planned. His obvious demands were written plainly on his face.

She backed as far against the wall behind her as possible as he approached her menacingly. A cold, wicked flash in his eyes accompanied a terrifying leer across his face– a look Kate hoped she would never have to see again in her lifetime.

"I've been waiting for this moment for a long time, Kate."

The threat was impossible to miss. As he approached, she began shaking, her blood boiling at the knowledge that she would have to exert some form of violence to escape. Her mind reeled; her legs quaked. She had never known such stark terror in her life. They were alone, and she realized that no one would hear her if she screamed.

His eyes roamed possessively over her, making her feel naked. The vulnerability was utterly foreign. Just as he pressed his body against hers, Kate heard a far outer door slam. On instinct, she took the momentum of him being caught off guard by the distant sound. Pushing him off balance, she rushed to the safety of the door and beyond. Two young colleagues had arrived. Intent on their conversation, they barely looked up as Kate exited. She was still trembling as she entered her apartment. Crawling under the sheets, she curled up in a tight ball.

Two hours later she arose reluctantly to study for her nursing classes. *You don't have time for self-pity and indulgence. Get yourself together*, she told herself sternly as she fought to regain her spirits, her courage, and her determination to overcome the harassment.

CHAPTER THIRTEEN

DELIVERANCE FROM EVIL

Kate worked to remain focused on her pressing decoding. Luckily enough, Mack was asked to lead a temporary project in another sector, and for the most part, her work distractions helped to take her mind off the frightening encounters with him. When she allowed these disturbing incidents to enter her thoughts, her concentration was exceedingly difficult to maintain.

She began working to sequence longer German ciphers sent on the same day, where repeat patterns were more easily detectable. If patterns were discovered, they were tested on the Enigma model. The longer messages often began with a phrase about the weather in Berlin, and Kate felt it meant the Germans were on the move. She conveyed this to one of her supervisors, and was asked to document these phrases in earnest to see if her theory was correct. It was often tedious work, and most times, unrewarding.

Two weeks later, Kate was invited to the center after her morning nursing classes to attend training for a new cipher sequencing machine under development. Engrossed in watching the demonstration, heavy breathing behind her caused the hair to stand up on the back of her neck. She fought to control the trembling, knowing instinctively that Mack was behind her. As she moved away from the intrusion, one of the instructors asked for some additional equipment from the storage rooms. Kate immediately volunteered to retrieve it, to remove herself from Mack's presence.

As she hurried down the hall toward the storage closets, the fear in her body was palpable. She turned the corner down the long, dim hallway to the storage area. Reaching for the equipment on the shelf, suddenly she felt arms creeping around her waist and a raspy whisper in her ear as she was pinned against the counter.

"You know what I want. I can make it good for you here at the center, Kate, if you'll stop resisting me." As he leaned in and kissed the nape of her neck, she whirled with the equipment, knocking him full force in the gut. Her knee jammed into his groin and she turned and sprinted down the long hall, rounding the corner in sight of the team of cryptologists. Working to control her fear, she let her rapid heartbeat cool down as she moved toward the group. Her friend Connor appeared to note that her face was flushed. But as he was absorbed in the demonstration, his momentary observation passed.

Kate searched for the right words to broach the subject to Connor about her problems with Mack, but there was no easy way to explain why the stalking actions terrified her. She wasn't sure anyone would believe her, and she felt like an idiot for voicing complaints. Reluctantly, she left everything as it was for the time being. This, she soon discovered, was a grave mistake. The weeks of stressful indecision on her approach for help affected even her magnificent health and stamina.

Finally, she wrote to Kerri asking for advice. The following weekend, she found a friendly visitor at the door of her residence, in the form of her brother-in-law, Tim. He promised not to cause her any harm as he assessed his approach. Kate found him to be charming, and devoted to easing her discomfort regarding the situation with Mack.

Having never had a brother or male cousins, she was relieved at the prospect of an older male who would shelter her somewhat, as her father once did.

Her newfound protector accompanied Kate to work that Saturday, where he was introduced to Mack only as "Tim" in an abrupt tone. At Tim's insistence, they gave Mack the impression that he and Kate were a serious item.

The two men shook hands, but Tim did not offer any conversation. He immediately moved back toward Kate's desk, watching her ostensibly work on her translations. After a few minutes, Tim handed Kate some money and with a wink, stated, "Honey, why don't you head over to the little sandwich shop across the street and pick up that coffee you've been bragging about? I need to make a few phone calls here at your desk. All local, so no worries about long distance bills, gorgeous girl."

The charming smile toward his sister-in-law indicated he wanted to be alone with Mack. Kate well knew that something was brewing regarding Mack and the stalking. She was supremely curious about what Tim had in store, but, surprisingly, not the least bit anxious about how he planned to handle things. In the short months since his and Kerri's wedding, she had learned through her twin that his judgment and discretion were as strong as his quiet confidence in managing medical school.

When she returned a short while later, Mack was at his desk but appeared to be leaving. He looked up briefly as Kate entered the room, his face somewhat mottled. *Anger, perhaps?* Kate observed. Otherwise, he appeared under control of his emotions. Tim was smiling and unruffled, leaning back in Kate's chair with his feet on her desk. As Mack left the building Kate remarked, "Gee, was it me, or did he just slither off looking sulky?"

Tim smiled and responded, "Honey, he just got his cojones handed to him, so I think he's pouting and probably out there frantically looking for them so they can be reattached for his next victims."

Kate laughed aloud at his comments, then asked curiously, "Would you mind telling me what was exchanged between the two of you? I've never seen him that subdued." "It was a short conversation— I assure you," Tim replied casually. "I simply mentioned that I have an uncle that works here in D.C. I also mentioned that *said uncle* is employed at the White House and used his connections to get you your job here, and that he manages the protective detail for the President. All true, for the most part, except that *said uncle* is actually an aunt, who *is* a secretary in the White House working exclusively for Eleanor. *Not* Franklin. She does, in fact, help schedule Eleanor's security detail," he winked. "So, a partial truth there. And… having a little fun with this," Tim continued merrily, running his fingers through his wavy blonde hair, "I casually mentioned that one phone call was a required call with my parole officer. He wants to ensure that I don't get into any more incidents involving a certain Italian stiletto given to me by my Uncle Vincenzo from Sicily. The same uncle who works in the White House on the security detail. I had even more fun, by the way, having a conversation with my 'also-paroled buddy', aka a fraternity brother named Giovanni, who entirely missed his calling for an acting career as a Sicilian Mafioso. I really enjoyed that exchange," Tim said with a mischievous gleam in his eyes.

"You owe Giovanni a beer, or a date, or both— for that graphic phone performance, which by the way Mack picked up on. As he was meant to. He's scared shitless now. Giovanni mentioned that the other guy was still in the hospital receiving blood transfusions. And recovering from the frontal assault on his balls, pardon my French, sis! All for flirting with Giovanni's girl."

Kate laughed heartily, opening her mouth to comment. Anticipating her following line of questioning, Tim looked over at his sister-in-law, with a final statement.

"Just to tie everything in, I mentioned that you have hinted that someone is harassing you on campus. You won't tell me who it is because I'm out on bail and can't afford another 'assault with intent' incident. But I gave him my number and told him that— as your boss— if he finds out, he can call me directly and I'll take the bastard to a little Sicilian necktie party Giovanni and I can arrange. 'Just' medicine for someone who is terrorizing my girl, don't you think?"

"Uh…what's a Sicilian necktie party, Tim?" Kate asked tentatively. Tim smiled at her.

"I've heard solid rumors about the existence of that particular form of death in Sicily to vile murderers— and enemies of the party. If you really want to know, little sis, I'll tell you. But don't say I didn't warn you about the graphic details."

Kate hesitated again. "OK, I'll bite. Just in case the bastard here asks about your experience with said method of execution."

Tim explained, "Well, first, you slit the throat," he indicated, with a gesture across his own throat. "Then I think you rip the tongue down the throat and out from the slit. If you're a nasty executioner, you cut the crown jewels off first, torturously slow, with a dull knife. Then you put them on top of the tongue. A disgusting and painful way to die, I might add." Seeing the color drain from Kate's face, Tim softened, giving her a reassuring hug in the way of an apology for the graphic details.

"Kate, dear. I'm not prone to *any* sort of violence. But I couldn't resist seeing that bastard have the same reaction you did when I mentioned cutting the cojones off of whoever happens to be harassing you. This might not eliminate the problem you're having. But it sure as hell will make Mack think twice about how many people he is actually messing with when he sexually harasses you."

Changing the subject before she could dwell on the possibility that this monumental effort by Tim did not deter Mack, Kate said casually, "Let's go grab a bite to eat, Tim. I know a great little French place that serves the most delectable beef tongue. Which I might just suggest tomorrow as a lunch item to my boss."

Tim tipped his head back and roared, finding sister Kate's humor returned, and her "biting tongue," as he put it, a fascinating part of Kerri's and Kate's unique twin-shared traits.

THE NEXT COUPLE OF weeks found Mack decidedly more reluctant to approach Kate. December came, and a quiet announcement was made that Mack was transferring back to the university. A relieved Kate made a celebratory visit back to Boston for the Christmas holidays. The sisters were ecstatic at being back together once more. Kate accepted the requisite date with Giovanni, with Tim and Kerri joining them at an Italian café in Boston. Over cocktails in a private room, Tim and Giovanni showed the sisters some self-defense moves. That night, while Tim was at the library, Kerri and Kate enjoyed a frank conversation on married life.

As Kerri offered, "I believe that sex was deliberately underrated by our overprotective parents. Once you get started, it's addictive. And they knew that," laughing as she spoke again. "The act itself is an incredible way to celebrate love, and I know it will be the same for you!"

Kate's mind flashed momentarily at the thought of this act with the likes of Sean. As she watched Tim playfully carry his wife off to bed when he returned home, she was grateful for her sister's happiness. She wondered a little wistfully if she too would find someone who appreciated the value of a wife with career-minded ambitions. She thought about the handsome Australian again, and just as quickly eliminated those thoughts. They meandered to a dangerous place in her mind.

She had an arranged date with Giovanni the next day. As she related to Kerri later that night, Giovanni was entertaining and engaging. "Still, his viewpoints on women were questionable, if not downright unacceptable, unless you were a complacent wife who lived for bedroom entertainment and cooking all day," Kate relayed.

They both laughed, and after a few more minutes of banter, Kate reluctantly went to pack for her return trip to D.C. the following day. The respite from her work renewed her spirits, and prepared her for the stressful schedule she had been committed to for months.

CHAPTER FOURTEEN

THE BRINK OF WAR

With the help of the naval command in D.C., Kate gained permission to accelerate the final courses for a college degree in biology/nursing, with a minor in foreign languages. Her two years of pre-college science courses afforded her the requisite college credits for biology. Not for the first time, she was very grateful for the strict parental upbringing.

By January 1941, she was well aware that the navy's keen interest in her work as a codebreaker eventually meant that her expedited training was, in fact, preparing her for medical bases near war zones. It soon became apparent that this was preordained as part of the navy's intentions regarding both aspects of her training. As she was receiving credible training at a prestigious nursing institute, she was comfortable with being moved to an active naval zone. There, she might see considerable activity on both ends of the career spectrum.

Unlike most of the men, female code breakers like Kate initially signed onto the army and navy as civilians. Kate was an exception with her naval connections. She also discovered after a friendly and informative pub outing with Connor and John that there were consistent inequities in pay, rank, and benefits to contend with. Connor, well into his cups, provided an inordinate amount of advice with this enlightening drinking session.

"Never mention your family or speak of strong domestic ties, little lady," he said. "You will be prohibited from holding any higher-ranking positions if it's known that these issues are hindering you in any way. Don't forget— a woman's place is *'in the home.'* If the home wants her back, she must return. And once married, you will have to resign, so if you're going to have a relationship," winking hard at her as he made that statement— "make sure it's not discovered. Your husband won't pay the price. You will."

Kate was furious at this introduction to sexism in the armed forces. But there was little she could do except to heed the proffered and well-meaning advice.

Despite these injustices, in 1941, women soon began arriving in Washington D.C. for work, and the city was spinning with activity. Exactly how many of these women contributed to wartime intelligence remained unknown. But as Kate had discovered, the women were profoundly capable of keeping their secrets, far more so than their male counterparts. They took the threats of court-martial from the military for revealing any aspects of their work seriously. So, no one knew the full extent of their training, their numbers, or their support to the armed forces.

Kate's continued efforts to advance her education paid off. She was conferred the full degree of a college graduate in biology and nursing, with a minor in foreign languages. As the June 1941 graduation neared, Kate was given her naval papers for transport to the Pacific, beginning with a month of progressive training at the naval base hospital in San Diego. Before she left, Kate received a much-anticipated package from Boston with some lovely treats from Aunt Maggie. Accompanying that was a considerable supply of herb seeds from her thoughtful Grama, and the fantastic news that Kerri was pregnant, due in early December.

Kate was ecstatic over the announcement, but also anxious that she would not be present for the birth. She hoped for some leave in the spring so that she could see the new baby. The sisters held several meaningful conversations, which spurred Kate toward one final visit before her transport.

Both sisters cherished the visit, and Kate learned more about how committed her brother-in-law was to Kerri.

She was relieved that he would take care of her sister during her confinement and delivery. Just before she departed for San Diego, she penned a letter to thank them for the visit and for the thoughtful send-off.

My darling Kerri,

I have been planning for my trip, the first leg of which will be sailing to the territory of Hawaii. That's all I am allowed to discuss, but I'm looking forward to the tropical sunsets and the relaxation. Unfortunately, the layover won't be for long! From there, who knows where we will sail?

Packing for the transport has been somewhat stressful. Virtually all the luxuries I take for granted will take months to ship. Our transport allotment is very limited, so I have to choose what I select carefully. You know me! I have categorized all my belongings several times. I've decided that most of my clothing, decorative items, and household linens can be purchased when we arrive. They will be inexpensive from what I hear, and more suited for the tropics. So, I have replaced that poundage with our mother's modern sewing machine and all of my sewing accoutrements and dress patterns.

The next priority is toiletries, stationery, and hosiery, and pictures to brighten my quarters. Books, especially my "bible" of aromatherapy, are critical to me. If I'm to be nursing in a primitive tropical zone, I have crossword puzzles, decks of cards, and some dice games for convalescing patients. For me? Grama's therapy teas and a generous case of our specialty coffee beans from Auntie's café were the last packed items. I will miss that so much!

I am delighted with the categorization of my medicines and antiviral provisions as "essential goods." With limited supplies and somewhat sub-par medical facilities in comparison to the states, I decided to requisition additional space on the transport ship for my therapy oils, herbs, cooking spices, and medical cabinets. A letter of recommendation from James Keighen in Kittery secured priority transport status for all of these items, so please tell our continuing "guardian angel" thanks again for me. I'll pen a note to him after we land in the South Seas.

I will miss you and I will definitely miss our lovely talks. As we grow older, and especially as we are apart, I find now that those talks have a great deal of meaning in my life ~ much more than I ever realized. Have Tim kiss you on "my cheek" and tell him how much I appreciate his outstanding love and devotion to my gorgeous sister.

Your adoring twin ~ Kate

HOPEFUL FOR THE potential for advancement in duties once she arrived at her assignment in the Pacific, Kate had asked Connor and John to initiate some training in Morse Code at the center, as a backup. Armed with their books and notes, she was most grateful for their attention to their favorite female colleague in the cryptology center.

Still, it was a mystery as to why the U.S. Navy had groomed her for work in naval intelligence, as well as the intensive medical training. At some point, Kate would be forced to choose which career path she would sustain. As she managed the long transport flight from D.C. to San Diego, these thoughts again passed through her mind.

It wasn't long before she found the answers to those questions. She was invited to a briefing at the San Diego Naval Hospital in mid-July which enlightened her on her work and her particular training paths. At least 50 young medical recruits were in the room, some of whom she recognized in her classes. She knew a few of the doctors who were attending the same advanced surgical courses with her. The briefing commenced with several naval officers presenting documentation regarding the current war efforts in Europe, and the U.S. involvement behind the scenes. An officer by the name of Commander Richard Evers rose to address the room. He began in a grave tone.

"What we are about to share with each of you stays strictly with the occupants of this room. Some of you know of the O.C.I. –the 'Office of the Coordinator of Information'. President Roosevelt recently founded it to expedite information sharing between competing and often fractious governmental agencies. There is a demand for a command center for classified information to be assimilated and evaluated, for us to better assess the European conflicts."

He waited for this to be absorbed by his audience.

"You may be wondering how you, as medical personnel, can assist in gathering and coordinating such intel. This is the precise purpose of this briefing." Kate watched him intently as he spoke.

"As high-ranking medical personnel, you may be called upon for utilization in several strategic projects, starting with evaluation and care of potential agency recruits in foreign lands. You may be asked to provide technical knowledge for U.S. armed forces medical studies. Those recruits will also be tracking enemy advancements in medical technology and treatment. The enemy being Japan, for these intents and purposes." He paused once more, this time for effect:

"Some of these activities involve being placed near or in Japanese-occupied towns on some of our remote transport islands, to monitor activities and report medical supply deficits. The focus is on any rampant diseases, combat distress and fatigue, and of primary concern, research of any germ warfare. Some may involve the storage, handling, and manufacturing of the medical supplies essential for our partisans. In other words, you may be interviewed for identification as medical professionals willing to take on the same risks in espionage as the operatives we release into these territories. This is for the advancement of U.S. military intelligence. We may not be at war, but we must always be on the defensive, and Roosevelt is supporting all such pre-war activities."

The room was silent as the participants absorbed the accompanying classified information being dispensed.

"We will all be under the purview of one William J. Donovan, appointed specifically by the President himself to oversee support of the war efforts in Europe. If the assignment is accepted, you will be briefed on potential areas key to your current work. That will be all. Thank you."

Kate was elated at the opportunities this briefing provided for her advancement in naval intelligence. She was somewhat impatient about *how* and *when* she would be asked to support these efforts. Reminding herself that both of her parents spent their entire careers in the advancement of naval dominance, she renewed her efforts to expedite all of her studies.

That evening, while walking home from the busy day, she stopped to look up at the California night sky, thinking of the long evenings under the stars with her parents' guidance. She paused for reflection, remembering that she hadn't had time to grieve in a long, long time. Speaking aloud to the heavens, she said:

"Mom. Dad. I want you to know that every day I remember what you taught me. I pray every single night that when you look down on me from Heaven when my day is done, I hope I make you proud. And I pray that I serve the family name well, and our country, as you did so honorably."

The tears streamed down her cheeks, but along with the tears, her resolve was strengthened by the love and guidance she knew was still a part of her heart.

CHAPTER FIFTEEN

INTO HARM'S WAY

When Kate's transport ship finally set sail for Hawaii in August of 1941, she was still unaware of her assignment until the brief stop at Pearl Harbor. Her final destination: The Philippine Islands in the South Pacific. The islands were already in a pre-war state. Preparations in Manila had begun in the months prior for an invasion the armed forces there suspected to be imminent. The big lumbering ship transported Kate and a crew of medical personnel, along with sailors, munitions, and civilian workmen, on the weeks-long voyage. It was crowded, but not miserably so.

Except for the exciting, all-too-brief layover at Pearl, the transport itself was a precursor to the potential hardships they would endure during the Philippines stint. As Kate wrote to her family before the layover in Hawaii…

…I actually tried my hand at a shift in the galley helping the beleaguered cook and his team. About those dehydrated potatoes they gave us— I worked hard, attempting to make them edible. I tried boiling them, frying them (which made them instantly turn to a wet mush!) and then steaming them with some of my spices. It was a waste of my valuable herbs, I assure you! They are just unfit for human consumption. And the powdered eggs… they went overboard the hard way, with me puking my guts out on an unfortunately stormy morning. The ship was tossing, and I was tossing my innards all over the place at the same time! I am prepared to eat some ridiculously crappy food until we land. After that, who knows?

The only thing tolerable in a powdered form is the ice cream. I am ever so eternally grateful for your tins of cookies and fudge that arrived before we departed from San Diego. The best thing about the package was the lovely notes that accompanied them. I am so homesick already, missing my darling family more than you can ever know.

and anticipating the impending arrival of my new niece or nephew with much joy! Well, I must run. There is a briefing to be held before we arrive in the far South Pacific. Yours forever and with all my heart…

~ Kate

During decent weather days, Kate busied herself on deck participating in relatively low-level discussions with two naval code breakers named Ned and Andy. The three met during their brief stopover at the base at Pearl. Kate still wasn't sure where she stood on the continuation of her code breaking career at the center in D.C. The navy would pay for her transport and salary during her stint in the Pacific Islands. She was under contract, and at their mercy on future assignments. So, she was envious that both men knew they were setting up communications outposts on islands far south of the Philippines. In preparation for those plans, they had access to details on MacArthur's current stance on the islands, as Commander of the Philippines' defense system.

Regarding the protection of the islands, Andy stated one evening over a barely tolerable shipboard dinner, "We learned through naval intel at Pearl that MacArthur has formed an underground intelligence web amongst the numerous American businessmen on the islands."

Ned interrupted with, "Messages are retrieved and forwarded to industrial mining executives and all the American-trained civil engineers throughout the Commonwealth. Both are fortunately high in numbers due to an abundance of natural resources on the islands." Probing the young man for answers, Kate asked, "What sort of messages are retrieved?"

Ned responded, "Our supposition is that the spies are managing information alluding to the nature of enemy movement, shipment tracking, and any uptick of government contracts. Of specific interest is the transport of a certain higher echelon of Japanese military leaders onto the islands." This knowledge confirmed Kate's growing suspicion that this Philippines assignment was far more encompassing than she had ever imagined.

Kate also discovered that MacArthur was proving to be a brilliant tactician in war preparation. Executing it was another story, though, and not so much of a success for him, according to Ned and Andy. Late one evening, watching the waning sun drop below the horizon, Ned offered another commentary on that subject:

"MacArthur knows how to subvert the hierarchy of the military's meticulous decision-making, and the command base in Hawaii knows it! The general is under no illusion that the U.S. would support his military operations should an enemy strike occur in the Philippines or the surrounding islands. They'd most likely consider that a lost cause."

As Kate absorbed the implication of that ominous statement, Andy responded, "Neither is he a fan of U.S. intelligence operations. The Washington-based intelligence units have never been integrated into his operation plans. We're certain the military echelon at Pearl and in D.C. are not fans of his open displays of defiance. He has managed to keep them at bay."

This statement was made in full admiration of the overt insubordination by MacArthur. Kate thought hard about the consequences of such actions. "Well, not having a chain of command to review his operations plans…that would cause absolute chaos on the naval base in Kittery. I'm not sure I approve." Both men shrugged this statement off, and the three left their thoughts to themselves as they headed toward their cramped bunks for the night. She decided to keep an open mind about the valuable information she received from her new compatriots.

MacArthur was preparing to wage an aggressive guerrilla war on the islands. His orders from Pearl and D.C. were specific: to fend off a Japanese attack until American relief expeditions could launch a support assault later. To this end, loyal Filipino reservists were recruited and trained to serve as guerrillas. This frenetic pre-war preparation was the state in which the Philippines regularly operated when the passengers of the transport ship would set foot on the island of Luzon.

These allied spies moved about naturally amongst the locals, thus not arousing considerable suspicion from Japanese spies known to have already infiltrated the cities. Some of the wealthy plantation owners on the islands supported these endeavors by hosting Soirées, for which socialization amongst the elite was a natural occurrence, and thus used as a safe conduit of information.

Also included in the general's web of spies was the almost exclusive use of cryptographers from Australia. Far more secretive than even their U.S. and British counterparts, only a few people had an inkling of their existence. This was undoubtedly one of MacArthur's more brilliant moves in waging his war in the Pacific. The small group of Aussies answered only to MacArthur's staff, which appeased his desire for total control over the island defenses.

Kate bent her keen mind toward learning all she could from her two colleagues about this select group of tacticians. She discovered that this band of Australian officers was comprised of collegiate scholars, many of whom spent at least part of their youth in Okinawa. Raised by parents in ambassadorship roles, as *attachés*, or in professorial positions at universities in

Japan, these men spoke fluent Japanese. Having parents with a former diplomatic status also allowed them to move with more ease among the Japanese elite on the islands.

This was the atmosphere under which Kate and the coalition of medical forces sailed smoothly into the waters of the Philippines to end an 18-day voyage on the *Bliss*. They docked in Manila. Most of her shipmates were unaware of the myriad military conflicts that marred the island's existence as a peaceful stop between Hawaii and China. Fresh from their medical training, the young men and women were just happy to end their voyage in the cramped quarters of the ship.

As the munitions and medical supplies were unloaded, the happy-hearted young nurses on deck waved enthusiastically to sailors on the docks. They were welcomed immediately at a lively party in the Manila Officer's Club. The naval nurses were soon transported across the bay to their final destination at the naval hospital on the Cavite peninsula.

Kate also discovered in the first few days that a superiority complex amongst the elite military officers completed the spectrum of full complacency behind MacArthur's staff. One stroke of initiative that he managed despite the complacency was the initiation of a series of covert relay stations to monitor Japanese movement. His own web of intelligence agents knew the surrounding archipelago and interior terrain like the back of their hand. To MacArthur's credit, he did submit a drafted guerrilla doctrine to his superiors in Hawaii, but his plans were buried under massive paperwork in Pacific Hawaii Headquarters (CINCUS), a moniker that Kate found to be comical.

The general had to content himself with the skills of the Filipino troops under Wainwright to monitor potential enemy aggression on Philippine beaches. His massive overconfidence in his ability to successfully plan a counterattack was shared by the American military on the islands. This cockiness spread like an epidemic throughout the military bases there. The young naval nurse found this legitimately alarming. As her dad had always said, "Cockiness breeds costly mistakes."

Kate sent a telegram as soon as she arrived to let the family know she had managed the voyage without incident, keeping it cheery, despite her growing concerns. Within two weeks, she received an uplifting note from her sister:

My darling Kate,

We received your telegram and were ecstatic over the news that you arrived safely in Manila. In fact, Tim and I drove to Maine to celebrate your safe arrival with the family. We also spent a weekend recently with Tim's parents. His father is delighted over the news of the baby. He has asked me to call him dad and I am honored to have him as a father-in-law. Unfortunately, Susannah (as she prefers to be called) has been somewhat recalcitrant. She is of the mind that the baby will slow Tim's career, and that we should have waited to get married. I don't understand that line of thinking. At any rate, there's no turning back, as I'm in my 5th month, and this darling baby will be here before you know it!

Tim has been nothing short of phenomenal in his support of the pregnancy! He is enthusiastic about being a father, intimating that he wants back-to-back babies, but I would love to wait a year to recover. As long as we can "practice," my accommodating husband is happy with that decision. That's my Tim!

Every morning I amble out to our tiny garden to view the sunrise. I think of you and wonder what you are doing at that precise moment. You are on the other side of the world and when I look up at the sky, I feel like the spot where you are standing at that moment is a million miles away instead of a few thousand. At night though... I can look at a bright star in the night sky and focus on you. I feel closer to you in those fleeting moments. I do miss you so, and cannot wait to let you hold our darling baby. Auntie Kate will be an incredible support for this child.

I am simply the luckiest twin in the world to have you as my other half.

Enjoy the scenic island life and bring some sand home in a jar for me. Kiss yourself on "my" cheek and remember how much you are loved.

Yours forever, with all my heart... ~ Sister
Kerri

Kate read the letter many times. She was incredibly homesick, but comforted by the knowledge that her short, two-year stint in the Pacific would likely pass swiftly. She would be home in Maine before she knew it, with a new medical and naval career to add much excitement to her life.

She hoped in the future to settle in Boston near Kerri and Tim. Together again, once more. The sacrifices she was making were all worthwhile, knowing that being near her adored sister again was the eventual end result.

CHAPTER SIXTEEN

ISLAND LIFE

With few pressing medical cases, Kate set out to study as much about the Philippine Islands' importance to the U.S. military as possible. Negotiated under an 1898 Treaty of Paris as an American territory, the archipelago of many islands surrounded the two largest islands, Mindanao to the south, and the largest—Luzon, in the north. Home to over 19 million islanders under the protection of the American Military, the U.S. believed it to be a highly strategic location between Japan and the rest of the vast South Pacific. That was precisely why MacArthur's presence was necessary; she would soon learn it was the reason for her existence there as well.

Peacetime duties for U.S. Navy nurses in the Pacific were reasonably rewarding. In late 1941, there were less than 100 naval nurses stationed in the Philippines, serving the entourage of military families. Cases were mostly familial in the small maritime hospital serving the base. The relatively easy work at Cañacao Hospital included jungle-related illnesses. Malaria, dengue, and various other tropical malaises were prevalent. These cases were interspersed with the occasional broken limb, personnel physicals, and routine tropical inoculations. The nurses worked efficiently. Luckily, playtime was abundant, with tranquil days on the beach and refreshing afternoon teas. Jungle expeditions, consisting of the occasional humanitarian forays into the surrounding hamlets, were instigated to provide care to the villagers. Kate volunteered for this work regularly.

Work usually ended at noon if you had the early shift. The afternoon relaxation came with pleasant ocean breezes, warm sunshine, and all the advantages of the lazy, carefree days of the tropics. Kate soon made several friends, including a young nurse named Callie who also hailed from Maine. The conversations were rejuvenating…talks of Maine blueberry pies, lobster dinners, and dance socials with the "boys of summer"—the vacationing upper-crust co-eds from Massachusetts. Life was easy, the medical cases were uncomplicated, and the officers' at the club were polite and socially adept.

With plenty of downtime, Kate's studies of essential oils, herbs and native remedies endemic to the islands began in earnest. The forays into the villages were helpful cultural experiences for her. At first, Carole Smalley, the young officer in command of her nursing ward, was slightly skeptical of the dilapidated suitcases that Kate brought with her. Kate appreciated Carole's curious questions.

"These are filled with curative dried herbs, organized seed packages, and essential oils from my grandmother. She is a healer and her remedies are miraculous!" Kate explained. "They will come in handy. We never know what we might face in the way of disease."

Eventually, Carole learned through watching Kate's experiments on minor wounds and post-surgical cases that there were considerable merits to Kate's knowledge. Carole was fascinated by Kate's handling of a formidable injury to a local Filipino, who had experienced an infected gash on his foot through misuse of a sharp farming tool.

The tool had evidently been used to spread farm excrement used as crop fertilizer. Thus, by the time the young farmer sought treatment, he was feverish and the foot and lower leg were mottled, red, and swollen. The small red telltale streak of sepsis was creeping up the leg. Soon after, the patient was nearly delirious with the ill effects of the ragged wound. Filled with pus and the sickly-sweet odor of gangrene, when the doctors discussed amputation Kate asked for their permission to attempt a homeopathic interventional treatment. Skeptical, but willing to experiment on a non-military subject, the medical team's consent was given, if somewhat reluctantly.

Kate looked at the young man's face and realized from his anguish that the loss of a limb took away his livelihood. She envisioned him hobbling painfully on a stump to plant crops. Her empathy for him ran inordinately strong.

"Yes," she determined resolutely, "We'll save this leg, young fella!" Kate placed one brown, calloused hand between hers sympathetically as she spoke. Out of that gentle, girlish gesture, a bond was formed between them. The determined nurse found to her surprise that he apparently understood some English and appeared to make out some of her words. She soon discovered that this patient was the youngest son of a long line of sons of a prominent Filipino plantation owner.

His name was Danilo. She smiled at him and said, "You're in my territory now. No surgery for you, I assure you." He was not a particularly garrulous patient, but his few words were calm and well-placed. He did know 'thank you' and that was whispered often. Kate felt confident as she promised him the limb would be healed soon and he seemed satisfied that she was capable of doing so. She moved Danilo's bed to an area where water and a stove were close at hand

Heading to her cabinets, she retrieved leaves from jars marked 'Comfrey,' 'Calendula,' and 'Lavender.' Working up a concoction she often used at home for infections, she took equal amounts of the leaves and crushed them. Wadding up the leaves, she added one or two generous drops of lavender oil. Using her mortar and pestle to crush the solution and open up their healing reagents, she then began boiling them in a small amount of seawater for several minutes, much preferring that to the dubious local water source at the hospital. Carole stopped by again, watching this procedure cautiously at first.

"Kate, don't you consider this a little primitive when we have alcohol for sterilization and wound care?" Carole asked. Kate responded with a smile.

"Alcohol is too caustic. It is a wonderful cleansing agent, but it dries the wound too quickly and damages the surrounding skin. And it doesn't allow for healing solutions to infiltrate the wound." Pausing slightly to let Carole absorb that statement, she continued confidently with, "I want the wound to be able to breathe while managing moist wound healing. The tissue will likely become macerated if the blood and pus are not cleared away. That's a dangerous kind of wound."

Carole moved around the bed to observe the wound closer. Elated with her interest, Kate added, "I am alternating with fresh air and then covering with breathable material to keep the moisture balanced," she said. Relying on her hours of memorizing Gattefosse's notes on wound care, Kate was, in effect, lecturing Carole. However, she was so elated with her audience that she continued on, certain Carole would approve.

"When a wound is just slightly moist, it affords a much faster migration of immune cells, promoting healthy new tissue growth. These cells pass easily through a damp, permeable host."

"Ah, interesting!" said Carole cautiously, commenting, "I think I am beginning to understand your thought process on alternative wound care methods. I want to know why you are heating the herbs. Go on, please."

Kate responded as she worked, "Heat can kill much of the bacteria, and for whatever it doesn't kill, this hot poultice will draw poisons, infection, and infiltrating dirt from the open sore. It also opens capillaries to help blood circulate." As she worked on the sleeping patient, she pointed to the wound's edges and continued her brief lecture. "This warm poultice draws your body's natural antibodies up to surround the wound and attack from inside and underneath. When we reduce the infection, you'll notice some inflammation go down."

She removed the hot herb paste from the heat source. When cooled enough to touch without scalding, she dipped her hands in a small bowl of alcohol, then hastily formed a poultice of the mushy solution. She placed it on a nearby sterile tray, then soaked a cloth in the remaining solution, pouring in a dark brown antiseptic mixture from her cabinets. Next, placing a separate steaming surgical cloth on the wound, she allowed it to cool, then removed it, taking some of the more ragged edges of the injured tissue along with surficial blood. This exposed fresh new blood to the surface. Kate immediately placed the hot herb poultice on the wound, winding a steaming cloth gently around the wound to hold the dressing in place. Finally, she laid a folded bandage soaked with the brown antiseptic solution on top.

"This process is my form of mechanical debridement," she mentioned casually to Carole. "It gently pulls off dead cells and any crusting and infected tissue. The clean, exposed tissue will create a stronger healing environment." Carole watched for a short while, then reluctantly departed to attend an officer's meeting, leaving Kate to capably manage her patient. Kate worked tirelessly into the night, changing poultices and watching for encouraging signs of healing.

By morning, the young Filipino's fever had abated and Danilo was stirring enough to take some healthy broth. Surprisingly, she discovered that he was intuitive enough to ask questions in passable English. She recognized her reaction as one of the American prejudices against the natives on the island. *They may not always speak our language, but that doesn't mean they are inferior by any means*, she thought, slightly ashamed of her unconsciously biased opinions when she had first arrived to review his case.

One of the young doctors on the morning shift watched quietly from a distance as she worked efficiently. Oblivious to her interested onlooker, she removed the dark liquid again from her medicinal shelf. Cleansing the area surrounding the wound once more with the antiseptic reagent, she placed a final mesh poultice on top. Still under the effects of Kate's moderately liberal morphine dosages, the patient remained calm and eventually fell back to dozing peacefully.

A few minutes later, she poured a splash of her peppermint oil into a pan of boiling water. Dipping a large cloth into the solution, she began wiping down the surrounding medical shelves and trays, the bed, and finally, the floor. She then added more drops of peppermint oil into a nearby steaming kettle. When it was steaming in earnest, she drew the drapes around the bed, allotting a small gap for her to exit. Allowing the pan on the stove to expel the continually boiling vapors, she raised the steaming kettle carefully around the drawn drapes. Across the hospital floor, the young doctor crossed his arms, pondering her curious actions. As the pleasant vapors permeated the white curtains, she closed the drapes completely, and the smell of fresh peppermint surrounded her peacefully sleeping ward.

Carole popped in during her mid-morning shift to see the progress on the wound care. The impact of the poultices was remarkable, attracting the attention of several former skeptics of her work. Still viewing her from across the recovery ward, the young doctor observing her was intrigued as he overheard the comments from her colleagues. After a few minutes of medical banter with the staff, Kate finally excused herself to rest her tired but elated body.

CHAPTER SEVENTEEN

A YOUNG LADY OF NO IMPORTANCE

Kate crossed the center of the wound care ward, entering the small anteroom where she kept her botanical herbs, salves, and healing jars. She had quickly changed from her nurse's uniform to a white button shirt and jeans. Still buttoning her shirt, she bent to repack the various jars into a cabinet on the wall. A shadow loomed over her, causing her to rise up unexpectedly. She collided unceremoniously into the broad chest of a tall young man she thought looked vaguely familiar. He quickly caught her, and politely backed off to allow her to finish buttoning her shirt.

"Umm….can I help you, sir?" she asked sheepishly, blushing profusely from the contact and her state of undress. Recognizing from his officer's emblem that he was a naval surgeon, she withheld a caustic comment about his untimely interruption. He smiled and seemed not at all taken aback by the contact or her state of dishabille.

"I wanted to ask about your work with the young Filipino," he commented. "I'm open to any new ideas on healing, and it's obvious that you are as well. Can we meet for tea later this afternoon for a chat?" He stopped, somewhat bemused, as her initial frown was rapidly replaced by the slightest hint of a pleased smile. Pausing slightly to take note of the smile, he said, "Forgive my manners, please. I'm Lieutenant Patrick Danforth. Call me Patrick, please. I recognized you this morning. I believe we traveled on the same Liberty Ship from Hawaii. You would be Ensign Kate Yeager, I understand."

She could tell by the way he cocked his head in a charming, confident manner that he was not ashamed to let her know he was interested in her. His eyes briefly perused the length of her body, but in a way such that the gentle, admiring look was surprisingly pleasant to Kate. Regaining her composure, she smiled in return, playfully giving a slight curtsy, acknowledging his rank in a more unique way than a salute. Giving a small, charming bow in return, he asked about her cleansing of the patient's wound care area.

Kate smiled, with a presence of mind she didn't feel under the attentive stare of what she noticed were large, expressive brown eyes. She immediately compared him with Sean and discovered that his looks were easily competitive enough with the Aussie.

"Oh, that! It's a peppermint oil concoction," she replied softly, answering his question. "It's used where I come from to keep mosquitos and other pesky bugs away. Mosquitoes are particularly dangerous here. So, wiping down the area and steaming the curtains repels them from the wound care area."

She paused, making sure he wanted her to continue. "Peppermint is a miracle plant. Sprinkling the leaves will also help deter ants, mice, and also snakes… if combined with cinnamon and cloves. And the vapors help to calm the patient as well. It has a soothing aroma." She stopped abruptly. Under the casual sensuality he exerted, she felt she was prattling on like a young schoolgirl. Patrick didn't seem to notice.

"This is all inspiring. I would like to discuss your wound care over afternoon tea if you don't mind." With a disarming smile and a look that said he would not take no for an answer, she agreed to join him after a shower and a few bites to eat. She exited the room before he could proffer a lunch meeting instead. Lunch was a "date" to her, and out of her comfort zone with a handsome and inquisitive male.

Back in his quarters, Patrick informed his suite mate of Kate's work— the one who happened to be the Chief of Surgery for MacArthur's Officer's Ward in Manila. Thus, in 24 hours, Kate's work had gained the attention of a number of medical elites.

She took more careful notice of her toilette than usual, searching for a casual outfit that accented her slender figure more than her usual loose, breezy island attire. She chose a blue pleated skirt, pairing it with a white fitted silk blouse. Both were sewn by Kate and thus enhanced her curves perfectly. She tied a patterned silk "island scarf " around her neck. *I just want to impress a surgeon who could influence others to review my work*, she convinced herself.

Patrick was waiting in the small canteen near the hospital. He looked charming, dressed in comfortable white linen. The white attire contrasted well against a lithe, tanned body. His brown hair was streaked with auburn highlights, the effects of the intense, tropical sun. The afternoon tea was refreshing, and Patrick completely disarmed Kate out of her usual shyness around a handsome male. She soon discovered she immensely enjoyed his company. As he talked, she noted his dark eyebrows and thick, sensual lips, and she again found herself comparing him with Sean. The assessment annoyed her for some reason.

Over tea and fresh scones, she explained her wound care process as she had with Carole, occasionally interrupted by probing questions from him.

"How did you come across the antiseptic solution, and how is it made? And can it be easily produced in larger quantities?" he asked pointedly.

Kate responded, "The formula itself is easy to make, so the concoction can be mass-produced if stored correctly. You take equal amounts of herbs— ¼ cup each of crushed comfrey leaves and calendula flowers and lavender, add 1 or 2 drops of lavender oil to a jar filled with sterile water. I use canning jars. Cover, shake, and leave it in a dark, cool area for a few days. Then strain off the leaves and petals. You only need the liquid. It doesn't need thinning and doesn't need a host agent. It's a powerful antiseptic that protects wounds, surgical sutures, and the like."

They conversed comfortably about the island's social events and medical practices for over an hour, when Patrick noticed that Kate was yawning considerably. He reluctantly excused himself, promising to meet her in the morning to study her medicinal herbs. The following day, true to his word, he was waiting by Danilo's bed when she arrived. Together they assessed the patient's wounds and found him recuperating rapidly. Patrick, like Kate, quickly became fond of the Filipino patient.

The young nurse and the handsome surgeon soon found many ways to enjoy each other's company. Patrick began squiring her to Manila soirees and hospital functions, and the two made a formidable pair on the social scene.

To that end, finding no time to sew, Kate had generously loaned her mother's modern sewing machine and accessories to a reputable Filipino seamstress named Mahalia. The grateful and talented dressmaker designed some elaborate dresses for Kate to wear to these events. Kate was happy to model them and bring in business for her new benefactor.

As the couple began to enjoy more outings together, Kate found that Patrick had many connections with the medical officers, as well as MacArthur's inner circle. She was somewhat envious that he knew far more about the general's military activity than she did.

Kate had been mildly disappointed when she was not immediately briefed for what she deemed "spy work" in San Diego after the medical meeting. She learned why at Pearl during her transport. Ted Dickson, the commanding officer and her primary naval liaison at Pearl, explained why during the layover. She was a fair-haired girl on an island filled with dark-skinned natives. Thus, she could never be inconspicuous. Both the Japanese and the Filipino societies were decidedly male-oriented, so her chances of being socially admitted where espionage was helpful were few and far between.

Little did she know, though, that the simplistic scheme designed to interject herself into the espionage work in Manila was solidified by her own suggestion at Pearl, during the same briefing. Once thwarted on the medical and military side, Kate had boldly discussed the idea of a dressmaking introduction, utilizing her sewing skills to work as an apprentice seamstress.

Commander Dickson was vehemently opposed at first, thinking there were limited opportunities to retrieve critical information amongst women. Kate was adamant that this was not the case. Uncharacteristically revealing a common weakness of her own sex, she retorted calmly, "In relaxed settings, women are known to discuss things they hear from their husbands and beauxs. Not anything that is requested *not* to be revealed, of course. But as military wives, they often overhear tidbits as the men chat, for which they are *not* asked to be silent and are *not* contributors to the conversations. The women share these at social events and only with a few highly loyal friends. That type of conversation is fair game. And to a woman's mind, that is not considered taboo."

While Commander Dickson mulled this over, Kate continued, "I lived and breathed this world back home in Portsmouth at the naval shipyard. Even my parents, sworn to secrecy, mentioned things casually while we were supposed to be busy and not listening to them. And this is less dangerous than having spies infiltrate the Japanese communities."

She paused to reflect on a final comment, "I learned in Washington that there is a longstanding tradition of wealthy Japanese taking mistresses. As you mentioned, it is a male-run society with multiple outlets for encounters. And these women *do* talk. They are not as loyal as wives. So, if I ingratiate myself into their midst, I will be privy to their world and their secrets."

She paused again, for final effect: "Eavesdroppers often hear highly instructive things," she continued, somewhat of a quote by Rhett Butler, her favorite movie character.

Dickson agreed to provide the opportunity— at his express signal— for Kate to instigate her plan. *IF* someone approached her, it would mean that enemy attacks on the island were potentially imminent. Kate was not hopeful that this was under consideration at all as they sailed to Manila. Thus far, her opportunities to contribute were nonexistent. She eventually found that prospect after reuniting with her two former liberty shipmates in a popular Manila bar near Sternberg Hospital. Patrick had escorted her there one night after a social event, and she was exceedingly happy to see Ned and Andy again.

Ned boldly approached her one afternoon shortly after their reintroduction, indicating that MacArthur's staff knew of her work in Washington.

Although the general himself was not a fan of the navy codebreakers in D.C., Kate's various skills were welcome, navy or not. After an intensive interview session and a nod from Pearl, she gradually became indoctrinated again. Thus, the timely introduction to Mahalia, the dressmaker.

For the first time in her life, she was most appreciative of her mother's insistence on the detested sewing lessons. Kate donated all her modern Butterick patterns and a stack of the latest mainland and French fashion magazines for Mahalia's design shop.

Fitting days were on Monday, Kate's day off at the naval hospital. Friday afternoons were set for final dress adjustments. By assisting in these, Kate was now privy to plenty of island gossip. To conceal her identity to the extent possible, she always wore a full Yakan headscarf, dressing herself in a long vestido with a dark pañuelo over her shoulders to conceal her skin and hair. She was as nondescript as possible in the native attire.

By avoiding eye contact, as the Japanese required of their servants, she gave all appearances of being a somewhat flighty girl of no importance to their social agendas. Thus, the women paid her no mind as they chatted during their dressmaking sessions. Mahalia translated the Japanese conversations for Kate, although most of her clients spoke English, with Mahalia being Hawaiian-born.

Kate discovered that nothing appeared to be off limits in their gossip, from their husbands' business associates, the Japanese functions they attended, and most critically, the government contracts and key economic endeavors between the local merchants and the Japanese.

The mistresses, of which there were plenty, were even more open, as it behooved them to extoll the high community standing of their 'escorts.' Kate absorbed it all and picked up the Tagalog language quickly. More importantly, her skills helped Mahalia gain a valuable foothold in the vast social circles of the rich Filipino patrons and the Japanese elite.

As the Philippines teams soon discovered, outside of the meetings at Pearl, Kate never discussed her work in Washington, or here. Her loyalty to the U.S. Navy was strong. Then too, her negative experience with Mack caused her to worry unduly that someone might know him. Like her, he could be assigned anywhere in the Pacific.

In a briefing managed at the onset of her assignment to the dressmaker, one of the commanders announced to Kate, "Be advised that you will not be spared the deadly consequences for treason by Japanese officials should war be declared and your work be revealed."

It was now terrifyingly critical to maintain silence. She knew her superiors would learn to value such discretion as well.

CHAPTER EIGHTEEN

SPIES, AND LIES

Patrick managed to permanently wrangle Kate onto his elite surgical team in Manila, allowing her to practice at the more modern Manila Sternberg Hospital surgical ward. He also introduced her to several high-ranking military officers, offering her remedies to manage their ailments. Word soon spread that she was a healer, and she moved up rapidly in social standing with the stories surrounding her medical expertise.

Notwithstanding the carefree atmosphere, to Kate, some ominous winds of change were sweeping in their direction. Like the tide, these could not be stemmed. Franklin Roosevelt was under no illusions after the brutal invasion of China that the Japanese would soften their military aggression in the Pacific. For this reason, Roosevelt had called Douglas MacArthur out of retirement to serve there and protect their investments. Kate also learned that MacArthur had been allotted resources to mobilize Philippine defenses *in the event* of a Japanese invasion. He deployed most of his troops on Luzon and Mindanao, forming what he deemed "key base points of the U.S. line of defense."

South and west of Manila, the Cavite Peninsula extended directly into Manila Bay. It was always an optimum, protected location for repairing and restoring naval ships. And MacArthur found it to be optimal as a supply depot as well. After the 1898 war with Spain, the military hospital rapidly progressed into a superb U.S. naval facility. In 1941, the Cañacao Naval Hospital primarily served naval forces in the western Pacific. Sternberg Hospital in Manila served the army.

One afternoon after a surgery shift at Sternberg, Kate and Patrick dined at a delightful tropical café where the conversation segued to the rampant romances on the island. After surreptitiously viewing a few clandestine doctor-nurse rendezvous from behind the vantage point of a potted palm, she mentioned it to Patrick. He responded after nodding curtly to a young married surgeon across the room with his date.

"Romances are more unguarded because it's a remote location. Given the element of danger to these tropics, with the invasions in China and in Indochina, that's a given.

Kate noted dryly, "This leaves the more inexperienced nurses dependent on the restraint of the men they encounter." Thinking that comment was a direct hint, Patrick retorted in a caustic manner, "You needn't worry, Kate. My mother and father have raised me to be a true gentleman at all costs. I'm following your lead on your propensity for strict propriety."

Seeing Kate's shocked look, he apologized, regretting the comment. Her experiences with Mack in the cryptology center had, in truth, left Kate eternally wary. She had incurred the nickname of "Ice Maiden" after a few attempts by one or two of the bolder military men to kindly relieve her of her shirt during several muggy tropical evenings. Thankfully, Patrick instinctively restrained himself when in close proximity. This restraint was not an easy task by any means.

On a balmy tropical evening a week later, he and Kate were socializing together at a local bar near the hospital. After some witty banter about hospital gossip left them laughing until they cried, Kate realized that she enjoyed Patrick's company far more than she intended. Having said that, she was shy about returning his attention past certain boundaries. Nevertheless, Patrick found many excuses to spend time with her.

Her military records listed her as a reputable linguist, so Kate was often called upon to manage translations for MacArthur's extensive team of aides, both in French and German. There was a small underground office near the entrance to MacArthur's headquarters. Ned was operating there after Andy had moved on to New Guinea to initiate a relay station there. Ned and his team worked in concert with the Australians hired by MacArthur.

Kate found that being in close proximity to the Australians, she relished the propinquity to anyone who grew up in the same country as Sean. She also enjoyed hearing the accent once again. When requested, she arrived before 5:30 am at the office where Ned worked, for her translation of documents received from Pearl. Surgical shifts with Patrick at Sternberg began at 8:00 am and ended by early afternoon. It was a hectic schedule, but she enjoyed the excitement and the work. Her shifts in the recovery ward in Cañacao across the bay were reduced. Most of the staff there merely surmised she was seeing a lot of Patrick. They knew nothing of her dressmaking assignment.

As an accomplished seamstress utilizing Kate's more modern sewing equipment, Mahalia's reputation grew further amongst the many Japanese clientele as well. With over 20,000 inhabitants of Japanese descent, there was no shortage of these customers. Thus, Kate learned a great deal about activities on Luzon and Mindanao. The ladies regularly shared details about whose husbands would miss key social events, where they were going, and how long these men would be absent. All of this was carefully documented by the younger seamstress.

Although she discussed none of this with Patrick, he missed little regarding her actions. He continued to encourage her work with the local dressmaker, if nothing more, Kate decided, than to entice her to look her prettiest at the Manila events they attended. For one of the most extravagant balls of the season, Patrick insisted on managing the expense of a ball gown for Kate befitting the young British Princess Elizabeth. Mahalia was happy to use Kate's alluring figure to present her work.

Held in the largest of the beautiful, stately ballrooms in Manila, this late November Christmas Ball was a highlight of the season. As Mahalia explained to her young apprentice, "Filipinos traditionally mark September 1 as the start of the countdown to Christmas. Known as the 'Ber Months,' the Filipino holiday season was considered the most extended timespan of any Christmas season in the world. And the balls and charity events become more extravagant as December gets closer."

Kate entered this late November soirée on the arm of a handsome Patrick, dressed in a form-fitting white tuxedo. Patrick soon discovered that "Miss Yeager," resplendent in a light peach dress, was an eye-turner. Outfitted in a lavish tulle and satin off-the-shoulder gown, it revealed a daring amount of cleavage for Kate. She had never felt so beautiful, shimmering under the effects of the swirling white globes and glittering chandeliers. Her hair, bundled into an elegant chignon, was a style that her sophisticated twin Kerri had taught her was forgiving on the dance floor.

Patrick was entranced. At his charming best, his eyes promised much as they glanced lingeringly over the tight bodice of her dress. The two danced the night away under the enchanting ballroom lights. During a pause in one of the dances, Kate retired to the lady's sitting area to re-pin her hair.

Entering a divided dressing compartment, she overheard several of the wealthy Filipino matrons talking in the adjoining walled seating area. Peeking tentatively around the partitions, she saw they were whispering to a few wives of MacArthur's military aides. Kate's ears perked up as one of the Filipinos mentioned indignantly, "This will most likely be the last ball of the season."

When a U.S. military wife mentioned that she was alarmed at the news, one of the Filipinos gossiped, "Then you'll be far more alarmed in what *we* believe is going to happen next, my dear."

A younger Filipino woman interrupted, stating, "I've heard that the wealthier Japanese residents are planning to exit the island within the week, using an evening merchant transport. They are leaving everything behind!" The wives obviously knew that this clandestine activity would set off alarms in the U.S. military that would effectively end their social season early.

As they gathered closer to chat, Kate overheard pieces of the hushed conversation. The Japanese were conducting military meetings in remote cities with some high-ranking Filipino military officers. This was managed to negotiate "protection" in the event of an invasion. And there was a credible rumor amongst the women regarding daily nighttime munitions supply landings on remote beaches near the Japanese enclaves. Through gossip at the dressmaking shop, Kate was aware that some prominent Filipino businessmen had also been parlaying with the Japanese bureaucrats to protect their businesses.

Most Filipinos remained intensely loyal to the U.S. and unforgiving to anyone with strong ties to Japan. The Japanese were often dismissive, condescending, and brutal with their Filipino servants. Therefore, the Filipino "American loyalists" were intrinsically aligned against the Japanese. This was apparent, especially at this particular ball where invitations to some suspected Filipino military spies mysteriously "went missing." Also notably absent at the ball were many Japanese bureaucrats, except for those invited at the express request of Jean MacArthur. So, the women, it appeared, could be equally as vicious as the men in their combative states. "Hell hath no fury…" thought Kate as she quickly exited the sitting rooms.

She reentered the ballroom, finding Patrick waiting patiently for their next dance. She was vexed about not knowing how to excuse herself to warn Ned's team about what she had heard. As she pondered this dilemma, Patrick commented observantly, "You look a tad flushed. Why don't we take a short stroll in the moonlight to cool off?"

He found Kate's wrap, and together they strolled down the manicured promenade of Dewey Boulevard. Under the majestic palms lining the wide promenade near the ocean, the ostentatious, beautifully lit mansions lining the avenue were a perfect backdrop for a romantic stroll together. The conversation flowed smoothly, with Patrick easing her obvious trepidation with some witty news he had heard, or most likely just made up.

Her attentive escort halted as they neared a dark alleyway beside the entrance to Ned's offices under the MacArthur headquarters. Kate also hesitated, turning to him and attempting to mask her surprise at the clear implication. Patrick bent, and in the soft, enchanting moonlight and the warmth of a perfect tropical evening, he kissed her, full and lingering, on the lips. She melted against him, swept away by this mysterious, handsome man full of many mysteries.

"Kate, dear," he said softly, "you might need to step inside and visit with our mutual friend Ned. I can wait outside if that will ease your concerns."

The astonishment was plain on her face. Many things— now explained— crossed her jumbled mind. Patrick was a part of their team of spies. His interest in her work with Danilo, the escorts to the balls… all of it now made sense, enforced as part of a more complex plan. Seeing the look on her face, he lifted her chin and kissed her again.

Kate hesitated as her mind assessed the situation and its implications. "Your interest in my surgical advancement and my medicinal concoctions…you needed to get close, to introduce me to our mutual friends. Is that what is happening here?" she asked pointedly. Patrick interjected, "No, Kate. My interest in you is genuine. Don't go thinking otherwise."

With that, he lifted her up to carry her down the steps leading to the underground room, adding, "The stairs are slippery from recent rains. You'd better not get your ball gown dirty." He opened the door, using a key he slipped from his pocket. Again, another surprise for Kate. 15 minutes later, they headed back to the ballroom, after a furtive look around to see if they had attracted any onlookers. For the rest of the evening, Kate danced merrily with Japanese merchants and Filipino officers, keeping the conversations flowing as innocently as possible toward their local businesses and merchant transactions, and of more importance, their export/import companies.

As Patrick supplied her companions with alcohol, she deftly pressed her dance partners on questions such as the natural resources on the islands they depended on in Japan, the crop outputs of food sources, and the hierarchy of potential mineral exports to the Orient. As charming and as interested as she could be throughout the night, Kate played the part of a flirtatious, inebriated blonde to perfection.

The couple lingered for many post-ball parties at the nearby stately mansions. Patrick had secured two hotel rooms at the Manila Hotel, so in the wee hours of the morning, he walked her to her room, unlocked her door, and gallantly turned to leave. Softened by his restraint, Kate placed her arm on his and offered, "Would you care for a cup of tea, Patrick?" He entered the room hesitantly. He wanted her. Very much so! But he wanted her to remember every aspect of their first auspicious night together…*if* it happened. It was clear this would not be that night, but the events of the evening had worked their charm on her. Her face pressed upward invitingly and she complied eagerly when he bent to kiss her. As a second kiss deepened, he took her in his arms in a slightly more forceful approach.

She hesitated immediately, quickly backing away, eyes wide. "No— don't. I can't. Please stop!" she said tearfully. Patrick sensed her mounting fear.

Working to calm her down, he sat her near the open window for some fresh air. Suddenly, the alcohol and the stress under which she was laboring during much of the evening caused her to wretch, barely making it to the basin in the bathroom. Miserable from the exertion, she curled up in the wide chair, rambling about past experiences with men.

Patiently coaxing her into revealing her negative encounters with Mack, Patrick now realized why she feared intimate situations. The lack of trust of men was glaringly apparent. Exhausted after their protracted, emotional discussion, she soon succumbed to a deep slumber. Patrick moved her to the bed, and gently removed her outer ball gown to ensure she would have no further mishaps in the expensive dress. Leaving her in her chemise, a silk slip, and a hotel robe, they fell asleep thus, with him on top of the covers at the edge of the bed — to placate her when she awakened. It would be a long, decidedly uneventful night, but he accepted that as the challenge of the promise of future intimacy.

Codebreakers in action ~ 1941

DEFEAT, DEFIANCE AND SHEER INGENUITY

Dec 1941–early 1942

War begins in the Pacific!

CHAPTER NINETEEN

INVASION OF THE PHILIPPINES

Kate awoke the following morning with a massive headache, wondering wildly about the course of actions that precipitated her state of undress. Showered, dressed, and toweling his hair dry, Patrick moved toward the bed, saying, "Good morning, princess. How's your head?"

Noting that her dress was on the chair, she shyly stated, "Pounding madly. And how exactly did that get removed?" Patrick smiled impishly, retorting, "You were sick. I removed it so you wouldn't ruin my investment. The ball gown, remember?"

She cocked an eyebrow toward him at the implication that she had received his unsolicited assistance in her disrobing. Patrick smiled again, "I left your slip and chemise and on as I removed your gown and accessories. It's not unlike wearing a bathing wrap and sarong on the beach. And I'm definitely not inclined to take advantage of a young girl 'under the influence,' so you're relatively safe with me. For now, at least."

There was an unmistakable air of intimacy between them that had elevated with the secrecy of the night's events, so he winked playfully, "Let it be a warning, though, that all bets are off later when you're *not* under the influence. So, take that as a threat. Or a promise if you'd like."

Kate could see that he was joking somewhat, so she smiled puckishly to lighten the mood further, saying, "Hmmm… that aspect of your plans might just require a marriage license!" Moving somewhat painfully to the bathroom, she changed into a skirt and blouse she had packed. When her toilette was reasonably presentable, they set out to find a local café for a recap of the night's events. Patrick spared few details of the work ahead of them. Her conversations with the Japanese officers had been highly enlightening, and the information required urgent relays to MacArthur's team.

During a slight lull in the discussion, Kate looked across the table and said, "Since I believe we've moved our casual friendship up a few notches, I'm curious as to how you managed to get assigned here on the island, and also," she said boldly, "how a man with your immeasurable charm and looks has managed to stay single at 27."

"Well, that may prove to be a long and titillating story, my dear." He smiled boldly as he spoke. Leaning back in his chair, he said, "Don't forget. You asked. So, the bachelor part is easy. My mother, Elaine, was a long-time friend of MacArthur's first wife, Louise. Hence, my military connections here, by the way, but I digress. My mother and Louise were debutantes together. As society pretty much dictates with the upper crust these days, one husband is never enough. Louise has had three thus far, with MacArthur being her second in line… her current husband being the English actor, Lionel Atwill."

Suitably impressed with this recitation, Kate's eyebrows raised. "Go on!" she commanded.

"By way of background information, Elaine was a great beauty in her day, I might add. Or at least Newport Society certainly thought so! My mother married three times, my father being the second round of the batch of husbands. When my father, Jack Kelly Danforth, married her, his family practically disinherited him. Divorce was taboo in Catholic society. Especially in his hometown of Philadelphia. And the Philadelphia Kellys and Danforths are strong, proud families. I have little to do with them these days. And equally little interest in most of the aspects of marriage, I might add. Up until now."

He looked across the table with a slight nod after she indicated she clearly understood the meaning behind those words. "As for the rest…Yale Medical School, after a dutifully distinguished collegiate career at Princeton… residency at Johns Hopkins…I was set for a private practice with my father in Philadelphia. I was bored to death with my prescribed life. The army took an interest in my application and the pay they offered was decent. I wanted far less of society and far more of adventure, so I asked for this assignment. So, there you have it, in a nutshell!"

AFTER THEIR NIGHT together in Manila, the two grew closer, and determined to team up for more of what Patrick humorously called "spy adventures." The days and nights began to be a blur. However, for the most part, all on the island still remained, on the surface at least, a tolerable coexistence between the islanders and the military presence of Japanese and Americans. Kate continued to assist Mahalia with dress fittings, which by now provided her with increasingly more portentous news relative to the islands' defense. A rapid increase in clothes orders told her that the military wives knew something was up. They were stocking up on clothing that would be in shortage with a war.

With no conflict in the Pacific yet, translating and decoding documents from the European front were still of crucial importance to MacArthur, for which Kate's French and German became acutely urgent. There were, of course, other translators on MacArthur's staff. They were vitally needed to monitor radio transmissions in his relay stations in and around Manila. Any documentation of German-to-Japanese contact was of supreme criticality, and that was deemed her focus. With Kate aware of his activities with Ned, Patrick could share what he knew about the Japanese movements. As they ended a surgical shift one morning in early December, he briefed her on events leading to an inevitable war.

"After the Tripartite Pact was signed by the Axis Powers in Berlin on September 27, 1940, it was a foregone conclusion to our government that Japan was eventually going to be pulled into the war in Europe. Therefore, as of now, it is simply a matter of *when* and not *if*."

When Kate asked how this affected the U.S., Patrick responded, "Well, this alliance was designed specifically to force us– as in the U.S.– into hesitating before jumping into a war on the side of the Allies. If we jump, that's it. We're committed to fighting and each of our allies will also have to commit. These treaties have that desired effect, on purpose! So we don't want to commit."

Kate knew from previous briefings in Washington that this practiced isolationism still remained prominent.

By early December of 1941, though, it was evident to anyone with a military background that the peace and tranquility of this island territory was well and truly under threat. MacArthur was increasingly in a perpetual state of preparation, requesting every type of military aid he could negotiate, requisition, or confiscate. Of critical importance were Boeing B-17 Flying Fortress bombers. In response to his urgent requests, the 27th Bombardment Group was eventually dispatched to Manila.

The bomber squadron had steamed boldly into Manila Bay on November 27, 1941. The personnel landed onshore promptly without their supplies, equipment, or the actual benefit of, say— any aircraft. For the next week or so, the crew unloaded supply ships by day and partied the breezy island nights away into the wee hours of the morning. It was always warm in this part of the world, so they enjoyed the respite from previous assignments in the freezing English winters.

The pilots were 14-carat gold in human form to MacArthur. And they were his only sure line of a mobile air defense should a Japanese invasion be imminent. At least, when the planes arrived they would be. Without these planes, the island was almost indefensible. Still, island life seemed promising for the men who accompanied this squadron's arrival, if only briefly.

These fresh-faced, ambitiously cocky pilots made fast friends with the young nurses, including Kate. She enjoyed their lively banter once she fended off some of their more persistent advances. Used to the allure of fawning young local ladies, and the unencumbered lovemaking with the relatively abundant local prostitutes in military zones, the men found that the challenge of the rebuffs of the nursing staff was an amusing pastime. As Kate said to her friend Callie one evening after a military party, "It's sort of like chasing persistent fleas off of a dog. Only the more consistent measures work with these brazen men!"

In that scant 10-day time, Kate grew attached to these men, especially one named Jimmy, who hailed from Boston. Through these attachments, she once again gathered ominous tidbits of the now-impending conflict with Japan. She braced herself for the eventuality of a war that was looming imminently toward the tropical island.

December 7, 1941 – Suddenly and Deliberately

By December 1st, the Japanese bombing patrols were regularly spotted over northern Luzon near Lingayen Gulf. Under the advice of military advisors, orders came from Pacific headquarters to move the 27th Bombardment Group B-17 bombers to Mindanao, out of range of the Japanese bombers in the north. As fate ordained, this move was postponed to allow the pilots to attend a lavish soiree at the largest hotel in Manila, under MacArthur's grace.

The MacArthur's residence hotel held this party in honor of Major General Lewis Brereton, Commander of the Far East Air Force in the Philippine Islands. Several of the nurses were invited. Kate politely declined, having pressing work at Cañacao the next day. The party was raucous, and full of rambunctious officers and unabashed drunken merriment. The festivities finally closed down at 0200 hours Manila time on December 8th, coincidentally, 0800 hours, Sunday, December 7th, at Pearl Harbor, Territory of Hawaii, across the dateline…the exact hour the Japanese aircraft began their raid on Pearl Harbor.

For everyone stationed in the Philippines on that Monday morning of December 8th, life as they knew it changed dramatically for the worse. Radio monitors in Manila picked up the famous *"This is no drill"* message at 3:00 am, informing them that an invasion of Pearl Harbor had begun. Further word crept out through chatter between California coast defense radio operators.

As it was still too dark for coordinated Japanese offensive operations against the Philippines, the Americans and the Filipinos had valuable hours to prepare preemptive airstrikes to strengthen their meager ground defenses. As one officer later said, "God appeared to be on our side initially." An unexpected heavy fog also presided over Taiwan at dawn, debilitating imminent Japanese air operations planning to take off from that site.

Unfortunately for everyone involved, this invaluable opportunity for preparation was never utilized. Ned had received word from sources in Major General Brereton's offices that Brereton, at 0300 hours, recovering impressively from any potential ill effects of his party, did his level best to get his aircraft in the air. He prepared for MacArthur's approval to attack the invasion fleet, or potentially target even the Japanese bases in Taiwan.

Patrick awoke Kate at 6:00 am in her quarters next to Cañacao, where she had a recovery room teaching shift that day for student nurses. He quietly informed her of the attack on Pearl.

"Brereton has attempted to prepare for a counterattack. MacArthur hasn't given the order. Literally from 5:00 am on, Brereton has been denied access to MacArthur to discuss a defense strategy. Kate asked, "Is an attack here imminent, or is this an attack against the U.S. military at Pearl, specifically?" she asked. Patrick replied gravely, "No one knows. But if it is an all-out war, this delay will be a fatal decision for everyone on this island. I'm not ruling out strict military orders from Oahu and Washington. That we are to be denied any opportunity for initial strikes here. I've heard military chatter that MacArthur could be negotiating a conservative approach on behalf of the Filipino government."

As they traversed the path to the hospital, he added: "If an attack is imminent, MacArthur might have felt it best to complacently accept what might be a limited landing. In other words, a peaceful negotiation toward their occupation could be better— to accept the inevitable and to prevent bloodshed. We will soon see. Let's get to the hospital and prepare. Ned will get word to us as he hears anything further."

If the brief but horrific attack on Pearl Harbor was a nightmare of epic military failure, the full-on Philippines attack was a disaster of biblical proportions.

At nearby Fort McKinley at 8:00 am, men were rising casually for breakfast when a loudspeaker blared orders to report for immediate duty. At Clark Field, nearly two hours northwest of Manila, the news about the Pearl Harbor raid was picked up from both commercial broadcasts and military messages. A military operator immediately notified MacArthur's staff. All combat units in nearby military fields and air bases were alerted to expect an attack on every military facility in the Philippines.

CHAPTER TWENTY

FIRE AND BRIMSTONE

Kate and Patrick soon received military word via phone, from Ned: "By 1100 hours, American aircraft that had been ordered earlier by Brereton as recon patrols monitoring Japanese air activity had to land to refuel. There have been no orders to launch preemptive weaponized patrols. We are unprotected and highly vulnerable at this point."

Other sources responded that it was almost 11:30 when MacArthur finally gave his approval, again with no one having any clear idea why the disastrous delay occurred. Thus, all military operations were rendered useless when the successive Japanese airstrikes began.

Rumors persisted that many casualties would have been averted had this order been given much earlier. It was not to be. At 12:35 pm, Japanese aircraft reached the airfield at Iba on the west coast of Luzon, destroying a flight of P-40 aircraft while they were landing for refueling. Almost simultaneously, the Del Carmen airfield to the southeast was also attacked, with its outdated P-35A fighters forming little resistance against the more modern Japanese planes. From what Kate later gathered through Ned and his team, what little resistance the Americans could have effectively offered was virtually blasted out of the air or destroyed on airstrips. The Japanese bombing attacks continued unabated, and steadily. MacArthur's air force was being annihilated.

On Dec 10th, with air superiority achieved and almost all semblance of resistance virtually nonexistent, the Japanese army landed on the island of Mindanao and then Luzon, quickly capturing airfields and other critical strategic positions. Further bombings to strengthen their landings were ordered by the Japanese Supreme Command.

December 10, 1941 – Cañacao Naval Hospital

With battles raging literally to the north and far south of Manila Bay, the carefree idyllic island life was over for good. Kate was busy at the naval hospital assisting with a pre-dawn inventory of the medical supply ward when Callie slipped up behind her, whispering softly, "I heard the Japs are headed our way. We're to prepare for pending casualties and an invasion of our area."

The tone of her voice registered the fear in her troubled face. She followed with, "They say it is imminent…not just probable, Kate. This is the real thing. There is to be an announcement at an emergency nurses meeting."

Kate's voice was soothing and she responded in a quietly resolute tone, "If it happens, we'll be ready. This is exactly what we trained for and we'll manage accordingly. Let's get the ward organized. Steady and ready, honey." Inwardly, she was quaking. She already knew from the decoding team that the traffic of messages had picked up significantly, a clear sign of impending action. The month-long training in emergency care back in San Diego kept her outwardly calm while they readied the ward.

As the nurses were rounded up, both Carole and the matronly naval officer who oversaw the surgical ward activities stated soberly that they could expect an imminent attack from the Japs any time after daylight. The mood was somber, expectant, but somewhat naïve. Many were under the illusion that with MacArthur nearby in Manila, robust military operations and fortifications would still prevail against an attack. Each was ordered to pick up additional tasks around the hospital to prepare for substantial surgical casualties. All leave, either casual or long-term, was canceled. So, Kate could not manage her regular transport to Sternberg in Manila.

Thus, the Japanese attack on Pearl Harbor forced the peacetime Philippines with a violent shove into World War II. The nurses at Cañacao braced themselves for wartime preparation. War was imminent, but they still didn't know *when*. They were not to wonder long. When the air-raid sirens blew at noon on the morning of Dec 10th, those few who were not on duty were dining in their quarters near the hospital. The previous mornings' message relayed was that sirens would not be for drills but reserved only for actual attacks, so there would be no confusion about an emergency situation and preparedness. This was real to all of them, and panic ensued.

Shortly after, the fear of death became conceivable, and then highly likely. When the sirens hit, everyone scrambled to find cover under the buildings. A few found shelter in a well-worn path between buildings that offered a small trench for protective cover. As quickly as they began, the air raid sirens stopped and the nurses shifted their positions to peer out from the relative safety of their shelters. Long, anxious moments of silence elapsed and they cautiously relaxed their vigil under protective but sight-limiting buildings. Still, they could hear no all-clear signal informing them that the danger had passed. *Perhaps no one was left to sound the alert*, many wondered anxiously. The naval base across the bay from Cañacao remained under heavy attack. Sporadic machine guns continued to strafe their area violently.

In the hospital, Callie and Kate were preparing makeshift surgical rooms and organizing the recovery ward. Suddenly, the terrifying, unfamiliar drone of a mass of planes filled their ears, followed by blasts of bombs exploding. They rushed to patients, moving them away from windows and flying debris. Soon after, a pitifully few anti aircraft guns strafed the air across the harbor, from the nearby U.S. Navy yard. The Japanese air attack was relentless. Some nurses prayed fervently out loud underneath surgical tables that became makeshift bunkers. Some were silent, in massive shock. Wave after wave of explosions shook the building above and the ground beneath them. Nearly an hour passed with torpedoes and bombs detonating around the area, creating a wide swath of devastation. Callie and Kate remained stationed near the patients, frantically covering the wounded as best they could. Terrified beyond any conversation, the nurses occasionally whispered soothing words to those post-surgical patients who were conscious.

No amount of preparation could have given them any reasonable expectation of what was yet to come their way. Word spread that more than 500 civilians and naval personnel were wounded or killed during the initial raid.

Before long, the ferry landing that transported goods and personnel across the harbor was bathed in blood and bodies. The shell-shocked nurses on duty were treating wounded and dying soldiers and civilians amid the final waves of the airstrike.

After 45 minutes of ear-splitting explosions nearby, silence fell upon them, equally deafening.

The nurses that took cover near their barracks crept from their hiding places, with shaking limbs and screaming nerves. Half a mile across Cañacao Bay, swelling clouds of smoke darkened the sky. Flames shot through the air, flaring from fuel depots and supply buildings. The shipyard and diesel depots were virtually leveled by the persistent and unabated bombings. Cavite Naval Shipyard looked to be totally demolished. The nursing personnel made their way fearfully to the hospital, finding any available cover under nearby palms, benches, and building awnings. They arrived to see the casualties streaming in. The terror was palpable, and absolute chaos soon became a bloody norm.

Patrick soon arrived from an emergency surgical staff meeting in a nearby building. Callie and Kate took action as he and other officers gave orders, "Any device on wheels that can carry wounded needs to be confiscated!" Callie turned to call this order out at the front entrance as the wounded started arriving at the hospital. Cars arrived, packed with battered, writhing bodies.

Bamboo mats, heavy carpets, small tables, and the like were also used for transport.

For Kate, who was immediately assigned to assess the wounded, any semblance of standard triage was almost impossible. She shouted orders over subsequent waves of bombings to nursing staff and orderlies, "Line the make-shift stretchers against the walls! Create a path for medical staff to assess as best we can! Move it! Quickly!"

The hospital was soon swarmed with patients… not a room or floor was left intact from the blood, gore, and broken bodies. With a medical cart of syringes she had set up earlier that morning, Kate made her way down a row of wounded with morphine. Callie and two other nurses followed immediately with tetanus boosters. It was all she could think of to do, the helplessness of the situation soon pressing on severely shattered nerves. Her mind screamed, but her voice was calmer than she expected.

"We need surgeons. Get a doctor over here!" she called out as her body moved almost mindlessly to the more severe casualties. Military personnel and frightened civilians carrying the wounded suddenly became ordained as medical orderlies. With a presence of mind she did not know she possessed, Kate began using medical tape and her cabinet marker to mark the patients by order of the type of wound and the immediate care needed. Those with relatively superficial wounds were marked "M" for morphine, to await attention as time permitted, with a giant check mark for those already administered with a dose. She wrote instructions on a white wall above them for all to see.

A double dose of morphine was potentially lethal, especially amidst the chaos. "S/A" was for immediate surgery/ limb amputation— and prompt carriage to the second-floor makeshift O.R.'s. "F" was for fatal or near-death— those who had no chance of survival. They were to be given morphine only, to ease them compassionately into eternity. None of the nurses giving these labeling orders had time to genuinely recognize what that meant to the patient. "P" was for primary critical care, requiring immediate wound closure to staunch bleeding or prevent organ failure. The marking system was repeated on walls, and passed on throughout the ward. In the continuing confusion, no one wanted to make fatal mistakes.

Within the first two hours, Kate's back was killing her, her body operating on equal parts of sheer will and courage. There wasn't time to rest or to find a corner where her nerves could calm. She soon made her way up to an improvised surgical ward on the second floor. As a trained surgical nurse, her skills were better served there, with triage the only area now under any semblance of control. The makeshift surgical wards overflowed– three or four O.R. tables to a crowded surgical unit. There were not enough doctors to go around, so experienced surgical nurses like Kate closed up surgical patients, tying off blood vessels while doctors moved on to more urgent cases.

During that horrific day, no personnel left the hospital, unless to rest under any stable object that could allow their battle-weary bodies a slight amount of respite. Casualties littered the first floor, and soon on the grounds beyond the hospital walls.

By the following morning, the hospital was rendered unsanitary by virtue of the sheer number of casualties. Patients who could be moved were transported to Sternberg, the largest and best-equipped hospital in the Philippines. Sternberg undertook care of the most critical medical casualties and Kate was requisitioned by Patrick for more urgent surgical cases there. This assignment coincided with the command from Medical HQ for her to supervise a post-surgical area for more acute patients.

With supplies dwindling rapidly, Patrick worked to help establish Kate's medicinal remedies as a primary source of wound care recovery. His constant support by her side was of great comfort. Together, they implemented the use of these as credible healing reagents. In peacetime, this improvisation of a new type of care would be thwarted by months of review and a lengthy trial period. With a massive deficit of medical supplies, Kate's processes were integrated rapidly and with continued measurable success.

CHAPTER TWENTY-ONE

THE FALL OF MANILA

Not long after Kate's permanent move to Sternberg Hospital, Patrick entered the wound care ward and announced quietly that her services were requested in the MacArthur suites. She took only enough time to change her soiled uniform and run a comb through her tousled hair. The urgent situation turned out to be MacArthur's young son, Arthur, stricken with a bout of malaria. With quinine sulfate in dangerously low quantities, General MacArthur recognized the ramifications of requisitioning medical supplies already under strict monitoring, for use on his young son. Having heard of Kate's prowess with medicinal herbs and oils, she was summoned by him to assist with little Arthur's care. She arrived in their private quarters and assessed the child.

Precocious, with huge expressive eyes, he had an unusual accent of the combined Chinese pigeon of his nursemaid Au Cheu and his mother Jean's Southern Tennessee drawl. This was coupled with his father's clipped military accent. He immediately took to his new nurse, mesmerized by her long blonde curls and wide, expressive, blue eyes. Surrounded since birth by dark-skinned Filipinos, his petite, dark-haired mother, and a Chinese nursemaid, a taller, fair-skinned model of the female species was a novelty to the small boy.

Kate requested a large teapot of boiling water, to which she added a liberal dose of peppermint oil. The pleasant aroma soon began permeating the room. Next, she made a potent tea mixed with fresh ginger slices and boiling salted water, laced with honey to entice Arthur to drink. Opening a jar with contents that resembled red tree bark, she began grating it into a tea strainer.

"This is a dried cinchona bark alkaloid. It has the same refined properties as quinine. I'll steep it and add honey. We'll start with this more concentrated form of cinchona and then use my tonic syrup later. This medicine will also increase his appetite. Arthur should drink this at 8-hour intervals for the first day, but it needs to be *carefully* measured. An overdose is dangerous," she added. "Here's a more precise dosage measurer." She handed it to Jean.

At his mother's curious look, Kate responded, "The ginger concoction and the cinchona tea will greatly boost his immune system." She turned to Ah Cheu and requested a bowl of Kalamansi, a fruit similar to limes but with a taste more reminiscent of oranges. Arthur was urged to eat one of these, and he managed it weakly. He was a darling patient.

To her delight, the young nurse found him to be a true military son, "soldiering on" with little complaint. Some pomelo grapefruit was scrounged up and washed and Kate again enticed Arthur to eat several spoonfuls of the liquid "gold." She explained that the concentrated juices worked to neutralize the effects of the malaria-inducing parasites. Peeling the grapefruit, she dropped the peelings in a pot of boiled water for later use. "We'll need a small glass of this Pomelo juice for him to drink every two hours."

Next, facing Arthur's mother, Jean, she said resolutely, "I'll need some chicken and immune-boosting spices to add to the broth. Boil the meat and some marrow bones down to a concentrated broth. Keep a large pot of this bone broth going strong for at least the next 72 hours. Take some of these grapefruit peelings and add them to this broth, along with some chopped vegetables. Add some cinnamon, paprika, luyang dilaw, and plenty of fresh garlic. These have healing properties."

She continued to examine little Arthur efficiently as she spoke, "I have a few bits of dried calendula and pepper to add to the soup. These compounds induce the growth of white blood cells."

Reaching down into her medical bag, she located these additional fresh spices. "Take a knife and scrape some lemon peeling into the broth and add five or six slices of lemon. You must be careful to wash the vegetables and fruits well to remove any dirt or germs. A bout with diarrhea will considerably worsen his condition."

As the staff scurried to do her bidding, she continued, facing Ah Cheu and Arthur's mother, "Last, take one or two drops of this peppermint oil and add it to a host oil like coconut or avocado oil if you have it. Use cooking grade tallow if not. Wipe the back of his neck, chest, feet, and the base of his spine at noon and repeat this every few hours. It will reduce the fever. But avoid the face and throat, please. It's not always good for small children to ingest this through the skin near the glandular areas."

Both Ah Cheu and Jean were immensely relieved at Kate's presence, and happy to be of use in helping to augment his healing progress.

Although his appetite was compromised by the effects of the illness, a small bowl of soup was also dutifully consumed by Arthur just after noon, with his mother promising that he would be ready to play by the next day or so if he cooperated. Filled with rich vegetables and the pleasant remnants of the added citrus and spices, the aroma was strong enough to arouse his appetite somewhat, precisely the effect Kate wanted. He dozed fitfully for the next few hours while Kate sponged him with the peppermint oilcloth. She fed him more of the rich soup the next time he awoke. She was rewarded with a slight color added to the wan little cheeks.

"If diarrhea becomes a problem for the little boy," Kate recommended, "a warm salt water enema is imperative to cleanse his system of bacteria and parasites." If the need arose, his mother promised to manage this with the staff. Kate performed the same mosquito prevention ritual she enacted with the young Filipino farmer, letting the steam seep into the netting surrounding his bed.

As she managed this routine, General MacArthur slipped in to check on his son. Noting Arthur's returning color and his more peaceful breathing, Douglas MacArthur smiled, with a tender look that almost masked the effects of the severe stress he was under.

"I cannot thank you enough for your help," he stated. "My wife has informed me that you have been nothing short of phenomenal. I understand from forceful sources that your services are essential at Sternberg, but perhaps a few minutes here tomorrow would help speed his healing."

Kate returned a smile in his direction, pleased at his kind mention of her work at Sternberg. She promised an evening visit and a morning repeat of the anti-malarial routine.

From then on, she found that both Jean and Douglas MacArthur's considerations of her needs at the hospital were gracious. Any requests to local Filipinos to help replenish herbs and oils were given full attention to every extent possible. Her dwindling repository of cinchona bark was mysteriously filled the next morning. She knew that the only ample source was on a farm in Mindanao, so she was grateful for the dangerous supply run. Jean MacArthur ordered a duplicate supply of every herb Kate used for a medicine cabinet in their family quarters. Kate was most appreciative of the continued assistance in maintaining her own herbal cabinets. From then on, they remained stocked.

The next days passed in a blur, and it was rumored that Manila was soon likely to be under attack. To prevent the slaughter of thousands of innocent civilians, MacArthur began negotiating terms to declare Manila as an "Open City"… abandoning all defensive measures to ensure a peaceful occupation. The destruction of military orders and ensuing documents was soon underway. The hospital staff continued to work in a frenzy, albeit with supplies, morale, and stamina running dangerously low.

Late in the evening of December 17th, a weary Kate walked to the docks, hoping to catch a glimpse of one of the few successful supply subs still sneaking into the harbor at dusk. Hoping for a final mail run from home, she spotted a submarine docked in the port with the familiar name *Sailfish* on the hull. She all but ran down the rickety bomb-damaged dock to ask for permission to board. Speaking to one of the sailors of her story about her sorrowful Maine connection, permission was granted.

As she reached the control room, she saw the Yeager cross still dangling from the controls. Kerri had hung it on that long-ago day when the *Sailfish* was christened for her first official dive after the rebuild. Kate closed her eyes as she touched the cross, wishing with all her heart that Kerri was there with her. Suddenly, a nauseating wave of dizziness overcame her. She worked to gain control of her senses, reluctantly heading back up to the hatch and onto the dock. As she breathed in the fresh air, Kate looked up at the spectacular array of stars above her, recognizing the ethereal Milky Way and the patterns surrounding them. Almost in awe, she looked up, finding the stars marking this constellation.

"The Southern Cross…" she whispered, looking up again into the night sky. As she continued to look in that direction, her heart started pounding in her chest, and she suddenly became faint again. Unsure of the cause, she went down on her knees, trying to control the second wave of dizziness. One of the sailors preparing to close the hatch jumped onto the pier to help her recover. Embarrassed, she made it to her feet and waved him off after balancing weakly on her own. Her mind was on her sister and she found that there was a troubling panic accompanying her thoughts…and an odd wave of pain deep in the pit of her stomach.

Kate passed the frightening spell off as some silly form of homesickness, but there was an inexplicable sense of emptiness and pain that she could not explain. She made her way back to her quarters and fell asleep with the unease of one who senses an irreparable crack in the universe.

The emptiness was still there throughout the next day, but the shakiness was gone. Kate forgot about the freakish incident when she arrived to find further chaos at Sternberg. Casualties were streaming in from the northern part of Luzon— the first combat on land. The war was looming ever closer with each passing day.

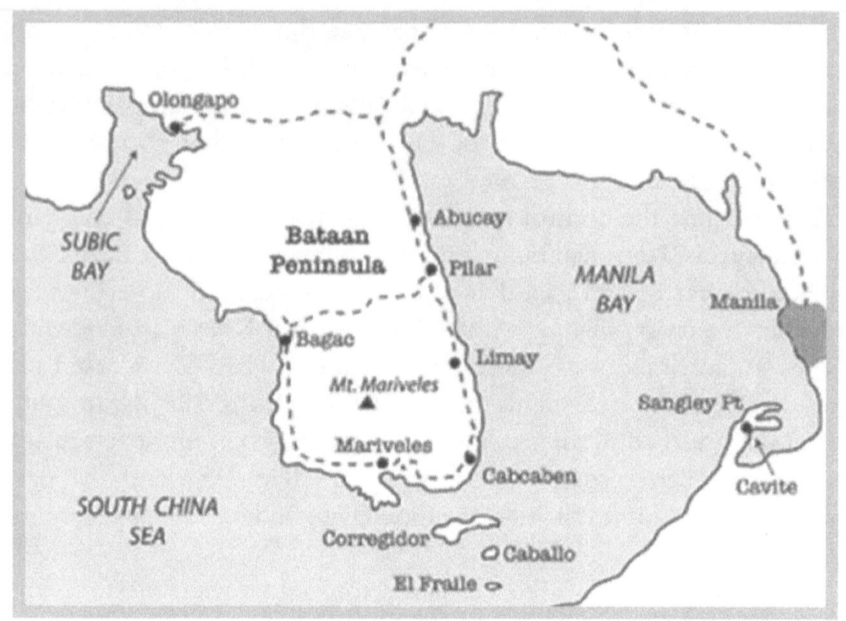

Map of the Bataan Peninsula and surroundings ~ 1941

CHAPTER TWENTY-TWO

ORDERS FROM WAINWRIGHT

DECEMBER 23, 1941

After several interminably difficult surgical shifts at Sternberg, Kate was catching some much-needed respite under a wide veranda when one of the pilots from the 27th Bombardment group woke her none too gently from her quick nap.

"Well, Jimmy, what's so critical that you felt compelled to kill my visions of lobster and wine? Was I snoring? Did I look too peaceful?" Sitting up abruptly, she stopped complaining, recognizing the urgency on his face. Jimmy responded with a request for her to head to the general headquarters for a medical briefing. No words were spoken as they made their way down a long hallway on the hospital's third floor. As they entered the room, she noticed some prominent officials there, both medical and military.

Seated at a desk, surrounded by no less than three of the highest-ranking medical officers Kate knew, was Lieutenant General Jonathan Wainwright. Two young Filipino scouts stood nearby, along with whom she assumed to be General Wainwright's aides. What Kate thought would have been a kind, congenial face was masked by terrible strain, and worn from obvious lack of sleep.

Kate knew that Wainwright commanded the North Luzon Forces, consisting of several Filipino divisions and the 26th Cavalry Regiment of Philippine Scouts. She also knew him to be fearless, charismatic and dedicated to his men. He held the respect of every soldier under his command, being a "fighting" general who was not afraid to get down into the foxholes and direct the combat. She felt a queer sense of awe in front of this famed officer whose respect she found she would greatly like to earn herself.

The Filipino Scouts under his direction were celebrated as among the bravest and most dedicated of the Filipino and U.S. Expeditionary Forces in the South Seas.

Under the influence of one too many bourbons one night, Jimmy and his band of merry men had let it slip that the U.S. had been funding the education and military training of several of these Filipino young men. At least a half dozen to a dozen per year were groomed at various military institutes across the U.S.

"It's the solid, English-speaking ones that have the best training!" Jimmy stated. "And they're under a protection statute by our U.S. Armed Forces. Can't let the Japanese get ahold of the top-educated men, so they ain't goin' about advertising that they know our language."

Wainwright explained the crux of Kate's requested presence. A doctor, a nurse, and two scouts were to head out under cover of the jungle to a beachhead area south of Olongapo, a coastal area northeast of Manila. They were on a mission to rescue two young reconnaissance pilots who were downed and injured while on a recon air patrol near Subic Bay.

"You're to head toward this area, using signals from the scouts in the vicinity who know the crash site. From there you'll rendezvous south of Subic Bay and get more instructions then." As the general spoke, one of his staff members cleared his throat, bending down to talk discreetly into Wainwright's ear. Wainwright looked up, nodding. Turning gravely to Kate, he continued his discussion.

"Ensign Yeager, you are officially being briefed about a military rescue operation where your assistance is needed. What you are about to embark upon is the retrieval of wounded reconnaissance scouts who are vital to us, and our defense." Wainwright continued somberly, "Your story is that you are traveling to Olongapo and back to Manila, seeking to bring back medical supplies to the Red Cross-designated hospital. The story will hold up if you're captured. It may end up saving your life. Frankly, the less you know of the actual mission, the better, for your protection."

A chill ran down Kate's spine, but she recognized that there were thousands of men in the jungles risking far more than she was gambling. She squared her shoulders and met Wainwright's stare with equally-matched determination. As Wainwright handed a stack of signed papers to one of his aides, they had a quiet, brief exchange. He glanced up, mentioning that there were changes to Kate's orders.

"I've just been informed that a decision was made to have the accompanying doctor remain here. If the enemy were to locate you, having a surgeon on the journey would not allow plausible deniability regarding the mission itself. I am assuming you will still accept this assignment, as a member of the U.S. Armed Forces. You will have the use and assistance of my best scouts for this mission."

Kate responded, "Sir, I am honored by the request and privileged to assist with the war efforts in any capacity," Kate paused, waiting for a further exchange of words. When none came, she saluted and turned to exit the room. Wainwright smiled at the gesture. As she departed, the general turned to his aide and said, "God bless the women of this damnable war. They'll keep things running back home and are charged here with keeping our wounded men returning safely home from the battlefields. They are the true unsung heroes of our fight for freedom."

With food, provisions, and medical supplies, Kate and three of Wainwright's Filipino scouts headed from the military headquarters to manage the start of their mission. The roads covering the distance between the two cities were still traversable, so they would travel them until darkness prevailed.

THE RESISTANCE movement in the Philippines was different from any other Pacific campaign, managed by organized guerrilla forces under the strong backing of a fiercely loyal civilian population. Kate was now a part of that organized guerrilla resistance by her acceptance of this rescue mission. She was considerably proud of her role in joining this dangerous sojourn.

Dressed in the thin green army fatigues they had provided, she had only enough time to swing by her makeshift dormitory and gather a military hat to tuck in her hair. She grabbed a rucksack filled with medicinal supplies, herbal salves, clothes, and a large, sharp Bowie knife, given as a present from a Texan she had nursed in California. She tucked this in its leather sheath and then into a pocket on the thigh of her fatigues. In a lower pouch, she packed a *Mark 1* trench knife that had been confiscated recently from a delirious soldier, after he unwisely brandished it at an orderly. She located a Red Cross nursing badge and placed it on her shirt, along with two Red Cross bands to wrap around her upper arms.

Meeting up with the Filipino scouts, they were joined by a young marine driver who was to act as a bodyguard for part of the way. They slipped out in a medical jeep with a Red Cross marking, traversing under the waning light of day. Traveling in the direction of the late afternoon sun, they headed from Manila, toward Subic Bay.

AT DUSK, WITH THE light of a full moon offering enough of a guide to expedite their journey, they continued to make a good pace. Eventually, they moved away from the more heavily trodden roads cratered by recently exploded bombs. Positioning themselves as close as possible to the shore where they were able to watch for any enemy patrol boats, travel was now exceedingly slow on the less traversed coastal path.

Although the trip was only a couple of hours by jeep, as they edged closer to Olongapo, distant, intermittent lights bouncing ominously through the thick jungle foliage necessitated abandoning the jeep to a patch of thick, impenetrable vines. They moved further into the swampy mangrove areas by foot. Movement through the mangroves was tiring, draining Kate's usual high energy levels. After an hour, as her boots sank far into the clinging mud, each step was a tiring struggle. She turned to the scouts, saying, "How long before we meet the other party?" It was her only complaint throughout the trip, if it could be called one at all.

As the scouts urged them to a faster pace, the occasional Macaques peered with great curiosity down at the intruders from high perches in the giant trees, chattering their alarms as the small group passed. Brightly plumaged birds added brilliant flashes of color as they swooped overhead, moonlight glancing on their colorful wings and underbellies. The intermittent shrill call of a bird of prey finding its nighttime target occasionally split the silence, terrifying Kate with the cries of a hapless animal meeting its grim fate. Otherwise, the silence was almost as fearful as the shrill calls. The sound of an angry protest at the invasion of their domain was welcome compared to deafening quiet, an alarming indication that nearby humans had already silenced the jungle inhabitants. *Morning could not come soon enough*, Kate thought, as she continued the exhausting trudge through the dense jungle terrain.

CHAPTER TWENTY-THREE

WHEN FIRST WE MEET AGAIN

For once, Kate was grateful that the sunrise came early in the tropics. That thankfulness, however, was short-lived. Two hours later, the mid-morning tropical sun turned the swamp into a steaming mist of oppressive heat. Scouts on the trails ahead radioed to her group with coordinates on nearby enemy positions, forcing them to move further into the swamps. The rest of the trip toward Olongapo was relatively uneventful for the exhausted party. They soon received word that their targets were within a kilometer, east of Olongapo City. A military jeep met them at this point.

Not long after, the scouts stepped ahead on the path to meet up with their intended rescuees. Making their way through the underbrush to a small clearing, Kate discovered a young Filipino hovering over a man on a makeshift gurney. As the Filipino stood up, Kate's mouth gaped.

"Danilo?" she cried out. "What on earth— ???" She stopped in her tracks. Standing before her was the young Filipino she had treated at Cañacao. The implication was clear. He was neither a farmer nor just the youngest son of a wealthy plantation owner. He was the celebrated Filipino scout she heard mentioned during their trek through the jungles. Danilo knelt down toward the young man on the gurney, indicating that she was needed for wound care.

"There's no time to explain, Miss Kate," he apologized. Beside him was a youthful, darker-skinned man tending to the man on the gurney. She placed her rucksack beside her and, kneeling, turned her attention to the man on the ground. Rolling him with caution from his side to his back, she looked at his face and leaned back, shaking, her mouth agape once more.

"*Sean?*" Her breath caught in her throat.

She could not have been more surprised had her parents been standing before her, alive and well. The piercing eyes were dull with pain and the terrible strain of his ordeal. He looked up weakly and said, "Well, g'day, Kate. I must be dreamin' or dyin', lovely lass. I've got an angel here takin' care of me." With that, his head fell back limply and he passed out. Almost paralyzed with fear,

Kate leaned over to hear even breathing, finding a weak pulse, but a pulse, nevertheless.

"Thank God, he's breathing. He's just passed out from the pain," she said aloud, more of a reassurance to herself. Still in shock, she busied her quaking limbs by examining his torso, resolutely taking control of the medical situation to help calm her screaming nerves. Palpating for broken bones and organ damage, Kate looked up at Danilo, stating, "There's no further bone damage, as far as I can tell." As Danilo turned toward the other scout, she turned toward both.

"What happened here? How was he injured? Where is he hurt?" she asked anxiously. Danilo stepped in to answer, bending down over Sean as he spoke. In almost flawless English, he responded:

"He was managing air recon with the U.S. forward air patrols over the coastal areas and the plane was shot down. The other two military passengers died. His right side took the worst of the crash. His right arm is broken and his right leg is badly twisted at the knee."

The darker scout interjected in a strong Australian accent, "There's a gash on his right side that needs attending. He hit his head pretty hard when we crashed and he's been in a fair amount of pain, as you can see."

Kate pulled the *Mark I* knife out from her fatigues. Bending down, she sliced Sean's pants from ankle to mid-thigh to have a look at the leg. She administered a dose of morphine and began a careful examination of his leg and side. The young nurse noted that the scouts who accompanied her had blended effortlessly into the penetrating darkness of the jungle, searching for enemies that might stumble upon their group. After assessing Sean's wounds, a vial of her liquid herbal astringent was pulled from her rucksack. She poured a liberal dose onto the leg and the side wound.

She then pulled out a shaker and dispensed copious amounts of a black powdery substance onto the wounds. When Danilo peered at her questionably, she answered simply, "Black pepper!" She continued talking as she worked. "It acts as a coagulant to seal the wound, forming a crust over the top. It also has great medicinal value."

Next, using a yellow powder labeled *Sulfonamide*, she poured it over the black powder and the areas surrounding the wound. Using a sterile gauze pad, she covered the area, following this with a dose of penicillin. "For now, that will have to do," she noted anxiously.

The arm was broken in two places. Under ample administrations of the morphine, Kate worked quickly to reset it. Using the Bowie knife, she chopped two strong branches to act as a sling for the arm, wrapping the whole of it in a strong gauze. She used bamboo to immobilize his hurt leg. The gash on the thigh needed treatment, and possibly, stitches. She cleansed it and poured a liberal dose of black pepper, with sulfa powder on top. Pulling the wounded edges together by crisscrossing surgical tape, the wound was wrapped tightly. By then, the scouts had returned and indicated that they needed to move quickly out of the area.

Taking a position near his head in case he woke during the transport, Kate helped carry Sean to the nearby jeep, and they moved onward into the heart of Olongapo. The morphine held him in a deep sleep and she was grateful that he wasn't experiencing the painful jolts of the arduous path. The darker scout never left Sean's side. Kate was grateful that he carried some of the burden of watching over her patient. She learned his name was Yarran and he was an Aboriginal Australian. The two had been friends since boyhood. Few words were spoken by Yarran unless needed to guide them along the trail, but she found that he was knowledgeable and thorough in his assessment of their selected path.

They reached the port of Subic Bay, finding the entire Subic Bay base area destroyed. As she discovered from the scouts, by December 24th, the situation at Subic had become hopeless, and an order by U.S. officials to destroy the station and withdraw was given. In the typical *scorched earth* policy peculiar to the armed forces, all buildings in the Subic Bay base were torched while Filipinos burned the entire town of Olongapo. The Marines had withdrawn toward Bataan.

Any ships that remained at Subic were towed into a deep part of the bay and scuttled. The area was ravaged, but Kate and two of the scouts searched around for any remnants of supplies they could salvage. Near what must have been a small medical outpost, Kate found a few singed medical tins of morphine and syringes, intact. That, along with a Red Cross kit filled with boxes of bandages, medical salve, isopropyl alcohol, and food were all they were able to scrounge up. The guides searched again throughout the ruins, finding two other salvaged remnants of potential use… a stray gun with ammunition and a large tin of U.S. Army food rations.

Here, they were to wait for assistance from other scouts. The smoke was omnipresent, frightening Kate almost as much as the morbid stillness of the surrounding jungle. There was not a bird, lizard, snake, or any other creature alive for miles around, she surmised. Under cover of a thick blanket of vines, she nursed Sean's wounds. The ragged wound on his abdomen still oozed. She was grateful there was no sign of infection.

The rendezvous party arrived soon, managing a rescue by way of a rickety fishing boat. From there, they rowed in silence, following the shoreline under cover of dark, hanging branches and moss. Sean slept fitfully. Kate almost held her breath, worried he would thrash around and threaten to tip the flimsy boat. The anxious nurse prayed that his condition would not worsen.

With little else to do as the small craft made its way with painful deliberation toward the relative safety of Corregidor, she assessed her emotions on the chaos surrounding her. Her head was still spinning at the events of the past day... on finding Sean here and managing dangerous military reconnaissance for the U.S.... on reawakening her emotions from that long-ago fateful night... and wondering what this might mean for her burgeoning sentiments for Patrick. Her mind was more than a little troubled.

Kate shuddered under a sudden realization. *Sean was the valuable man they wanted to be protected at all costs. If the enemy had found a way to capture him, he would be tortured and then executed,* she thought, horrified. She looked down at his sleeping face, the contorted look of pain softened by the effects of the morphine. His utter helplessness affected her far more than his physical prowess had when they first met. As the boat rowed through the water, her thoughts wandered, reliving the memories of their time together in Maine.

They approached the start of the Bataan Peninsula near Morong, just below Subic Bay, meeting up with a small contingent of Filipino scouts. After a few minutes of discussion, Danilo stepped back toward the boat, informing Kate that they were not returning to Sternberg.

"MacArthur has declared Manila an 'Open City.' He plans to move military personnel here to Bataan, so we are to head toward Corregidor and await further requests from him. Our scouts have secured a Red Cross jeep for our additional travel. We leave in 15 minutes, so prepare him for transport Miss Kate. They have scavenged around for fuel and we have enough to get us there."

Kate sat down on a large rock, recognizing the implications of Danilo's words. She was now separated from Patrick, both hospitals, and her friends in Manila. She had no idea whether they were safe. A tight lump crept into her throat and she blinked to hold back the tears. But she had no time to dwell on this fear for her precious friends. She was on a mission to save Sean's life.

CHAPTER TWENTY-FOUR

BY FIRES UNSEEN

The group traveled by jeep through the rainforests to Morong. They stopped there, finding shelter and food for the next day as they awaited further word from MacArthur's HQ. The natives in the area were friendly, but they were unfamiliar with Americans– and, in particular, fair-skinned blondes like Kate. She decided to pull her hair up under her cap, and remove her Red Cross markings to remain as nondescript as possible. If the Japanese were to infiltrate the area, word of the passing of a Caucasian nurse with a wounded man and several guards would be a sure sign that this person was of importance to the Allied forces. Kate did her best to pass off their trek through the town as a malarial study of the surrounding jungle, which Danilo translated to their innkeeper. It was a plausible story since the army had instigated such area studies during the first months of 1940.

Their long journey had begun at dawn that morning. They had skidded and jostled their way along long stretches of pot-holed dirt roads and she was sore from the constant jostling. Having nothing to eat but K-rations they had confiscated, she was starved and undeniably filthy.

The innkeeper managed a small but tidy hotel that promised warm showers and clean beds. Kate set about finding a healthy soup for Sean. Anxious to bathe, she pulled out a clean set of clothing from her rucksack and stepped into the tiny shower in the room set aside for Sean. A short time later, she exited the bath area with a towel wrapped around her, finding Sean propped up somewhat woozily on the pillow of the bed, watching her. Inherently shy, she moved a bamboo screen over to complete her toilette. After dressing, she walked over to the bed to examine him. He was still weak, but his eyes were penetrating as they watched her work.

She began a sponge bath to clean the grime from his body. Sean seemed not at all concerned when she somewhat sheepishly began removing his pants. Managing this regularly for male patients, she quickly transformed into her 'nurse mode'. Leaving a folded towel to cover private areas, she removed all of his clothing and began scrubbing him with strong soap. Sitting on the bed, their eyes locked.

After a moment, she broke the silence. Placing her hand on one of his, Kate began with, "I'm thrilled to see you again and very happy that you're in my care so I can get you healed." There was a pregnant pause as each worked to find words to cover the unsaid apologies they both felt were needed. As Sean watched Kate, she added ruefully, "For what it's worth, I'm sorry that we had a fight that night. I was so young and wary of men."

Sean smiled, caressing her hand in his, saying in a low, husky voice, "No need to apologize. We both made mistakes. It's enough to know that I am also mighty keen to see you too, Kate. That's all you need to hear for now." His accent and the sound of his voice were music to her ears. Her eyes filled with tears and she turned her head to keep him from seeing her cry.

Her voice faltered. "I looked for you, Sean. I thought you left Kittery because of me— because of my anger."

He smiled wanly and said, "Darling Kate, I left under orders, and under stricter orders not to *discuss* my orders with anyone. I am mighty sorry that you were not allowed to know why I left or where I was going. If that caused you any pain, I could never apologize enough for that."

The conversation seemed to cost him a monumental effort, and his weakness affected her deeply. Her eyes welled up again, her lower lip trembling. She placed her hand over her mouth to hide the momentary weakness.

Seeing that he was exhausted, Kate responded in a soft tone, "We can speak of all of this much later. Let me play nurse now and work on getting you healed."

Administering another dose of morphine, she smiled, continuing with, "Get some rest now. I'll find you some clean clothes that won't be military in nature. We must burn these." He pointed toward a second rucksack and Kate reached in to pull his clothes out.

Scrounging around in the bottom of the bag, she was astounded to find her blue shirt from that long-ago day in Maine folded neatly in the bottom. She was thrilled at that revelation, and the implication that their time in Maine had held significant meaning for him as well. When she pulled it out, Sean grinned weakly, saying, "In case I saw you again," but his accompanying wink made Kate blush a little, secretly pleased at this admission.

That night, she slept beside him on top of the bed covers, careful not to jostle his leg or arm, surprisingly untroubled to once again sleep in a bed beside a man she cared for. She found herself comparing Patrick with Sean, and wondering how one could evoke such strong emotions for two such different men. It was a mystery for the centuries. Both were handsome, captivating, and obviously holding secrets they might never be able to reveal. It would have been a troubling sleep had she not been exhausted.

At sunrise the next morning, Danilo and Yarran met with Kate. Danilo's orders were curt: "Per instructions directly from MacArthur's staff, we are to meet up near Corregidor with the *SS Mactan,* which is in port there reloading supplies and refueling." When Kate questioned the next steps, including the ship's destination, Danilo responded, "The Red Cross is negotiating for the *Mactan* to be utilized as a hospital transport from Manila to Australia. Sean is to be on that ship and, Miss Kate, you are ordered to be transported with him to Australia as Red Cross staff."

Kate knew that these orders meant that Manila had fallen and there would be as many key military personnel exiting the Philippines as humanly possible. They traveled the arduous distance to the port where the *Mactan* was harbored. Under cover of darkness, Kate and Sean were transported onto the ship, along with Yarran and Danilo. From there, the ship sailed across the bay for Manila, to transport wounded soldiers on their arduous journey to Australia. The U.S. Naval Base at Cavite had by now been almost fully evacuated. For reasons unknown, the medical personnel at the naval hospital were told to remain at their posts at Cañacao. Therefore, Kate's friends and the entire nursing staff were ordered to stay to serve those under their care. Kate was distraught at the implications of this order.

As the untenable status of Manila became glaringly apparent, by New Year's Eve, 1941, all army personnel, including 80 army nurses, were evacuated to the Bataan Peninsula and then down to Corregidor. Retreating from the Japanese beachhead landing at Lingayen Gulf, the Allied Forces had regrouped from military points throughout the Manila Bay area, most withdrawing onto the Bataan peninsula. Many reconnoitered on Corregidor to defend the strategic entrance to Manila Bay.

The unenviable position of Allied Commander of the Philippines fell to General Wainwright. Kate admired his fortitude, his courage, and his unfaltering support toward his men. He was all but worshipped by those who served under him. Already by the 28th, the transport docks at Sternberg had become overcrowded, with the last patients finally evacuated from Manila on New Year's Eve. MacArthur had directed that only the worst cases be evacuated to Australia.

To that end, Douglas Steamship Company operated a coastal China trade, under which the *Mactan* had sailed. Although it would not have been the first choice as a hospital ship, it was the closest one available that could be utilized for this task. The U.S. army had chartered the *Mactan* days earlier, but the urgent need to evacuate the most critical patients led to the ship's confiscation by the

Red Cross. Under an agreement being brokered and carefully negotiated with Japan through persuasive Swiss Intermediaries, the *Mactan*, under captain Julian Tamayo, was then released from an army charter. This avoided any military undertones during the painstaking mediation by the Swiss. The Japanese were playing hardball with this exception to their occupation.

The ship had been unloading supplies near Corregidor, where she picked up the four passengers: Kate, Sean, Danilo, and Yarran. She was recalled to Manila to be designated with Red Cross markings.

On the evening of December 31st, 224 patients were loaded for transport. Under the strictest negotiations, only a scant few medical personnel were permitted aboard to manage the patients. The course of sail and the destination were conveyed to the Japanese government. Any weapons or contraband items were thrown overboard, as the Swiss expressed to the Japanese that *Mactan* would comply with all requirements as a medical transport ship. The Swiss Consul ship inspected the vessel for compliance with *The Hague Convention*.

Although functioning as a hospital ship, she was undoubtedly not equipped as such. Medical supplies were hurriedly loaded from Manila. Patients were crammed onto open decks, precariously close to the ship's rails. An operating room was hastily organized in the ship's salon. Having considerable difficulty obtaining a response from the Japanese regarding the final negotiations, Kate was listed unofficially to the Swiss as international Red Cross staff. As yet, there was no confirmation that the ship would be granted safe passage to its destination. The determined nurse requisitioned her medical supply cabinets in Sternberg as they waited for this confirmation. Her request was granted, but silence continued to mark the communiqués between Tokyo and Geneva.

Somewhere, it was rumored that the ship's status was honored, but that never became official. The officers were under tremendous stress as they were made aware of this tenuous situation. Just after midnight on January 1st, before the Japanese officially entered the battered city of Manila, the *Mactan* set out, escorted by a U.S. naval vessel for guidance through the minefields defending Manila Bay. *Mactan* had the dubious honor of being the last civilian ship to leave the Philippines before Japanese occupation of the city.

Kate busied herself on deck securing patient cots as well as she could, plying the wounded men with blankets and soothing words. She provided soft, reassuring hands as she checked their wounds. There was little else she could do. The few other nurses on board were below, securing critical patients to bunks prior to departure. She moved to the port side of the ship to watch as they headed toward their patrol escort. As she observed the last vestiges of the twinkling lights, Manila was lit up with explosions, amid massive fires throughout the city.

Not the kind of explosions you'd expect on New Year's, she thought, as she watched from the confines of the ship, worried about Patrick, her friends, the townspeople, and the city itself. She was not hopeful as to any measure of safety for those left behind. The fires burning throughout the city were proof enough that the occupation by Japan would be fateful for many.

CHAPTER TWENTY-FIVE

CORREGIDOR TO AUSTRALIA

Having been declared an "Open City," Manila was supposed to have been accorded the protection of that neutral occupation status, but once again, the elegant municipality was afire, with explosions shooting up all over the beautiful boulevards, stately mansions, and merchant buildings. Walls of bright orange flames cast a pall of horror over the once-glorious city, most of them set by allied forces. The army was dynamiting gasoline storage tanks at its fuel depots on Engineer Island to prevent their use by the enemy. Once again, the bare remains of Cavite Navy Yard were smoldering. As if by some macabre order to light the skies at midnight, the last of the enormous gasoline storage tanks blew up with a horrendously-timed set of detonations, looking like a New Year's fireworks disaster, with a much more sinister meaning.

Soon after, Kate was joined by the ship's captain and two other medical personnel. The ragtag, emotionally-spent group on the *Mactan's* bridge was silent, contemplating the devastation left behind and the unknown fate of the people they had come to know throughout their stint in the Philippines. Kate soon headed below, unable to withstand the pain of watching the city under destruction. As the ship set sail, her chest physically burned with the pain. It would be an excruciating night for the weary crew.

She found her way to the radio room, determined to learn if they had made contact with Ned's team. She discovered that Yarran and Danilo had been put to use there, having trained as radiomen. Yarran relayed to her that all of Ned's team had been relocated to Corregidor in the underground bunkers of the fortress on the island. While in the radio room, she also discovered that the *Mactan's* journey had begun haphazardly, a bad omen for their long voyage.

In the strain of preparing for the departure, the *Mactan* was forced to improvise with geodetic maps from another ship, so her captain felt she was ill-prepared for the journey. In the chaos, communication was also sketchy with the escort ship. The radioman on the escort ship informed the radioman on board that the *Mactan* had made a potentially fatal turn. Already smack in the middle of the minefields, their escort ship signaled frantically of their imminent danger. By either miracle or divine purpose, the *Mactan* was able to recircle the waters and return to the safe designated path. While the ship was dragging across the bay on a zig-zag course, Kate remained in the radio room during the tense period. *Mactan* passed the guns of Corregidor, and at long last moved into the safety of the open seas.

With their journey commencing, Kate made the rounds to keep patients as comfortable as possible for what could potentially be a month-long journey to a safe harbor. Taking a nurse's cot near Sean, she succumbed to sheer exhaustion. The weary nurse felt as if the entire world was on fire and the ship was falling into the abyss and burning with it. Darkness eventually fell upon her restless, tortured soul. She slept like the dead.

After their harrowing ordeal escaping the deadly minefields in Manila Bay, the first days were long and arduous but thankfully, not life-threatening, considering the omnipresent fear of Japanese attack. The noxious fumes below deck left Kate clamoring for the fresh air on the ship's surface. This was experienced only on the rare occasions Kate was given permission to manage a shift of wound care on the upper deck. With few exceptions, when not tending to patients, the medical staff were requested to stay below for safety.

The nurses took turns sleeping on a "hotbed"... a bunk that they joked absolutely never cooled since the occupants took 6-hour shifts sleeping in the cramped four-bunk sleeping quarters. They were ever grateful for a private toilet and their makeshift toilette…a slop bucket converted into a sink for sponge bathing and other purposes. The dilapidated ship was overrun by males, and places for such privacy were hard to find.

When they weren't serving in the capacity of full-fledged nursing, Kate and the medical staff on board spent most of their waking moments working to provide comfort to the patients on the crowded ship. At first, there was little time to even converse with these men. Kate was able to locate Sean below on the first break after a day of sailing. He had been moved twice, and on the crowded ship with wall-to-wall cots, it was no easy task for her to find him. The surgical team had palpated some shifting shrapnel in Sean's side, so he was in and out of consciousness after the surgery. Kate had to content herself by knowing that he was nearby.

On the third day of the voyage, she passed by the radio room, discovering that Yarran and Danilo were still taking turns on shift with the overtaxed radiomen on board. Finding a few moments to talk, Kate asked Danilo for the details about how Sean came to be rescued and whisked aboard the *Mactan*. They found a quiet area and Danilo relayed the story.

"Sean reported to MacArthur's team and the general knows him pretty well. Wainwright was given direct orders from MacArthur that Sean was not to be captured, at all costs. And Yarran was given orders that should they fall into enemy hands, Sean was to be given a pistol. If he was unconscious, the duty fell to Yarran, for both of them."

Kate felt dizzy at the finality of that implication, and Danilo held her shoulders to keep her from fainting. Her face white as a sheet, she said in a voice so low that Danilo had to bend to hear her words, "What in God's name could he know that the Japanese would want to get ahold of?"

Danilo chose his words with deliberation.

"Any Aussie in the territory would be known to have ties with the Allied Signal Services from Australia, which supplies most of the recon air patrols. And Sean also works as a language expert on their code breaking team. He knows the size, make, maneuverability, and weaponry of every Allied submarine in the area, as well as each sub's refueling capabilities. He is well-versed in their depth and dive response times and knows the captains on board. And he knows these captains well enough to know what they likely would or would not do in an imminent battle situation."

Danilo let that sink in and added, "He knows every weakness in the underbelly of every hull and exactly how much torpedo power it would take to sink them. All deadly information in the wrong hands, Miss Kate."

"And," and these words hung out in the air sharply, "Sean speaks Japanese. Fluently enough to translate written documents and certainly enough to translate verbal messages and understand their meaning. He lived in Okinawa as a young boy, so he understands the spoken inflections far better than the written ones. He's been of great use in translating radio messages. Under any of their more hideous torture methods, that may have come out."

Kate shuddered again at that thought.

As all of this sank in, Kate asked, wonderingly, "And what about Yarran? Why is he here?" Danilo responded, "Yarran and Sean were boyhood friends. He's an Aboriginal… a *Wurundjeri* from the Kulin nation. Sean learned to track from him. Yarran's the best tracker I've ever known. He can look at a print on the ground and tell the type of animal, the size, the time it passed by, and practically the age. An infant couldn't get within a mile without him knowing it. He's absorbed everything about what I've taught him regarding most plants and animals in our jungles. He's exceptionally loyal to Sean and a good man in any fight or fix. And he knows the constellations, so he's at home navigating. A good man to have around, no matter what your needs are."

"And you?" Kate asked. "You speak flawless English, which you hid well from me when I was nursing you, I might add," she smiled impishly. "What's your story, young man?"

Danilo smiled, an amusing, lopsided smile indicating he rather enjoyed playing that game with Kate when he was ill.

"I was sent to America to be educated. The last son in a long line of sons has little chance of inheriting his father's riches. So, I made my own way in the world. I got selected at an early age. And this is just the end product of a grateful young protégé's education process. Flawless English is but one of my many talents now," he laughed.

"A wee bit modest, aren't we, Danilo?" Kate retorted, smiling. "You're a young man of many secrets and also a good man to have in any fight, I would say." Danilo smiled again and said, "I'll return that compliment back to you, Miss Kate. And by the way, Sean is aware of your work as a codebreaker, as well as your admirable dressmaking skills, I might add," he winked as he made that last statement.

Kate's heart skipped a beat at this comment, inordinately pleased that Sean was aware of her background, but also wondering how he knew. That conversation would have to wait, as "Ensign Yeager" was called in for an emergency amputation. In some respects, it was fortunate that she had little time to spare for long-desired conversations.

She needed time to process her attraction for Sean. Mere infatuation for a talented and mysterious man? Or something more profound? She suspected the latter, she told herself as she scrubbed up to assist the surgeon.

A few hours later, she found herself on deck, seeking a few minutes of quiet respite after the stressful surgery. As she watched the waves rising up against the ship, the waning sun bathed her face and she closed her eyes to rejuvenate her beleaguered soul. She was joined by Red Cross Director Irving Williams, enjoying a frank discussion about what the war meant to both of them. The ship was entirely at the mercy of any marauding Japanese, and Irving felt the weight of that fear on his shoulders. Like Kate, he was fiercely protective of every passenger.

Suddenly, they found their conversation interrupted by Yarran, who had joined them on deck to view the stars. Kate introduced the two.

"Yeah…I was under the impression that we were headed to Darwin, fellas," Yarran looked directly at Williams with his intense brown eyes. Irving answered evasively, "We are following the precise course directed under the Swiss negotiations." He met Yarran's stare squarely.

Yarran's gaze fixated on the darkened skies and spoke.

"Well, mate, the moon is on the wrong side of the ship if Darwin is our projected destination and we're currently heading in an easterly direction, not south." Yarran pointed out two separate constellations and explained their positioning with respect to the ship's current location. Kate smiled at his direct, penetrating stare toward Williams, and watched Irving shift his body as he carefully responded.

"We are avoiding some dangerous reefs while sailing through some smaller Japanese-held islands under cover of darkness. It's best to keep this conversation between you, me, and Kate."

Yarran agreed. A healthy respect between the two men was born, with Irving Williams enjoying the Aboriginal constellation lessons that Yarran provided Kate and him. Kate was also fast gaining a considerable amount of respect for the Aboriginals, and for Yarran. Yarran's quiet confidence was contagious; his knowledge unimpeachable. He reminded Kate of her father in this aspect. She felt a sharp pang in her heart as long-ago childhood memories were stirred. The painful moment passed, and soon afterward they parted ways for some much-needed rest.

During the next few days, Kate was ordered to remain below deck to help with surgeries and wound care, and she vowed to make the most of this enforced confinement.

When off duty, any spare time was spent cleaning and sterilizing surgical equipment. Kate used up much of her supplies, keeping the surgical and wound care areas disinfected. Germs were their enemy; malaria, and dysentery their biggest nightmares. The quinine was so scarce it was under lock and key, along with the penicillin and opiates. The opiates were used to ease a soldier's pain for surgeries in the absence of proper anesthesia. And to ease a soldier out of life when, and if, death was the inevitable outcome. The medical staff on board did their level best to ensure that did not happen, but unfortunately, it happened twice on their fretful journey. In truth, the trip to Australia so far was just on this side of tolerable, but the unknown alternative in Manila was far worse. Kate was obsessed with worry for Patrick, Callie, Carole, and her many friends. She prayed fervently that the Japanese would be more merciful than they were rumored to be.

Sleep was often elusive, given a violently pitching ship at high speed. A couple of the bolder nurses cajoled their way into the mess hall during those rough sleep shifts, to help bring some cheer to the depressed patients on board. There, they added feminine touches to the dishes and helped the beleaguered cook serve the crowded ship.

Kate found that the many dried cooking spices she had packed away in small tins were put to excellent use in the mess hall. The chives, pepper, fresh lemon peel, and parsley added a perfect touch to the potatoes and greens. Those were accompanied by gallon cans of beef stew, fricasseed spam, homemade bread, and coconut raisin rice pudding. They had plenty of that dessert, as the *Mactan* originally sailed as a coconut transport ship. The sunshine-bereft men were heartened by the morale boost.

An elated Kate found a recipe in her supply cabinets for a "war cake" that her Grama had often made during the depression. Comprised of raisins boiled with brown sugar, water, and lard, the concoction was cooled and mixed with flour, hot water, and baking soda, and then baked. The small crew in the mess hall managed the subsequent baking so she could return to nursing.

There were no fridge ships in the area. Enemy strafing had left those unarmed ships with orders to remain in safer waters. During the stop at Corregidor, the resourceful chief from the mess hall happened across a few chickens and a "freshly dead" cow that met its untimely demise by straying too near a strafing Japanese bullet, as he mentioned in his mess hall journal. Had one looked closely, an autopsy of that stray bullet— and the cow— might have revealed the truth: that a U.S.-issued armament helped to end that errant cow's life. The steak for the next few nights was a resounding success with the exhausted, morale-bereft shipmates.

Like the quartermasters on land, the mess chief's efforts to raise these men's spirits were monumental. The officers "looked the other way" at the chief's creative story about the stray Japanese bullet, recognizing the dangers he braved in trying to feed the men under his culinary responsibility. Kate struck up a friendship with this crotchety gentleman, one Otis Steadman. She found that underneath his crusty exterior was a sweet, convivial, and lonely old man. And together, with her spices and his skills, they found they could make Spam taste as good as fried chicken on a Sunday picnic.

CHAPTER TWENTY-SIX

WELCOME TO OZ

Three weeks into the journey, the crew and patients had reached the end of their endurance. Tempers were sharper, the tension was high, and sleep was rare, if at all. At dawn one morning after a restless night at sea, Kate entered the mess hall to find Otis reading a letter. She sat down, somewhat embarrassed at witnessing him wipe tears away hastily as he put the note in his pocket. The kind look on her face encouraged him to speak, saying, "It's a note from my wife. The last one I received before she died in an accident at a factory back home. She's been gone six months, and this ship here's my family now."

Kate sympathetically reached for his hand, not at all sure that the gesture would be appreciated or accepted. But once again, a strong friendship was borne out of that characteristically sweet, girlish act. She responded in a voice that could be willfully soft and kind.

"I lost my parents within one 24-hour period back home from two freak incidents. So, I know the pain of such a loss, Mister Otis." She told him a little of the *Squalus* story and found him to be taken aback, almost as if he were sitting next to a celebrity. Another bond was formed as he recognized bits and pieces of the story, and remembered hearing about the *Squalus*.

For the next few days, massive storms continually challenged the overtaxed ship. Patients were strapped in their beds with enough medicine to keep them from vomiting from the pitching ship's continual imbalance. Surgeries were canceled. Kate busied herself again assisting Otis in morale-boosting, his pastime of late— unless you counted the massacre of rats, beetles, and giant cockroaches.

Once again, Kate was grateful for the restaurant work with her Aunt Maggie. She discovered a pack of her mother's handwritten recipes in her medicine cabinets that were transported onto the *Mactan*. She again found value in the painstaking efforts of her mother's resourceful cooking lessons during times of rationing. Kate showed Otis how to make the tasty Ginger Cakes from

Catherine's Kittery church socials. And her eggless cakes were a hit among the men on a miserable, stormy day that closed the Sick Bay due to the heavy wave action.

The boost to the men was not lost on the captain or the few officers on board. There was a lovely angel, the chief surgical nurse named Miss Flora Feldmuth, who was a miracle worker with the men's wounds. The unsung hero of this fated journey, Lt. Feldmuth sought Kate out to thank her for the morale boosts, and the two became fast friends. They steamed toward Australia, and the medical staff was fully aware that the sanctions against strafing the ship could be rescinded at any time.

In the Sulu Sea, the presence of a dangerous reef necessitated waiting until dawn to pass it, ever more terrifying with still no confirmation of Japanese safe passage. They scheduled a few surgeries during this lull and Kate was requested to assist. They were grateful to have her additional skills on board. She was a Godsend to the lone surgeon on board, as she was not listed on the official manifest of medical personnel.

A reef and a small string of islands marking the entrance to the Celebes Sea were successfully navigated just as reports from the radiomen were conveyed regarding Manila's violent occupation by the Japanese. A rumor persisted regarding the Japanese belief that MacArthur was wounded and on board their ship. The occupants were even warier that the Japanese would torpedo the hospital ship, Swiss negotiations or not.

There was abundant distress as the Filipino medical personnel worried about family and friends left behind. So, a few of the nurses busied themselves pulling together steaming kettles of chicken and vegetables with Otis and his team. Where once the smell of old fish, stale grease, and aged meats like water buffalo were nauseating scents for the patients within smelling distance, the refreshing aromas of parsley, salt, tarragon, rosemary, lemons and pepper soon permeated the galley. Kate's assistance was a grateful payment for the safe passage of Sean and his companions.

The ship entered the waters of the Makassar Strait and the Captain radioed Swiss Red Cross representatives that the vessel was dangerously low on fuel and water. They refueled, which was risky, given that another deviation from their path would provide ample excuse for an attack. The potential for enemy strafing was terrifying. Boredom was never a concern, but how thankful they would have been for that tedium in a sea rife with potential enemy ships and planes!

Japanese warplanes often taunted them. The patients who could be moved off the bridge were transported below to safety from possible strafing bullets. When she was sent on deck, Kate gulped in the fresh air like a prisoner allowed out of solitary confinement for a few moments of respite. On one rare occasion, when Kate was given the all-clear to allow her a few minutes of reprieve from the fumes below deck, the familiar drone of planes sent her scrambling below again. The last rays of an evening sunset bathed her face as the hatch closed unceremoniously, locking her below in the presumed safety of steel. The lack of sunshine began to take its toll on her spirits.

One evening, Kate managed her rounds with the patients on deck and made her way to the ship's bow. The night was still, and the seas, for once, were calm. She looked above to the thousand twinkling stars in a brilliant, moonlit sky. It was a rare, peaceful moment. She was wistful, thinking myriad thoughts of home, especially of her darling sister. Kerri would be enjoying her first month of motherhood by now. She prayed fervently that her twin's labor wasn't difficult or dangerous, and that she could reach Australia soon and telegraph news that she was safe from the Philippines. She was lost in her thoughts as she continued to worry about the family back home.

A low, husky voice with a distinct Australian twang broke her silent reverie. "My darling Kate…still searching for the fault in our stars?"

She turned, her eyes filling with the thrilling realization that Sean was beside her. "They brought us back together again, you know," she responded. Her heart skipped a beat as he moved closer to her, blocking any sudden gusts of night air, much as he did that long-ago night at Nubble Light. She noted that he was limping from the leg injury and stitches, with his arm still in a cast from the recent breaks. He had a lone crutch he was using to steady his right leg. It must have cost him an inordinate effort to make his way on deck with the recovering tendons and ligaments on the knee, but she was extremely grateful that he did.

Smiling into his eyes, Kate reached up to adjust his arm sling to better balance the weight of the cast. It was a tender gesture to keep his shoulder from aching later. As she did this, Sean's unencumbered hand reached out to entwine in hers and he bent down to kiss her. Completely enamored by this captivating, handsome man, Kate forgot where she was— only that the vast universe was spinning around them wildly. It was a long moment before they parted. She sat down and he moved beside her. Her head rested softly on his chest, the tears flowing freely now. She was no longer afraid to let him know how she felt.

Kate clasped her arms around his strong neck and somewhat awkwardly, he attempted to wrap his arms around her. They both laughed as his cast bumped her head. Sean leaned back on the small rickety watchman's nest and she leaned a little into his chest again, mindful of his stitches from the recent surgery. His arm rested naturally around her body, each of them basking in the physical contact and cherishing this bittersweet moment together.

After a minute, Kate realized that she hadn't had a decent bath or even thoroughly combed her hair in days. She said forlornly, "I have dreamed of this moment, with both of us looking as we did on that wonderful picnic day. And here I am, looking like the Wicked Witch of the West. Why can't I look like other women when they're being held by the man of their dreams?" Sean laughed, obviously pleased at the promotion to the position of 'man of her dreams.'

"You look like a princess to me," he said. "A sight for exceedingly sore eyes, Kate Yeager!"

Sean looked up at the speckled Milky Way, showcasing precise whorls and patterns across the canopy of stars. Pointing up into the vast darkness of the southern hemisphere, he said in his lovely Aussie accent, "You once asked me to show you the beauty of our 'Southern Cross.' Well, there it is, Kate." He pointed out the particular stars, giving their names and their specific part in the constellation pattern. She was again enraptured by his voice and his captivating storytelling.

Sean started to say something as he looked into her eyes and then turned away, changing his mind and staring again at the sky. After a moment, he moved back to the safer subject of the constellations.

"According to Aboriginal legend, emus are the 'creator spirits' that used to fly and watch over the land to protect the people." He glanced up again to the Southern Cross and continued with his story. "The dark cloud between the stars is the head. The neck, body, and legs are formed from the dust lanes patterned across the Milky Way."

"I have seen photos of emus but haven't ever seen one in person," Kate said wistfully, finding nearly everything in Australia magical to her mind, including Sean. "Ah, they're incredible creatures, Kate. Feisty, aggressive, and ever curious, like your ostrich, only the ostrich is a mite bigger," he smiled. Finding her interested in the subject, he continued further:

"The Aboriginals use the stars in ways we can hardly imagine. The stars tell them the seasonal supply of food in their area. They know precisely when the annual dingo migration is underway and they can track them as a food source. As the stars align in certain directions, they know exactly when to prepare the land for the planting season. This is life-or-death knowledge for them in the arid areas where they live. They rotate their crops with the rainfall patterns."

Sean's interest was more than just a passing understanding. He held a profound respect for the people, their culture, and the knowledge they contained.

Realizing that he was moving the discussions away from the subject of 'them,' he hesitated. "I'll teach you more about Yarran's people later, Kate, when you can visit the lands and speak with them," he promised her. Once more, he became quiet. *How I wish I could read his thoughts!* she said to herself. Not knowing where to begin her next conversation, Kate's words faltered. Her eyes were downcast as she started with another apology for the night in Maine that seemed eons ago.

"Sean, about that night in Maine. I really—"

"Shhh…Kate." He put his fingers to her lips in a gentle gesture. "I'm having none of that! I'll explain my actions. I reached over to re-pin your shirt, but I timed it wrong. It looked like I went for your charming attributes, sweet girl. That wasn't my intent." His eyes were a marked green as he stared into her deep blue ones, now brimming with unshed tears.

"Well, maybe I was thinkin' of it, but thinkin' and doin' are two separate things, as my father used to say. I was mad as a cut snake that night, but it was directed at myself."

He added softly, as he moved a strand of hair that whipped across her face, "I was aware that you were not experienced with men. So, I knew you would not be game for any sort of shenanigans. Anyway, we'll not speak any further of it unless you have something you want to get off your chest. Pun not intended!" he laughed.

She had one more nagging thought, but hesitated after the finality of his comment. Seeing that hesitation, he said, "Go on, girl. What's your burning question?"

She blurted out, "Did you go home that night or did you head out to the pubs to find someone else to end the night with?" She asked the question with force, as if she felt there was an answer forthcoming that she didn't want to know. But there was strength there, a conviction about where they stood if the answer was not what she wanted to hear. She did not want to be part of a long line of conquests or to have any part of a man who sought out promiscuous women on a regular basis.

"Ah, Kate, you let your imagination run away with you that night, didn't ya? I went back home and was flat out like a lizard drinkin'. Which means, since you don't know Aussie terms, I went back to work at my desk, whilst soaking up all the wine we left open. And I paid for it dearly in the morning." He laughed at the memory of the painful hangover.

"Believe me— I wasn't out trolling for an easy conquest, after spending the day with the likes of you. That'd be senseless. Like having powdered milk in your tea when you can have real fresh cream straight from the source. If you're patient enough to wait for the right cow! And I most definitely am!"

He glanced down fleetingly at her breasts as if to make his point. She thrilled at that meaningful glance… Sean boldly showing a keen interest in her body.

Laughing out loud at the comparison, she was satisfied with his answer and let that last nagging doubt go, relaxing in his arms. They sat together, reminiscing again about that long-ago day. No words were needed for the moment as they both embraced the first treasured moments together again. Minutes later, Kate broke the silence once more.

"Sean, I've never been known for holding back and I'm not one of those girls who can make up some mysterious feminine excuse about my emotions. You sometimes seem to have this cool, casual air about you. Like nothing matters. And I don't know where we stand right now."

He smiled, touching her small, upturned nose with his finger and saying, "You are incredibly charming when you are troubled. You get this cute little wrinkle on your brow, like so!"

"I'm being serious, Sean!" Kate continued. "I don't want to ever experience the pain I did after you left Kittery." She sighed and exclaimed, "See? I can't hide my emotions. I am not good at this. I so wish I had my sophisticated sister here to advise me."

Sean smiled at her disarming honesty. When she looked up at him with those expressive, imploring eyes, he realized the seriousness of her statements.

"Darling Kate, it isn't hard at all to say that *that* night meant more to me than any other experience I have ever had with a woman. We never ran out of things to say and whenever I caught myself looking your way, I was tempted to take you in my arms and make love to you. It wasn't at all sexual. Well, I reckon it *was,*" he laughed out loud, "but not in the way you think. I wanted to possess you, to hold you, and make you mine forever."

The power of that statement was profound.

He faltered, somewhat surprised at this frank admission. "I felt alive, like for once my work wasn't the most pressing parcel of my life. And there I was with this beautiful, intelligent young girl enjoying my company. And we had so much in common. So, when I blew it and I frightened you, I was arced up at myself. I never blamed you. Not once!"

She looked surprised at his words. "And I thought you walked away because I was inexperienced around men!" She looked away, ashamed of that admission. Sean shifted, his right leg somewhat pained by sitting still.

"Kate, you might think that most men want experienced women so that they can have a good time. Maybe for some men that is the way of it. For me, one of the most amazing things about that day was that you went to great pains to *not* show your inexperience, but it was out there, which adds such mystery to the chase. This extended absence did nothing to change my attraction. Let's pick up where we were, and are. And if the innocence— and the intense attraction— is still there, as I think it is, we'll work through everything." Silence followed that little soliloquy. He cocked one eyebrow up and stared right down into her eyes, stroking one cheek as his eyes penetrated hers.

"Well, charming girl? *Is* it?" he asked bluntly, in a joking manner. But there was somewhat of a pained expression on his face, wondering if she had found some dashing young doctor. Or a commanding officer who had finally swept her off her feet and made her forget all about him… and her virtue. Kate adjusted her body against the hard steel of the ship and looked up, saying impishly, "I've been pretty married to my work, I'm afraid." He smiled, much relieved. Once more, his mouth found hers. Her eyes closed, cherishing that auspicious moment together.

They were sharply interrupted by the drone of planes, and they both scrambled up to look toward the sky. "Jap Zeros," Sean exclaimed, watching the moonlight dance across the planes' insignias. Throwing caution to the wind, she ran closer toward the men stretched out on deck under tarps. Sean ambled after her. They crouched as the Zeros swooped toward them, their hearts pounding in their throats. The Zeros dived down again, much closer this time. At this point, the captain was on deck, watching intently. "Damn the little bastards— they're playing with us!" He exclaimed. The planes circled for a moment and took off into the clouds. Captain Tamayo turned to Kate and Sean and said in halting English, "We need to get to Darwin. They're frothing at the bit to get to this ol' girl. They already broke their word to the Swiss in Manila."

Never more than an inner-island transfer ship, it was miraculous that the old, rusty bucket of tin had not sunk under the weight of the additional cargo, and the pressure of the precarious trip in roiling seas. At long last, in Darwin, an Australian gunboat escorted the *Mactan* into the harbor to a welcome from the Australian Red Cross. News of the embattled ship and beleaguered passengers had made it to the mainland U.S., and the *Mactan* was a celebrity ship on both continents.

The welcome to the Australian mainland included food, fresh linens, chocolate, cookies, and various and sundry hand-made items, compliments of the Red Cross and the Northern Territory defense. The respite, though, was brief. With Darwin itself under direct threat, immediate orders were to proceed to Townsville and Brisbane, with a final stop at Sydney.

The ship arrived in Brisbane on January 24th. Winding their way for about eight miles from the Pacific Ocean, the fast-traversing Brisbane River took them into civilization. As they neared the city, cheering residents lined the river banks, waving colorful handkerchiefs. As they docked, they were greeted by the American Consul, the commander of the American base in Brisbane, and military attachés from Canberra. The ship and its passengers were now famous.

Mactan departed the next day for Sydney. By then, the exhausted team of medical personnel was running on frayed nerves when the summer heat, the stench, and the sheer exhaustion became overwhelming again. The sail was to be short, though, and they were much heartened by the enterprising quartermasters in Brisbane. The latter had provided them with gallons of fresh milk, ice cream, and a plethora of fresh Australian fruits and vegetables to keep their spirits up.

After a final bout at sea with a horrific storm that threatened to break the ship in half, the *Mactan* made it to Sydney by January 27. The sun was shining intermittently through the clouds as they entered the colorful sandstone cliffs that heralded the majestic Sydney North Heads. Kate was awestruck as she and Sean stood on deck watching the ship sail toward Sydney, several kilometers beyond these staggering, rugged bluffs.

They had reached their final destination… the breathtaking waterway of the vast expanse of Sydney Harbor.

CHAPTER TWENTY-SEVEN

PARADISE FOUND

There was much fanfare as the ship's weary occupants began disembarking. The bone-tired passengers were greeted by U.S. and Australian officials, as the Australian army boarded with stretchers and Australian Red Cross ambulances. Sean reported to a contingent of officers to be debriefed, and Kate left for a nearby telegraph office to inform her family that she was safe.

Director Williams, who was lauded for his meritorious service, now officially represented the American Red Cross in Australia. He pressed local officials to initiate a drive to find domiciles and employment in Australian hospitals for the Filipino doctors and nurses. Irving then met with Kate to offer her a position as a Red Cross naval liaison to U.S. troops already en route to Australia. Kate accepted, most honored by the request.

She found out later that the soldiers who had all been saved on the *Mactan* had collectively signed a letter to recognize Irving Williams, directed to the U.S. Red Cross in Washington D.C. She received a framed copy of the document to place on her bedroom wall. Kate found time later to write to every soldier who signed and left their address. It made her heart happy to tell them how meaningful their lives were to her as a nurse on board.

On that first night in Sydney, after refreshing, long showers and some rest, Sean made a booking at a quaint Italian café for a romantic dinner together. With her small advance stipend from the Red Cross, Kate found a lovely red ruched form-fitting dress and some matching heels. Sean, too, had purchased a fitted white shirt, black slacks, and a jacket for the occasion. The young couple turned heads as they entered the restaurant that night. The owner refused to allow Sean to pay once he discovered they were from the *Mactan*. They were both grateful for the many kindnesses of the Australians that day. Walking hand-in-hand on the old, bricked streets of "The Rocks" together, they passed by a small chapel and Kate asked if they could step in to pray. Sean was touched by the unexpected request.

The small church heralded intricate archways, grand staircases, and polished stained-glass windows. Kate was deeply moved by its beauty, and the painstaking work that detailed the wood carvings inside. She knelt to pray near the altar at the front and the tears soon followed.

Overwhelmed by their welcome in Sydney, and utterly exhausted from the constant month-long fear for each of her patients on board the ship, Kate was overcome with the enormity of the world at war. She was homesick for her family, weary to the bone, and infinitely sad for those mired in the horror of what they left behind. It was a long time before she could get control of her emotions.

The pain of the hellish war was seemingly etched upon her heart and, once again, Sean moved to hold her. She tearfully began with, "My heart aches for every young soldier who goes into battle. When love and life are most precious, their youth and inexperience make them believe they're simply invincible. But in those first few moments, when chaos and absolute mayhem surround them, they see the terror of their own death, and often of those right beside them. The human soul isn't meant to process such horrors."

She tried vainly to dry her eyes as she continued.

"Think about it. You're just a boy, really, with your entire life ahead, when love is the freshest and best it will ever be. All at once, your youth flashes before you; you see every tiny possession you once owned, every beautiful girl that once smiled in your direction, and every positive, nurturing life lesson by a loving mother or father. Each of these wonders has such tremendous depth of meaning at that moment in time. But of each of these things…love is the one thing that really truly matters."

Sean began worrying that she might make herself sick with all of the pain. She moved to the altar again, then turned again to speak.

"When all of these memories flash by, the love created in those moments is like balm creeping over your heart. I hope that stays with each soldier faced with their fate. I pray every single day with every fiber of my being that those who die a violent and untimely death in this war will be holding the strength and memory of that love in their hearts when they die, and not the absolute terror of their horrific end." With those sad words, her sobs grew stronger.

Her chest heaved with the pain. It was as if she was witnessing those violent deaths as they occurred. Sean moved behind her, turning Kate toward him. The look on his face clearly showed that he breathed in the wonder that this passionate, kind, willful girl loved *him*. The moments passed and Kate calmed herself, allowing him to escort her from the sanctuary and away from her troubling thoughts. They strolled in silence toward the hotel, reflecting on an eventful day.

Sean was quiet and solicitous when he escorted Kate to her room that night. "Good night, Kate," he said in his husky Aussie voice. He bent to kiss her, another long, lingering kiss. Leaning close, he let their bodies touch.

Then as if something switched off inside him, he turned reluctantly to head toward his room. Kate looked after him and whispered with some hesitation, "Would you like to come in and talk? There's so much I still want to talk about and I'm still half afraid that if I let you go, I'll never see you again."

Without a word, he entered the room and shut the door. The finality of that one act left the sorrows of their journey and the world at war resolutely behind him.

KATE TURNED SHY once again when he shut the door. Sensing her nervousness, he broke the ice by teasing her, "I reckon you did not hesitate much there at that open invitation for me to join you. Do you often invite wayward men into your room?" She smiled sheepishly and said, "If we're confessing all things tonight, let's start by saying that you're not exactly the first."

Sean looked expectantly at her, waiting for her response. "Righto. Let's have a go at an explanation there, please," he responded in an even tone, crossing his arms and leaning casually against the door. The only indication that he was concerned as to where this confession was going was a somewhat puzzled look and a raised eyebrow. Kate blushed under his frank, penetrating stare, marveling at how he never lost his calm demeanor. In reality, it took all of his resolve— and a fair degree of pride in never displaying his emotions— to keep his thoughts to himself.

"Well, just so you know, I had a good friend… a young doctor that was my escort at some of the social functions in Manila. He took me to my room one night after a cotillion. He stayed overnight, but only because I was inebriated and Patrick just wanted to ensure I didn't choke if I passed out. Call it a medical intervention, if you will," she peered at Sean cautiously to see his reaction. "Nothing happened, Sean."

Continuing his casual air, his long legs crossed at the ankles in a relaxed pose, he said in an even tone, "This uh… Patrick guy. Did he mean anything to you, Kate?"

Kate moved around the room toward the window, peering out from the curtains into the dark night. She turned to him with an innocent smile, saying coolly, "I'd be lying if I said he didn't. But I kept him at bay, much because of that night with you in Maine. I felt like I was cheating on you, Sean," she added with alacrity, "See? There's that 'honesty' gene. I'm a definite failure at this."

She shrugged her shoulders as she turned to face him. Her face was carefully blank, but she was somewhat regretful about that admission.

Allowing her a little more leeway because of her charming disclosure, he retorted, "I *am* jealous, sweet girl. But if you kept him at bay, *as you said,*" he clipped in an even tone, "*and* he played the part of the gentleman all night, *as you said,* then there isn't anything else to be discussed. Unless you want another go at that admission, Miss Yeager." Kate shook her head, irritated by the suggestive tone— her eyes flashing sharply at the challenge there to defend her honor.

Sean almost laughed out loud at her glare. The quick glimmer at once showed the fire and ice coursing through her veins. "Fire and ice!" he smiled calmly. "That quicksilver temper… it's what made me love you, Kate. Long ago in Maine."

Once more the chameleon, Sean closed the conversation before Kate could delve further into that subject. Deftly, he moved onto less emotionally invasive waters, asking how Kate came to be in the Philippines. Kate responded, "I'll ask the same of you, Sean."

They sat up most of the night talking about her sister Kerri's wedding, Kate's move to Washington for nursing, and his work with the submarines that took him across the seas to the Philippines. She hesitated when discussing her work in Washington at the cryptanalysis center, for several reasons. Sitting next to the window with a cup of hot tea they had ordered, she watched Sean move over to the chair across from her, pouring himself a cup as well.

"Just so we hold no secrets between us, Kate, I know about your work. When I arrived in the Philippines, I was told to memorize the names of the small group Ned ran. Given to me for contact purposes, we were to discuss nothing of our missions with anyone other than Ned's team. I was a mite curious when the name 'Katriana Yeager' came up, but I had no earthly reason to believe you and she were one and the same."

"And while we're at it, this Patrick guy… would he be Lieutenant Patrick Danforth, perchance?" Kate looked at him in surprise but responded in the affirmative.

"I understand he's a good man— intuitive, intelligent and acutely loyal to our cause," Sean replied. "He's one of the best Ned has. So, I reckon I won't hold that against him. At least, not until I size him up fair and square. I've not met the man," he grinned widely at her.

Kate looked up at him and said, "Well then, I guess I can say this is now a 'dedicated relationship.' But," she added, "if so, how do I know if it's more than any relationships you've had in the past?"

Sean moved over to sit on the bed, stretching his long legs out, saying, "I'm not hinting here. I'm just stretching my achin' leg out so it doesn't start paining me again." He patted the bed next to him, repeating the words almost verbatim from that long ago night: "I'm pretty harmless, Kate!" he announced in a teasing, tender manner.

Kate sat beside him on the bed, putting her arm around his waist. She gingerly touched the bandage on his right side. The long, raised scar was healing well but still tender to the touch.

"Sean, it may be a foolish question to you, but I really *need* to know. Kerri and I discussed this during my last visit with her. She asked Tim the same questions. He answered that before her, he couldn't remember any other encounters. Is that how you feel?"

There was no hesitation in Sean's response.

"First, I've never felt this way about any other girl. And, yes, this is more than a relationship in both depth and intensity. We've already shared a lifetime of events together. There are only two more things to anticipate at this point: sex and marriage. And I think you're knowing by now my thoughts about at least one of those subjects," he said, grinning broadly. "And I can freely admit that I want to marry you, charming girl. Soon, if I'm lucky enough. If I'm being dinkum, the sex thought entered my mind the minute I first met ya, Katie girl." He smiled again and, once more, her heart skipped a beat.

"I remember the day you both rode up on your bikes to the *Squalus*. You had those white capris that showed off your gorgeous legs and backside and a beautiful orange shirt that showed off your attractive cur—" she popped him on his good arm to warn him, but her smile and a slight blush showed she liked where the conversation was going.

"Hmmm…me? And not Kerri? When people meet her, they all think she's beautiful, sophisticated, and always so poised! And she is." Kate said with admiration. Sean smiled.

"It's the chemistry, I guess. Kerri is beautiful, yeah. But you looked like a challenge to me, and one that I wanted to take. You were staring at me from behind those lovely sunnies, and meeting my gaze square on. And when you sat down near me, the chemistry was right solid. I couldn't take my eyes off you when you weren't lookin'. I still can't." "I felt the same! I watched you on that platform and I have never had those thoughts about a guy before. I thought you could look at me with those penetrating eyes and see exactly what I was thinking, so I kept my head down as much as possible." She laughed at the remembrance of that moment. As she laughed, Sean turned toward her, his casted arm resting gently across her stomach. He kissed her, saying, "Keep those thoughts coming, Kate!"

A pregnant pause followed, and Kate turned shy once again. "What's your middle name, Sean? I have to know it if I'm asking what I'm about to ask." He answered quietly, "Sean Douglas." His left hand reached for hers as she began to speak again.

"Well then, Sean Douglas, do you want to stay for a while longer?" she asked shyly. She spoke nervously, but resolutely determined, even if the night went further than expected. He turned to her with a soft smile directed her way that made her heart skip once again.

"Kate, darling. Soon, my love. But not tonight. You may well be ready for more, but I'm not. I'd not be up to my superb performance levels in my condition," he stared at her after that bold statement.

"Performance levels?" She asked, surprised by the comment.

He raised his casted arm and pointed to the healing knee, his crutch, and both sets of stitched wounds and said, "I can't have you thinkin' I'm a sub-par lover. Especially not our first time, and your— you know– your first Broadway performance." He rolled off the bed in one swift movement, wincing as he landed on the right leg. He moved to turn a small corner lamp off. The room was lit only by the rays of a full moon glancing off the bed.

"Stand up, my love!" he requested. She did and he moved again to kiss her. Perhaps in a small way to punish her for his nagging doubts about that night with Patrick, he deliberately aroused her. They stayed thus for a long time, building up the fires between them. With slow, tantalizing moves, his hand moved to trace the V-neck on her dress, inching one finger down to touch the crest between her breasts. Her eyes grew wide, but there was no protest, so he kissed her deeply. Moving his hand to her shoulders, he unzipped her dress and let it drop to the ground. Her silk slip fell next.

His hand glided down her back and he undid her bra deliberately, with one swift move, left-handed. It fell to the floor as his hand moved around her waist to tease her, then moved up to cup one full breast. *Still no protest*, he smiled to himself.

The dim room made it easier for Kate to accept that she was almost naked and vulnerable against his onslaught. Against the backdrop of the windows and the soft rays of the ambient moon, Sean could only see the outline of her body, but he was stirred like he had never been before with a woman. His hand moved up to her lips, tracing them with one finger, letting his lips follow. As his hand moved downward further, Kate gasped, fully intoxicated by his lovemaking. She absolutely could not move. Not if the entire Japanese army were beating their door down.

Parting her lips again, his tongue demanded more. He stroked her belly, circling with one finger. Moving lower, he found the lace on her last remaining stitch of clothing. Teasing her, the shadows of the moonlight traced across the intensity in his face. His eyes burned into hers, and Kate's head tipped back. She forgot where she was as nearly all vestiges of nervousness slipped away… wondering what would happen if he took all of this further. He pulled her in closer so his hard, insistent body was against the soft curves of hers. His eyes were penetrating as they looked into hers.

"THAT'S one-handed, my love. Just wait until my dominant hand is free."

Her large, soft eyes were clearly wondering why he hadn't continued.

"Not now, Katie girl. That's the tip of the iceberg, my love. It will be stunning for both of us, I promise."

She started to say something and, putting one finger to her lips, he whispered, "Shhhh, love. Soon enough."

He turned to exit, locking the door behind him and leaving a trembling Kate, shaken by her raw emotions. She edged blindly toward the bed. Moving under the covers, Kate fell into a deep slumber, exhausted by Sean's intense lovemaking.

CHAPTER TWENTY-EIGHT

A WAR BRIDE

Kate slept like the dead that night, completely spent by the emotions of the previous evening. Sean slept little, sitting on the windowsill of his room and looking out at the moonlight across the bay. He suffered much in waiting for the awakening of this beautiful girl, but he was determined to do it all proper and right for her. When Kate met him in the lobby the next morning, she kissed him, turning rosy at the recollection of last night's lovemaking. He marveled once again at the changing moods of her personality.

She asked him if he could take her to the hospital to see the patients and meet with Chairman Williams, taking Irving's request for her assistance as a legitimate, serious offer. Sean escorted her, meeting up with her again in the late afternoon.

Shopping once more with the small salary advance provided by the Red Cross, Kate found a black sleeveless swing dress with a tapered, curved waist and a full skirt. She was back to being teasing, but mindful of how close they had come to taking their relationship further.

Sean located a charming bistro near a tourist spot he called "Mrs. Macquarie's Chair," and together they strolled to the bistro on the warm summer night. Over cocktails and entrees, Kate removed a small gift from her purse and placed it on the table, her eyes brimming with unshed tears.

As Sean opened it, she said in an emotional voice, "When I'm with you, Sean, time seems to stand still. The world is once-again balanced and we're the only two people in it." She smiled, as her tears fell onto the white linen. "I thought this would be a wonderful reminder that we can live in the moments we have right now, but we also have to move forward and let time take us to where we both need to be in life."

He leaned across the table, kissing her, appreciative of the gift. Reaching into his inner coat pocket, he placed a small rectangular box on the center of the table as well.

"I have something for you as well, Kate." She opened it and found a strand of pearls and matching earrings with a small diamond drop. He added, "I saw these and knew that they would go perfectly with whatever you were wearing tonight." He smiled with that half-crooked smile she loved. "The white pearl is for 'innocence, purity, beauty and new beginnings.' That is everything you are to me, but there's so much more to you. How lucky am I, my love?"

Sean took her hands in his, both turning to view the stunning lights of the Sydney Harbor. He paid the bill, and they strolled off through the charming Sydney Botanic Gardens toward Mrs. Macquarie's Point. They reached the point at the end of the small spit and rounded the path to where the chair was, a giant stone icon constructed for then-Governor Macquarie's wife in 1810. The exposed sandstone rocks, smoothed and polished by age and wear, were painstakingly carved into the shape of a large bench for Lady Macquarie, known to watch the ships in the picturesque harbor.

The night was perfect— with light winds from the ocean giving them a cooling summer breeze. The stars were out in all of their splendor, with the backdrop of the currents in the harbor lapping gently over the rocks below them. Hundreds of shimmering lights from homes around the surrounding hills and the secluded coves glimmered at them from a distance. Staring across the calm waters before them, Kate was mesmerized, hoping fervently that the war never touched its peaceful, scenic inlets.

A few sailboats and small yachts dotted the bay on this clear, starry night, making a charming backdrop for the two lovers. She turned to gaze at the Sydney Harbor Bridge, marveling at the magnificent steel structure that crossed the expanse of the harbor entrance. When she turned to face Sean again, he was down on one knee with a carefully balanced box in his casted hand. Her heart caught in her throat as she looked down at him. He clasped her delicate hand with his larger one.

"Darling Kate," he began, "this harbor has always been a safe place for me to reflect on every memorable moment I've had. Until you, I never thought that there was more to come. I had no plans for a future with a wife. Now, that's rightly the one thing on my mind since we've found each other again."

Bystanders stopped to watch the enchanting scene, but Sean and Kate forgot there was a world beyond them.

Sean continued, "You're the only dream I ever had that didn't get lost in the face of my drive and passion for my work. Now I can't think of a life without you by my side. This is my safe harbor here. I plan to share that safe harbor with you. Will you marry me, Kate?"

"Yes, Sean. Yes, yes, yes—I'll marry you."

Her soft, lilting voice was music to his ears. He stood and moved to kiss her, slipping the ring on her finger, and then they both looked toward the gentle clapping of a small crowd gathered behind them. They wound their way again through the Royal Botanic Gardens in full summer bloom. Back at the hotel, Sean had ordered a bottle of champagne at a candlelit window table with a view of the water.

There, as they sat and talked about their future, Sean brought up the subject of their wedding and honeymoon.

"Kate, darling, neither of us knows how things will go for us or where we will be directed next with this war. I'm not always patient, especially considering you, and marriage and all that entails, So I'm offering up another proposal to you!" He smiled as he spoke.

"Well?" she asked softly.

"I want to get married straight away. Even if it's only with a Magistrate here in Sydney. I have thought of every impediment, I believe, that a young bride would fancy. Firstly, you would want your family here, but that isn't feasible, so I'm proposing that we have another ceremony with them at some point. Secondly, I've found a dressmaker who can whip up something for the occasion, as a bride would want. Thirdly, we should keep the marriage a secret so you can resume your career path." Kate waited for him to finish before she responded.

"And lastly, I promise to be gentle on our honeymoon night, when I'll be taking advantage of that beautiful body with both my dominant hand and my backup," he winked, "but I want that to be *soon*." He stared at her, daring her to say no.

"Yesterday would have been perfect for me. Tonight would have been exceptional as well. Getting the idea?" he taunted, his eyes flickering over the daring cleavage of her black evening dress. He leaned forward, his eyes dark and shadowy against the softness of the candlelit table.

"I'm a pretty impatient bloke right now, Kate."

Kate whispered in a low, soft voice, "Well, Sean, you leave nothing to chance. I think I can most definitely be persuaded to see things your way on the marriage."

Her expressive eyes promised everything as she looked into his own. As he walked her back to her room that night, he kissed her, his arms encircling her body. A minute later, he pushed away, eyes gleaming. As he made his way down the hall toward his room, he turned, his jacket and tie enhancing his broad shoulders and slim hips as he favored her once again with that incredible smile.

"By the way, this bloody cast is gone tomorrow." He let that sink in, finally adding, "And as you've noticed, I'm not using my crutch tonight. All bets are off on you keepin' your virtue much longer, Katie girl." With his eyes raking over her, once more, she entered the room and stood, trembling, as she gathered her emotions together. *Soon enough*, she smiled. She would be his wife.

~ele~

ON FEBRUARY 10TH, Sean and Kate were married. They received a special dispensation from St. Mary's Cathedral to have the ceremony at the exquisite altar at the church. Sean's mother was a devout Catholic, so Kate had to make a promise to convert to allow for the wedding to happen in this historic Sydney icon. Yarran, Danilo, Captain Tamayo, and several shipmates were witnesses, all sworn to secrecy to protect Kate's new government job at the Red Cross.

Kate wore a floor-length gown with intricate lace sleeves. The dress was of white chiffon, gathering at the waist with a beautiful small satin bow. Her hair was pinned loosely on one side, cascading down the back and the left side of her neck in a mass of loose curls. The veil was a simple one, held with a pearl barrette, fanning out at the neck, down to her waist. She wore Sean's pearl necklace and earrings as her only jewelry.

Sean watched as she moved down the aisle to the organ music, on Captain Tamayo's arm, holding a small posy of white roses. Standing at the altar, he wore a dark suit and tie along with a white shirt, all of which was tailored to his handsome frame. As Kate made her way down the aisle, she noted four women near the front of the church. She thought they might have been errant worshippers who had slipped in, but those thoughts left her mind as she saw Sean at the altar.

It was a simple, prayerful ceremony, with candles lit for Kate's parents and Sean's dad, and a white rose added to the altar for his grandmother. They left in due time for a small reception at a nearby hotel. The young couple received an ovation as they entered the lobby, tourists and guests alike acknowledging the lovely newly-wedded pair. To show his appreciation for the gesture, Sean raised their entwined hands and turned and kissed his young bride. All eyes were on them as he twirled her once to Glen Miller's music in the reception area.

In a corner of the lobby, under an immense chandelier, were four decorated cocktail tables with the word *Lawrence* tagged on short name stands. Kate was touched by Sean's apparent thoughtfulness for their small number of guests. As they moved to the area, Kate noticed the four women from the church entering the spacious lobby and approaching them. In the next instant, she was astounded as an older woman with dark hair and a youthful, vibrant face kissed Sean on the lips, turning to Kate next, taking her hands. In an accent eerily similar to Sean's voice and inflections, she said, "Welcome to the family, Kate.

You have made my son a happy man." Sean smiled. "Kate, my lovely mother, Madeleine Stuart-Lawrence."

The three younger women were busy hugging their brother. All three turned to Kate, each bearing features remarkably similar to Sean's. "Sean's sisters?" Kate questioned. Sean introduced them to his new wife. "Laurel, Veronica, and Stella," he pointed to each, touching Laurel's cheek, kissing Veronica's forehead and affectionately tugging at Stella's hair. Kate turned to Sean, eyes brimming with tears.

"How— how did you manage this surprise?" she asked. Laurel, the oldest in the family, said, "Sean is married to his work. When Mum got the telegram, we knew he had either gone daft, been hit in the head, or was caught by some beautiful sea siren. We had to witness this for ourselves."

Veronica rushed in. "Obviously, our brother is head over heels, and who wouldn't be? You're stunning, sister Kate!"

Stella, the youngest and quietest of the three, responded, "We are most happy to welcome you to the family!"

After mingling with their few guests, the family moved to an intricately decorated table in the dining area. With an affectionate look at his mother, Sean explained that she had arranged for the cocktail tables and for dinner. It was obvious the Lawrences were close, which Kate found to be charming.

As the girls chatted with Sean, Madeleine explained the sibling lineup to Kate. "Laurel, here, is 31. She lives in Toowoomba, outside of Brisbane. She has a twin, Lilibeth, who lives in Cairns. You'll meet her later. Veronica is 29; Sean is next at 27, and our Stella is 23."

By that time, Stella had joined the conversation. She turned to interrupt, but with a firm look of admonition, Madeleine warned her, "There'll be time enough to regale her with all of the particulars of your siblings, Stella!"

As they all were seated at the dinner table, a flash passed between Sean and his mother, but she changed the subject abruptly with an unassuming smile. It was evident to Kate that his mother and sisters adored Sean, but he undoubtedly returned the affection as the protective brother and son. Over a memorable meal, Kate enjoyed listening to riotous tales of Sean as he was growing up. As the night wore on, his mother, smiling discreetly, said, "Girls— we need to unpack and get settled for the next day or two."

Soon after, they rose from the table and said their goodnights, and Sean, well into the happy occasion, carried Kate up the winding stairs to the second-floor ballroom landing. They disappeared toward the elevators, heading to the suite that Sean had reserved for the next few nights.

The room overlooked the harbor, with a stunning view of the shimmering waters. Beside the large bay window, a small table was covered by a white tablecloth. A tray of cheese and fruit was sitting in the middle. "We'll be famished later. That happens, you know." He smiled down at her upturned face. As he popped open the champagne, Kate noticed an intricate, mauve-colored satin negligee and a matching lace jacket on a chair beside him.

"From your groom, my darling wife." He kissed her neck as he unzipped her wedding dress, whispering huskily, "You look absolutely divine in that wedding dress, my lovely bride, but I believe I have something much more comfortable, Kate."

Kate disappeared, and a few minutes later, she stood at the bathroom door in the revealing satin negligee. The lace-sleeved jacket made her look feminine and enticing at the same time. Her eyes were wide and intensely blue as Sean turned to her with two glasses of champagne.

His shirt was off, his belt unbuckled as he walked toward her. His dark hair was slightly tousled, raking down onto his forehead. He handed her the champagne as his eyes swept over her curves. "Have a drink, Kate. It'll take the edge off of a long, eventful day." They both sipped their glasses and placed them on the nearby mantel.

Sean took her in his arms, his fingers lightly moving down the lace on her sleeves. He removed the lace jacket as he kissed her. Lifting her up and carrying her to the bed, he dropped his pants onto the floor. He was naked underneath and, as he moved closer, he smiled about the object her eyes were intensely focused on. In one quick move, he was above her on the bed, his knees holding most of his body weight as one hand reached out to stroke her hair, then moved to unbutton the hook on her negligee. Her hands reached out to caress his chest and she felt the corded muscles flex as he balanced his weight above her.

Sliding one strap of her negligee, he kissed her smooth shoulder as he removed it, then moved to the other side to do the same. His lips traveled down the center of her negligee, slipping the lace away to kiss naked skin. Inching the satin gown up, his hands explored tantalizingly. Kate arched her body instinctively, her senses on fire. Kissing her inner thighs, he lifted the negligee over her head. Poised above her again, he let his full body glide sensuously along hers as he shifted toward her neck to caress it with his tongue.

His mouth covered hers and she melted once more with the intimate caresses below. His lips traveled lower once again, caressing her skin as his hands explored her body. Moments later, eyes focused on hers, he finally traced back to her mouth. With his lips still locked with hers, he gently slid between her thighs to enter her. Kate gasped at the sudden pain, her breath catching in her throat. Sean slowed as she tensed. Hesitating for a few seconds, he finally penetrated further, holding back when she cried out again. He moved against her for a minute, and then withdrew as her resistance grew further. She began shaking softly, knowing that she had stopped his lovemaking and sensing she had failed her husband. He kissed her, full, on the lips.

"Katie, girl. You're not going anywhere and I'm not going anywhere. We have heaps of time to make this work. No regrets, love. No regrets allowed." She curled up and he moved to massage her back and shoulders until she relaxed. Exhausted by the emotions, Kate willed her disappointed body to sleep, with his long body curved against hers.

A short time later, Sean moved to the bay window. Taking a draught of brandy from the bar, he let the warmth of the liquor burn slowly down his throat. He was content knowing that this was a minor setback in a long life ahead. Knowing full well that if he went back to bed, he would be more than tempted to press for sex again, he wrapped a robe around his body, letting his long legs relax. The patient groom finally succumbed to sleep in an uncomfortable chair as his new wife slept peacefully in the oversized bed. Much later, he rose, looking out over the harbor as the moon drifted across the sky. Suddenly, two small hands undid his robe from behind. Kate's body cradled tightly against him. She said softly, "I can't sleep, Sean. Shall we find some other activity to occupy us until morning?" Turning, he smiled at her suggestion, responding, "My mind is slow at this time and I have just one activity I can dream up at this moment, my beautiful mate."

She kissed him deeply, replying, "Well, what are you waiting for? Your competitive bride does not like to be last in her class, Sean." He took her hand and led her to the bed. An hour later, she was soaking in the large tub, white suds covering her as she relaxed blissfully in the hot water.

A freshly-showered Sean sat beside her at the edge of the tub. His hand reached in to search for parts that had piqued his interest during the night. Kate sighed, looking up impishly, saying, "Good Lord, Sean, I'm exhausted. And I'm really sore. I need some time to recover from that massive assault." Noting his readiness and staring at that offending member with a somewhat dubious look, she whispered, "I'm begging for mercy."

"And mercy you shall have, my darling wife. I've a few more things to teach my young bride to put her at the top of her class." Kate sat up, the foamy suds deliciously covering the soft curves of her breasts. "There's more, Sean?" she asked. Sean looked up, as if praying to the heavens.

"I'm about to open up a can of worms— and there's no turning back now, love."

Her interest mounting, he followed with, "It's all in the vows, my darling wife. You promised to love, honor, and obey. And so, you must obey." She looked at him questioningly as he toweled her dry and led her to the bed.

"Holy God… Sean— what the ——————————"

"You asked for mercy, love. I'm givin' it to ya, sweet girl— the only way I know how!"

CHAPTER TWENTY-NINE

WAR AND PEACE—IN AUSTRALIA

Three short days after their wedding, Sean and Kate were again immersed in the war efforts, ordered to report to Melbourne to the offices of Station FRUMEL, Fleet Radio Unit, Signal Intelligence Corps.

At MacArthur's express request to Director Williams after they had landed in Sydney, Kate's nursing work could continue as part of wartime training measures, but she would split her time as a part of the joint army-navy code breaking services.

They moved the few possessions they owned to Melbourne, grateful to be offered a small cottage on the Lawrence property, which would allow Kate to become better acquainted with her new family. The family homestead was breathtaking, and somewhat intimidating to Kate. As they pulled up in the long, circular drive in front of a sprawling two-story home in the country near Melbourne, she turned to Sean, saying, "My God, Sean, you're rich. Why didn't you tell me your family came from money?" Sean smiled at her awestruck look. And Kate added modesty as another one of his admirable traits.

The surrounding land was scenic and powerful. She had never seen such majestic hillsides amidst the vast stretches of the endless untamed valleys that heralded the Melbourne countryside. Varying shades of green carpeted the lush farmlands, and the rows of trees bordering each property line were tall and splendidly arrayed.

"The tall hedgerows were set up as windbreakers," Sean explained, "but most of the countrymen prefer their land to be separated with natural tree breaks." The result was a vast array of imposing, statuesque tall spruces, Australian Beech, and colorful Grevillea. Brightly-plumed Banksia and imposing Illawarra flame trees added to the pervasive beauty of the land. Each farm appeared to compete to outdo its neighbor in height, color, and design, enhancing the regional landscape and displaying the astonishing arboreal colors endemic to Victoria and southern Australia.

In typical Australian custom, the Lawrence house was built a few feet off the ground with a wide veranda porch surrounding it. The porch was decorated intricately with beautiful plants, tropical shrubs and white Queen chairs.

A picturesque table and tea setting was displayed in a sitting area next to the front doors. Giant open birdcages dotted the landscape surrounding the house, and feeders were attached inside the cages for the large, brightly plumed birds to enjoy. This provided an eclectic touch by way of aviary ambiance. The house itself was surrounded by vibrant Illawarra flame trees and equally unusual Grevillea. It was a scenic, peaceful little settlement in its own right… with a large, neatly-adorned vegetable garden on one corner and tropical flower gardens and walkways on the opposite side in the backyard.

Kate soon learned that Stella, the youngest, visited home almost every weekend with her new husband, and she often kept the gardens up for her mother. She was two years older than Kate and the quietest of his siblings, but Stella and Sean shared several 'like' traits. Both were giving— in fact, generous almost to a fault, and Stella displayed her affection toward others, but in an unobtrusive way. A small hand placed on Kate's arm, a shawl strategically resting on her shoulders on the cooler nights on the veranda, or a cup of tea to coerce Kate to rest while gardening around their little cottage…all of these were predominant displays of her thoughtful attentiveness. Kate grew to love Stella's kind nature, as she did her mother-in-law, who surprisingly worked hard not to interfere in their married life.

When Kate asked Madeleine about her hands-off approach one night, Madeleine responded, "My dear, you have every right to privacy as you adjust to married life. I know from past experience that Sean values his alone time. So, when you need space, you can and should treat me as if I live 100 kilometers away instead of 100 meters."

Kate appreciated Madeleine's discretion and her timely advice. As they settled into Victoria, she also learned to love southern Australia, especially, the city of Melbourne. She and Sean were exploring the distinctive countryside every spare moment they had, which was somewhat rare in the first few weeks. Kate nearly wore herself out setting their tiny cottage up. Sean also found another endearing trait to love in his young wife… a domestic streak that was as strong as his mother's.

While waiting for the Red Cross personnel to move from Sydney, and for circuits and equipment in the cryptanalysis center to be set up, new curtains were made by the young wife. A rich Aubusson rug was purchased in Melbourne. And Kate discovered a plethora of hanging tapestry and various artisan bowls and decorations from their first trip to Yarran's tribal lands. She was impressed with the talents of the Aboriginals, and the cottage was soon dotted with artistic displays of vases, paintings, and the like.

In an effort to continue providing income to Yarran's tribe, Sean's only domestic request was that all dishware be ordered from the tribe. Kate willingly obliged. Her first visit to the Yarran's settlement left her indelibly touched by the plight of the people. Forced onto so-called tribal lands, the days of their ancestral foraging, hunting, and gathering were over. The acclimation to tribal domesticity was glaringly painful. Unfortunately, the infiltration of liquor was to the detriment of many of the men. Kate offered up any free time on the weekends to work in a makeshift clinic, which was their only medical support. Sean often worked as a handyman, repairing roofs, houses, tribal centers, and village stores. It was a pitifully small gesture by both, as it was a never-ending battle to preserve their dignity and their livelihood. Nevertheless, both Lawrences pressed on with their help. Sometimes Sean was painfully morose upon returning to the cottage.

Through relaxing chats on their veranda in the tranquil countryside, Kate learned to love her husband even more as she helped him work through the pain of seeing Yarran's people in such dire straits. She continued to cheer him with bits of help to the community and free medical advice to tribal elders to implement across the settlement. The decorative sofa Madeleine had provided them as a wedding gift was soon covered with rustic pillows ordered from the tribe. The sentimental handmade patchwork quilt from Sean's bed in Maine was prominently displayed on the back of their sofa while a new bedspread was ordered from the talented Aboriginal seamstresses.

On their first official weekend at the Lawrence homestead, Kate made dinner for Sean, Madeleine, Stella, and her husband David. If there was any chance of her new family thinking she could not provide adequately for her husband, Kate was determined that there was to be no doubt after this dinner. Not for the last time, she was grateful for the painstaking culinary lessons from her collective family back home.

Serving cocktails along with a sizable varietal tray of cheeses, fresh tropical fruits, and homemade scones, she managed a cracking lamb roast, accompanied by mint peas, garlic mashed potatoes, and marinated Brussels sprouts, capping this off with a fruits-of-the-forest pie for dessert. She was so exhausted after spending the previous day preparing that Sean asked over lunch if "overwrought wife" was going to be served on the menu as well.

A playful pop on the cheek was followed by Sean's favorite new pastime: a wrestling match with his wife. She was pinned in about 30 seconds— also about the time it took for their clothes to be shed. Their passions mounted quickly, but he delayed his entry into an erotic tease, making her wonder blissfully how she had resisted in the confines of the room in Sydney. The requisite long, relaxing nap afterward left them drowsily content.

Paying great attention to every detail in her newfound domesticity, Kate had also gone to the trouble to find an English oak kitchen table, a comfortable armchair for Sean, and a table setting on the outdoor veranda, to make the atmosphere as warm and inviting as possible.

Their dinner affair was lovely. Sean reached over affectionately to caress her hair and Kate returned the gesture, clasping his large hand with her small, dainty one.

That night, with the balcony doors open to the scenic valley far beyond them, Sean made love again to his young wife. The sounds of the bush track— birds and beasts alike— lulled them to a blissful sleep afterward. Kate boldly initiated it, gaining confidence steadily in her ability to judge whatever temptress his moods desired, from coolly seductive, to sweetly romantic, to the wildly passionate, which she was discovering often occurred outdoors, or as close to that venue as possible.

She had entered the small open living area in a new negligee, while a shirtless Sean was clearing the table, having stripped down partly with the oppressive summer heat. He approached her deliberately, and with every licentious intent on display in his searching eyes, easing off the rest of his clothes as he moved. This time, there was no slow undressing. The negligee was dropped to the floor and in one fell swoop, Kate was picked up, legs locked around his waist as they fell somewhat ungently onto the Aubusson rug. Sean was more eager this time— slightly forceful in his lust. He entered her quickly, his pent-up emotions from their perfect family evening building as fast as his response to her initiation. Her passion met his, almost equally as fierce.

It was a swift taking and a raw encounter, with both of them somewhat surprised by the naked boldness each showed in the act itself. Somewhere in the midst of their passion Kate cried out, and Sean slowed his pace, using a gentler approach for the rest of the lovemaking session. Kate was finding that there were many facets to sex, and Sean was a disciplined lover who could make their encounters last or boldly take the lead in a quick lovemaking session. Thus far, she found, as Kerri had mentioned, sex was wonderfully enchanting.

Had anyone, friend or foe, happened upon this "scene of domestic tranquility" afterward, they would have found the sofa askew, the rug mussed, and a young, stark-naked couple intertwined on the floor, fast asleep in each other's arms. As it was, the scene was only observed by a large, errant, and most decidedly poisonous red-bellied black snake crawling across the veranda steps… and a small goanna who happened upon the inset of their open doors.

Had she been awake, Kate would have openly preferred the indelicate situation of a live family member witnessing the carnage inside, to these two terrifying intruders.

When Sean discovered a piece of new snakeskin embedded on a slightly protruding porch nail the next morning, Kate begged him to uproot every piece of furniture in the tiny cottage to search for the offending reptile, which was long gone by that time. Sean was much amused by her abject terror with each overturned cushion or rug. That was the last time she allowed the doors to stay open all night. Thus, he discovered another one of the relatively few fears she possessed. Underneath the steel exterior of the vastly adaptable wife he married, any forked-tongue, slithering reptile was an uninvited and most unwelcome inhabitant in their charming little abode.

Being a man who meticulously plans all aspects of his life, Sean had already organized a short honeymoon trip in South Australia. Kate was not expected to work full time at the Red Cross center in Melbourne until Director Williams managed a full setup there from his headquarters in Sydney. She and Sean headed out on the Great Ocean Road trek early one morning, soon after getting settled into their cottage on the Lawrence property. As they headed toward the start of this scenic road, Sean explained with considerable pride that it was built by returning soldiers after the Great War as a long-term project to keep them employed. It was also set to become a vital transportation link for tourism and for the timber industry in Victoria.

Before this iconic road was built, the rugged south-to-west coast was accessible only by sea or by traversing rough, untamed bush track. The land surrounding the area was pure wilderness— rife with myriad exotic birds, a plethora of snakes, dense, untrodden bushland, and a variety of animals that Kate had never imagined.

Cape Otway was the home of the first of many koalas that Kate was able to view up close. These incredible marsupials moved with intentional, sloth-like slowness, so observations at eye level were a regular occurrence. Kangaroos dotted the wilderness as they drove to stopping points with picnic areas and scenic overlooks. She was enamored with their bouncy, energetic personalities, especially the young joeys.

Kate spotted her first emu as they hiked down a well-marked trail where the long-ago remnants of a smoldering volcano once stood. Sean explained that the males rumble, while the females make what is called a "boom" sound in their chest— all intriguing parts of the untamed Australian wildlife, Kate felt. As she headed closer to examine a female cautiously approaching her, the *boom* was almost mesmerizing in intensity. She was like a small child in her wonder, as she learned about each new creature they encountered. Sean marveled at

Kate's enthusiasm and boundless energy as they explored the haunts of his childhood. As they traveled near precarious cliffs on some of the more dangerous byways, Sean inadvertently discovered that Kate also had a supreme fear of heights.

They rounded a corner of a small winding lane with sheer cliffs a few inches from the edge of the paved road. As he turned to show her the splendid sight of the calm seas out toward the ocean side, Sean saw that her eyes were closed and she was holding her hands toward her heart. He reached out to take one of Kate's hands and found the palms sweaty and cold.

Immediately, he searched for a small inside pullout and stopped the car so he could help her calm down. While Kate gained control of herself, Sean spoke softly, "You're as tough as nails, as you proved capably through the enemy-infested jungles in the Philippines. And now I am finally learning about your fears!" From then on, he was careful about traversing the narrowest sections carved from the tall majestic cliffs on the ocean.

As Sean continued on the road, he gave an explanation of the highway's initiation.

"The "Ocean Road," as it was first named, was planned towards the end of the First World War. The chairman of the Country Roads Board was a friend of my father's. The committee asked the State War Council for funds to help returned soldiers find work on new roads in sparsely populated areas of Australia." He gave Kate's hand a squeeze as they rounded a harrowing curve in the road.

"Dad had served on the initial board, and he and the chairman had requested that this south coast road be dedicated as a memorial to those who lost their lives in the Great War. It was to be paid for in tourism tolls until the debt was cleared. The road was then to be gifted to the people of Australia. I like that, and also that this also includes Yarran's people, to me. Dad managed some restitutions to Yarran's tribe for the use of their land." Sean was immensely proud of his father's part in this endeavor.

⁓ele⁓

THEIR HONEYMOON journey wound them across one of Australia's most incredibly scenic road treks to their final destiny, in Port Fairy, Victoria. He explained the many iconic landmarks they passed along the roadside.

Kate was enamored with the scenic early morning jaunts across the country roads. Spectacular ocean sunrise panoramas with picturesque farmlands on the inland side suddenly turned into views of luxurious tropical rainforest areas as they rounded one corner after another on long stretches of the country drive. The views were of a charming coastal plethora of scenic seaside cliffs, dotted by imposing off-shore geologic structures, limestone caves, and blowholes. Centuries of dangerously roiling seas formed these features, along with the massive oceanic storms of the unpredictable Southern Ocean.

"I could stand on one of these platforms for hours and hours and watch the waves roll in!" Kate exclaimed with her arms outstretched. Sean watched as she closed her eyes and basked in the sun and the ocean breezes.

That evening, they sat outside their cabin in the tiny seaside town of Port Fairy, watching the sunset and drinking robust South Australian wine. The tall grasses that separated their cottage from the ocean's pounding currents were swaying gently against the scenic backdrop of a waning sun. Enveloped in the warmth of her husband's arms, Kate sighed languidly. "There is nowhere else on Earth I would rather be at this moment than with you!"

A man to seek all tempting sights, Sean looked down at his wife, having the advantage of height over some inadvertent cleavage as she relaxed in his arms. He moved to unbutton one button and have a further peek. She smiled as he did, saying, "Your mind never strays far from the prospect of carnal encounters, does it?" He laughed, kissing her to take the moment onto a romantic twist.

Refilling her glass of Shiraz, he carried their drinks next to the toasty, crackling fire inside. Sean had won the wife lottery with Kate. Enticing and seductive at times, charming and coquettish at others…her moods were ever-changing. He never knew exactly where the moment would take him. Nor did he care, as long as she was by his side. It was a peace amidst the hells of the war efforts they knew were only beginning.

Monterey House HQ - Melbourne

A
CRACK
IN THE
PACIFIC WALL

The best and brightest minds
convene…

CHAPTER THIRTY

SPECIAL FORCES– THE SIGINT GROUP

In due time, Kate and Sean reported full time in their respective positions. Although Kate held an official position with the Red Cross, her work had as yet to be defined as they opened the offices in Melbourne. Initially, Kate was assigned to the 75-man code breaker unit, many of whom transferred from Corregidor after they were under siege. With her fluency in German and French, she was a valuable translator for the group at Victoria Barracks in Melbourne.

As a Royal Australian Navy officer, Sean was assigned to the naval cryptography unit, consisting of naval personnel, university professors, and linguistics graduates. Sean's specific team specialized in voice surveillance from radio, and the "leaking" from telephones or wiretaps. He was adept in verbal Japanese, his fluency continually improving with the help of Japanese linguists. In a hotly debated first meeting between him and his new boss, Commander Eric Nave, Sean came out fighting for some of the Japanese linguists he was working with. Nave's superiors insisted that they phase all Japanese employees out of the interpreter work. Sean insisted just as hotly, "I am adamant about being trained by first-generation Japanese natives!"

When his commander demanded a reason, Sean retorted, "The nuances of inflection and tone can be more easily discerned with first-generation native tongues." Nave had responded, "I have a strong sense of unease about using anyone connected to the Japanese nation. In keeping with naval requirements, I will agree *only* if you agree to phase the Japanese out so that only Aussie, American, or British officers will be the primary radio translators."

Sean accepted the request for now, but his dislike for the condescending tone and possessive nature regarding information intensified.

Lieutenant Lawrence had a brilliant mind, and proved to be a quick study. As a recognized expert in submarine design and the tactics of submarine battles, he headed the traffic analysis regarding naval positions, pinning the location and frequency of transmissions from the Japanese fleet. Movement from island to island was a critical aspect of understanding when and where pending battles might be fought. He was a highly-sought commodity with his pragmatic approach, and extensive submarine training.

In late February 1942, the RAN Cryptographic Unit also transferred to the Monterey Apartments. Sean had initially reported to this unit, which was also originally housed at the Victoria Barracks. Commander Nave was known as a knowledgeable but eccentric man who was not always well-received in the Melbourne spy circles. Sean respected his infinite knowledge, but eventually, Nave's singularly secretive behavior ended up being an impasse in the intelligence field, despite his vast experience.

For now, Sean acted as the group's primary liaison for the Australian Naval High Command. Being respected in British, Australian, and U.S. circles, he was allowed privileges that many Aussies, and most Brits, did not receive in MacArthur's headquarters. Sean's ability to convey important information with a logical, intellectual twist did not offend his superiors. In a short time, he was promoted to report directly under the leader of the "ultra-secret" classified group that intercepted and decoded all Japanese military and naval messages. He made it no secret that he detested the competitive nature of the numerous teams and leaders. Any divisiveness was a positive boost for the enemy. For this reason, he was trusted to run interference with the messages conveyed between commanders and units. His practiced approach allowed for the conveyance of only what was deemed necessary.

This prevented extraneous details from being misconstrued, taking the communiqués off track.

As Sean was a loyal Australian, and a British citizen as well, this arrangement also provided for less animosity amongst the leaders in Australian and British chains of command. The American officers respected his strong appreciation of their submarine expertise. If he felt in his own judgment that a message warranted further discussion, or that one team or another could shed better light on an interpretation or code, he initiated those conversations in a roundtable discussion. He was authorized to act as a negotiator should arguments arise. The Americans were pleased with this approach, and later, MacArthur himself endorsed it by having his staff members attend occasional roundtable discussions with the young Aussie.

When Commander Nave was transferred to a position to create field units monitoring Japanese signals, Sean remained cordial, recognizing that Nave's vast experience was valuable for faster interpretative relays of codes.

As the group gained ground and began to operate as a dedicated, cohesive unit, Sean's team soon discovered he was quite thorough in his work. He immediately organized the transmissions in his sector into location, divided by whether they were moving or stationary, and by time, duration, and frequency of the transmissions. Extensive maps were overlaid on the walls, with cities, ports, and radio stations. These were pinpointed down to details on particular coves and geologic formations, such as extensive reefs in each area. In zones where Sean knew there was heavy radio traffic, he ordered intricate topographic information.

One morning, when monitoring the transmission activity north of Port Moresby, Sean and Nave's team reached another impasse. Sean requisitioned two oceanographers from the Melbourne Uni Meteorology Department, requesting that one study deep-sea thermoclines in the North Pacific, key to submarine warfare in that the thermoclines accurately reflect active sonar and acoustic signals. The other oceanographer was to provide detailed information on navigation bathymetry, to provide more accurate ocean floor topography.

In a briefing that morning, an irritated Sean bounded up from the table to confront Eric Nave's team lead, who stated to Sean, "I have absolutely ZERO interest in working with a bunch of college professors who are obsessed with some rare underwater phenomena that may or may not be useful to us in the war efforts!" He was overruled by Rudy Fabian, from the combined Australian Navy/U.S. Navy Ops Center, who had an appreciation for Sean's thoroughness, if not yet a complete understanding of the importance of such information. Secretly elated with the support but subdued in his response, Sean added one further request for his intelligence group: "My colleague Yarran and several of his tribal members from the Kulin nation are needed to set up a group of surveillance specialists in Port Moresby, in Papua New Guinea."

Sean was interrupted with another contentious conversation regarding this request, for which he held his own decisively. Being overly dismissive of Sean's new approach, one of the ranking officers spoke his mind plainly about the waste of staff and resources. It was to be one of his last acts in Sean's roundtable group. Sean listened to the arguments, then responded even more decisively to the faces around the room.

"Yarran speaks the dialect of the Wurundjeri people– the *Woi Wurrung* language of tribes surrounding the Melbourne area." He clipped abruptly. "It is a distinct language not understood by the Japanese, but it is well understood by me and several others, including linguists at Melbourne Uni. The use of this language will provide an added measure of security as they translate codes and positions of the Japanese carriers and their naval fleet."

After several naval staff members around the room agreed, Sean was given approval for a trial experiment.

He pulled a map down from a screen above him to provide further detail. "We are receiving consistent Japanese communication directives from the Philippines. Our lead Filipino radio communicator, Danilo, is to position himself with this group in New Guinea, as he is obviously fluent in Tagalog, the predominant Filipino dialect. He is fluent in other derivations on the surrounding islands and he is decently proficient in Japanese."

Sean continued, watching the faces around the room digest his suggestion. "Danilo is also skilled in calculating from the derivations of Filipino dialects the approximate locations where they are transmitting from," explained Sean confidently. "And that is of key importance to our assessing precise positions of the Japanese transmissions and movement. Together, both Yarran and Danilo will have a strong command of the channels from the Philippines to Port Moresby and then to Melbourne." The group agreed, but Sean left the meeting knowing that his battles with competing team members were far from over.

On March 21, 1942, MacArthur arrived in Melbourne, immediately ensconcing himself and his entourage– nicknamed the "Bataan Gang," in the most expensive suites in the luxurious Menzies Hotel. He was held in adulation by much of the Australian populace. Still, his preference for luxury and his disobedience of orders from Washington demanding that he have only one aide accompany him from Corregidor did not go over well with the higher echelon in the armed forces. To garner further sympathy and support of the Australian people, MacArthur informed the press in Melbourne that his aircraft was in perilous danger throughout the transport from the Philippines, having been chased by Japanese Zeros. This was, in fact, strenuously denied by none other than the wireless operator on his plane. They were never in any danger on the journey to Australia.

Although he and Sean were well acquainted with each other, Sean began to distance himself slightly from the self-aggrandizement that became MacArthur's *modus operandi* after his retreat to Australia. Sean and Kate preferred to focus on their own work relative to the war efforts. And too, Sean had no use for luxury and refinement when he knew many of his naval colleagues were aboard ships mired in life-and-death struggles. Thus, his apartment near the Menzies was spartan. Kate insisted on adding enough touches to it to help Sean relax when he was there, with Sean's mom and sister Stella assisting generously in this endeavor.

Sean's Port Moresby plan, code-named "Southern Cross," took some convincing. But eventually, the Ops Center realized this was a monitoring setup that the Japanese could not break. To MacArthur's great credit, he endorsed Sean's unorthodox plans, sensing that Port Moresby was a strategic transference and surveillance location. In fact, he welcomed the Aussie's ingenuity regarding the proposals for Aboriginal assistance. In a fit of magnanimity soon after, MacArthur requested an audience of the young naval officer, and the two were cordial in the subsequent discussions.

"I am aware of your submarine prowess in the Philippines, Lieutenant Lawrence. I was also informed that you were wounded during the reconnaissance runs I requested from Ned's group during the initial attacks. I value your ingenuity and bravery, and I am interested in hearing more of your ideas," he said congenially, as Sean acknowledged the compliments in his usual non-effusive way.

"I understand you have had some resistance in your efforts, and I fully intend to make sure this is not continuing from anyone under U.S. purview. This creative genius is how we win wars, Sean," MacArthur said, dispensing with the formal titles and asking Sean to call him "Douglas." The two men planned to meet on the occasions that MacArthur was required to report updates to Washington, a request which automatically elevated attention to the New Guinea efforts.

As Sean saluted and stood to leave, Douglas MacArthur stood before he saluted in return, in a rare gesture acknowledging his appreciation of Sean's efforts. He accompanied the salute by adding, "I also understand you are seeing a lot of my young American acquaintance, Miss Yeager. She's quite a catch, that one, and continues to be a valuable asset in the war efforts in virtually every position her considerable talents are requested."

MacArthur's face turned stern for a moment and he closed the meeting with a sharp quip, "Don't run off and marry this young lady just yet, Sean. We'll lose her in our talent pool and that would be a pity."

Sean grinned and responded somewhat sarcastically, "Well then, don't let your valuable assets go as soon as they find happiness and end up with a bloody marriage proposal by the likes of me. They'll reward you tenfold with their loyalty and appreciation, Douglas!" The two men shook hands and a friendship was born out of this propitious meeting.

Soon after Yarran had set up the Comms center in Port Moresby, their team broke a Japanese code while monitoring radio transmittals near Manila. Translating the messages by *Woi Wurrung*– Yarran's Aboriginal language, they relayed to Melbourne the exact positions of Japanese destroyers in the vicinity south of Java. Simultaneously, Sean's Melbourne Naval Center assisted in finding intricate reefs for two battle-damaged U.S. subs hiding from the destroyers' sonar. A portentous biological discovery for evasive maneuvering against the Japs, Sean immediately incorporated it to protect these two crippled subs. The two subs headed for Brisbane for repairs, with the submariners living to fight other battles for the Allies.

Sean was pleased that his Melbourne and New Guinea units had proven their value within the first weeks of their existence. As the war progressed, this biological warfare knowledge would indisputably prove to help hide Allied submarines from potential Japanese destruction.

In a second meeting requested by MacArthur a week later, Sean explained his work in detail:

"The marine biologists from Melbourne Uni have discovered that pistol shrimp, a species endemic to certain tropical waters of the Pacific, make deafening 'signature noises' with an oversized claw, sounding much like the noise of a pistol being fired." He continued with, "This claw closes at remarkable speeds which the shrimp use to stun their prey. The subsequent loud 'crack' that accompanies this closure, if grouped together in masses, can cause significant distractions to sonar readings which are based almost entirely on sound echoes. This breakthrough will undoubtedly save many lives as we fight these underwater battles."

MacArthur was impressed at the sheer ingenuity of the enterprising young Australian. Under his good graces, and with the favorable protection, Sean pressed forward rapidly with his work.

ELATED WITH SEAN'S report of a highly successful meeting and MacArthur's full support, Kate rearranged their weekend schedule to head to the countryside for a brief respite.

A few hours of hard work at the Aboriginal settlement clinic were rewarded by an enjoyable evening with Madeleine, Stella and David. Madeleine's cook spoiled them with one of Sean's favorite meals, a delightful, crispy lemon butter Barramundi, with smashed potatoes, asparagus, and mint peas. They were ever-grateful for her continued efforts to keep their sanity amidst the chaos of the war.

CHAPTER THIRTY-ONE

NAZIS ON NAURU

To Kate's chagrin, she arrived for work on the following Monday and found a note on her desk, asking her to make herself available to translate more documents for MacArthur's senior officers. This time, the request was specifically relative to a small island due northeast of the Queensland Territory, called Nauru. Despite its diminutive size of only eight square miles, Nauru was critical to the Allied war efforts, being a primary supplier of phosphate. This phosphate— over a million tons per year— was used as the predominant source of fertilizer for Australia's agricultural crops. In turn, these crops were used to help feed the massive influx of new troops on Australian soil.

Although of keen importance to Australia and New Zealand, the tiny mass of land was virtually undefended, and thus became prominent as the *only* area targeted by the Germans in the Pacific during the entire war. In briefings held by MacArthur's staff, classified information regarding Nauru was dispensed to the few people in the briefing for further code breaking endeavors. Kate had been requested for these briefings.

"In December of 1940," announced one of MacArthur's senior staff members, "German commerce raiders attacked the massive steel jetty on the tiny island used for loading valuable cargo ships headed for Australia, and in some cases, Japan as well. The focus of the Nazi marauders was on the destruction of all phosphate facilities on the island. Foiled by precarious weather, the Germans at this time retreated, leaving several sailors stranded on the island, scattering quickly to avoid capture," he paused briefly.

"General MacArthur has concluded in subsequent staff reviews that the island remains critical to the Axis powers."

Turning to Kate, he added, "Miss Yeager, at General MacArthur's express request, your presence is required to translate German encrypted documents and communiqués regarding any subsequent strikes on South Pacific islands, including Nauru. We're monitoring all natural resources in this vast area in case other islands are targeted. There are several French Protectorates in the vicinity, for which your translations and code work will be required."

Although MacArthur's team certainly had other linguists capable of joining his staff, most of them were briefing generals, troop leaders, and active-duty commanders. Thus, reluctantly, Kate proceeded with the requirements to add regular translation routines to her hectic schedule. Inadvertently, this had the unintended effect of her becoming involved in the only military action of the Nazis in World War II to take place in the vicinity of the South Pacific.

Kate's translations, and the simultaneous strategic interrogations of German sailors who had been imprisoned on the island, allowed the Allies to maneuver merchant ships from the shipping alleys that the German freighters were tracking in order to confiscate the phosphates. Still, she felt as if she was of far too little contribution to the war efforts, and of more significant contribution to the singular appeasement of Douglas MacArthur. Not that she minded, but Kate was far more interested in the cryptanalytics with members of the Monterey teams.

Unfortunately for Kate, the Japanese also felt that Nauru was critical to their war efforts. Sean explained the importance of her work at a late dinner in his apartment one evening. While listening to her frustrations about the translation demands, he felt inclined to shed more details about both the Australian and U.S. need for her interpretation.

"Japan's interest in Nauru is twofold," Sean stated to her over a relaxing glass of Australian Red and a broiled emu steak as they sat on his small patio overlooking the streets of Melbourne that evening.

"They too want the phosphate deposits and they also have plans to attack the sea route between Australia and the western coast of the U.S. Verifiable transmittals between the two Axis nations have already indicated that Tokyo was incensed by the German's previous attacks, and their subsequent focus on this tiny island," he reiterated.

Kate agreed, adding her observations to the conversation. "Communiqués between Japan's Emperor and the Führer have intensified. According to Naval Intelligence, this is threatening the Tripartite Pact itself. I guess I'll be needed for a while as long as MacArthur knows the scrutiny is warranted."

Because of pressing air raids on Darwin and the continual Japanese threat against Brisbane, MacArthur remained interested in this tiny independent nation. Knowing the nation's critical food chain was under continual threat, 'a while…' became an enduring duration of months. So, Kate continued her monitoring.

She worked on translations three early mornings per week in the vast expanse of the MacArthur Headquarters; the rest of the day was spent at

Victoria Barracks. At least two evening classes were managed in the Red Cross building at the Royal Exhibition Hall, at the request of Director Williams. On these evenings she taught a two-hour "combat surgical unit" class to U.S. nurses, and the Australian surgical medical staff from the Melbourne Hospital. These discussions included mobile surgical unit set-up and medical triage under combat conditions. Her knowledge was based on her considerable nursing experiences after the Manila bombings. She was managing little as a practicing hospital nurse these days, but the classes were deemed critical, so her teaching efforts continued. They also boosted her salary, which she graciously spent on the Aboriginal settlement clinic.

The Saturday classes on pacific island botany, which she taught at the Red Cross HQ, were voluntary. But these were of value to the military. They began as informal classes of her therapeutic wound care and herbal medical pharmacopeia, taught to new military personnel. She lectured on food sources and medicinal herbs on the tropical islands, using her Philippines experiences as a guide. Malaria prevention and dysentery cures were prominent discussions.

Among her students was Miss Hannah More Frazer, who was slated to be appointed Director of the American Red Cross Service Club in Melbourne. Using copious props, animated firsthand stories, and live plants from a Botany professor loaned from Sean's staff at Melbourne Uni, her classes soon became a prerequisite for military nurses and surgeons in Melbourne. Miss Frazer later relayed these training efforts to officials at the American Red Cross HQs in Sydney and Brisbane.

As Kate's escape on the *Mactan* became known, she also became something of a celebrity among the Aussies and the Americans in Melbourne. She managed her newfound celebrity status through somewhat self-deprecating wit, professing that her rapidly growing audience was there to poke fun at her Maine accent, interspersed with entertaining Australian phrases. Humor notwithstanding, Sean was openly proud of his talented fiancée (and secret wife). He admired her energy in balancing several complex jobs in her weekly routine. Since she was a young girl, Kate had always required far less sleep than most others. Here, it was a great asset for her and for the war efforts as well.

WHILE THE ENTERPRISING translator/nurse/spy was busy appeasing MacArthur's staff, Sean took pains to plan a live demonstration of his recent biological shrimp discovery at a university auditorium. This monumental effort was managed to impede any further resistance which might be making its way through Monterey. He enjoyed the pronounced shock effect when Douglas MacArthur walked into the lecture hall and sat in the front of the room. The value in producing such a distinguished audience was immeasurable. Sean invited several strategic Allied staff members to the demonstration. He was in full Australian naval uniform, preferring to promote his Australian background for the more formal briefing. After introducing the Sigint Research Group staff members and their impressive academic credentials, Sean initiated the meeting.

"Gentlemen," he explained, "we are here today to demonstrate what we call *biological warfare with a twist.*" He paused for effect. "With the capable staff of the University of Melbourne, the SRG was able to uncover a natural biological phenomenon which we believe will assist us when our subs are entering enemy waters or, even more critical, seeking shelter from enemy radar in a battle." Sean explained the science of acoustics, adding a short lecture to aid the demonstration.

"The objective of 'passive acoustics' is to detect the sounds produced by a submarine, such as propellers, engines, and pump noises. One would deduce that when a sub is hiding, this equipment is shut down. Therefore, passive noise cannot be detected as easily.

'Active acoustics,' however, is the natural enemy of hiding subs. Active sonar is where sound waves are sent out, bouncing off objects to create what the Navy calls a 'sound signature.' It is one of the few effective ways to quickly find a silent submarine. However, it is incredibly challenging to perform active acoustics effectively under certain marine conditions…around large rock beds, near a continental shelf, in barrier reefs, and the like. So, these areas are mapped and used by submarines all over the world. Including our enemies, I would presume. We'll demonstrate how to effectively disrupt active acoustics using marine beds."

With a sizable portable sonar device and radar screen running on one side of the room, Sean gave the signal to raise the volume for a minute, waiting for the meeting members to adjust to the loud, rhythmically acoustic *ping.* At his signal, a recording of these pistol shrimp was played by the SRG Staff on the opposite side of the room. The cacophony of crackling, a recorded sound remarkably similar to that of frying bacon, capably disrupted the sonar readings. Sean managed the same demonstration again, producing the same effects to prove the phenomenon was legitimate.

The lights in the auditorium then lit a darkened stage in the room, where live pistol shrimp from a giant biology aquarium were swimming in an intricate replica of their natural habitat. Members of his Sigint staff passed out maps of the Pacific Ocean where these shrimp were known to migrate. Sean had incorporated such bio maps from Melbourne marine biology professors. The SRG staff members had memorized the locations of these beds in their most prominent habitats— the massive coral reefs in the Pacific. As larger-scaled maps of these areas were pulled down onto projector screens behind him, Sean explained his methodology in more detail.

"In studying further, my team and I have discovered that these alpheid shrimp inhabit many of the rich tropical and subtropical coastal waters in the nearby Pacific, where zooplankton, their predominant food source, is abundant. The biologists at the Uni have been asked to provide all available details on *when* these shrimp migrations occur to the various massive zooplankton beds where they are known to hover."

As he continued to point out details from the maps, Sean shared the story of the two recent submarine saves near Java. He let it be known that his staff in Port Moresby had been instrumental in the save, communicating the necessary submarine movement into the alpheid beds to Sean's team in Melbourne. The messages were relayed in the Aboriginal language. The Melbourne team directed where the subs were to hide, in Aboriginal naval code, while the Japanese were searching diligently for their prey. He continued with, "Our Comms team will additionally have biologists available to provide updated migration detail reports, whenever available, and these will be provided to the radio operators on the subs. A briefing will be provided to the captains daily when close to known enemy waters. Our land radio operators are working with the biologists to memorize new migration patterns and the exact coordinates of each coral reef where these shrimps inhabit and incubate." He added, "In just the few short weeks that we have utilized this information, this knowledge has saved the lives of every submariner on these two subs. It will save countless other Allied vessels as well."

This statement was not lost on anyone in the room.

"On another related note, our naval team is requesting that all of the equipment for repair work in the engineering rooms on our Australian subs must be rubberized to every extent possible. We're recommending fully rubberized soles on shoes as well. Dropping one metal tool against a hull is a dead giveaway as to position. Emphasis on *dead*."

He paused again: "A good sonar man can hear a ship 60 miles away if it's not running silently. A better sonar man can tell you whether it's coming or going from the exact sound detected." Not content with the acoustics demonstration, he had the biologists set up a live pistol shrimp feeding, snapping up their prey of krill and mysid shrimp. The sound in the large aquarium was amplified to replicate the noise when traveling underwater. The audience was riveted.

Sean was elated that the Melbourne Uni staff members proved useful to the war efforts. Any measure that saved the lives of Allied troops was a worthy endeavor. The meeting was thus a resounding success.

THE FOLLOWING WEEKS saw both Kate and Sean's workload increase at a rapid pace as both soon gained reputations for being obsessed with their work. They reluctantly agreed to keep their marital status secret. Each was aware of efforts to sack females, including higher ranking officers, who were thus expected to maintain and raise their families. Called a *marriage bar,* the practice of restricting the employment of married women, particularly in professional positions, was well in force. Although neither liked dishonesty in any form, Sean, in particular, detested the dismissal of someone operating as a solid contributor to the war efforts.

Through contacts in MacArthur's HQ, Sean managed to secure an empty apartment for Kate in his own building so that they could be with each other as often as possible. They saw each other on a social basis and were genuinely assumed to be an "item" as a newly engaged couple, which was, of course, permissible by all employment standards.

On every possible weekend they made a getaway to Sean's homestead, finding peaceful respite, and time for what Sean pronounced humorously to Kate as his much-needed "less risky conjugal visits."

Sean's Melbourne Uni contributors continued to achieve rapid success. Some weeks after the inaugural demo, the two crippled subs that had hidden in the pistol shrimp beds arrived in New Farm, Brisbane for repairs. Sean arranged to have giant Australian prawns delivered with an accompanying feast, upon their portage in Brisbane.

The gift arrived with a note from Sean, proclaiming that he was ensuring the Aussie crustaceans would forever be the submariners' favorite meals. He knew both captains personally. And thus, they appreciated the humor in this gesture even more. The message that the "biological measures" had saved the lives of the submariners was a deliberate one that Sean intended to be conveyed to joint U.S. and Australian naval staff. The kind act and the humor were also not lost on U.S. commanders in the area. The news reached MacArthur's attentive ears yet again, and Sean was thus able to permanently secure his team of professors into his folds.

His academic team of biologists, oceanographers, and geoscientists helped to bring even further notoriety to the overseeing Sigint Intelligence Group. Sean was eventually assigned to work in the command center of the SIG, but he preferred to continue active involvement in much of the message tracking. He remained a participant on rotational shifts to cover transmittals from Yarran. Sean was proficient in tracking specific Japanese operators by the tones and inflections of their voices. By monitoring individual radio operators, his team could ascertain when senior officers were transmitting messages… a detail of critical importance. Their signal characteristics were elevated to a higher level of analysis, contributing significantly to more defined cryptic evaluations.

This effort was aided by some of the more careless Japanese operators who translated newer codes by resending them again with the older methods. Thus, Sean's team could more quickly decipher recently changed codes. He and a great many other dedicated men and women were putting Australia on the map in the world of espionage.

CHAPTER THIRTY-TWO

THE LAND DOWN UNDER

As they headed rapidly into the pell-mell pace of employment, they found that their time together as a couple diminished as they both became intensely absorbed in the war efforts. Using artful attempts to distract Kate from an almost-obsession with teaching and code breaking work, Sean soon discovered that anything having to do with Australian wildlife was a big hit with his young bride. With that in mind, he sporadically planned a second honeymoon break. A three-day scenic trek to Phillip Island was initiated, to see the fairy penguins.

In a fit of nostalgic vibrancy unusual for Sean, he explained to Kate that they were the world's smallest penguins and, as a young boy, the night show where they waddled onto shore in masses into their burrows, was enthralling for him to witness.

He convinced her to cancel her Saturday class that week and head out the Friday before. They took off early that morning on the 135-km journey from Melbourne.

Recently, three enterprising Phillip Island residents had decided to start tours, taking interested sightseers by torchlight to watch the pint-sized penguins' sunset arrival on the beach in the Summerland Peninsula. Sean reserved an excursion with them through an accommodating hotel concierge. The bridge access road was reasonably new, erected in 1939 to connect the diminutive island to mainland Australia. Before the bridge was built, the Lawrence men rowed out to the island for their camping trips, braving the challenging currents in a family fishing boat.

The island divides the Western Port Bay and the Bass Strait, and the heavy currents and winds where the two headwaters meet contribute to a windy beach at night. Sean had the forethought to bring a heavy blanket for them to huddle under during the late-night avian show. He had arranged for a room in Cowes at the Isle of Wight Hotel, in the northernmost sheltered part of the island. The island was just 20 km long and 10 km wide, but there was so much wildlife to see that Kate perpetually asked him to stop the car to view animals by the roadside. Her eyes wide with excitement, she was enraptured by every encounter. Sean thrilled as she embraced every new species.

Both were chatty on the drive, with Sean reflecting on trips with his father many years earlier. He glanced at Kate in the passenger seat as she listened. She looked particularly fetching in a white shirt and blue pants, with her hair braided down one shoulder. She wore an intricate diamond cross on her neck that Kerri had given her for their last birthday. Her eyes were shining as she listened to his childhood stories, enjoying the opportunity to know more about her husband as a young boy.

"We used to come here a lot when we were kids. Aidan and I would set up the tent while dad built a fire and set the lines for fishing. Mum would pack a huge picnic basket—" Kate caught something in his voice and interrupted him, questioning with, "Who is Aidan, Sean?"

Sean was quiet for a moment, wrestling with a response.

He hesitated, and then said, "He's my brother."

Kate looked at him, surprised that he had never mentioned this, but guessing that, like her parents, he was no longer living. Her hand reached out sympathetically for his and he turned to Kate with a small, half-smile. She thought she caught a glimmer of a tear in his eye.

"Is? Or was?" Kate asked, finally registering Sean's use of the present tense. "Is he still alive, Sean? Why haven't I met him? Or even heard about him?"

"I guess this is as good a time to tell you as any," he said, staring at the road as he drove. "Aidan is about two years younger than me… in between me and Stella in the family lineup." He glanced over again to see her reaction as she listened.

"When we were little, we were inseparable. Aidan, dad and I went hunting, camping, and hiking… all the things boys like to do with their father. The three of us had a unique bond. And Aidan and I shared an even stronger one. We learned to hunt and fish with bows and spears, taught to us by Yarran and the elders in his tribe. Aidan spent a good deal of time at the tribal village… often hitchhiking to their encampment when I was busy at school. He was 16 and I was not yet 18. I was an obsessed student who was quite properly absorbed with the prospect of getting a much higher education." He smiled at the remembrance of pushing himself so hard in school.

"One day, the chairman of the Country Roads Board, who was also dad's good friend, approached the tribal elders and told them they would have to move. He had official papers, and the law with him to ensure the tribe had to obey them. Parts of the road under construction were running through their lands and the village itself, I guess." He paused for a moment, absorbed in the memory of this painful incident, even years later. Finding a small scenic pullout, he got out of the car to sit on a nearby picnic table. Kate followed, sitting beside him.

Sean was quiet for a moment, gathering his thoughts. With the sea breezes whipping through his hair, he looked inordinately handsome, Kate thought, with a considerable amount of wifely pride. His eyes were glassy as he reflected on this past and what it meant to him.

"For Aboriginals, land is central to their identity, their heritage, their spirituality, and frankly— their very existence. Once again, the Aboriginals were being evicted from *their* land. Aidan was present when the councilmen arrived. He had a spear in his hand and he threw it, principally to hit a nearby tree just to annoy the councilmen who had accompanied the chairman. One of the fellas moved and it hit the bloke in the shoulder. It was just a glancing wound, but dad was there as a member of the council. Dad was pretty well forced to make a show of upholding the law and Aidan was arrested. So, at 16, he was thrown into the gaol. Dad wanted him to learn his lesson, but I disagreed, rightly so. I drove to the gaol and bailed him out. I took money saved for my education from my parents to do that, but that's another story."

After a short pause, he continued, "When he got out, Aidan made his way back to the Aboriginal village. This time, mum drove out with me to try to make sense out of his behavior. She told him he had to support his father— that families stand together, especially in times of strife." Sean paused once again.

"Mum understood his anguish, but she felt the need for the road to be a great success, with dad having been a war veteran himself. He felt a huge responsibility for the returning soldiers."

As he faltered again, Kate realized that the incident was still an emotional one for Sean.

"Anyway, Aidan told her to go to hell. He told me I could go with her if I sided with dad. It was a veritable nightmare for our family. Lilibeth, Laurel, and mum sided with dad, whilst Veronica and Stella took Aidan's side, with me. So, I went down to the county magistrate's office to find a solution for Yarran's people to keep their land. I found some workarounds and one that was manageable, but it was too late. They were evicted from the land and the tribe moved further into bush track… wild, untamable land with little food or natural resources. They were destitute. Aidan went with them, vowing to never see the family again."

Sean turned to look at Kate again, absorbed in his story. A small tear rolled down her cheek as she said, "I cannot imagine how difficult it was for you,

Sean. You must have been devastated over this rift in the family." She moved to gently push a strand of hair out from his eyes, looking at him tenderly. Sean smiled at the comforting gesture, continuing his story.

"In fairness to dad, he insisted that war reparations be utilized for housing the displaced families.

That softened me somewhat, but Aidan was young, headstrong and impressionable. He was the most sensitive child in our family– similar to Stella. Dad and mum were devastated when Aidan pressed on to help the Aboriginals rebuild.

I was angry at my parents for caving in to 'progress,' and that was back when I was ready to graduate. So, I opted, instead of a local scholarship to Melbourne Uni, to move to Sydney and accept another scholarship offer. I never returned home to live again. And for a long time, I didn't reckon I'd visit either. I found a scholarship for Yarran and several tribal youths to help them attend college. That was my way of helping the tribe."

Reflecting on the moments, he scooped Kate in front of his seat on the table and she leaned against him as he continued.

"You see, Yarran's father and several villagers served in the Great War as trackers, and the Uni couldn't get around the scholarship programs they 'gifted' to children of war veterans. I made sure of that. So that's why Yarran is so intelligent and well-bred. He was one of the lucky ones, Kate." Sean was silent again. Painfully so.

"Dad died a year or so after that. We never reconciled and so he carried that cross to his grave. Mum said it almost killed him to lose both of his sons in just a month. His health went downhill rather quickly after that. Of course, he died from the shrapnel wounds from Gallipoli. The shrapnel started penetrating some of his organs.

We weren't to blame for that, obviously. But his loss softened my mum considerably. She grasps Aidan's and my protective stance of the Aboriginals now. That's about the end of the story. Now you know who Aidan is."

"Where is he now?" Kate asked. "Don't you ever see him?"

"Dunno, Kate. It's a mite hard to track people in the bush when I reckon they don't want to be tracked. He could be anywhere. Yarran knows, but he was sworn to secrecy. And I honor his friendship too much to test it by demanding the answer to that. Yarran will only say he's happy and doing well. That's all I can get out of him. And I guess it's enough. For now."

Finally, Sean got up and said, "Let's get you to the hotel so you can change. The beach is windy at night."

They left, making their way to the hotel in Cowes. At a quaint little romantic bistro nearby with a scenic water view, they enjoyed a quiet evening together before they headed out to the south part of the island and the penguin beach. Armed with a couple of bottles of rich Australian Cabernet Sauvignon, they were ready for the show. They reserved one bottle for them and Kate donated one to their guides. The men appreciated the gesture, and thus, the couple received a more private tour of the beach and a better upfront viewing spot.

They even treated Kate to a visit at an animal rescue center where she and Sean got to nurse an injured baby penguin. Once again, her enthusiasm was boundless. She vowed to return and help with their rescue recoveries.

As Sean had suspected, the much-touted penguin parade was a remarkable experience for Kate. The actual number of these small, flightless seabirds was almost close to 300 on this night. They kept coming in from the sea… wave after wave of these tiny, sleek little birds with a striking bluish sheen to their coats. Kate watched from a close vantage point as several bolder ones waddled onshore, marching in an orderly fashion and then stopping to observe their uninvited visitors. She was close enough that she could have reached out to touch them as they ambled by and turned uphill to find their perspective burrows.

Surfacing from the rough tides, it was fascinating to observe as they found their own particular sand dune and path. Often, they strutted amiably, side-by-side, but sometimes they argued, like shrewish little humans, bumping and preening each other as they marched. Kate found more than a few to be showmen, appearing to enjoy their captivated audience.

Always inclined to protect the underdogs in nature, an inquisitive Kate asked one of the guides, "How do these helpless creatures defend themselves from Leopard seals, great whites, and the like?" Most appreciative of Kate's interest in his lifelong work, the guide said, "They swim in packs, called 'rafts.' By massing close together, it makes it harder for predation to occur, as their predators have to seek out a stray penguin. They can also swim at remarkably high speeds," he finished, happy to have an audience for his research.

The young couple stayed until the last penguin found its way to its burrow, then returned to the privacy of their secluded hotel room. Sean celebrated the successful penguin foray by pulling a large quilt onto the balcony to watch the moon rise over the waters of the vast ocean. It was bright and cheery next to the inviting fire, and they were further buoyed by the generous wine, fruit, and cheese basket supplied by the hotel staff. He opened one bottle of wine, and his arm moved under the blanket into the even more accommodating warmth of Kate's robe.

She caught her breath as his hand slipped further, undoing the ties on her pajamas to explore other inviting parts. Emboldened by the wine, she readily reciprocated on the upper balcony. They celebrated the enchanting evening under the protective cover of the warm blanket, the crackling fire, and the added warmth of two fully-entwined bodies.

Much later, Kate succumbed to a sound sleep, hastened by the combination of the wine and a second energetic session of lovemaking. As Sean watched his young wife, he prayed fervently that they would always remain this much in love. And at least this much in lust, he added, smiling at their last playful session. He prayed the war would not separate them, mentally or physically.

The next morning, Sean and Kate rose early and hiked for half of the day. As the afternoon sun was waning, they discovered a secluded platform standing just offshore, erected for whale watching. As they were leaving, they happened upon one enormous great white shark who swam underneath the platform, circling for fish offal. Kate shivered, watching its massive, powerful jaws open and close to let infinite schools of small fish inside.

Everything about the island fascinated her. And thus far, virtually everything Australian awakened her senses in an astonishing way, including her Australian husband.

CHAPTER THIRTY-THREE

THE VALLEY OF THE DARKEST SHADOW

"When someone you love dies and you're not expecting it, you don't lose her all at once; you lose her in pieces over a long time— the way the mail stops coming, and her scent fades from the pillows and even from the clothes in her closet and drawers."
–John Irving, A Prayer for Owen Meany

They returned from this three-day Phillip Island trip exhausted, but elated with their brief honeymoon foray. Sean was carrying the suitcase inside as Kate unloaded the seashells and souvenirs onto the veranda. Madeleine opened the door for her son, with a foreboding look that told him something was seriously amiss. He walked inside the door, leaving the suitcase in the front foyer.

A young man was sitting on the ottoman next to his mother's sewing chair– a handsome guy who looked vaguely familiar, but one whose face looked hauntingly grave and stark to Sean. He had time to make an introduction, discovering that the visitor was Kate's brother-in-law, Tim, who he remembered from the sisters' birthday dinner years ago. The air in the room was tense, so Sean moved over near the mantel across the room to observe Tim's interaction with Kate.

Tim's face was not a positive omen for Kate, and an inexplicable sense of dread came over Sean as he waited for his wife. Opening the door, she looked from Madeleine's face to Sean's, then down to a stranger on the nearby ottoman. Her surprise registered as excitement at first, and as Tim stood, she flew into his arms, saying, "Where's Kerri? Where's my beautiful sister? How on earth did you get here, Tim?" Tim let go hesitantly, taking her hands in his and holding her at arm's length so he could see her face. The expression on his own face was telling.

"Kate, darling, sit down please."

Kate refused. "I'll stand, at least until you tell me what's wrong. What's happened? Is Kerri sick, Tim?"

He shifted to grasp her shoulders as he looked down into her eyes. Sean and his mother felt like outsiders as they watched the tense scene play out in front of them. "Kate, honey, I don't know how to say this. I'm so sorry, but Kerri is dead. Oh God, I'm so sorry to have to tell you this!"

Kate stared at Tim for a second, not registering the words. Then she let out a small cry, collapsing in his arms as her legs went weak.

"No—no—NO! Oh Tim, please, No! Please, God, No. Not my sister, too!"

She began pounding his shoulders, her head falling onto his chest as he held her up. Fighting not to faint, she clung to him, sobbing out Kerri's name almost incoherently. Her mournful cries were wrenching to each of them witnessing the scene. Across the room, Sean moved forward in a protective gesture, but his mother held his arm back, saying, "Give them a moment, son. Let them grieve together. This is a tremendous loss for both of them."

As Madeleine faced him and moved in front to gently block him, Kate abruptly let go of Tim and bolted out the front door. Tim looked over to Sean, running his fingers through his hair, saying in an anguished tone, "Jesus, Sean. Help me. It's killing me to do this to her. It's absolutely killing me."

They headed out after the stricken girl. Glancing through the line of trees in the front, they looked to see if she had headed down the drive toward the roadway. Seeing no sign of her, they rounded both sides of the house in separate directions, heading toward the grounds in the back. As they did, they heard a bloodcurdling scream from the far back of the property. Both men bounded toward the open fields that led into the Bushland track.

Kate was a decent runner, and her anguish quickened her pace as she took the long, arduous path that led to the large reservoir on the back acres of the Lawrence property. She showed no evidence of tiring or slowing down, but Sean's powerful legs were longer, and he was determined to catch her. He kept a steady pace, and after some time, caught her at the cliffs above the lake, grabbing her from behind. They both almost lost their balance as Tim quickly approached Sean to help pull her away from the sharp precipice on the edge of the overgrown trail.

Sean held her in a death vice as she fought against them both. Struggling to breathe from Sean's tight hold and short of oxygen from her run, she fainted, a merciful blackness falling over her tortured body and soul.

It was a long way back to the house, and both men were emotionally and physically exhausted, so Sean said calmly, "Tim, can you please have my mother bring the car around? I'll keep Kate here and wait for you." He added, "I can't put her down on the ground. This part of our land isn't cleared and we have Tiger Snakes and Eastern Browns on the property. Their bite is sharp and deadly."

Tim turned to head back to the house, but dust rising from a nearby tractor path showed that Madeleine was already on her way. Sean carried Kate to the front seat of the sedan, holding her in his arms and stroking her hair gently. She was out cold. He brought her into the house and placed her onto the sofa. Madeleine headed into the kitchen for some hot tea and a cool towel, leaving Tim and Sean to handle Kate. Tim took control at this point.

"Can you move over, please? I'm a doctor. I need to check her vital signs, Sean."

Reluctantly, Sean moved and Tim began to examine Kate. Checking her pupils and looking at her pale face, he touched her cold, clammy skin and took her wrist. Finding her pulse rapid, he said gravely, "Her pupils are dilated. She's going into shock, Sean. Get a blanket and a couple of pillows to elevate her feet."

Sean returned as Tim moved to unbutton Kate's shirt, leaving her chemise on for modesty, but allowing her to breathe unrestricted. As he wiped her face with the cool cloth, he said, "Madeleine, please go and grab my medical kit from the car. It's the black bag on the back seat." Kate moaned as he patted her cheeks, willing her to respond.

When Madeleine returned, Tim opened the kit and pulled out the stethoscope, listening to her heart. He reached in for a vial and a syringe, working to fill the syringe with fluid. When Sean stopped him, saying possessively, "What are you doing to my wife?" Tim flinched, looking surprised, but he recovered fast.

"I'm giving her something to raise her blood pressure. We need to find a way to regulate the heartbeat."

He swabbed her arm and injected her quickly. It was Sean's turn to flinch as the needle went into Kate's arm and her face registered the pain with a brief flicker. Tim rechecked her pupils. Frowning, he requested a second blanket to help pull her body temperature up.

"If you have some brandy, it will help to revive her," he stated flatly. "We need to be able to sit her up and get the blood flowing normally."

Rubbing his hands together swiftly against hers to warm them, he waited as Madeleine returned obediently with brandy and a spoon. Tim placed a small amount on her lips. A second spoonful caused her to sputter and choke slightly, some color finally returning to her pale cheeks.

After a few seconds, Kate stirred. Her eyelids fluttered, and Sean nudged Tim away, with Tim moving behind his shoulder to watch anxiously. Kate opened her large soft eyes, pathetic to both men in their wide, bewildered look. They were glazed, the violet shadows dark and humid with agony.

As she moved from Sean's face to Tim's, not fully registering either of them, Sean picked her up to hold her against his chest. Tim handed him another draught of brandy and Sean urged her to drink. Finally registering Tim's face again, Kate remembered what had transpired.

The wrenching sobs began once more. Tim stood silent, arms crossed, agonized once again by reliving the loss of his beloved wife, the memory even stronger seeing the remarkably similar features on her twin.

Sean let Kate cry, continuing to rock her gently. The sobs seemed to come from deep within her soul, as before, in the small chapel in Sydney. After a while, the tears abated and she began to calm down a bit. She wrapped her arms around Sean's neck tightly as if afraid to let go for fear of losing him as well. Finally, she pushed herself away resolutely, willing her shaking legs to stand.

Sean helped her up and she moved straight toward Tim, seeing the look of pain on his face. She reached out to provide comfort with a hug. "I'm so sorry, Tim… you lost your beautiful wife. She loved you so much. And she was happier than I had ever seen her before." Both men were moved by her tender gesture to acknowledge Tim's renewed grief.

Once more, Sean recognized that their sorrow wasn't exactly his to share. For the first time in his 27 years, he felt a tiny pang of something bordering uncomfortably on jealousy as Tim held his wife in his arms, both bonded by their intense grief. Tim recovered first and Kate moved to sit on the sofa, staring blankly out of the large picture window toward the veranda and manicured gardens. It was only a short time, yet it seemed like hours, with none of them knowing how to comfort her. Sean finally moved beside her and she reached out to hold his hand. After another eternity, she looked at Tim, willing herself to ask tough, as yet unanswered questions. Madeleine watched the process quietly, with much sadness toward the agonized girl.

Seeing her expectant look, Tim began haltingly, head down as he spoke, his hands holding both sides of it, as if pained by his thoughts.

"Kerri went into labor about a week after her due date. She was coming along fine, but the baby was breech and bigger than expected, being a week late. We got him turned around, but something went wrong and we didn't catch it in time. Kerri panicked because of all the activity in the labor room and both went into cardiac stress. We all did everything we knew to do, but we lost her and the baby. A boy. Timothy Phillip— our little Timmy."

Tim's face showed the agony of that moment, and Sean reached for the brandy snifter, recognizing the grief of a young man who never had a chance to kiss an ecstatic mom or hold that tiny sprawling baby that would have grown to be a much-beloved son.

With a catch in her voice, Kate asked, "Did she suffer, Tim? Did she know she was dying?"

Tim looked straight into Kate's eyes, answering with a resounding, "No, Kate. No, she didn't."

He was lying, and praying to God that Kate would never know the truth.

"She never knew what was happening. She fainted solid, Kate. She died thinking she would be holding her little baby in her arms soon."

It was Tim's turn to stare out the window, the bitter taste of the anguish of those moments like acid in his throat.

Madeleine eased out of the room to prepare dinner, recognizing that some comforting food would help the emotionally drained group. Kate turned to both men, saying, "I need to just think for a while. I want to go for a walk. By myself."

Sean moved toward his wife, looking into her eyes as he spoke. "Kate, I wouldn't advise that. The bush is filled with dingos, snakes, emus, and the like. Emus aren't exactly abundant in these parts but they're not unknown. And they could be aggressive toward humans if startled. You aren't familiar with the risks. He watched with deliberation as she registered his words.

"Tim and I can follow at a safe distance if Tim doesn't mind."

Tim responded, "I need to do something physical myself. Alright with me."

Kate stared blankly at them, shrugging her shoulders. The vacant expression on her face caused both men to instinctively reach out to help her down the back steps and onto the outback trail once again.

CHAPTER THIRTY-FOUR

SEPARATION OF TWO SOULS

Kate ambled down the same path and into the lands behind the homestead. Relatively alone, she walked along somewhat numbly, her thoughts jumbled and distorted by pain. Several yards behind her, Sean and Tim talked quietly, getting reacquainted, finding a common bond quickly through a shared love of the two sisters. After nearly an hour, Sean made his way up to Kate, saying, "Kate darling, mum was making dinner for us, and I reckon it's time to head back so you can get some rest. You must be zonked by now."

She stared at him, acknowledging the words by shrugging her shoulders. Reluctantly, she turned to head back to the house.

SHE ATE LITTLE at dinner, pushing her food around on her plate and registering something resembling a frown as Sean prodded her, the first sign that she was coming around from the shock of the grief. Madeleine had insisted that Tim stay the night and, indeed, for as long as he needed while he was in Australia. Kate's interest was piqued after he accepted, saying he had no plans to return to the States. She refused to sleep that night, asking for more details as the night wore on. As they sat down in the family room again, she wanted to know when Kerri died, even though there was no real correlation to a timeframe. She had already missed the funeral and any chance to say goodbye to her beloved twin. *War and distance had that effect on many people these days*, she thought bitterly.

At her insistence, Tim began to relay the scenario in greater detail. It was around 7:00 pm on December 16th when Kerri went into labor, and the contractions progressed in phases throughout the long night. As soon as the date registered with her, Kate suddenly stood, her face white as a sheet.

"6:03 am. December 17th. Oh God. Oh my God. I was with her. I was there. I felt it. I felt her leave."

Her words made no sense. She stood, and began pacing while Tim and Sean looked at each other, wondering if she was losing her grip on reality.

"Dad. Dad's birthday. The *Sailfish*. It was an omen. Oh my God, I knew something was wrong. I should have known something was happening to her."

With the more frenetic pacing and mumbling, she began to sound as if she had truly lost her sanity. Sean finally stood up, taking her by the shoulders to force her to sit. As if in a trance, she sat down somewhat obediently beside him, rocking back and forth pitifully. Tim finally began to pick up on something, saying, "Kate, how did you know the exact time? I didn't say anything about a specific timeframe."

Kate looked up, staring across the room absently as she spoke. "The *Sailfish*. The new name for *Squalus*… It was in Manila Harbor. I was on board that night, looking for the cross Kerri and I hung together in Maine. The one we asked to hang on the control panel on the day of the christening. You remember our request, Sean. Anyway, it was still there. I touched it and I felt something so powerful…so intense. At first, I thought it was dad reaching out to me. I started shaking, so I finally left the sub. When I stepped out onto the docks, I looked up at the stars for a moment. At the Southern Cross. Something passed over me. I couldn't breathe. Everything got dark and I just could not catch my breath."

She continued rocking, talking, more to herself than anyone in the room. "My chest hurt. I felt as if I were dying. As—as if my body wasn't my own, and I thought I heard voices calling out to me." She stood, and moved to the center of the room to continue her sad soliloquy. "When I looked at my watch, it was 7:03 pm Manila time.

Which would have made it 6:03 in Boston. 6:03 *AM*." She began pacing once more. Looking at Tim, she continued: "That was when Kerri died, wasn't it? And dad… that was—that was when dad was born. On that same day and hour, December 17th, 45 years ago."

Sean began to finally see where she was going with her thoughts. Her rambling suddenly started to make sense. He remembered reading something about the telepathic bonds of twins. Now he began to believe there was something to it. A chill ran down his spine as he thought of what Kate must have felt on that night, and what she was relaying to them now.

Tim looked at Kate and finally spoke. "Kerri said something when she— uh— passed out. Do you know what she said, Kate? Do you remember?" His eyes were intent, his face devoid of all color.

Kate turned to him, her blue eyes suddenly blazing with the realization of what had happened on that fateful night. "The Cross. 'The Southern Cross.' She whispered about the cross. She saw it too. She was with me and I was with her. I believe I was dying at that moment. I was having heart fibrillations and she was trying to keep me alive. Our souls were separating, and God wasn't sure who to take. Kerri willed me to live. Those were her last words. 'Come back, Kate! He wants me.' Oh, God. Oh my God. It should have been me."

Tim dropped down to one knee, the look on his face confirming to Kate and Sean that everything Kate had relayed was exactly how Kerri's death had transpired, including her last words. It all made perfect sense to him now. Kate took one last look at Tim, saying, "You lied to protect me. She knew she was dying. She let go for me— to let me live."

The tortured girl was beyond coherence at this point.

"Why? Why, God? WHY didn't You take me? She had a son and a husband. She had everything to live for!" she sobbed in unmistakable pain. Once more, her heart was beating far too fast. The blackness enveloped her and she could not catch her breath.

Sean moved quickly to catch her as she passed out for a second time. As he did, he dully remembered a long-ago phrase his father told him about the losses during the Great War:

"The most painful goodbyes are the ones over the agony of a long distance, because you were never there to physically let them go."

THE FOLLOWING DAYS were exceedingly difficult. Kate's guilt was immeasurable, as was the searing pain in her heart. During that week of grieving, Kate discovered that Tim had little else to draw him back to the States.

In mid-November, his father had died of a sudden and massive heart attack, leaving Tim's mother to manage the estate. This mistake would be emotionally and monetarily costly to Tim. That sad letter from Kerri never reached Kate. By that time, the war had hit the Philippines.

Tim's mother lost little time in seeking a replacement husband. Shocking by the standards of that time, within weeks of his death, Susannah was seen regularly being squired by one of her husband's colleagues. In January, Tim discovered that she had amassed massive debts, which he assumed angrily were, in part, the cause of his father's untimely death. The remaining funds that had been set aside in a protected account by his father to help Tim pay for his surgical fellowship were reallocated by a narcissistic, self-promoting mother. She worked to keep appearances up, "at least until she could land another wealthy husband," he told Kate and Sean bitterly.

Harvard had fast-tracked Tim through medical school, but the surgical fellowship in New Orleans was no longer feasible for him. With Kerri and the baby gone, Boston held nothing but wrenching memories for him. His home in Maine was full of the bitterness of seeing his poor excuse of a mother wreck the family finances. Tim left before she could ostensibly find a way to charge him for the debts he had incurred during med school. He took transit on one of the medical transport ships bound for Australia.

Kate felt immense sorrow for him, with so many losses and heartaches in such a short period. In the next few days, she arranged through the Red Cross for his surgical training at the University of Melbourne. Sean was happy to find an apartment in their area near the Medical School, for Tim to continue a surgical fellowship. Asking for help from one of her naval friends, Kate called in a few favors to ensure the U.S. Navy would pay for his residency. This was negotiated in exchange for one year of service… training combat surgeons, medical corpsmen, and combat nurses for the navy. Tim found this to be a favorable arrangement, and he was grateful to Sean and Kate for their help in keeping him debt-free.

Life moved on in its own way. Kate's enormous grief was channeled into her work, which kept her sanity. Like Sean, she had to keep moving, balancing many projects simultaneously. In short order, they were moved permanently to their inner-city apartments in Melbourne, housed separately to keep up the premise of being an unmarried, engaged couple. Sean was perplexed at how to lessen her pain. She seemed happy only when she chatted with Tim about Kerri or took brief sojourns to the country estate to see Madeleine. The Lawrences were, in effect, her only immediate family now besides Tim, whom she would forever consider a brother. Kate found purpose in immersing herself in her work.

Sean accepted that he was only a distant emotional part of this grief process, and he knew that it was a more significant loss than he could comprehend. So, he reluctantly gave her the space to grieve.

IN THE RAN CRYPTOGRAPHIC Unit, once again, Sean reported to a new officer, in his position as the group's primary liaison for the Australian Naval High Command. Being well-respected by British, Australian, and U.S. command alike, the young Australian was allowed privileges that many Aussies and most Brits did not receive in MacArthur's Melbourne Headquarters. His career was thriving. Not that he cared. He was singularly focused on winning the war.

His submarine knowledge was superior to many of the naval men he worked with, as was his ability to convey critical information with a pragmatic, intellectual twist that did not offend his superiors. It was a trait he inherited, or likely learned, from his father, during his father's days as an attaché. In a short time, Sean was promoted to report under the commander of the "ultra-secret" classified group that intercepted and decoded Japanese military messages. His work was stressful, and often he spent the night on a couch in a back room of the decoding center.

Kate learned that it was useless to fuss over him. He was inclined to respond that he was sacrificing far less than those on bloody battlefields in Europe or the Pacific. Nevertheless, she continued delivering small dinner plates and glasses of wine to help him on these exceedingly long nights.

Early one afternoon she was exiting the Victoria Barracks and preparing to head to the Red Cross, on a determined mission to refill her dwindling botanical and medicinal supplies. When she turned to check traffic on one side of the wide street, she noticed a familiar gait that caught her eye. She stared at a handsome man in a U.S. naval uniform walking several yards away. As by now, the city was rife with U.S. uniforms, and this alone would not have been enough to catch her eye. Had he not been whistling a tune that Patrick used to whistle on occasion while escorting her to events in Manila, she would not have noticed him.

The melody caught her attention at once. Her heart skipped a beat when she peered upward and saw the face. She ran into his arms, overjoyed at seeing Patrick alive and well. He bent down and kissed her, swinging her in the air wildly as he did. It took a few minutes for Kate to catch her breath, but she eventually did, saying, "Do you have time for coffee? How did you escape the Philippines? God, it's so wonderful to see you again!"

He looked the same. Perhaps a little thinner, though, from the time he spent in the Philippines after the fall of Manila.

Patrick turned to look at the building, saying, "I'm not due to report until later this afternoon. Let's go grab a bite to eat."

They found a nearby café and an hour later, they were still chatting when Sean entered the restaurant. Kate had not had a chance to bring Sean into the conversation, except to say that she was seeing someone and that it was "very serious." As they were chatting, Sean approached their table and placed his hand on Kate's shoulder. Patrick stood, saluting to acknowledge Sean's rank in the Australian Navy. Sean saluted back.. Both men shook hands afterward, and Kate stood to introduce them.

"Lt. Commander Patrick Danforth… Lt. Commander Sean Lawrence." She placed her hand on Sean's arm.

If Patrick was taken aback, he did a remarkable job of not showing it. Other than telling him the man she was seeing was an Australian, Kate had let the subject of Sean drop for the moment while they caught up.

Both men were immensely handsome in their uniforms, and Kate felt a surge of pride in introducing them to each other. If Sean sized Patrick up, as he had mentioned weeks ago that he would, Patrick evidently met his estimation, judging by Sean's look. Also, Sean had the advantage of the marriage to Kate, so, in effect, he could well afford to be magnanimous about his purported rival, although any form of gloating was not inherent to his nature.

Pulling up a chair, he sat down, asking how Patrick had escaped the Philippines. Patrick obliged with a careful, noncommittal answer at first. Sean stopped him politely, interjecting, "I'm familiar with your work there and your right solid reputation. General MacArthur requested that I memorize the Manila staff in Ned's office as well as their capabilities and talents."

"Very well," Patrick clipped. "Then we both know a little about each other. I take it you're the Aussie who captivated Kate's heart before I had a chance to do so!" he stated bluntly, looking from Kate's blushing face to her slightly possessive hand on Sean's arm. Patrick smiled as he spoke, a disarming smile that showed an appreciable measure of respect. Sean held a fair amount of admiration for Patrick as well, whom he had also heard much about in Manila through Ned. It appeared that all three had at least one solid association: MacArthur. And the two men had a further connection. Both were attracted to Kate.

Sean surmised that Patrick was part of the Navy Signals Group that had escaped from Corregidor by submarine. As such, he now worked in the Central Bureau under the Allied command of the SW Pacific area. This group reported all intelligence data to the U.S. Navy Office in D.C.

Rumor had it that MacArthur was not exactly thrilled with this linking of command. Still, the general vastly respected Patrick, Ned, and his small unit. So, he tolerated the network, albeit with an eye toward control over the code breaking group through his own subordinates.

Patrick reported to Lieutenant Fabian of the U.S. Navy, along with the rest of the 75-man unit of FRUMEL. And although he was a surgeon by profession, his medical connections with the elite Japanese and Filipinos in Manila had served as a conduit for critical spy information. This was precisely why he was moved to Sternberg Hospital in Manila, despite his obvious naval connections at Cavite. It was also why he was evacuated as part of Ned's team.

The three spent the better part of an hour chatting about the past months. They were well on their way to becoming fast friends, for which Kate was grateful. After two hours had passed, Patrick reluctantly decided he needed to inspect his new office space in the Monterey Building. His residence, they determined, was one building over from theirs, in the same apartment block as Tim's.

With Sean's working hours, Kate had been spending many tough evenings alone after the loss of Kerri, so she scheduled some late dinners with Patrick and Tim after work. This was a relief to Sean at first, but as time passed under this new arrangement, Sean noticed that he and Kate were spending less and less time alone.

It began to bother him somewhat that she was spending so much time with Patrick and Tim. He was perplexed over this concern, especially when he was too busy to spend time with her himself. Nevertheless, he was perturbed enough to feel it necessary to arrange a short break by way of another weekend trip.

Sean decided to have her accompany him to a short meeting in Sydney, and a weekend of respite from their work immediately after the meeting.

CHAPTER THIRTY-FIVE

STARRY NIGHTS IN OZ

After a brief transport flight arranged with some Australian naval connections, they arrived at noon on a Friday for requisite Sigint meetings. The next morning, they set out on a long, invigorating harbor hike around the natural coves and inlets of the vast Sydney Harbor.

Ending their trek one day later in Bondi Beach, this was Kate's first real Australian experience at one of the spectacular sunny beaches in this sublime, ocean-bound country. It was precisely the break she needed to lift her spirits after Kerri's death.

She found a stylish bathing suit at a beach hut that piqued her husband's interest, much as it did a few interested men on the beach. She made a pretty picture with her long, wavy, blonde hair flowing down her back, and the blue suit accentuating her bright eyes and darker complexion.

Her skin was tanned after two days of hiking, and the swimsuit fit her extremely well, as she wanted it to— but for Sean's eyes only. To Sean's vast amusement, she was shy about taking off her wrap and accepting a few catcalls and whistles as they meandered out to the crystal blue water to swim.

Later, Sean headed toward a beach café to pick up some drinks. Subsequently finding himself on display for a few nearby ladies, Kate was more than a bit intrigued by the attention he drew at the beach bar. This was her first experience in sharing a "nearly naked" husband within the interested view of other attractive women. Sean took it in stride, grinning at her over the head of a stunning brunette who sauntered up with a female friend to chat with him.

Obviously, by now, he well knew that his looks afforded him more than just a passing glance. And with no ring on his finger, he was fair game for all intents and purposes, much to his wife's chagrin.

Kate sat there, brooding, unable to put her finger on why. The lingering pain and emptiness caused by her sister's death contributed pointedly to that sudden lapse into melancholy. There was a slight but nagging fear that someone more sophisticated might coerce Sean into sex and she would lose him as well.

She knew this was absurd, but with every member of her immediate family now gone, it was natural to fear such a loss again.

Kate was subdued on their walk to the ferry terminal, and Sean wondered what had transpired on the beach to make her so quiet. When they should be enjoying the culmination of a perfect day together— and looking forward to an even lovelier evening, he was frustrated at his inability to read his wife's changing moods. Shortly after, the ferry began its journey across the harbor and Kate moved upstairs to stand at one of the rails and catch the ocean breezes. Sean soon joined her. They had the entire deck to themselves, with the wind whipping incessantly from the channel entrance that led to the ocean.

"Well, bugger! I'll take the bait. What's caused your impertinent little nose to be out of joint, Kate?" he said.

She looked at him, her transparent face unable to mask her irritation.

"I have nothing on my mind, Sean. I'm enjoying the evening air."

Undaunted by the brush-off, he took her gently by the shoulders, saying, "That horse won't run with me, darling. I may be a newlywed, but I *do* know women. I've been virtually surrounded by them my entire life," he retorted in a low, unthreatening tone.

The comment… and the relaxed, even inflection in his voice annoyed her. The calmer his tone, the more frustrated she became.

"I'm sure you do, Sean Douglas. Plenty of them! I watched some of them fawn over you on the beach. You were pretty happy to flirt back with them. So, what happens when I'm not around to monitor the situation?" She was gearing up for an argument.

"First of all, I don't need monitoring. I'm not a monk, nor am I a saint. But I do use discretion and I always have. I don't just jump at every opportunity that arises, Kate. Good Lord, give me credit for having some reasonable restraint, will ya?"

She turned and said in a vitriolic tone, "Restraint, huh? How many women were you with before me? I'll be the judge about your restraint, Sean Douglas Lawrence."

He glanced toward her and responded in a calm, even tone, "Oooh, all three names now, is it? Slow down with the angry taunts. I will acknowledge your questions when you stop acting like some 16-year-old girl who thinks everyone should be celibate until the day they are wed."

"You're mocking me," Kate responded. "I cannot believe you are twisting things around. You're making me look like some flighty little girl who couldn't ever get a date before you, and fell for the first charming guy who was *willing* to seduce her silly, naïve, untouched self."

She turned to walk away and he grabbed her arm, more roughly than he expected. Kate moved away, but he caught her with one hand, holding her until she calmed down.

"You are a temperamental little thing when you are aroused like this. I learn something new about you every day, Katie girl. Some of it puzzles me, I have to say."

"Let go of me, Sean!" she struggled, bristling that he easily pulled her into his body and held her against him in a tight restraining hold. "I hate you right now. I do, I really do." Sean knew he had struck a raw nerve when her eyes filled with tears.

He softened his response and his grip. "It's okay, Kate. I love you enough for the both of us right now." He bent and kissed her lips, and the tears started flowing down her cheeks.

Sean took her by the hand, moving to a nearby bench and facing her, saying more tenderly, "Now, let's start at the beginning, shall we? Before the part about you hating me. And I'll see if I can come up with the rationale behind your vehement behavior, my little spiky echidna. You and your tough little exterior!" He kissed her forehead.

"You're all hard-shelled on the outside right now, but you have a soft little underbelly and you're afraid to show it. You are such a charming, fascinating young woman, Kate Lawrence. So, tell me. What is it about me that you hate?" he asked softly, blinking rapidly with an expectant look. His expression made her laugh out loud, his neck stretched out deliberately, like a turtle sticking out of its shell to peer around at the world.

Kate spoke in a low voice, somewhat challenging in her slightly reproachful tone, "I watched you on the beach today, and I thought— with all of those beautiful ladies interested in you, what would it take for you to be in their arms, making love to them, instead of me? You're so practiced, so confident, and so bloody gorgeous that you get these looks everywhere we go. So why in God's name did you choose me when you can have fun with any pick of a lot more experienced women? It seems as if I'm running in this race and you're crossing the finishing line and just hanging around waiting for me when you could be at some local pub drinking beer and having a fabulous time with your bevy of admirers. What kind of relationship is this for you, Sean?"

He smiled, knowing exactly where this conversation was heading. "Hang on a minute, will ya? I'll give you a fair chance at all that anger. It's a normal approach to the first year of married life, especially with a young, inexperienced wife." She started to frown, and, smiling again, he used his thumb to work the wrinkle out from between her eyes.

"Kate…whether you believe me or not, this is all an expected part of being a young woman of just 21, marrying a man of 27. So, let's take your argument one step at a time, beautiful girl. Lean back against me and we'll have ourselves a little chat about sex. I'll call it your 'Introduction to Marriage 101." Kate turned to look at him in surprise, wondering again if he was mocking her. He turned her head right back toward the ocean.

"I don't want to see your face when we talk. It'll make me laugh. Your expressions are inordinately telling, you know." Kate obediently turned and leaned her head against his chest. Thus so, he began the frank discussion.

Stroking her hair as he spoke, he initiated with, "So I've had women before you, yes. A few encounters, in fact. But I *was* selective. I'll tell you about one or two of them. I've had no one-night stands whatsoever. Unless you count that charming little temptress in Maine who swept me off my feet."

She poked him in the ribs playfully and he gave a pretend grimace of pain. The warmth of his body made her relax, and the night air and the array of stars above were enchanting. She was falling out of anger rapidly.

"My first encounter was with a young professor. As I've said before, I was angry about the strife with my parents when I first settled in on campus. So, I was less than reserved about my natural reticence around older, more experienced women. She was charming, easy on the eyes, and intelligent. It lasted four or five months and we both moved on." He paused for a moment to see if Kate wanted to ask questions.

"My second encounter was one or two months later, with a college student nearer my age. We saw each other socially for a month or so and one night we simply carried it further. It was a natural progression for both of us and she had already had at least one or two encounters before. So, neither of these women was a virgin and I did not take advantage of them in any way. Nor did they take advantage of me, either."

He moved to look at Kate's face. She was listening calmly and taking what he said in stride.

"About a year later, we broke up. She found a graduate student and they married, if memory serves me. I certainly think that was meant to be, as I was not interested enough for marriage, which is what she wanted. At any rate, I got properly involved in my schoolwork and by that time was preoccupied with helping Yarran and his young Aboriginal friends navigate the college realm. It was foreign to all of them, and the challenges were daunting. So that became my 'project' of sorts…helping them all reach their goals and initiating some educational endeavors with Yarran's people. I pretty well was consumed with it, and you know how I am when I'm consumed with my work. That's about all there is to it."

He maneuvered his arm around her neck affectionately and kissed her on her cheek as he spoke.

With little else to say at that moment, they both peered up at the majestically cloudless night sky, knowing that for them, so many poignant nights together had been initiated by their favorite pastime of stargazing, followed by a stretch of meaningful interaction. Thus far, this pastime appeared to be the most effective way for them to communicate their emotions.

The ferry was reaching its destination in Sydney— the large Circular Quay Terminal. They disembarked and headed for a restaurant on the Quay, finding a quieter corner table to finish their conversation without prying ears. Over a perfect salad entrée, prawns, and rice pilaf with some delicate lemon asparagus spears, he continued his dialogue.

"Still want to hear these stories?" he asked, pouring two glasses of Pinot Grigio as he spoke.

"Yes, I do!" she responded, relatively engrossed by the details of his youth.

"So…I was just about ready to graduate and I met this attractive young hostess at an upscale restaurant here in Sydney. We met up and hung out for a few dates, stretched out by a couple of weeks in between my studies and her work schedule. One thing led to another and I found myself back at her apartment on about our fourth or fifth date. She wasn't easy, but she could be 'had' as the saying goes. We became somewhat of an item and that lasted about eight months, though my first few months of graduate school, I became obsessed with my education at that point. She demanded more of my time, and we ended up breaking off the relationship. It was for the best for both of us. At about that time, I moved to London to finish a second graduate degree. Obsessed with school and subsequent work, about three years later, I met this wonderful young beauty in Maine. I was absolutely smitten. No one else compared." He smiled charmingly.

"Anyway, there is a theme you should be taking away from this discussion, Kate. First, I am not inclined toward one-night stands. And second, these were long-term encounters, all of which I walked away from. I mean no disrespect to the women, but the relationships were never important enough for me to wonder if I was missing anything after we ended them. I wasn't disinterested in getting married, just so you know. I told you I had my nights where I walked down to Mrs. Macquarie's Chair and sat, looking out over the water. Sometimes I would wonder just what it would be like to be well and truly in love. So, there you have it all now. Not much to tell, really," he finished.

Kate opened her mouth, hesitating at what she was about to ask.

"Go on, girl. Ask away if you still need answers," he said disarmingly. She looked up inquisitively.

"Ok, Sean. So, you're a proficient lover. You know that, don't you?" His eyes moved to her breasts, eyebrows raised, wanting this conversation to continue.

"All these moves that are pretty new to me… sometimes I wonder if you enjoyed them more with these young ladies you dated. Do you ever wish you were with them, enjoying the sex that I am maybe not proficient at yet? Do you men actually rate your lovers?" she asked in a wistful tone.

"Darling, Kate. You're reading far more into this lovemaking thing than you should. I'm not mocking you for doing that. We all navigate the 'newness' as we first start out. But I will say that what Tim said to Kerri is true. I don't really remember *any* of those encounters. And if it's acceptable for you to hear this, I didn't have a whole lot of desire to have to *practice* on my wife whenever the time came, so I'll share with you that as young boys, Yarran, Aidan and I used to climb the trees in the village. Some families kept house in sturdy tents, some in small huts with thatched roofs, and some elders had homes. But all these structures had a few features in common: large windows, few curtains, and an inclination toward a view of the open sky in their sleeping areas.

Aboriginals are uninhibited in their lovemaking. After all, they've been making love under the stars for centuries. And they're oblivious to 'unsuspected peepery,' which we were proficient at, I might add. So, I learned far more from those free shows than I ever did from practicing on a woman."

Kate nearly choked on her asparagus, laughing at the vision of a much younger Sean up in trees and watching the sex act as a willing voyeur.

"Men are such funny creatures," she said, fairly amused. "That kind of behavior never would have crossed my mind as a girl."

Watching her smile, he asked, "Is that all you need to know?" winking at his beautiful, honeymooning bride.

"Weellll…I'm actually afraid to ask you!" Kate responded shyly.

He looked at her intently, and said, "Alright. Let me guess. About the only thing we truly haven't covered here pertains to the actual act itself, between us. So, what you *really* want to know is, do I regret not marrying someone with experience who can already make love passionately while hanging in trees, leaning precariously over cliff ledges, or perhaps, say, roughhousing on an expensive Aubusson rug?" he asked playfully.

Taking a bite of the delectable sticky date pudding he had ordered for dessert, he moved to share it with Kate, smiling tenderly as he did. "I may have to let this one sink in your stubborn little head as I believe I have already demonstrated it physically, at least once or twice." He offered her another bite as he continued. "I love every single thing about you, Kate."

Most men don't ever talk about their first carnal encounters with the love of their life. And often, women *really* need to hear it! That first night of our marriage, I loved that you were nervous and trying hard not to let it show. I enjoy your shyness, especially now— when you *still* wrap a towel around your body the minute you see that I'm watching you when you step out of the shower or the bath. And I fell even more in love with you that first night. Your eyes held this natural curiosity in what we were about to do. But most of all, they held a trust in me— in what I was about to do to you for the first time. I have never felt more alive, as a man with a beautiful girl to protect and cherish— than I did that night." His eyes searched across the crowded room for a moment, reflecting on that first encounter.

"As I said then, we'll grow together as a couple. I am a lucky man, being your first lover and the man who will happily attend this particular class with you for the rest of your life. And if we're grading, you have earned an 'A plus' for arousing me like no woman has before. Kate watched his eyes dance as he spoke. As they walked out of the restaurant arm in arm, she was a contented woman. They were best friends and lovers, sharing life as a united couple. *How great was that gift?* she thought as they entered a nearby hotel where they had secured a room for the night.

Sean went to move their car to the hotel car park. By the time he had returned, anticipating an amorous lovemaking session, his little wife was showered and fast asleep, her head resting on her hands peacefully. Somewhat disappointed, he stripped down, crawling into bed and spooning up against her. His eyes rested upon her young profile as the moonlight shone across the bed and onto her peaceful face. *There's always the morning*, he said to himself, smiling.

The window was open and the curtains were swaying gently with the evening breezes from the harbor. The cry of an occasional seagull broke the silence of the peaceful night… a sound he loved as a boy when boating with his father. A wind chime on one of the harbor boats soon lulled him to sleep, as he succumbed to the exhaustion of the day's events.

CHAPTER THIRTY-SIX

THE END JUSTIFIES THE MEANS

Returning to the city from this brief vacation, Sean and Kate were fully immersed in their duties again, finding little spare time with their frenetic schedules. Determined to carve out more time for each other, late one afternoon during the following week, they met for a quick break. Sean decided to apprise Kate of some of Patrick's previous medical activities in the Philippines, to gauge her reaction to several military medical experiments under conduct. The two of them strode down one of the wide Melbourne boulevards to a meeting in a building Kate had never seen. As they entered the building, Sean showed his credentials and added Kate to the clearance list for the meeting.

He briefed her as they walked into the session.

"Some of this, you may already know, Kate," he explained in detail. "Patrick routinely informed MacArthur's staff of the various Japanese ailments, from mysterious maladies to serious medical conditions among their elite. He also learned of their own practices and remedies for these conditions."

As Kate remembered conversations with Patrick that appeared pretty innocuous in the past, Sean continued, "By treating their families as well, this ultimately provided critical information about the Japanese high command on the islands. The stresses they were under, troop movements, secret orders… all of these contribute to serious and lingering health ailments."

While waiting for the meeting to begin, Sean mentioned that Kate, and potentially Tim, might well be pulled into similar work. What the U.S. army deemed as human biological warfare.

"In the Philippines, Patrick was briefed on Japanese medical research, such as malaria experiments, inoculation initiatives, the extent of their medical supply depots, and shipping routes. Including their current venereal disease treatments underway. We also learned that the Japanese used some of the Filipinos in their so-called 'friendly inoculation experiments.'"

Somewhat surprised about Patrick's participation, Kate asked, "How did the U.S. Navy convince a prominent surgeon and a ranking naval medical officer to medically spy on these families?"

Sean retorted frankly, "Patrick was briefed in a meeting in San Diego prior to his departure from the mainland. Let's just say it was an enlightening briefing. He was approached immediately after the briefing, and he readily agreed to manage the medical needs of some of the more prominent Filipinos and Japanese."

Kate interrupted him. "Well then, I'm certain Patrick and I were in the same briefing. San Diego Naval Hospital. July 1941. I felt no concern whatsoever about spying. I'm glad he could be of service."

Somewhat taken aback, Sean continued further with the discussion, deciding it was the perfect time to take Kate one step further. As he continued talking, Patrick and Tim walked in, and Sean recalled that Patrick asked Tim to join in the meetings as well. The two had become fast friends after their initial introductions.

Their entrance was timely. The discussions began shortly afterward, with an introduction of a roundtable panel consisting of Allied medical officers. The room was filled with doctors and medical staff, most of them of a higher ranking than Kate. A few minutes later, Kate was surprised when Patrick stood to speak to the audience in attendance.

Behind a lectern, he began with, "Credible evidence has been provided of the Japanese army's extreme, grievously torturous medical experiments on Chinese and Russian prisoners in Northern China. Unit 731."

Patrick's words were terse and clipped. "You will hear about Unit 731 later. The entire world will, eventually. Vivisection, germ and biological warfare experiments, weapons testing…we are aware of it all."

One of the audience members raised the question cautiously, "What do you mean by 'vivisection?" Patrick turned to the questioning doctor.

"Prisoners are strapped to tables, and then dissected, while alive, without the benefit of anesthesia or any form of painkillers— minor, medically ethical or otherwise. Organs are removed, sometimes just to determine how long it takes the victims to die. Some of them are injected with virulent diseases so they can review their effects on live organs. The experiments have no medical merit whatsoever. Zero. The prisoners also know they are going to die. It is a matter of how long they survive and how torturous their deaths can be made."

He continued, letting the effect of his words seep into his audience's minds.

"Sometimes limbs are removed, only to be sewn onto opposite parts of the body, purportedly to 'see if arterial flow, etc. can be restored.' Again, no medical merit, as no efforts are made to keep them alive or to even provide anesthetics in the process. Some of these experiments have been filmed and documented."

Patrick continued, "I have been briefed, and have also seen some of the films snuck out of these encampments, so yes, Unit 731 exists, and these Draconian forms of torture exist as well."

He moved from behind the podium to the front of the room to face the audience closer.

"Each of you in this room is being briefed here in order to request your assistance in several classified medical experiments that the Allied Forces are initiating. Any detail you may uncover will provide valuable input on how the Japanese army is managing the medical aspects of their war efforts. As well as how our Allies could use this knowledge to defeat them."

Sean glanced at Kate to see how she was reacting to the discussion. She was riveted by Patrick's enlightening information.

"In the Philippines and other islands where Japanese were a part of the island culture before the war, the Allied Forces spent time monitoring their activity after the Tripartite Pact was signed in 1940. We observed Japanese medical activities and key surgical and epidemical experiments, right down to advances in equipment and diagnostics. We also took great pains to ensure that misinformation regarding our own surgical expertise and advancements was supplied back to the Japanese. 'Medical espionage,' I believe is the term we now use," Patrick smiled at the term that had recently been coined in clinical circles.

"We know the Japanese are testing 'Field Bombs'— infecting prisoners with plagues, biological epidemics, and the like, for eventual use on our Allied troops. To that end, you may be requested to manage, supervise, or perform similar research. You will be active contributors in our experiments to combat these weapons. This will be top-secret work. The penalties are extensive if *any* of this information is conveyed outside these walls. That must be made abundantly clear. We cannot win this war without the cooperative efforts and the loyalty of men and women such as yourselves."

With that, Patrick stepped down, and another ranking officer stepped to the podium to provide a further briefing. After another 10 minutes, the meeting adjourned, and the four friends left the building to head to a local pub for a bite to eat. They were silent as they walked together, each of them deep in their own thoughts. As they sat down to eat, Kate quizzed Patrick on some of the details, focusing on one aspect in particular.

"Have MacArthur's staff and officers been apprised of this medical activity?" She knew full well that if he wasn't informed, there might be hell to pay for Patrick and the officers involved. Sean smiled at her comment. "To ensure continued strong relations with MacArthur, Patrick was astute enough to provide an abbreviated briefing every two weeks to MacArthur's staff, so I believe we are covered on that aspect, Kate."

Patrick laughed at that statement, retorting, "Keep your friends close but your enemies closer. In this endeavor, I report to Washington, but I know where my bread is buttered. MacArthur provides cover, *and* he gets things done. If he likes you!" he added.

Sean continued, "I learned of Patrick's work through an Australian biologist hired on my Sigint team. I pieced the two together soon after we first met that day in the café with you, Kate."

Highly interested, Kate added a few key tidbits of her knowledge to the conversation.

"Maybe this is related. And maybe it isn't. But at the beginning of the Pacific campaign, it was discovered that there was a critical shortage of quinine in Australia. Most of the world's supply is produced in Indonesia, which lies directly in the path of the advancing Japanese forces. Australia never had trouble managing the supply routes before, but they've been interrupted since the start of the war," she interjected as the three men looked on.

"The Australian army is working on establishing an experimental malaria group in Cairns where the disease is still prevalent and strong at the time. Colonel N.H. Fairley, whom I've actually met through the Red Cross, will most likely lead this team. There are Australian Malaria Control Units and Mobile Entomological Sections. The group is looking at the components of sulphamerazine and atebrine. This experimentation is continuing as we speak. And the patients will all be volunteers, just so you know."

Kate finished her short dialogue with a few final comments.

"Patrick, I am impressed with your tenacity and your dedication to this undercover work. I never knew. I haven't been asked to participate, but I *was* briefed and it seems at the same briefing you attended. I am working on holistic medical treatments and natural remedies for malaria, dysentery, and the like, but still, it's not been officially promoted, although MacArthur is aware of my work. So, it's only on Sunday afternoon sessions with a small team of medical staff. It may not be scalable, but I'll continue my work there. If it benefits even one stricken soldier, I'll be happy."

There was a short pause as each of them absorbed this information. Finally, Kate asked, "So, this is all enlightening, but where's this conversation heading?"

Tim opened another discussion from that point. "Melbourne Medical Uni is also conducting germ protection experiments to reduce the effects of malaria and other illnesses on Allied soldiers. But they are taking it one step further. What if, let's say, we had the malarial components in a liquid form and dropped them onto known enemy territory to expedite the advancement of the disease?

Or the same with dysentery? They're stricken, not dead. And it would reduce the loss of lives on our side considerably."

Neither Tim nor Sean was opposed to germ warfare experiments. Kate nodded in agreement. Except for Sean, however, they were all opposed to chemical weapons that induced death on a massive scale. Sean made one last ominous comment on the subject:

"I just want to make it abundantly clear that unless we take some drastic measures, hundreds of thousands of innocent lives will continue to be lost, if not millions. Don't rule out the use of chemical warfare on a massive level. Which means, there *will* be some testing that we all may have to implement and certainly live with afterward. Our collective consciences will be compromised. But ultimately, the end might justify the means and the methods we use to get there."

They were aware, though, that with MacArthur in Australia, scientific efforts on Australian soil would be stepped up. It remained to be seen how far the germ and chemical warfare would go. Still, the four friends agreed to keep each other apprised when any experiments were initiated, or if their own involvement was requested.

Patrick's medical involvement in the clinical research was expedited. For the time being, Kate continued in her own slow work, being fully immersed in the translations and analytics. With the movement of MacArthur's expansive team into Melbourne, her frenetic pace would continue indefinitely.

CHAPTER THIRTY-SEVEN

THE BROWNOUT STRANGLER

Soon after MacArthur's arrival in Australia, there was an influx of American troops…over 30,000 to be exact…who were quartered in Camp Pell, Royal Park, Melbourne. At first, the Australians welcomed these soldiers with resounding, seemingly endless parties. However, overcrowding, and the raucous behavior that accompanied these celebrations soon began to wear on the residents of Melbourne. Ever sensitive to criticism, MacArthur's commanding officers warned the U.S. soldiers that punishment would be severe for crimes committed against the peaceful citizens. Soon after their arrival, the citywide "brownouts" made the citizens fearful of traipsing out after dark.

In the waning Australian summer months, accelerating in January, there was credible evidence of a man assaulting women in residential areas around the camps. He was dubbed *The Brownout Strangler* for his vicious attacks, Sean was informed about the violent incidents in a military briefing. The protective husband unwisely chose to be forceful in his conveyance to Kate, his remonstrations attributable to a stressful week of negotiations between Nave's team and Ruby Fabian, the U.S. Naval liaison. Sean demanded that Kate restrict her travel around the city and use an escort at dawn and dusk. She did not appreciate his forceful insistence.

"I understand the concern," Kate countered. "But you're not giving me credit for having the sense to be cautious of the dangers surrounding me," she faced him after he ordered that she obey his wishes.

"You're my wife, Kate. And I'm requesting an escort at dawn and dusk. For your own safety, you have no choice but to obey me. If you remember correctly, 'obey' was in our wedding vows." He smiled, but the forced smile showed he would not accept a refusal.

"I most certainly did *not* promise to obey you!" Kate responded vehemently. "Those were just words that everyone repeats when they get married!" Sean reached her in one quick stride, spinning her around, calmly saying, "Those were sacred vows of marriage, my dear, made before God Himself. And you will obey me on this, Kate."

Kate opened her mouth to reply, but finding no argument to his vehemence, she left the room, muttering as she exited. It was a trait of hers that Sean had found to be vastly annoying, as she often did it on purpose when exasperated. After some protests, she seemed resigned to her fate. He was grateful that she took the advice he had proffered, but his demand of her obedience was somehow the start of a brief estrangement between the two.

Sean waited for Kate one night at the end of the following week, hoping to join her and her escort on their walk home. He was aware that she had been avoiding him, and was more than curious as to why. Watching her exit the building with no escort in sight and no pretense of waiting for one, his concern grew. Frowning, he followed her through the dark streets, his anger rising as she ignored her surroundings and walked into the enveloping darkness of the Melbourne night. He made up his mind to confront her again about the escort when he noticed a man approaching from the opposite direction. Sean stopped, standing in the shadows of a dimly lit street, watching to see if the man advanced toward Kate.

He did, asking if she had a light for a cigarette, to which Sean heard Kate reply sweetly, "I don't smoke. I'm sorry; I don't have a lighter." As she started to move on, the young man grabbed her arm, pressing his weight against Kate and pinning her aggressively to a nearby wall. She tried to break away, her screams muffled by a hand over her mouth and one large hand wrapping around her throat, choking her. Suddenly, she was freed by a violent jerking motion to her side. In the darkness, she could only make out two figures, one taller, in the act of protectively blocking her, and the other rising from the ground and making a hasty retreat. She recognized Sean standing beside her, and said shakily, "Sean? What are you doing here?"

Sean said nothing as he half-dragged her by the hand to the grounds of their apartment building two blocks away. Safe inside the confines of the building, she said, "I – I think I recognized that man from one of the parks nearby. I've seen him twice." Sean shook her, giving her a furious, thinly-veiled look of anger. She opened her mouth to convey that her attacker was probably just a vagrant with too much to drink. Sean stopped her, warning, "Don't say one word. I could throttle you right now, so do NOT tempt me, Kate. I dislike losing my temper. I have told you to use an escort on your walks. Do as you're told or there will be consequences you won't like. That I can promise!"

Kate mutely walked inside her apartment and shut the door posthaste, recognizing the wisdom of keeping her mouth shut. She had little experience with Sean's anger. In fact, virtually none. And it had shocked her into a prudent silence. She had genuinely been frightened by the incident, but Sean's fury brought her out of that fear and directly into a wordless protest.

The next day, Sean approached Tim and Patrick after a meeting, sharing the story of her recent stalking and attack, asking for their help in protecting her. Both Patrick and Tim looked at each other knowingly, with Tim mentioning at once, "Given her past history, it is extremely odd that she allows herself to be so careless in this situation."

Sean whirled on Tim, backtracking immediately into the conversation Tim had just opened up. "Past history? What are you saying?" Sean questioned. Both of the other men glanced at each other again, reluctant to continue the conversation. A pregnant pause followed.

"Is there something I'm not aware of about Kate?" the tall Australian asked menacingly, his jaw tightening with justifiable anger. Both men instantly recognized there were elements of their friendships with Kate that were potentially problematic for Sean. Patrick gave a curt nod in the direction of a small, empty conference room. Albeit reluctantly, the story of Mack emerged.

Tim conveyed the story of Kate's months-long stalker in Washington D.C. He mentioned Kate's letters to her sister asking for advice. He ended with his part in attempting to thwart Mack. Sean turned to Patrick. Patrick hesitated, not from fear, but from understanding why Sean was angry. He decided on the truth.

"Kate told me. I escorted her to some social events in Manila and she got a little testy one night when we were at a function."

Noting Sean's narrowing eyes, Patrick put his hand on Sean's shoulder, saying, "This was well before she knew you were on the island and I suggest you take it exactly for what it was… two good friends, and colleagues, at a social gathering. Although she never admitted such, I gather she told me about Mack because she was wary of being with men in private situations. She was pretty frightened that night. There was no trigger for her fear, only me helping her when she got sick from imbibing too much alcohol." (In fact, there was a slight trigger— a kiss that Kate had encouraged in her state of inebriation.) Still, Patrick added dryly, "Let's focus on the matter at hand and not a rehash of the past, Sean."

Sean respected his honesty, even though he suspected there was more to the story than Patrick shared… an admission that Patrick wisely left out, given Sean's volatile mood.

The story of Mack mystified Sean further, and he was hurt that Kate had not confided this crucial part of her past to him. All three were undeniably perplexed by her current inexplicable behavior. They moved to a nearby bar to continue their discussion over drinks, each more worried than they cared to admit about the attack on Kate. Hours later, Sean's senses were somewhat dulled by alcohol, but he remained sharp in his ability to read body language. Over their fourth round of strong drinks, Sean sensed that all three men sitting at the bar table had sentiments for Kate in varying degrees, and for complex reasons. He wondered if Kate knew. He also began to wonder if she somehow encouraged it, but that was an unfair assessment on his part that he would not have made when sober. His wife was a great many things. Experience as a temptress was not one of her strong points. Even as a married woman, at 21, she was still a novice at sexual baiting. He liked this particular trait. In fact, right now, he damn near worshipped it.

Near midnight, the three men walked the scant few blocks back to their respective apartments together. Drunker than he had been in a long while, Sean was in rare form when he arrived at Kate's apartment. She let him in and he flew at his surprised wife.

"So, what makes you withhold your past from me Kate? I'm your *husband.* Or have you forgotten that part in your efforts to keep the charade going about our relationship?"

"Sean, you've been drinking and you're scaring me. I think you should leave. *Now!*"

She tightened the belt of her sheer robe around her slim waist, pointing toward the door. Sean wheeled on her, saying, "Why Kate? Bloody why?" holding her shoulders as he spoke.

"Why what, Sean? I don't know what you're angry about and I'm a little afraid of you right now!" she responded, shaking at his uncontrolled anger and the force in his voice.

"Why didn't you see fit to tell me about Mack? Why did you have to let me hear from both Tim *and* Patrick? They seem to know a lot about you that I don't. You're my wife, Kate. And these secrets are bloody painful for me." He searched her eyes as he spoke.

"You're spending more time with the two of them than with me! Do you have feelings for either of them?" The agony in his voice was wrenching. As his wife paused to search for the right words to calm him down, the silence triggered Sean's anger again.

"Answer me, Kate. What exactly is the nature of your relationships with Patrick and Tim? Is there something I need to know? As your damned *husband?* I know they have affection for you! Have you encouraged either of them?" He never used foul language in front of a woman, and she was infuriated by his lack of respect.

Wanting to cause him the same pain he had just inflicted upon her, she said, "If I *were* close friends with another man, it's because you said 'separate lives, to protect our careers.' Well, your career is well-protected, isn't it? And you bloody well live for your work! In fact, you're *married* to your work! So separate and independent it is! And if I choose to walk home alone, that's also my business, Sean Lawrence. Just like I did tonight. I do not need the likes of you— or anyone else— telling me how to run my life or my body! My body is mine alone to protect!"

Sean's fury was at its peak by now, "None of my business? I have the right to know! Are ya wanting to make love with one of them, Kate Lawrence? Cause you're sure not managing the likes of that with me lately! You've been mad as a cut snake since I ordered you to obey me!"

Rife with pain, he half dragged her across the room into the small bedroom, saying as he worked to subdue her resistance, "I told you not to walk alone. You didn't listen to my demands, so now we're in this sorry state of affairs and hatin' each other. I'm bloody close to giving you the punishment I said I'd give ya for not listening when I told you to obey. You are *ordered* to heed my warnings."

He loosened his grip, but with his anger still rising, Sean was close to punishing her for her disobedience.

"You do *not* own me, Sean Lawrence! Let go!"

She backed away further, falling onto the bed as he fell with her. Kate struggled futilely as his arms held her, the solid weight of his body pinning her down. Desperate to stop the argument between them, she called out, "Sean, please stop! The baby— you'll hurt it!"

His grip loosened, shocked sober by her words. Pulling Kate up with him, he was considerably gentler with her. The anger on his face was replaced by a combined look of fear, disbelief, and unabashed joy.

"What did you say?" he asked Kate, his face full of shock.

"You heard me right. You're going to be a father," she whispered softly. Sean came to the abrupt realization that he could have caused potential harm to his pregnant wife.

"We're having a baby?"

The room was quiet again and the astonished look she saw on his face softened her approach considerably.

"Yes. I'm pregnant, Sean. I was going to tell you tonight, but you came home in such a state that I didn't dare broach such a delicate subject!"

Kate's tears flowed freely, and she was filled with relief now that the announcement was finally out in the open.

CHAPTER THIRTY-EIGHT

THE YANKS INVADE!

They both sat up together, in silence, until Sean gently moved Kate onto this lap. It took a few minutes for him to calm himself enough to ask her the questions to which he badly needed answers.

"Kate, why couldn't you tell me this? Are you so upset about the pregnancy that you couldn't share this kind of news with your *husband*?" He searched her face for answers.

"God, no. To be honest, this isn't exactly the right timing with the war. We're both so immersed in our work. Whatever you might think about questioning my love, there's been no other thought of anyone else. You can't imagine how hurt I am about you even *thinking* that."

"Then why, Kate? Why are you worried about losing me? You know you're every single dream I've ever had!" he said, almost reproachfully. She smiled at that overt admission.

"I'm not worried about losing you, Sean. I'm worried about *leaving* you. About dying. Because what happened to Kerri wasn't an anomaly. It runs in our family. My Aunt Maggie lost her first and only child in childbirth and she nearly died herself. Aunt Caroline, who I never knew, *died* in childbirth. My mom? She had twins, but she nearly died too. We're alive because we were born over six weeks early. Like Aunt Maggie, mom was told not to have any more babies either. So, you see, there's a good chance I'll die too, like Kerri did. We can't bear children. We're highly defective in that area," she added bitterly.

Sean held her in his arms tightly, recognizing the pain and hearing the overwhelming fear in her voice.

"Is this why you've been so distant? And flaunting my demands about protecting yourself? Are you mad at me for getting you in this state? Cause I've done my part for sure, my darling wife!" he laughed at that admission over the intimacy during the first months of their marriage.

He added, "I won't let you die. Not on my watch! If I have to employ Tim, Patrick, and every doctor in their hospital, we'll make certain this baby arrives safe and sound."

Kate sat down on the bed, desperately wanting to make him understand that her fears were not irrational. She began rambling about past family memories, reflecting on a long-ago conversation between her, Kerri, and her Grama Helene.

"During the last months of 1939, we spent most of our time in Boothbay. We both really enjoyed and needed the company of Grama Helene." She sighed wistfully, remembering that particular day and time vividly.

"One morning, Kerri came right out and asked Grama if she minded talking about Aunt Caroline. I'm sure it must have weighed heavily on Kerri's mind with marriage right around the corner. I remember Grama saying Caroline was tall and slender, but her hips weren't meant for easy childbearing. Unfortunately, the childbirth came slightly earlier than expected and the midwife didn't make it in time. The baby girl was breech, and too weak to turn itself around. Things just happened and Caroline lost a lot of blood in the process," Kate sighed. Sean squeezed her hand as she continued:

"I remember the look on Kerri's face most vividly. She was scared. She remembered hearing about Aunt Maggie and our mom both struggling during childbirth. It was as if she *knew* she would also have trouble with childbirth. So yes, I'm afraid right now." Kate responded, with a tear trickling down her cheek.

Sean said protectively, "Again, we'll ensure this baby arrives safely. Patrick and Tim won't let anything happen to you either, Kate." At the mention of their friends, Kate looked up at him and hesitated, remembering the reason for their argument. Resolutely, she said, "Let's turn toward other pressing issues. And you and I need time to adjust to the news I just blurted out."

The room was silent again for a moment. "And about Mack. About Patrick and Tim knowing…let me explain please. Tim knew only because Kerri asked him to come to D.C. to help protect me. He was phenomenal. I'm so grateful to him for doing all he did to help."

"And Patrick?" Sean asked, searching her eyes again with his own piercing green ones.

"He knew because we were on a mission together. Spying. At a Christmas Ball in Manila. He escorted me to my hotel room and helped me out when I got sick. I had too much alcohol, and I panicked when he got close. It brought everything back about the stalking and assaults. Patrick was most understanding," she finished, "and he's an honorable man."

"OK. I'll give you that. Frankly, I appreciate that Patrick didn't leave you to your own devices. I've seen ya tipsy. You're one huge mess." He kissed her forehead tenderly. Continuing, he said, "But why couldn't you tell me over the last few months? We've been married now for 3 months." His voice carried pain with his words.

She sighed heavily. "Sean, the timing has to be right. You don't just blurt out over dinner, 'Oh, by the way, honey, I've been sexually assaulted. And I was stalked regularly for months by a deranged man. How's your steak there, darling? Is it cooked to your perfection?'"

He smiled at her marked point by way of a dinner conversation. She continued, "As you've conveyed, there are things we still don't know about each other. Would you somehow blame me? Because *I* did. This kind of thing haunts you because you're a female working in a man's world. You *know* it can happen at any time."

Sean waited patiently for her to continue.

"There's a fear of telling people something like this. That they might share it with others. If *you* know, and *Patrick* knows, and *Tim* knows, you all might discuss it. I don't want to be the topic of that discussion. And my innermost nightmare is that somehow Mack will be approached. I trust you with my life, Sean. But what would you do if you ran into this man who terrorized your wife? And being in the same field, this could happen. It just might become personal with you, you know!"

Kate added, "When we first met again, I *still* thought most men think it's ok to touch a girl who isn't willing. So, I worried you *could* pass a chat about Mack off as another 'men will be men' discussion. This is a society where men rule at home, and at work. That's why I was so mad with the 'obey' thing...like you were some 'lord of the manor.' And this pregnancy thing... I'm looking much like your own personal broodmare in this state." She swept her hands over her stomach to emphasize her point.

Sean sighed, hesitating with his thoughts, "Let me have my say and we won't speak of this again unless it's of your own accord. If you *ask* me to never talk about this to anyone, I won't. And if I ever ran into this man, I might be tempted, but I wouldn't cause a scene. As for the fact that he regularly harassed you after you repeatedly said 'no'— I could never blame *you* for that. I expect you were fairly terrorized. Maybe one day you'll tell me what happened. But maybe not. And so be it, if that's the case," he finished. Intent on showing his support by comforting her, Sean turned Kate toward him and began massaging her shoulders. After a few minutes, he patted her belly gingerly. Resolutely, he asked, "Is making love safe during your pregnancy?"

Kate responded, "Here's where, if I absolutely detested sex, I could tell you 'No,' and you would have to leave me alone for the next seven months. But the truth is, as long as we're not too aggressive and don't manage anything precarious, the baby will be just fine."

"Well then, Kate Lawrence, I'm seeking permission to have carnal knowledge with my pregnant wife. If ya say 'no,' I'll back off, but I might be walking with a stoop for a while. You asked me for mercy once. Now I'm begging the same of you," Sean countered. She giggled at his nonsense, her silence acting as her expressed consent. The gown came off, and the memory of their argument was erased as Sean proceeded to show his appreciation to the mother of his impending child.

After that night, Kate was under protective watch in the darkened streets as she left her late night shifts at both the hospital and the Victoria Barracks office. Soon after, her unit moved to Monterey with the other codebreakers. All things considered, the following months of the pregnancy passed by rapidly.

IN LATE APRIL, KATE exited the offices at Monterey one evening at dusk and waited for Sean. Exhausted from the early stages of pregnancy, after 20 minutes, she decided to head to their apartments herself. There was still some residual light in the area, so she felt safe. Walking three blocks and rounding a corner, she headed up a small flight of steps. Noticing a lit cigarette in the shaded area of a low tree, Kate felt a stab of fear as she tried to hurry past a dark, shadowy figure. Too late, she recognized an unmistakable scent from the previous attack. A mixture of alcohol, sweat, and cologne. Seconds later, she felt arms around her neck from behind and a hand wrapping around her throat. Struggling against the pain and blackness, she vaguely remembered a move Tim and his friend Giovanni had shown her after the incidents with Mack. She gulped in air, screaming as loudly as she could. Her shirt was ripped down the front and an enormous hand roughly grabbed her throat again. She struggled violently, kicking her attacker hard in the groin. Wrenching free and crying out again, she heard footsteps in the distance and she found her voice again, screaming, "Help me, please! Someone help!" The man grasped her a final time, launching her backward down the steps she had just traversed. For Kate, the devil had taken the form of her worst nightmare— fear of losing the baby. Then unconsciousness mercifully set in as she blacked out.

SEAN HAD BEEN DELAYED in meeting up with Kate. Cursing himself when he found her missing from their meeting spot, he knew she had decided to head home. Running lightly to catch up with her, he rounded a corner when he heard a distant scream. He turned in the direction of the sound and another scream pierced the darkness, along with a woman's cry for help. He neared the area just in time to see a slight shape in the dark being hurled down the steps about a half block away. Reaching the motionless body, a sharp stab of fear pierced his brain as he recognized his wife, bleeding and unconscious.

"Call for an ambulance, now. We need to get her to hospital!" he said to some onlookers who showed up to help. They arrived at Royal Melbourne Hospital minutes later, with the medical staff getting word to both Tim and Patrick to meet Sean there. Tim was on duty, and Patrick arrived from a surgical lecture shortly after. The lead trauma surgeon met them in the hallway, facing Sean bleakly.

"Your wife has a concussion, and she may have some bleeding on the brain. We won't know until we get her in to have a look. Her condition is serious."

As he headed back to move Kate into surgery, Sean took Tim and Patrick aside, informing them that Kate was pregnant. Both men registered surprise, for different reasons. Sean grabbed Patrick's arm, saying, "I'll explain later. Just help her. Please."

As a senior trauma surgeon, Patrick was allowed into the surgery, leaving Tim and Sean in the waiting room. An hour later, Patrick entered the waiting area and Sean stood up, grabbing his shoulders. "Is she okay? What about her concussion? And the baby?" Sean asked anxiously.

Patrick pulled them into a private waiting room.

"A small shunt was placed in the back of Kate's skull to reduce compression on the brain. She has some bruising and facial swelling, but no broken bones, thank God. You can see her in about two hours."

He put his hand on Sean's shoulder.

"I'm sorry, Sean. Kate lost the baby. The trauma was too much. I'm truly sorry for your loss."

Sean sat down, utterly broken by the news. After a few seconds, he looked up, with the agony registered on his face.

Knowing the pain Sean was experiencing, Tim said, "Let's take a short break while she's in recovery, Sean."

The three walked to a nearby café. Sean detailed the marriage, the secrecy, and the surprise pregnancy, for Patrick's benefit. All three agreed on keeping the marriage secret. Losing her job was a huge barrier to her recovery from the loss of Kerri, and from the loss of this child.

It had been reported again through military channels that the attacker around the vicinity was a U.S. soldier. The three men felt it prudent to place the entire community on elevated alert, but that was not their call. As it was, tensions were exceedingly high with the thousands of American troops infiltrating Melbourne.

Their primary focus now was on helping Kate recover.

CHAPTER THIRTY-NINE

A CITY STEEPED IN FEAR

"The Australian Government …regards the Pacific struggle as primarily one in which the United States and Australia must have the fullest say in the direction of the democracies' fighting plan. Without inhibitions of any kind, I make it clear that Australia looks to America, free of any pangs as to our traditional links or kinship with the United Kingdom."
-Prime Minister John Curtin, 27 December 1941

In the military echelons, word got out about Kate's attack, although details were downplayed to thwart a city-wide panic. The American leaders feared if hostile relations continued to build, Australia might turn to Churchill for direction. The same Churchill who wanted Australian troops under his complete command. Curtin had balked at this after Churchill moved a mass of Australian troops to the far Eastern British battles, leaving Australia vulnerable to attacks by Japan on their northern coast.

A plethora of military guards were placed in and near the U.S. camp, ostensibly for "top-secret security measures."

For now, that was all MacArthur's senior officers could manage without inciting further alarm amongst an already terrified community.

Back at the Melbourne hospital, the three friends were in the room when Kate regained consciousness. Her face was healed except for the pale bluish eyelids and the bruising on her forehead from the fall. While Patrick and Tim stepped out, Sean told her about the loss of the baby. She turned her head and faced the side wall of the room while he watched her large, soft eyes fill with tears. Her hands were shaking, but there were no words for a while. Sean silently lifted her in his arms, letting her cry on his shoulder.

After a brief period elapsed, the two friends reentered the room and Patrick sat by Kate's side, examining her head and the bandage for the tiny shunt. Taking her hand in his, he said, "Kate, we need to ask some questions about

the attack. The constables need answers. It would be best if one of us could convey this information to them without traumatizing you further."

Sean nodded for Patrick to continue. "We need to ask if it's possible you were sexually assaulted. If so, the evidence must be presented to a magistrate to get a higher bench warrant for this man's arrest. You may need to testify if this comes to a trial."

Kate faced Patrick evenly and said, "No, Patrick. It happened so fast. He didn't have much of a chance."

Her voice was strained as she thought hard for a moment. Summoning her strength, she responded, "I really can't remember much about the attack, but I know I fought back. I kicked him very hard in some vital parts. I think it would have been difficult for him to perform."

All three men concluded separately that a full sexual assault was likely implausible.

Patrick asked several questions that had been requested by the constabulary's office. Kate showed signs of tiring with the energy it took to talk, and her answers made it obvious she couldn't add much further detail to the police investigation. The two friends left the room, leaving Kate and Sean alone to grieve.

A week later she was released, and immediately moved into Sean's apartment. She was emotionally drained, being taxed from the strain of the assault, and from losing the baby. Sean cared not one whit about any backlash concerning their living arrangements. They needed to work through the pain of their loss.

ele

NOT HAVING CONSIDERABLE practice delving into his deepest pain, Sean turned his attention to the pressing political arena in Canberra, a current hotbed with the Allied Forces. He also surmised that the ensuing war discussions, which were causing a distinct buzz around Melbourne, would help keep Kate's mind off the loss of the baby and the attack.

Most of Australia's troops were already committed to fighting with the British in the Middle East when Japan attacked Pearl Harbor and the Philippines. To complicate matters, two months earlier, on February 19th, Darwin had suffered a massive air strike by the Empire of Japan. This was the first time the Australian mainland had ever been struck by enemy forces. In the period following that attack, Churchill demanded that Australian troops be diverted to Burma, a request which Australia's Prime Minister John Curtin promptly refused.

Bringing these boys home to protect the Australian continent remained his prime concern. Curtin, concluding that Australia was Japan's next target, vehemently demanded reinforcements from Churchill. This was the first of several well-publicized heated discussions between the two men concerning the British lack of commitment to the defense of Australia.

Angered, and turning to the U.S. for support, Curtin announced a critical historical event: he and U.S. President Franklin Roosevelt had agreed that Douglas MacArthur would permanently preside over the entire Pacific defense plan in Australia. To continue securing the protection of Australian people, Curtin agreed to place the Australian forces under the command of General MacArthur, who became "Supreme Commander of the South West Pacific." As Prime Minister, Curtin had thus presided over a major shift in Australia's foreign policy. For the first time in its 41-year history as an independent nation, Australia decided that the U.S. took precedence over British interests in its geopolitical arena.

Kate was complacent over this precedent, having a fundamental belief that the United States, as a protector and "big brother" would ensure the safety of the former British colony. Sean had sincere doubts about the U.S. role. He believed that Australian troops could better manage the protection of their own country working in concert with MacArthur... not *under* his command.

This was the first time they had disagreed over politics. Kate had finished teaching her Saturday morning class and they met for coffee. Both were dressed in formal military attire on this cool, breezy fall morning. While teaching her classes, Kate had agreed to wear her naval uniform and represent the U.S. Navy and the Red Cross with armband insignias. Sean had just presided over a briefing with MacArthur's staff regarding a recent uptick of Japanese radio activities in New Guinea.

Sitting at a private table near a window, their discussion started out amicably and ended up rather heated. Kate was recovering well from her attack and looking strong and resolute as they chatted. The paleness from the loss of the baby had thankfully been replaced by a rosy color.

"I *do* agree with Curtin," Kate retorted to Sean's initial statement that MacArthur might be inclined to mobilize Australian troops toward somewhat vainglorious battles.

"To an Australian," Sean interjected, "this means potentially losing men at the same casualty rate they did in the Gallipoli offensives of World War I."

Kate continued in her defense, "But MacArthur won't step on Curtin's toes. He is far too preoccupied with his reputation on foreign soil to do that. I'm evidence of that concern. He has asked that Americans show themselves in full dress uniform and comport themselves in a positive light at every opportunity.

He will initiate a strong military plan to ensure Australia can engage in protecting herself," Kate responded again.

She continued with "This is something the Brits are currently not doing, and we're still part of the British Commonwealth, I might add." Sean smiled inwardly at the "we" in her comment, but he continued to press his argument.

"Kate, darling, the British forces are over-extended as it is, defending their own country against Hitler. Curtin is a charismatic leader. He can mobilize forces *and* Australians. We can and do need the U.S. forces to prevent war from invading Australia. But that should be an agreement for us to work together. Side by side. Not as MacArthur's minions." He stirred his coffee as he continued pressing further:

"MacArthur's an absolutely brilliant tactician. But by some accounts, he strikes aggressively, jeopardizing thousands of men in battle." Sipping her second cup of coffee, Kate watched as a captivated group of young ladies stopped to view Sean in his military attire, surreptitiously, from across the café. He looked charming and handsome, displaying his most persuasive arguments in such an animated discussion.

Kate lost her train of thought as she smiled at Sean's admiring, captive audience. "You're sexy when you get so forceful, my darling. You've attracted a nice little audience," she said, trying to deflect the argument into a more peaceful start to their weekend. Still exasperated, Sean nevertheless softened the finishing assessment of his opinions.

"I agree with him on one thing: that full-on aggression to protect us is preferable to attempting to establish hasty defense mechanisms once an invasion has already occurred." He glanced out of the corner of his eye toward his bevy of admirers, then turned to nod at Kate.

"A compromise is needed to manage warfare more efficiently. Let's hope Curtin's diplomacy, MacArthur's massive military strength, and Roosevelt's forward-thinking can prevail. Preventing needless loss of life. That's all I care about," he added.

Kate wisely let the conversation end there and they both left for the countryside and a much-needed break from the overcrowded city, the political drama, and the site of her recent attack. Madeleine spoiled them. She was reticent about verbalizing her recognition of their private pain, but her support was in the way of care and relaxation during their brief visit.

When they reached the city limits Sunday night, the traffic was heavy, as the continuing influx of U.S. troops into the city had been steady since February of 1942. By the end of April, when Kate was attacked, the streets were crawling with newly-arrived U.S. troops.

Melbourne was on edge. With the invasion of foreign accents and the more aggressive American mentality, the citizens were growing weary of these newcomers. Windows and street lamps were covered to prevent targets for Japanese air strikes. Car lights were dimmed on the streets and the darkness was more ominous than ever.

IN THE NEXT FEW weeks, Sean and Kate pressed on, striving hard to ignore the tensions. Sean continued familiarizing himself with Japanese radio operators. He soon learned that the input from his team was reaching the offices of Admiral Chester Nimitz. The latter was now in command over the entire Coral Sea area.

Nimitz held daily briefings, with much of his intelligence coming from FRUMEL and Monterey. Although neither Sean nor his colleagues were given attribution for their intel, it was universally known that Nimitz preferred briefings from Australian personnel familiar with the Japanese language and culture. Thus, Sean continued to provide critical regular communiqués to both U.S. and Australian-based commanders.

Through painstaking efforts by Yarran and Danilo's team in Port Moresby, it was detected that Japanese carriers were active now in the Coral Sea. The accurate assumption was that Japan was preparing for intermittent air raids on Northern Australia. Thus, Sean's team in Melbourne stepped up their tracking of calls. American intelligence teams also concluded the Japanese were planning attacks as far south as Brisbane.

By now, Patrick was absorbed in the medical endeavors and experimentation by the U.S. Armed Forces. Patrick also felt it worthwhile to brief Sean regarding specific initiatives on the middle floor of Monterey under FRUMEL. The valued briefings advanced Sean's work tenfold. It was Sean who picked up that Japanese operators were transmitting messages via Truk radios, to deflect the location of their carriers in the Coral Sea. The Japanese also dispatched a flurry of dummy traffic from the Mandated Territories, German islands in the North Pacific under the Japanese administration after World War I. The analysts in Melbourne immediately recognized the bogus call signs on the dummy signals.

While Sean was solving the political concerns threatening his team's success, Kate was able to convince MacArthur's aides that the surveillance of the island of Nauru did not require a full time translator. She agreed to arrive at dawn and translate any German communiqués from her vantage point of the third floor of Monterey, where the actual decoding work was managed. She was placed under Commander Jack Newman as his liaison at Monterey.

Kate reviewed and summarized reports from Moorabbin, Newman's collection center, and the enterprising young woman quickly proved herself as valuable of a commodity in Newman's realm as she did on the translation team. The work was fast-paced and stressful, but rewarding for her.

CHAPTER FORTY

FAMILY SKELETONS

In early May, tensions in the overcrowded city were further escalated by continuing attacks on local women, including the first fatality on May 3, 1942. A woman was found strangled in Albert Park just before sunrise. Six days later, a second victim was discovered. Last seen alive with an American in uniform, the local constabulary and the U.S. military police were on alert for suspicious American soldiers. Melbourne women now walked the streets in abject fear. The threat from Japan was, at best, far-stretched. The biggest threats lived and thrived in their own fair city. The brownouts, once merely a sacrifice, became a veritable nightmare to the citizens.

Unsurpassed in their field, Aboriginal trackers assisted in reviewing the crime scenes to help piece together the clues about the perpetrator. As the saga continued, the three men continued to be vigilant about escorting Kate, and Sean remained in contact with the trackers, whom he knew through Yarran. As the intensity mounted, Kate was called in one morning to a second interview at the constable's station. After the murders, she readily agreed to help.

Tim offered to escort her there and then back to the Monterey building where Sean was conducting critical meetings. Kate entered the station in full military uniform, affording her a measure of confidence as she faced a room of male detectives. After about 10 minutes of questioning, she was asked to speak to the lead on the tracking investigation. She was still talking with one of the detectives when minutes later, she looked up to see a tall, dark-haired young man walk into the interrogation room. Kate stood up, startled, staring wordlessly at the man in front of her.

Noting her shaking hands, the interviewing detective kindly left to retrieve a glass of water for her. She recovered her senses, still staring at this man who could pass for Sean's twin. He had a slighter build, but his face and eyes were the same, right down to the smile. Obviously, standing before her was her

brother-in-law, Aidan Lawrence. Kate found her voice and said in a soft, beguiling tone, "Aidan Lawrence, isn't it?"

Taken aback slightly, he responded, with a similar voice and inflection to Sean's, "Yes, that's correct. Should I know you, miss?" he asked inquisitively.

Holding out her hand to shake his before he sat down, she responded, "Well, yes, you probably should. I'm Kate Lawrence. Your brother's wife."

His eyes briefly flickered over Kate's trim figure, saying, "An American, eh? Brother Sean has apparently done well for himself," he commented, with a bemused look on his face.

"And when did this blessed event occur?"

Kate noted he had the same slightly lopsided grin his brother often used.

"About three months ago, Aidan," Kate answered, with a warm tone, introducing herself. "Kate Yeager Lawrence," she said, as Aidan directed her to her seat with a polite gesture. As Kate sat down again, she said, "I am thrilled to meet you and happy to say your incredible brother is an amazing human being. And husband. He thinks the world of you, and I suspect the sentiments are mutual."

On occasion, Kate was overt with her emotions, and this poignant family introduction was no exception. Now recovered from the surprise, she changed the subject to return to the meeting at hand. "My apologies for taking the meeting off focus. I understand you and the lead tracker are here to ask questions about my attack."

Aidan turned and signaled for others to enter the room. A middle-aged Aboriginal man walked in with a younger companion, both sitting opposite Kate and next to Aidan.

They began by relaying facts about the case, with Aidan translating for the older Aboriginal, who understood English but preferred conversing with Aidan in his native language. This particular banter lasted for about 15 minutes. Kate lost her composure once, when she detailed her attacker's second attempt at the chokehold. She now was aware she could have lost her life. Aidan interrupted with an abrupt question to the Aboriginal elder, speaking the dialect of the Wurundjeri, and then turned to translate for Kate to respond.

"Do you remember him removing some of your clothing, Kate?"

She seemed taken aback by the question and her hands shook slightly. "No, I do not recall that. I do know my shirt was torn." Aidan translated again, receiving another question from the Aboriginal. He translated, and Kate listened. "Yes, we know it was torn down the front. This appears to be the signature of this serial attacker. Are there any physical traits that may assist in identifying him?"

She turned away, frowning. Aidan seemed to understand where her thoughts were trailing. "I could not see his face well, nor did he speak. But he had unusually large hands," she offered. "Only one hand was used to wrap around my neck. The other was ripping my shirt. I only know he reeked of smoke and alcohol. And a peculiar cologne mixed with sweat. He was definitely tall, and quite strong."

Aidan pressed further. "Kate… if he is, in fact, your attacker, a signature mark of this killer is that he strikes fast with a fatal assault and confiscates some of the clothing as a souvenir. He doesn't appear to be capable of following with a full-on sexual assault."

Recognizing that she was getting traumatized as she strained to remember details, Aidan decided to conclude the interview for the time being. Since she did not see the attacker's face or hear his voice, in a court of law, the crown prosecutors could not provide definitive evidence that her attacker was the same as the killer who murdered the women.

Aidan walked Kate out to the lobby where Tim was waiting. She turned to her new brother to say goodbye, and in a voice that could be enchantingly soft and entreating, she asked if he would have dinner with her and Sean. Her eyes were misty with unchecked emotion as her hands joined Aidan's. She stood on her tiptoes and kissed her tall brother-in-law on the cheek when he agreed to the dinner.

"Thank you, Aidan. You will make Sean happy tonight, and nothing in the world could please me more than that!" She introduced Tim, who was enjoying the scene, having guessed what had just transpired. *And, like everyone else,* Tim thought, *Sean's brother has fallen under the Yeager spell,* remembering that Kerri had that same calm, entreating ability.

———

SEAN AGREED TO an early dinner, glad to oblige his wife's request for what she deemed a "delightful surprise." His shock at seeing his brother was tempered only by the amazement of seeing his wife chatting animatedly with Aidan as he approached the table. Sean could only guess at whatever miracle Kate had performed to entice Aidan to meet them. She had a quiet way of bending people with her charming will and captivating demeanor.

He was thrilled to see his wife so vivacious and spirited again. Wearing the red ruched dress she wore on their first night in Sydney, she had taken the trouble to put makeup on, conscious of a strong desire to have Aidan find her to be a positive addition to the family. Aidan appeared to immensely enjoy her company and her sincere affection. It was a solid start at a reconciliation.

The two brothers were surprisingly candid with each other, and eager to catch up on lost time. Aidan agreed to meet up with them later on the weekend, and to plan a visit to see their mum…another entreaty by Kate. Before dinner was concluded, he smiled at his new sister and said, "I must say, Sean has had a strong go at this marriage thing and looks a mite successful in his endeavor. Do you have a twin that might help to edge me toward the light at the end of that tunnel? Might be worth a go, eh?"

Kate was slightly startled by his unintentional reference to her twin. She smiled softly, and said, "Hmmm… we'll have to do something about that, Aidan." She added as casually as possible, "I had a beautiful twin. She's no longer with us, but she would have approved of you had she not been a happily married woman."

Aidan commented genuinely, "I am terribly sorry about your loss Kate. She must have been an extraordinary lady, quite like you." He grew silent, somewhat curious about Kate's sister. He surmised that the story would come out later, as time passed.

Kate excused herself to freshen up, and at the valet booth in the car park, Sean told Aidan briefly about Kate's twin Kerri. When she returned, Aidan reached out to Kate before she stepped into the car, and he kissed her lightly on the cheek. His eyes were consoling, and she determined that Sean must have told him about her twin.

As they drove back to their apartment, Sean reached over to hold Kate's hand, knowing she was thinking of Kerri. Neither felt up to speaking about the loss. The warmth of his hand was enough. As she was exiting the vehicle, Kate said reflectively, "Sometimes it hits hard, that's all. I don't know how to answer questions about my twin. People are so sad when I mention it, but I don't want to stop sharing her life with others. It's like I am being punished for grieving her. I didn't mean to spoil our lovely evening, Sean."

He led her into the building, kissing her sweetly on the stoop of the front entrance. "Not to worry. You didn't spoil a thing. And there is no need to apologize, Kate."

It was a long time before she fell asleep that night, but her pensive mood was not necessarily a movement into depression, so Sean left her alone with her thoughts.

❧

AIDAN AND THE ABORIGINAL trackers would remain active leads in investigating the attacks. The trackers were certain it was an American, with the distinctive markings of American army boots at the scenes of the murders. Nine days later, on May 18, another woman was attacked and killed while walking home from work. An American soldier was seen running from the crime scene, his description matching that of several women who had survived recent attacks.

Kate was questioned again in her apartment, as it appeared that all signs now led to her being an attempted victim of this serial killer. She was unfortunately of little assistance, having never seen his face. But she was further traumatized when it was concluded that her attacker was a violent murderer.

The latest attack led almost straight away to a young American soldier who, under lengthy questioning, finally admitted his guilt in these heinous crimes. Other survivors were able to pick out Private Edward Leonski from a line-up. Kate was asked to join in this lineup review, but she could not identify him by face. She did recognize his voice as the same man that had asked for a light and attacked her, before Sean's timely intervention weeks earlier. Having a face now attached to the attacker made it frighteningly real, and Kate was shaking when she left the police headquarters.

The detective sergeants informed her that Leonski had stalked his other victims for weeks and he had admitted to stalking Kate as well, wanting to take her "voice" away, enjoying her soft inflections, American accent, and lilting tone. Leonski confessed to the triple murders, admitting to a violent upbringing with a mentally disturbed mother. By taking the victims' voices away, he "stole the abusive voice of his mother." He was mentally deranged, and it was now a sensational case throughout Australia.

Sean noticed a marked change in Kate's behavior after that shocking admission by the killer. She was visibly startled if Sean walked up behind her. She avoided walking the streets after dark, even with Sean by her side. At night, she cried out in her sleep, sometimes in a full panic. At Sean's request, the three men met up again one afternoon to determine how to help her.

Both doctors had a clear medical perspective on her trauma. Sean looked straight at Patrick and questioned, "She admitted to me that she panicked with you one evening. What was your experience with her? I'm asking you only to assess her past trauma level. I need to know."

Patrick's look was direct and challenging. "There was no move on my part to precipitate her fear. Let's settle any doubts about that night please, once and for all."

Watching Patrick's eyes, Sean assessed his thoughts, then turning to Tim. Tim stated, "Regarding the stalking with Mack… after I met him, I told Kerri that clinically, the man had the markings of a true psychopath. There was something in his eyes that clearly terrified Kate and it unnerved me as well," Tim offered. "Kate's fears were well-founded. So, I would say that she is reliving the real fear of having a stalker once again, and also facing the fear—rational or not— that she is somehow a magnet for psychopaths."

Patrick reiterated, "To Kate, this Melbourne incident started out as a possible alcohol-induced mugging. This is traumatic enough in itself, but not on the level of attempted murder. She recognizes now that she could have lost her life during both attacks. The two attacks signify that Leonski staked her out with the intent of making her one of his intended victims."

Tim added, "From a clinical standpoint, signs of traumatic stress for a victim include flashbacks, hallucinations, nightmares, difficulty with intimacy and sleeping, and especially, hyper-vigilance. She may have difficulty concentrating as well," he offered helpfully. "Kerri was working for a famous psychiatrist in Boston. This professor was garnering much attention regarding how the mind reacts to such prolonged stress after such shock and trauma. All of these are tangible symptoms. The intense flashbacks, of more importance."

Finding this medical approach beneficial, Sean answered, "No hallucinations, no flashbacks that I can speak of. Nightmares, yes. She wakes up crying out at times. She does have difficulty concentrating."

Sean hesitated. "And the surgeon said that any intimacy can't happen for at least eight weeks. So, I won't know that for a while." Tim recognized Sean's emotions from the pain he experienced with the loss of Kerri.

"In the majority of these cases where a rape isn't involved, the intimacy returns, often on the level it was before the attack," Tim offered.

Sean responded, "Well then, we should be in excellent shape there, mates. My wife can't keep her bloody hands off me." All three men smiled as the humor lightened up their little "psychology" session.

Patrick added one further observation, "While assessing Kate's trauma, let's examine you for a moment, Sean. We've discussed that either of us could have been her escort that night. And no one could have predicted that *any* man was out there waiting to attack her. So let that blame go. It will help her work through all of this emotional trauma."

Tim finished the conversation.

"Let's drop this chat for now and go have a beer, fellas. The three of us can take Kate out to dinner tonight. The distraction of fending off three alluring, virile men fawning over her incessantly should be enough to charm any woman out of her fears of attracting the wrong sort of men."

He put his hand on Sean's shoulder, ensuring Sean knew they were all in this endeavor together. And he was right about the dinner. Kate was enchanted by the attention of the three men at their charming best.

CHAPTER FORTY-ONE

THE BLUE MOUNTAINS

The cooler fall weather glided smoothly into the wintry month of June in Melbourne. Between Kate's attack, the sensational murders in May and the continuing political concerns from Canberra, Sean's focus was somewhat off. The largest distractions threatening the success of Sean's team were caused by several Pacific units competing against each other for favor among the navy's senior officers. A few of them worked to encroach on FRUMEL's responsibilities, while distancing themselves from the bickering between groups. Sean worked hard to keep his team together, and duly focused.

Fortunately, U.S. Naval cryptanalyst Joe Rochefort in Station HYPO, Hawaii gave the Australian the impetus to draw the team back together again with a critical task. Joe had been decoding key messages regarding an impending offensive near Rabaul, off the coast of Papua New Guinea. The opportunity to work with Joe's team was a huge catalyst for the Melbourne unit. They quickly began honing in on a decrypted intercept regarding repairs to the Japanese flagship *Kaga*, for an impending campaign near the Coral Sea. This gained the heightened attention of OP-20-G in Washington, a faction of Kate's old D.C. team.

The result was that Joe and his lead codebreaker, Thomas Dyer, were instrumental in determining that the Japanese were planning an attack on the Midway Islands. The Allied forces were still licking their wounds from the May defeat in the Coral Sea. They seized the opportunity for retribution, and the June 4th battle decisively defeated the attacking fleet under Yamamoto and Nagumo, the masterminds of Pearl Harbor. The battle inflicted crippling damage to the Japanese Imperial Navy.

It was now heading into July, and the Leonski murder trial was underway. Sean wanted Kate distanced from the sensationalized chatter surrounding it, so he planned a stopover to his sister Veronica's in the Blue Mountains, near

Sydney. After two days of Sydney meetings, they headed to Veronica's for their brief visit. Madeleine was there to help Veronica during her latest pregnancy.

Once again, Kate was captivated by the scenic drive. The rolling hills were dotted with small farms and a vast expanse of breathtaking forests. Narrow, winding mountain roads, exotic wildlife, and the quaint little roadside cafés along the way made the long trip more bearable. They arrived in Katoomba at Veronica and Daryl's homestead soon after sunset.

These were Kate's only 'siblings' now, so it was important to her to get to know them all. She immediately observed that Veronica was far more vocal than sister Stella, and Veronica and Sean shared the same quick humor. Kate enjoyed the steady influx of commentaries about their childhood. Taller than Stella, with black hair and hazel eyes, Veronica favored Sean, while Stella, at Kate's height of 5'6", had dark brown hair and vivid blue eyes, like her father had, according to Madeleine. Sean's 9-year-old nephew, Darren, was the spitting image of Sean as a child. 6-year-old Jacqueline favored her grandmother.

Over a lovely Aussie brekkie on their veranda, Madeleine explained early the next morning that Sean, like Darren, was always "doing things" as a small child. He was obsessed with climbing trees, exploring the woods, reading for hours, and studying voraciously when he was not in school. Now that Sean's mum knew Kate was aware of Aidan's existence, she regaled the family with enchanting stories of the two boys as they were growing up.

The young Lawrence couple undertook a long hike in the Blue Mountains on the second day. Kate was fascinated by the blue haze and eucalyptus oil vapors that gave the aged majestic peaks their signature name. Sean explained the phenomenon to her as they hiked.

"The haze is caused by highly volatile terpenoids emitted in enormous volumes. They emanate from the dense population of oil-emitting eucalyptus trees in the area. Your American eucalypts have a far lower volume of oils. By the way, this is one of Australia's best-known tourist sites," he mentioned casually as they trekked down a narrow trail toward one of the valleys. Kate had never been around vast forests of eucalypts, but she was adept in the properties of terpenoids, which were used by her Grama in traditional herbal remedies.

These mountain ranges were but a small part of the *Great Dividing Range*, a name Kate thought made them sound immensely rugged and Australian. They bent and twisted from the Nepean River to the Hawkesbury River on their Easternmost border. The series of ranges were divided by gorges as deep as 2,500 feet. Massive waterfalls, tumbling brooks, and fast traversing streams cut the rugged landscape further, each stream and waterfall more astonishing than the last, to Kate. They made it to the iconic *Three Sisters* rock formation and

Sean took her to a ridge nearby, where the sheer, rugged cliffs near the trail's edge climbed vertically for hundreds of feet.

They rounded a corner of a less traversed bush track on one of the heavily forested areas opposite the peaks. The pervasive smell of the eucalypts, the crisp, refreshing air, and the misty sun creeping across the blue haze of the sheer cliffs deeply stirred Kate's blood. She turned to Sean, exclaiming, "I never want to leave Australia. All this vast wonderland of beauty… I love everything about you and our Australian home, Sean Lawrence."

She tipped her head up to kiss him, pulling him tightly against her body. In the way of love, deeply-stirred emotions quickly led to a rise of different passions. Sean commented jokingly, "What if we're discovered by some wandering park ranger, my darling?"

She looked into his eyes and said, "I'll tell the judge and jury 'I was merely appreciating nature in its highest form,' my dear. I'd like to see them sentence me for that!" she answered cheekily.

❦

KATE AND SEAN departed early for Melbourne the next morning. Madeleine was to accompany them, but stayed behind to help out while Daryl was away training troops, so their return trip was taken at a slow pace. During the journey home, they broached the subject of their recent loss. For the first time since the hospital stay, Kate broke down and cried, recognizing that the tiny baby they would have had together, untimely or not, would have been a most welcome part of their lives. "I'm not sure I can even carry a child to successful childbirth, Sean. But that doesn't mean that I'm not willing to try. Especially knowing as I do now that you really are happy with the thought of fatherhood. So, it hurts knowing that we lost that chance. And yes, I do hold myself responsible. Had I waited for you that night, we would not be where we are today. And I'd likely be looking like I was ready to explode by now," she smiled ruefully, patting her flat stomach.

Sean abruptly pulled the car over to a small café on the road's edge. "Let's pop in for a bite to eat and we can continue this conversation. First, you can't fault yourself any more than I can blame myself for being late to meet you that night. Let's put that aspect to bed once and for all. And I greatly need for you to understand that this is a terrible loss for me, as well. I too need to heal. The talk will be beneficial for us both."

Together, they sat on the small veranda enjoying a hearty bowl of soup, a delightfully overstuffed sandwich, and some lamington cakes. Much heartened by the scenery, the friendly hostess, and the quiet solitude of the small table outdoors, they spoke of their loss of the baby.

"Well, darling— let's start with some assessments of where we are in our marriage," Sean said, staring out at a scenic babbling brook not too far from their table. He watched the water traversing across the large weathered boulders, quiet for a moment as he gathered his thoughts.

"First of all, as newlyweds, we're navigating intimacy amazingly well," he winked, "and you have settled into domesticity so well that you're spoiling your husband rather immensely."

"Communication appears to be a great strength. And a necessity, I might add," he continued, "considering that my lovely little wife has a fertile imagination that gets away with her. Unless I head her off at the pass before she goes down some ridiculous path with that overactive mind of hers."

Kate responded with a small glower, which amused Sean greatly. "Case in point?" she asked, part in jest, but somewhat serious in tone.

"Well, let's start with the little incident on the beach in Sydney, with you thinking I was interested in bedding every beautiful woman within a 100-kilometer radius."

"Ok," she said grudgingly. "I'll give you that one, Sean Douglas. My imagination was soaring that day. But in fairness, you had a bevy of admirers to influence the direction of my thought process." Stirring her tea, she remembered the enlightening conversation they held afterward.

"Righto. Back to the subject at hand," Sean continued, "we're so comfortable in our marriage that having a child was a natural progression for us. So, I would be delighted at the prospect of fatherhood. And I have no qualms about seeing my lovely wife morph into a 'doting mum' whenever a baby does come along."

Kate nodded at this statement and opened her mouth to interrupt, "With that said, what would happen if I cannot bear children?" she asked wistfully. Sean faltered once more, gathering his thoughts. The cool breezes on the wide porch were blowing through strands of Kate's long blonde hair and he looked across the table at her, exclaiming how pretty a picture she made against the blue sky behind her. He smiled as he spoke:

"I've thought of that myself. But first things first. We certainly know you *can* get pregnant now. But with that said, *if* you are in any danger at all, then I would not be willing to take any chances. Second, if we cannot have children, we can adopt. It matters not whether it's our blood child we're expending all of our time and energy and love on. It will be ours from the moment it arrives at our doorstep."

A tear traced down Kate's cheek, and he reached across the table to wipe it away. She smiled and said, "Well then, I think we're on our way toward making a family of tiny little Lawrences. So, we'd better find a bigger cottage, my dear. Twins *do* run in our families, so we're in for a large brood, I'm thinking."

Sean raised his cup to that thought and as she stood, he moved around the table to wrap his arms around her.

"Between the two of us, my mum, and all of our Lawrence siblings scattered hither and yon, I think we'll manage this little army remarkably well. Don't you? And I, for one, don't mind practicing until we make this successful reproduction process absolutely flawless in every way. Practice makes perfect, you know."

They reached the car and both laughed as a large, scurrying water dragon moved across their path, startling Kate and making her scramble into her seat.

"*Still* getting used to the wildlife here, Sean, so mark that on your list as part of my vast learning process to conquer as an Australian wife."

Brownouts in the streets of Australia

STRATEGIC ALLIANCES

*The Australians and Americans
find common ground*

Oct 1942 ~ Oct 1944
MacArthur's Exit from Melbourne to Brisbane

CHAPTER FORTY-TWO

A HASTY EXIT

The two returned to Melbourne late Monday evening, plunging back into work at 5 am the next morning.

The young couple both worked to heal in their own ways as they were thrust further into their duties within Monterey. As Jack Newman's primary liaison, Kate was grateful she had far more visibility into the analytical material, and thus a bigger piece of the puzzle.

Some weeks later, Kate was asked again to report to MacArthur's HQ for some additional German translation work, this time reviewing correspondence between German POWs and their families back in Europe. Compared with the Axis-run POW camps, the German and few Italian prisoners in Australia were on "holiday." The Australian government took its Geneva Convention obligations so seriously that the prisoners were unanimous in their praise of the humane treatment they received from the Australian military authorities. At one of their large encampments, there was a "HOP IN—You're Welcome" sign across the mess hall, and here, locals mingled on a regular basis with the POWs. The cordiality was vastly different from the punitive and torturous treatment the Allied POWs received in Germany.

Certainly, one of the more comical and enlightening aspects of the war occurred with a few regularly escaping POWs, which was almost viewed as some morbid therapy for the bored German prisoners. The POWs plotted breakouts not dissimilar to how ordinary people would plan regular travel routes on vacations, having come to the fast determination that they would not be lined up and shot. They were often abetted by the locals, who gave them food, and conscripted them into short stints of farm work.

Perhaps the Aussies recognized that the escapees meant them no harm. "Or perhaps better yet," as Sean mentioned to Kate one afternoon, "the Australians well knew what the Germans did not. Beyond the camps were a few scattered farmlands. After that was impenetrable bush track and almost numberless

precarious river crossings and gorges. Highly poisonous snakes, emus, goannas, thorny devils, and dingoes turned most men back posthaste," he joked.

So, in due course, they surrendered and returned to camp, grudgingly grateful for hot meals and a bed.

As part of the Geneva Convention covenants, the prisoners were allowed to write to relatives, and receive correspondence from their far-off homes in Germany. Hundreds of letters poured in and left the encampments weekly, and thus, needed to be censured for content. Once more, Kate pointed out that there were many linguists in the HQ. Again, she was told with painstaking finality that these other capable translators were working on critical war-related documents. So, Kate agreed to arrive early and translate pre-screened German letters. This time, though, she requested and received another compromise… to remain on the third floor of Monterey while she performed these tasks, where the actual code breaking work was being managed.

Kate's previous Morse code training aided her scrutiny of the German transcripts. German orders weren't just spoken by radio, but also sent routinely from ship-to-ship, so the series of long and short beeps the Germans used to open these messages were all written in Morse. The previous training alerted her to letters from their country with suspicious markings and repeated patterns.

More often than not, the translation work was tiring and unrewarding, but the work at Monterey compensated for the tedium. She was quick to convey suspicious patterns to security officers for closer observation. Still, this assignment consisted primarily of perusing mundane German letters, so she requisitioned two trustworthy female linguists in Jack Newman's group to assist her when the mail backed up.

One morning in late July, Kate reviewed a few patterns in translated phrases that seemed to repeat themselves throughout various letters. She felt them to be military in style and pattern, rather than genuine family messages. She also noted that these, and similar letters to unrelated POWs were sourced from a centralized town and address in Germany. She might not have noticed the similarities had she not kept an organized pattern to her filing system.

Walking into the offices of the MacArthur security services, she stated to Lt. James Bryan, "Excuse me, sir. I might be off base, but several letters need further review. See the patterns in this phrase? It's only visible after translation. The letters also show a consistent array in the first letter of each paragraph. They spell out the name "Arthur" in Morse code. There were three this week and at least as many in last week's mail. These letters are from Germany to the POWs here. Same address. Same town. Sent to several unrelated prisoners. I checked."

She handed the letters over to Lt. Bryan and mentioned her theory: "These appear to mention 'Arthur' and a park in Melbourne. Again, I could be off base, but the Germans may be targeting General MacArthur's young son."

Bryan immediately picked up a phone to ring Colonel Sidney Huff, the primary guard to Arthur and his mother, Jean. Huff arrived immediately, listening to a briefing by Kate. Armed guards were assigned to MacArthur's personal quarters as a precaution. MacArthur was notified of the danger and asked to meet with Kate personally regarding the translations.

Complicating matters during this time, the incident coincided with the recent Leonski trial. With the trial press in full force, credible threats against his family, and cold weather also causing a variety of illnesses for his small son, MacArthur made the abrupt decision to move his family north. After he personally signed the orders for Edward Leonski's execution, he wanted to distance himself entirely from Melbourne.

Kate was assigned even more time in the MacArthur offices, ordered to monitor all of the German letters on the third level of screening to and from the European front. She was in the MacArthur HQ during the final packing, when credible sources arrived bearing irrefutable proof of a German plot to kidnap little Arthur MacArthur on his way to Brisbane. It was organized in Germany, to be orchestrated by escaped POWs in Melbourne. She was asked to stay and report on the German communiqués found on recaptured prisoners.

Once more, the Aussies tended to follow the Geneva Convention to the letter, and as such opposed torture as a means of gleaning information. The Americans did not, especially when it came to plots against little children. The Aussies deferred to the Americans due to the attempt on MacArthur's young son.

The recaptured Germans were immediately led into interrogation rooms, and Kate was asked to translate for the American officers. The Aussies had requested her presence, thinking that the interrogators would not cause considerable physical harm with a young woman in the room. To their surprise, the Americans approved. She knew valuable details of the communiqués between the prisoners and their plotters in Germany.

Her professionalism during the interrogations provided them the ammunition they needed to determine how to protect little Arthur and the MacArthur entourage. Sentinels were dispatched along the planned train route from Melbourne to Sydney, and then to Brisbane. Additional guards were posted alongside Jean MacArthur and her staff. Thus, the plot to kidnap Arthur never came to fruition.

Safely ensconced in Brisbane, the grateful mother sent Kate a box of highly rationed chocolates, nylons, and perfumes, along with a profound letter of thanks from her and her husband. Kate had arrived home the morning after two successful days of interrogations, utterly exhausted, but elated that her work with Army Intel was fruitful.

Once the threat against MacArthur's son was thwarted, the new SWPA headquarters were quickly established in Brisbane. On July 21st, MacArthur and team settled into Queensland, commandeering the posh Lennon Hotel as their residence. They inadvertently took the problems of Melbourne right with them when they requisitioned movement of the bivouacked U.S. soldiers in Melbourne to Queensland.

While Melbourne's population thankfully diminished, Brisbane's population grew by 80,000 overnight as American troops occupied strategic locales surrounding the downtown. Areas along the Brisbane River… Bulimba, New Farm, Kangaroo Point, and Fortitude Valley were concentrated with combat training camps, naval repair bases, and medical training areas. The rapid increase in population resulted in widespread congestion and a taxing demand for essential goods and services. For the remainder of 1942, over 96,000 of the 119,000 U.S. servicemen bivouacked in Australia were transferred to the northern state of Queensland.

Kate, Sean, and many others hoped that once the Americans were transferred north, the military reduction in Melbourne might settle most of the antipathy toward the American servicemen. As they drove out for a quick weekend stopover at the Aboriginal encampment and an extended visit with his mother, Sean mentioned, "Our team has received credible evidence through radio dispatches that Japanese propaganda is intentionally encouraging the rift between the Americans and Australians." This rankled him mightily, knowing that shortsighted, highly-ranked officers on both sides were not the least focused on this plot to 'divide and conquer.'

They dropped off supplies at the Aboriginal camp and chatted briefly with Aidan, who had agreed to join them for dinner that night. This softened Sean's tension considerably. Arriving home to their little cottage on the Lawrence homestead, they opened the doors to the veranda overlooking the beautiful bushland.

Taking advantage of the fact that "mum" was out for the afternoon, Sean escorted his wife into the living area. There, he slowly undressed her, letting the prevailing breezes and sounds from the outback ease the tension from their work stress. With her husband still somewhat tentative about how to treat her after the loss of the baby, Kate laughingly responded, "For God's sake, Sean… quit teasing me! I think I've missed this far more than you have!"

He left caution behind, rolling her onto the soft rug below, bodies still entwined and impervious to anything but the passion between them. Had any hapless fauna wandered onto their veranda doorstep *this* time, they would have been frightened off by Kate's moans and Sean's rather unholy "Holy God, Kate!"

Exhausted by their lovemaking, Kate finally came back to earth, saying, "Sean, what if someone heard us?" His following peal of laughter annoyed her, as it was a legitimate question. He disappeared into the bedroom, returning with a red scarf. She asked curiously, "What on earth is that for? Have you taken to dusting after sex?"

"Hardly," he retorted. "When this little prop is tied to the curtain rod in our window, mum knows not to disturb us… a signal I worked out when we first moved in," He smiled, unperturbed at her astonished look.

"You WHAT?" she asked. "Your mum knows when we are making love? She must think I'm an absolute harlot!" Kate scrambled up to make herself presentable, as if anticipating Madeleine at any moment. Sean laughed heartily, "Kate, dear…mum knows you're a wife, and particularly, the wife of her darling son. If she wants me to be happy, then she is aware that for me, 'happy' means this little signal is up often and for fairly long periods… like me," he grinned. Kate headed to the bathroom, entering the shower to remove all traces of their intense, amorous session. A smiling Sean soon joined her.

Much later, they exited, with Kate noticing that the red scarf was on the floor in the living area. She turned to him with another slightly annoyed look, saying, "Well, if that's not up, and you *are*, then how will we maintain our dignity if she happens upon our domicile when we're in the 'act'?"

Sean retorted, "I like to live on the edge a little!"

He promptly pulled her towel away. "With you, Kate, living on the edge is every single moment of the day. I love my life with you! I am quite a lucky man."

Dinner that evening was a jovial event. Grateful that Madeleine had busied herself shopping while they "occupied" themselves in the cottage, Kate produced a "New England Seafood Boil." This spiced steaming pot of corn, prawns, potatoes, onions, and sausage was a huge hit with the Aussie family. Seasoned with spices, butter, olive oil, pickled banana peppers, and fresh lemons, Aidan, Stella, and David devoured the New England staple with gusto. Sean whispered to his wife, affectionately saying, "Your family in Maine would be so proud."

Kate leaned a little against his shoulder, filled with a momentary pang for home.

They returned to the city that Sunday evening with renewed vigor toward the next few weeks of work. Unfortunately, their hopes for fewer distractions were short-lived.

Two weeks after MacArthur left there was a briefing at Monterey. MacArthur, it seems, intended to move the entire Central Bureau with him to Queensland. The headquarters were to be established in Nyrambla at 21 Henry Street, Ascot.

CHAPTER FORTY-THREE

THE QUEEN'S LAND

Kate and Patrick were among the first of their teams to be requisitioned to Brisbane, and the orders were carried out posthaste. By September 1942, the Signal Service Unit of the U.S. 837th would also be a part of the new Central Bureau relocating permanently in Queensland.

Central Bureau had been formed in Melbourne with a substantial mix of about 50% American armed forces, approximately 25% Australian Army, and 25% Royal Australian Air Force (RAAF) personnel. Later on, especially in Brisbane, more Australians joined as capable and noteworthy members of the upper echelon of their elite staff.

In the meantime, as Commander Eric Nave moved to other projects in Melbourne, Sean and the Australians took more of a primary role in the decoding requirements. Sean was intensely focused on the airwaves and reviewing translated material from the Japanese Embassy in Canberra. He had no desire to vie for leadership positions or deal with military politics. His work on the ground was too pressing. As soon as the messages arrived, codebreakers decrypted them and forwarded them to Japanese translators, a process that Sean supervised himself. As a result, he was highly engaged. This allowed for considerable progress in their decoding, focused primarily on the Coral Sea area.

Kate's transfer orders were as part of MacArthur's permanent military entourage. Her previous medical devotion to little Arthur, her work as a German translator, and her participation in the recent interrogations had left an indelible impression on Douglas MacArthur. When informed of the move up north, she asked Sean, "I'm somewhat curious about the name…Queensland. How did that come about? Was it a move to show Australia's subservience to the Crown?"

Sean responded, somewhat bemused by her slightly accusatory tone, "It was named in honor of Queen Victoria, who signed documents to separate that colony and give it independence from New South Wales. You Americans are bloody fond of that kind of independence, eh? So, it's not exactly 'The Queen's Land' and technically, she made damn sure the people were treated honorably in the process. If you're going to be an Australian, you will bloody well need to know the history." Sean laughed as he spoke. Kate shrugged her shoulders at his correction but duly absorbed the informative history, finally exiting the room to pack for the move.

Patrick was requisitioned under the same orders. Initially sent along with the US 837th to the crowded quarters at U.S. Camp Doomben, he was moved with the officers into apartments near Nyrambla. There, spurred on by MacArthur and his staff, the U.S. Army instigated a team designed to head a sequence of critical medical studies.

Soon after arriving, Dr. Patrick Danforth requisitioned Dr. Timothy Taylor officially into a team he was tasked to lead— directing a band of malarial medical researchers and pharmacologists at a newly established Army Medical Academy. There, they inaugurated research for a successful anti-malaria vaccine. The epidemiological experiments carried supreme importance in creating an effective replacement for quinine, which had far too many drawbacks in efficacy and long-term usage. MacArthur and his commanders were intensely interested in expediting this project, and thus Tim was a welcome addition with his former U.S.-based medical training and a short stint in epidemiology.

Douglas MacArthur was interested enough in this project to join in a roundtable with high-ranking doctors on Patrick's team, emphasizing the key importance of their work. He was introduced at their inaugural meeting, stating, "This will be a long war if for every division I have facing the enemy, I must count on a second division in a hospital with malaria and a third division convalescing in the barracks from this debilitating disease!"

The general was *almost* less concerned about defeating the Japanese than he was about the failure, up to that time, to annihilate the Anopheles mosquito, a terror during jungle warfare. As he stated at the end of this roundtable discussion, "I count on the outstanding assault of these deadly enemies by antimalarial personnel; this is the true key to a short and successful war in the Pacific, just as Eisenhower counted the invention of the Higgins Boats as the key to the successful amphibious invasion of Europe and North Africa. Get to work men! The armed forces are dependent upon you all."

The city of Brisbane had been the first Australian port to welcome the arrival of the American forces, and the passengers on the *Mactan* witnessed this same joyous greeting. But now, the arrival of the new soldiers was met with more suspicion after the negative press that leaked regarding the *Brownout Strangler*. Thus, the 'friendly' American occupation of Brisbane had a more profound influence on the lives of the Brisbanites than anyone had anticipated. Nevertheless, they were here to stay.

The continuing work Kate provided in the translations, the previous work to protect Arthur, and a decent friendship with MacArthur's wife, Jean, ensured that she would be somewhat protected under the realm of the MacArthur entourage. She was moved into the Lennon Hotel on the far opposite hallway from the MacArthur suites.

Kate took advantage of the chaos of the move by ensconcing herself in the initial setup of Central Bureau in Ascot. They were busy installing banks of IBM Tabulators which were used by the cryptanalysts to intercept Japanese messages. These machines were placed in the rear part of the large house and manned 24/7.

While strolling one evening with Tim and Patrick, Kate took time to explain her frustrations over the lost time in getting set up, "It's taking considerable effort to overcome the difficulties encountered by varying the frequency standards. The Aussies use a 220 volt-50 Hertz frequency and the U.S.— where the new machines were built, is at 110 volt-60 Hertz. So, our first weeks here will be taking them all apart, painstakingly rigging them for proper voltage, and recalibrating them. It will be months before we can recover the loss of time in code breaking efforts."

Both men sympathized with the interminable wait, as they were waiting for the extensive testing laboratories to be set up, calibrated, and manned. The 837th Signal Service was tasked with the efforts at Ascot, as they had successfully built complex cipher machines in Melbourne. The machines were used to encipher messages from plain text into a secret cipher text for use by the Allied Forces.

Almost every adult in Brisbane was now actively involved in some aspect of war preparation and support, so it was impossible to retreat from the tension and the massive influx of the war materials and servicemen. Large encampments opened up all over the small city, the result of which was entirely predictable. Even before Kate's arrival, the bustling, overcrowded city was on edge, perhaps more so than Melbourne had been with the blackouts.

Sean took time off from his Melbourne work to help Kate settle in. On the first night of his visit, they met up with Patrick and Tim, both working to get acclimated to their surroundings. Together, they learned the nuances of where the Central Bureau activities were located. They explored the areas surrounding the beautiful, winding Brisbane River as it meandered through the city, its banks now crowded with soldiers and encampments. Kate fell in love with the Brisbane botanical gardens and the massive parks and walking trails dotting the countryside.

The morning before he departed for Melbourne, Sean and Kate headed for breakfast at a nearby café in Brisbane. There, they met up with Sean's two sisters…Laurel, from Toowoomba, and the twin that Kate had not yet met— Lilibeth, from Cairns. Dale and Glen, their respective spouses, were entertaining and fun. Once again, the Lawrence family resemblance was remarkable. The sisters favored their mum considerably, but the eye intensity— a crystal blue color— was remarkably similar to Sean's. The family reunion boded well for the move up north to Brisbane.

As Sean told a mournful wife the next morning, "I promise that this arrangement will be short-lived, Kate. I'll end up here before you have a chance to really miss me." After a prolonged, emotional hug, Sean had to jog to catch the train as it was ambling out of the station.

Kate made her way on that rainy morning to the American PX/Postal Exchange to meet up with Patrick and Tim, as Sean had asked them to lift her spirits when he departed. The two men were all but inseparable now that they worked together, having recently found a large apartment in New Farm near the city. This morning, both were slightly hung over… the effects of bar hopping through the fair city the night before.

The PX was situated on the ground floor of a building not too far from the Lennon Hotel. It was both an emblem and an indicator of the simmering turbulence between Australian servicemen and their U.S. counterparts.

A gloomy Kate observed dryly as they sat down for a late breakfast, "The PX here is drowning in American luxuries that are being heavily rationed throughout the rest of the city. Cigarettes, nylons, high-quality alcohol, luxury food supplies….don't forget the chocolates and ice cream. We appear to have exclusive availability of every item. We're stirring up trouble by not rationing like the rest of the city!"

Tim responded, holding his head as clear evidence that he had imbibed in too much of the high-quality alcohol she spoke of.

"The U.S. Navy took the trouble to export these goods, using supply routes that aren't exactly secure. We provide all of the protection on those supply routes. So maybe, the U.S. soldiers *should* have first dibs on these lofty items." This provided another perspective for Kate to ponder, which made her even testier that morning.

"Really, you two. I'm conflicted about how we're presenting ourselves as Americans, and I talked with Sean about the Australians' emotions regarding this. The citizens of London need close protection because they are literally immersed in the war in Europe. They rely largely on British 'stiff upper lips' and their sense of country to understand and best appreciate our American support."

Deftly evading a rather imposing water dragon sunning near the path as she spoke, Kate skirted across the walkway, much to Patrick and Tim's amusement.

She was somewhat somber after these discussions, so when Patrick and Tim mentioned a planned trip to the beach, Kate was uplifted by the prospect. The three friends headed for the shores of the South Coast. The countryside heralded lush farmlands and stately Queenslander houses dotting the roads along the way to Surfers Paradise. An hour or so later, they rounded the main boulevard and parked the car near the sand dunes protecting the beach.

Kate was the first to traverse the pathway that led to the water. She could hear the waves just beyond the dunes crashing into the shore. A small curved wooden bridge added to the charm of the scenery. Stepping out over the dunes beyond the bridge, she held her breath. The palm trees above her were swaying in the balmy breezes. The mesmerizing, crystal blue body of water stood before her, pristine white sand edging over her feet as they sank in. The mist from the waves breaking along the shoreline enhanced the ethereal beauty of the vista.

As Kate watched the waves roll in, the sounds of distant gulls broke her quiet reverie, followed by the trills of exotic tropical birds. Tim and Patrick caught up, noting that tears were streaming down her face. The hypnotic scene was deeply stirring to her young soul. She missed the presence of Sean by her side to revel in the paradise of the tropics before her.

"The Queen's Land…" she whispered. "No wonder she couldn't give it up. There's nowhere else on earth like it."

CHAPTER FORTY-FOUR

LETTERS FROM MAINE

Amid the chaos of the Nyrambla setup, a much-welcomed package arrived from the Red Cross on September 15th, Kate's 22nd birthday. Two boxes contained letters from home, an advanced French Lessons book, a cache of cookies, and sealed jars of Grama's homemade antibiotic crème for wound care. Buried in the bottom was a new bestseller, Agatha Christie's *The Body in the Library*.

Kate opened an envelope first:

My dearest granddaughter,

I am hoping these jars and books survive any scrutiny from military sensors, which I hear is a requirement for every outgoing package these days. The German language book is a gift from your Grossmama Yeager, and the French one is obviously from me, to help you continue your studies. I am keeping myself well and active in support of all of the war efforts here in Maine.

This grand old house here in Boothbay will be yours one day, and I cherish knowing that my beautiful young granddaughter shares my love of life here in this tiny harbor town, and my love of medicine as well. Speaking of healing, write back when you can, and let me know that your heart is mending as well as can be expected, with the loss of dear Kerri. Knowing that we cannot change what happened, we only move forward as best we can. I hope you receive this package on your birthday and that you remember

how much everyone back home loves you. You will never be alone as long as you know this.

> ~ I remain yours very affectionately, and with
> heartfelt kisses, always... Grama Helene

The German book was missing. Confiscated, most likely because "Grossmama" only wrote in German, and this could be perceived as a potential message from the enemy. A second envelope was bound with a pink ribbon, and it contained two letters inside:

My sweet niece,

The good ladies in the Kittery community are busy into the wee hours baking these cookies for the soldiers, as we hear they are great morale boosters. I hope you enjoy them and know that my hands touched them at some point as I made up your birthday care package. The Agatha Christie book is a bestseller here and I had to barter to get it second-hand from our new minister's wife! You're worth the 10 pies for the local bake sale at the church rectory. I just hope you enjoy it, as you may have preferred a whimsical, fun read instead of murder and mystery. At any rate, it is probably in your hands and knowing you, you're enjoying it under a nice shade tree with an apple in your hand, as you did when you were young.

Now for the tougher news. The second letter was sent by Kerri weeks before her death. It was returned to us and I believe postmarked from Hawaii, as by the time it arrived there in December the conflict was in full swing. I did not have the heart to open it. It was meant for your eyes and there it shall rest, no matter what the content is. Know that my heart is with you as you read it and I hope you have a safe place from prying eyes when you grieve again, as you will.

Uncle Frank and I are doing well, and the bakery and café are in full swing. We miss you every day, and often wonder where you are and if you are happy and well. Our love is steadfast and our hearts contain many beautiful memories of you and Kerri to comfort and sustain us. Remember us at night when you say your prayers, and rest *knowing that our hearts are never far away from our beautiful surrogate daughter. With many prayers and full hearts,*

Your loving Aunt Maggie and devoted Uncle Frank

Kate held the letter to her chest and calmed her aching heart before working up the courage to open Kerri's note. With shaking hands, she opened the second letter, addressed on light pink stationery with an embossed seal bearing the initials **KYT**.

My darling twin,

I write here in the easy chair that used to be dad's as it is the only seat in this tiny apartment that I can be comfortable in with this baby making my belly so cumbersome. It is late here in Boston. Tim is out studying, so this is a perfect time to write, as the baby is in no mood to sleep right now. There is not much time before he/she arrives and the nursery is prepared as best as possible.

Tim is still the doting husband and he will make a fabulous father to this darling child. I don't know whether I hope for a beautiful little girl dressed in pink and frills with adorable little curls, or if I want a precocious boy, all bouncy and energetic and full of mischief for my Tim. I guess I just pray for a healthy baby and an easy enough delivery that the recovery is quick, so I can spend every moment spoiling this little darling. I am anxious to get on to the business of motherhood.

I cannot wait for this little miracle to be in my arms!

Here, a tear fell from Kate's eye, dropping onto the letter as she continued reading, her heart aching with the words on the page.

The letter continued with:

…I so wish my darling sister were here with me to help hold my hand and watch over me during labor. But it isn't to be. I will take comfort that the next time you see me, you will be holding the product of this great love between Tim and me; knowing that you will be a perfect aunt to this child makes my heart sing.

Remember how much I love you, and that the miles will never separate two hearts that love each other as much as we do. Faith can move mountains and I have great faith that we will be together soon enough. The reunion will be magnificent.

Oh, and as you requested, Tim is working on a career for his wife, and is so very supportive of my educational plans. I am sad to say that his mother has been pretty vociferous about my performance as her son's wife. She believes that my place is to bear the appropriate children when the timing is right (which according to her is not now!) I am most definitely not of this mindset, but I do want Tim to be happy and fulfilled. However, our greater needs as strong, loving and attentive parents are my focus right now.

I do hope to hear from you soon, as I am anxious to know that you are well, resting as much as you can, and most importantly, safe. I fear this conflict will be a lengthy one, but we will persevere with the Grace of God and our strength in this world— as a country that leads a powerful army and the hearts of strong, resolute, and compassionate human beings. I sometimes wish we were young again, so we could still be the innocent babes that dad and mom nurtured and cherished. I don't know how the world became so dark and foreboding, but I look to our God to right that soon enough.

Ever your adoring sister, with all my heart and soul forever. -Kerri

Kate held the letter to her heart, sobbing uncontrollably. The severance of the bond that began at conception was still so raw that phantom pains from the emptiness in her heart would not subside. She let her emotions resolve themselves in the way that grief often does, through tears. Knowing that nothing could ever assuage her heartache over losing the other half of her soul, she picked up a pen and wrote a letter she knew her sister would never receive.

My Heavenly Sister,

I write here in my little apartment in Brisbane, Australia, looking down upon the city with its beautiful winding river and lush tropical landscapes, all of which are rapidly becoming a part of my heart in an indelible way. Your Tim is here with me now, but

I'm sure you know that. I'm taking excellent care of him, keeping him busy helping with the war efforts. You would be so proud of him, so engrossed in supporting our armed forces in this great conflict.

I miss you with every fiber of my being. I never knew it was possible to endure such a loss and be able to function as if my world wasn't falling into a dark abyss and a part of my soul wasn't lost forever. So many times, I have thought of you and wished you were here, providing advice and love to your adoring sister. I wish this so badly my chest literally aches with the pain. We complemented each other in ways that no other siblings can ~ as only twins can possibly do. And no matter how much time passes, or how many treasured life events come my way, I will always have this giant hole in my heart because you're not there to share in these meaningful moments. My heart aches as I travel these paths alone, knowing I always will travel them without your love and your gentle spirit.

Remember when we would walk along Marginal Way for one of our "sister picnics," and stand before the ocean beyond us and cry because it was so perfect in every way? We wanted those life-giving moments to last forever. And you would say, "It wouldn't be half as perfect if I were standing alone, without someone to share it with!"

Just last week, I stood on the most scenic ridge near Mt. Tamborine, looking across the landscape of lush, green rainforest valleys. The blue waters of the Pacific were far off in the distant horizon, and the vibrant tropical birds were chattering and singing. The crescendo of the cicadas was almost deafening... but I felt such loneliness when the striking views should have been so profoundly stirring to my blood. The happy lilt in my heart was missing. _You_ were missing, and it is simply impossible to describe the emptiness. We were one from the day our hearts first started beating in tandem in the womb. And now my heart beats alone, singularly, as if it will never quite have the strength again that I felt with you by my side.

I mustn't feel sorry for myself. You would not want that. I have Sean now and I'm so happy he got to meet you. He makes my heart strong again when I need it most... a ballast against the winds of the strife that we face with this horrific war.

I cannot end this letter without letting you know how profoundly the void has been etched onto the very depths of my soul. I cannot say which was worse: the shock of the terrible loss or the ache of what is never again to be. I wrote a poem for you, and I *hope these words find their way into your heart, in Heaven, as you smile down upon me and raise up my soul.*

Your loving earthly sister, Kate

WATCHING THE SUNRISE, she reflected on their last birthday picnic, on their 19th birthday in 1939... the introduction of their future husbands to each other:

It had been an absolutely glorious sunrise, boding well for a sunny fall day on the Maine coast. The girls had appreciated the 'Godly' cooperation, this being their first birthday without their doting parents to help them celebrate. After their visit to the naval base and their brief work at Aunt Maggie's bakery, they headed to Ogunquit. They parked near Perkins Cove and headed up the walkway toward Ogunquit's claim to fame... the vibrantly blooming "Marginal Way." The steady cadence of the waves crashing onto the rocks never failed to take their breath away in the first few moments of that propitious view. A light morning fog was still hovering over the small cliffs and a slew of seagulls circled above, the quintessentially fat gray and white birds perusing with sharp beady eyes for any telltale movement of hapless prey lurking in the tidal pools below. The air was heady with the fragrance of salt, and of the equally pervasive smell of the colorful flowers that marked "The Way," as the girls called it.

The high footpath hugged the coastline, and looking out at the bay to the right, the waters were a deep hue of blue, with white sprays of waves cresting onto weather-beaten rocks. Far off in the distance, they could see delicate white clouds moving gently across in exquisite sworls. The girls found their familiar grassy plot near the highest cliffs and spread their blanket to set the picnic basket down. They read together for a while, arm in arm. Kerri had broken the silent reverie first:

"Do you suppose this will ever grow old to us? I always wanted to be married on this exact spot! Just a little archway with a small cross on top, looking out at the backdrop of the ocean."

Kerri watched her twin's eyes while hugging her knees protectively against the cool bursts of sea breezes.

Lying on her side and picking at the remnants of a piece of cold, peppery fried chicken, Kate said briskly, "Well, that could happen sooner than you think, my dear. It seems as if you're ready. More so than me at this age," Kate had observed. The accompanying sigh was deeper than she had intended, but she welcomed the change in life plans if it would make her sister happy once again. Impetuously, Kate turned to give Kerri her impression of Tim.

"He's a good looking fellow, Kerri. But he doesn't take himself too seriously, and I like that. He really cares for you, and for now, that's enough for me. If he plans to take my sidekick away from me, he'd better treat her right," Kate smiled merrily. Kerri responded,

"He's wonderful to me. I want the love to stay this way always." They both got quiet again, looking out at the vast ocean before them.

After ages of watching the clouds float by, Kerri broke the silence again. "So, what did you think about the young man we met this morning? I caught him glancing sideways at you several times!" Kate laughed heartily, with a lighthearted retort, "Who, Sean? I'm certain that never really happened. So, if he was looking, it was because he was wondering why you were so perfectly put together and I looked like something stiff and overripe that the cat dragged in." Still, she was pleased that Sean had favored her with at least a glance. The more social of the two, Kerri shared gossip about Sean that she now explained to Kate.

"Every time he shops, a mob of young ladies finds a dire need to manage their grocery shopping, according to James' secretary. But he's apparently married to his work. So, he's even more mysterious to the ladies of Kittery."

While packing up, Kerri continued, "I thought he was great fun. So, I asked Uncle Frank to invite him to dinner tomorrow. Also, Tim would have a male to chat with," she finished. Kate turned toward her sister, horrified, saying, "You did NOT do such a thing! Did you?" She asked the question in a near-terrified tone, which she knew amused Kerri greatly. Kerri responded, "Well, I asked Uncle Frank to stop by and see if he was available. We'll know the answer when we get home." The girls were silent for a moment or two.

Somewhat reluctantly, the two sisters finally retraced their steps down the long path. Both hearts were lifted by the prospect of a lovely weekend with some captivating young men…

Kate looked out the window again, pensively watching the Brisbane River traverse through the city. She fashioned a cold compress over her eyes to reduce the swelling, and reluctantly dressed for work.

The knock on the door startled her. Working to rub the storm of emotions from her eyes, Kate opened the door reluctantly, to greet her untimely guest. A tall, striking man in a naval uniform held a vase of sunny flowers and a small velvet box. Joy put strength into her flagging soul, and she flew right into Sean's arms.

"You have the rest of the week off. As do I. Let's make the most of every second together, Kate," he said, bending low to kiss his wife.

TAKING A MUCH-NEEDED break from pressing work at Nyrambla and Sigint, Kate and Sean explored the South Coast just southeast of Brisbane. She was in awe of the picturesque villages and quaint towns that dotted the twisting roads on the mountaintops. The vast ocean was visible from atop many scenic overlooks. They drove, found a promising hiking spot, hiked the trails, then took the scenic roads to another trail.

At one pullout, Kate twirled around, basking in the sun's warmth and breathing in the heady air of the nearby rainforest. A cacophony of whipbird calls, buzzing cicadas, and clicking frogs was at once deafening and entrancing. A nearby waterfall was roaring over small boulders, with mists of silvery, white spray cascading through the cracks of the rock faces.

"Aren't you exhausted from all the hiking, darling?" Sean asked as he watched her, looking down over the railing to the verdant valley below.

"No, I'm not tired Sean. I just want to absorb every minute. All this awe, the grandeur of each scene… this wonderful gift of nature from God. How lucky are we to share this perfect place on earth together?"

He smiled, grateful that she loved his country as much as he did.

"There's plenty more to see. We're still in the honeymoon phase with our traveling, darling. Speaking of honeymooning… let's head back to the little cottage. I've got a bottle of wine chilling. You're vastly amusing when you've been under the influence," he added suggestively.

They left for the rented bungalow, the respite being the precise dose of inspiration needed to resume their difficult work back in Brisbane.

CHAPTER FORTY-FIVE

THE BATTLE OF BRISBANE

{the Aussies v. the Yanks}

Two Americans walk into a bar, spot an Australian, and say, "You can go home mate, we're here to save you." The Australian looks them up and down, commenting "I thought you were refugees from Pearl Harbor."

Their time together passed by far too quickly. Just before Sean left for Melbourne, he was requisitioned for a meeting with MacArthur, where he learned that his team had been commandeered for a permanent move up north to Brisbane. In contrast, the month of October passed at a snail's pace, as both of them waited to be permanently reunited. Thankfully, Kate immersed herself in her work at Nyrambla. The assignment with the Red Cross continued, but was an easy, pleasant break from the more pressing cryptanalysis efforts.

Things were starting to settle down somewhat regarding the negative press of the late July Brownout Strangler murder trial until the Review Board upheld his death sentence. It was confirmed on October 28, 1942, and MacArthur had personally signed the execution order for Leonski, a distasteful task he permanently assigned to his aides once the trial was over.

Private Edward Leonski was hanged on November 9, 1942 in Melbourne— a celebrated event in Victoria. It was yet again a controversial topic of conversation in Brisbane and Melbourne social circles. An American court had presided and imposed their justice and the requisite sentencing. Yet an Australian rope, executioner, and prison managed the execution in a country where capital punishment was all but abolished. Kate, unfortunately, found

herself once again reliving the trauma of the attack, the loss of the baby, and the trial.

As part of the investigative team, Aidan Lawrence had been called as a witness, which meant he had access to the trial transcripts, whereas details to the public were severely censored. Only the final outcome was announced: the hanging at Pentridge Prison. Remembering the trauma Kate had experienced after Leonski was captured, Aidan paid a visit to Sean's Monterey offices in Melbourne to relay information from the trial. During his testimony, Leonski had admitted to stalking other women before and after the murders he committed. He freely admitted to accosting a woman after asking her for a light for his cigarette. It turned out that this intended victim was Kate, and the attack was immediately thwarted by Sean's timely arrival. Both Kate and Sean had agreed that the two attacks were unrelated, but they had reversed the attackers.

As Aidan relayed to his brother, "It appears that with the second attack on Kate— the one where she was injured, Leonski was in the stockade for 30 days. So, all evidence of her physical attack pointed to a local Aussie farm worker with a lengthy assault record. He was imprisoned afterward." Aidan paused.

"Kate was selected entirely at random, by an alcoholic who had a propensity for violence after drinking." A relieved Sean promised to convey this to his wife when he returned to Brisbane.

IN A MEETING SEAN attended the next day with Australian officials from Canberra, spies had discovered details of prominent discussions in the Japanese army regarding concerns that Australia posed a grave threat to Japan while the country was in alliance with the U.S. The Japanese intensified efforts to blockade the shipping lanes between the two countries, but they stopped short of an invasion, although it *was* a genuine consideration. Instead, they worked to increase tension between the allied nations. Commander Thomas Moreland, one of MacArthur's many chiefs of staff, commenced with the top-secret discussions:

"The generals of the Japanese army general staff, and the Prime Minister of Japan, General Hideki Tojo, are aware that Australia poses a serious threat to Japan while it remains an ally of the United States. Our spies in Tokyo have conveyed that as early as January 1942, the Army and Navy Sections of Imperial General Headquarters had planned to blockade supply from Britain and the U.S. to strengthen the pressure on this southernmost continent." He paused reflectively to allow the room's occupants to assess this information.

"However, when the Japanese Navy requested troops for an invasion of Australia at a meeting of the Army and Navy Sections in March of 1942, the

Japanese generals were adamant about not committing massive troop and logistical resources to the conquest of the Australian mainland. The capture of Rabaul on 23 January 1942 and the first bombings of Darwin in February convinced the Japanese Army that Australia had little with which to defend itself from invasion."

Moreland continued, "Japan has been heavily overextended by massive territorial conquests. Their generals are assured that Australia could be pressured into surrender by isolating it entirely from the U.S. They plan to intensify the blockades, and therefore apply concentrated pressure on the two countries. The Japanese plan to sever Australia's lifeline to the United States has been given the code reference 'Operation FS' (also known as FS Operation)."

In the meantime, tempers in Brisbane were continuing to flare. MacArthur made no secret of his criticism of the Australian general leading the bloody Kokoda Track counteroffensives in nearby New Guinea. At a time when Japan was concentrating on New Guinea to the north of Darwin, Australians were leading the battles in the horrendously bloody terrain of the Kokoda Track. MacArthur's opinion raised tensions exponentially.

Emotions also ran high over the Leonski execution. As Kate relayed to Sean, the sensationalism over the *"Brownout Strangler"* was not the direct cause of the ensuing violence. But it certainly didn't help the rising animosity between the two countries. Kate was heading for work with two nursing friends when they learned during a stop at the PX that MacArthur had just relieved Australian General Sydney Rowell, commander of I Corps in New Guinea, of his command. A rash decision, this sparked pronounced anger toward MacArthur. This negative sentiment in the Australian forces ran extraordinarily deep. As a result, opposing and vociferous viewpoints escalated with great speed into an emotional furor that could not be stemmed.

Some of the commentaries were fairly humorous. Kate was at a movie with two nurses watching the Walt Disney movie "Bambi" when in one scene, Bambi cried out for his dead mother, *"Mother, where are you?"*

From the balcony in the back of the theater came a male voice, *"She's out with some damn Yank; where do you think she's at?"* The theater roared with laughter. Still, Kate worried as ads for the American Thanksgiving holiday began circulating in November. A notice in a Queensland newspaper read:

~Townsville Daily Bulletin, 27 Aug 1942~

"United States forces in Australia will celebrate Thanksgiving Day on November 26, with the traditional turkey and pumpkin pie. Arrangements

have been made for a shipload of frozen turkeys to come from America to Australia in time for the festive celebrations. Each man will have at least one lb. of turkey, accompanied by the usual garnishing of cranberry sauce. Thanksgiving Day has a deep religious significance in the States, where it ranks with Christmas. It began in 1621, when the Pilgrim Fathers celebrated their first harvest.

❦

AFTER ABOUT TWO months of such notices, when the Kokoda Track Battles were at their apex, Kate felt it was like pouring salt on a gaping wound. She was outspoken with one of MacArthur's aides when she greeted him at the hotel elevator one morning.

"I am assuming this is a public relations attempt to acclimate Australians to their visitor's holiday traditions, but it has gone terribly wrong," Kate explained. "We have wounded and crippled Australians from the Kokoda Track walking the streets like they lost a one-sided battle with the devil. And with food and luxuries severely rationed for locals, it's no wonder people are angry," she commiserated.

The officer politely listened and just as politely ignored her, Kate felt.

As they moved further into November, tempers were escalating as fast as the soaring temperatures. And they were rapidly moving into the start of the hottest season— the Australian summer. On November 26, this escalation and the enmity between the two nation's armed forces turned deadly in the city of Brisbane.

There was a minor skirmish on Albert Street downtown that moved to the PX on the corner of Creek and Adelaide Streets. This intensified into a rioting mob, which oddly enough began with several Australian soldiers defending a rowdy American "mate" against U.S. PX M.P.'s who were intent on reigning the inebriated man in. This scuffle was followed by a sudden attack on the PX. It was Thanksgiving Day in the U.S., a holiday neither recognized or warmly received in Australia.

Kate was exiting the Red Cross building across from the PX after an afternoon of training classes when this mass of servicemen gathered. As she left the building, she noted that many were yelling at the American guards and order was rapidly disintegrating. A few turned in her direction, recognizing the American military uniform. She leaned against the door, uncertain whether to retreat inside or head quickly toward her residence. One Aussie soldier yelled out, "Here's a real live one! The Yanks can take our women at will. Let's get friendly with one of theirs!"

From behind him, somewhere in the crowd– a voice yelled, "Leave her alone mate! She's an Ami nurse and they've done us no harm!"

Kate watched, wide-eyed, as the crowd moved on, directly in front of the PX. Furious, seeing that their anger was now directed toward a couple of vastly outnumbered guards in front of the American service center, she jostled her way toward the front of that building. Not knowing why, but hoping in vain that tempers would dissipate, she pushed her way right next to the mass in front where several leaders appeared to be directing the crowd's rants. It was a careless maneuver, Kate quickly surmised. She reached the leader, touching his chest, and calling out, "Is this going to get you anywhere, mate? Stop this madness now before someone gets hurt! We need to work this out amicably!"

He turned and looked her in the eyes, saying, "Right. You're one of the damn Yanks and part and parcel of the problem!"

"I'm one of you now. I married one of you Aussie blokes, you bastard! If you weren't so bloody stupid, you'd realize I am trying to help!" He grabbed her shoulders to swing her in front of him, but before he could respond further, an arm reached out, yanking her unceremoniously away from the front of the mob.

Patrick had been notified of the impending trouble from his residence in New Farm, so he and Tim had driven toward the Red Cross building to provide protection for Kate. They had watched from a short distance as she jostled her way to the front of the mob by the PX. Dressed in casual clothing, the Aussies let both men through, as someone near the front yelled out, "That nurse must be looking for trouble, eh?" Patrick shoved him away, responding in a nearly perfect Aussie accent, "I'm her husband, mate. You can bloody well let her go, or you'll get the best of my temper and my fist!" The Australian backed down. Tim was already edging Kate from the crowd. Throughout the evening, throngs of Aussies attacked hapless American GIs escorting Australian girls. The trouble might have dissipated rapidly had Australian MPs and Brisbane police intervened to restore order, but none of them seemed inclined to do so.

At 7:45 that evening, the mob erupted into a full-fledged riot involving over two thousand men. By some witness accounts, the count was put at over four thousand. From the windows of her apartment, Kate, Patrick, and Tim watched as M.P. batons flew and more Australians joined the growing fray outside the American PX. Local pubs had just closed and the streets were filled with soldiers and civilians fueled by alcohol. The American M.P.'s were pelted with rocks, bricks, and other projectiles.

When an M.P. finally raised a shotgun with the idea of shooting it off to disperse the crowd, there was an immediate scramble to control it. The gun discharged, striking Australian Gunner Edward Webster in the chest. Webster lay dead, and all told, eight other Australians were wounded and eleven U.S. soldiers were attacked and sustained injuries. The violence finally subsided, but at least 20 other Americans were now hospitalized. The rioting continued until 10:00 pm, when peace was temporarily restored, but not before the main floor of the American PX had been destroyed and scores of individuals on both sides suffered severe injuries.

With the American PX under heavy guard, the following night, which was November 27th, a crowd of Australian servicemen gathered across the street outside the Red Cross. The rioting began just as violently as the night prior. Patrick and Tim felt it best to get Kate out of the city for the evening, so they met with some friends from Nyrambla in New Farm. Kate and Patrick were pleasantly surprised to see their old friend Ned, now stationed in Darwin. Ned was opinionated about the animosity between the allied leaders. As he stated, "The dissension is at the top. Thomas Blamey is Australia's Commander of Allied Land Forces. He and MacArthur are both strong personalities. Their clashes undermine our efforts to win this war! Don't see why neither of them can see that!" Kate added, "The provosts on both sides should agree to sequester the soldiers on the street. I will approach MacArthur's staff to support an end to this violent backbiting."

Patrick supported her. "The Axis powers encourage this enmity. Japanese propaganda in New Guinea is focused on spreading rumors that while the Australians are fighting in the jungles there, the Americans in Australia are having a grand time with their girls."

Leaning back in his chair, Tim responded, "Well, that may well be, but the Aussie women seek us out. We're not monks, so we enjoy their companionship when they offer it up."

Kate turned the focus back to the animosity. "All joking aside, it's up to us to *not* help the Japanese stoke their war of aggression between the two Allies." With that, their small party adjourned, all agreeing to do their part to prevent the conflicts from escalating further.

A free American Red Cross clinic and an adjoining market were established. Goods from across the seas were sold below cost, and an abundant garden of free herbs, vegetables, and spices was introduced, for use by the Australians. Australian merchants were told to reduce the severely inflated "Yank prices"…the markup in goods whenever U.S. troops paid for basic food, entertainment, and services. An Australian guidebook distributed to arriving American servicemen explained the Australian's humor, their fondness for drink, and their readiness for a brawl.

The events surrounding the "Battle of Brisbane," as those two days were called, were decidedly glossed over, with military reports redacted significantly.

Both Allied nations decided, rightfully so, that the incident would reflect poorly on each, and the Axis Powers would relish the news that their propaganda was working. Genuine efforts to turn the focus toward goodwill between the two countries finally achieved significant progress.

And gradually, the war once again became the primary focus.

CHAPTER FORTY-SIX

CENTRAL BUREAU

1943 rolled in auspiciously, with the new year bringing some helpful changes to Kate's routine. One Thursday evening after her Red Cross teaching assignment, Patrick was waiting at the door as she exited, and they headed toward the PX to grab a bite of dinner. Kate asked somewhat sarcastically where his sidekick was, and Patrick grinned back, retorting, "He's squiring a very attractive young Brisbane gal named Jacky around these days. I'm not seeing much of him after work hours." Seeing the disappointed look on Kate's face, he asked, "Does that bother you? Are you missing your bevy of loyal admirers, Kate?"

Popping him on the arm playfully, she answered, "Nothing like that, Patrick."

Looking forlornly at the bustling pedestrians on the opposite sidewalk, she sighed briefly, "He's my twin's husband. Life moves on, as it must. And I know that eventually he will find someone and marry her. It hurts, that's all. It's hard to swallow, knowing Kerri will be replaced someday. It's like she's being erased from a chalkboard… almost as if she never existed. It's a cruelty I never thought I'd have to imagine until perhaps at an old, old age."

The pain that accompanied that remark was enough for him to turn and take her by the shoulders, saying in a more serious tone, "This might be for the best for you, Kate. Tim's lonely. And frankly, he is still grieving the loss of your sister and the baby. He hasn't spoken much to you about it because he senses it will add to your pain. But it's been hard on him too. And I will add that I think it might be best for some separation. It appears that some of the loneliness may be manifesting itself into an interest in his wife's twin, despite his new Aussie companion."

They walked into the canteen area of the PX and sat down to order, but the surprised look on Kate's face as she sat across from him caused him to backtrack a little.

"I think I've struck a raw nerve," Patrick announced. "Tim's been devoted during your settling in. Not that you would allow any impropriety, but grief does inordinately insane things at times and he might believe any misdirected affection from you was an encouragement."

She put her menu down on the table abruptly and countered, "Do you *actually* think that he would make a move on me? A married woman? And practically his sister? When he could have any number of females that would love to have his affection?" she asked.

"Yes," Patrick responded. "But not intentionally. Men are egotistical bastards at times. We often think every attractive woman will die unless she gets to possess us. Married women are not always off limits, you know, and war does have a number of effects on the stresses of even the most devoted couples' separation." He looked over at Kate from above his menu as he spoke.

Hesitating for a moment, he pressed the issue, "I'm not going to say I'm above those temptations myself, Kate. However, I do know your limitations and I greatly respect them. I also respect Sean enough to strictly manage the current boundaries you and I have between us. Just so you know, the interest has *always* been there. The friendship remains strong despite that, and I want to keep it that way. We're both mature adults and this is my issue to handle. I can deal with my emotions. I always have."

They were interrupted by a young waitress approaching their table. Ordering a sandwich, Patrick finished the subject with, "Enough said on this. I think you get the gist of the direction this conversation is heading." He looked into her eyes, daring her to protest the facts he pointed out about both friendships. Kate ordered and then fixed her eyes on Patrick, somewhat discomfited by his candor.

"At any rate, this enlightening confession is not why I picked you up, Kate," he continued. "This little meeting was actually requested by your husband to ensure that you were not running yourself ragged these days in a thousand different directions. Sean wants you to slow down and focus on one project at a time. So, I'm here to encourage that to happen. You're wearing yourself out, little lady, and this pace isn't good in the long term. I'm afraid this is going to prove to be a long war. So, you need to make sure you can manage it at a reasonable pace yourself."

Kate pondered his words, appreciating Sean's thoughtfulness and the tact which Patrick added to the discussions. She was tired. And getting crosser as each week passed with no sign of Sean, and no word about the definitive date of the eventual transfer.

The two friends left the restaurant and walked the scant few blocks to the Lennon Hotel. At the door of her building, Kate turned to Patrick to speak. Her response was pragmatic and thoughtful.

"I do appreciate the talk, Patrick. On all of the subjects we broached. And I value our friendship, likely even more than you do, as I keep everyone in my heart compartmentalized and nurtured to every extent I can. It keeps my heart beating on the right track, you know— all this camaraderie." Kate smiled, continuing with, "Please don't ever let anything get between us. Promise?" she pleaded, blinking away the threatening tears.

Patrick looked down at her and smiled back. "It's a promise." Hesitating slightly, he put his arms around her and hugged her tightly, saying, "Goodnight, Kate." He escorted her in, turned, and headed back through the doors whistling that same melodic tune she heard on the streets of Melbourne when they were reunited.

～ele～

WITHIN THE FOLLOWING weeks, Kate worked to back out of most of the German translation work, finally able to focus on the code breaking at Nyrambla. This was easy enough for the time being, with MacArthur attending meetings in Australia with the Canberra government. After the plot against little Arthur, the POW camps had tightened up the correspondence between the prisoners and their relatives back in Germany. A translator was hired at the camps, and only the most critical letters met Kate's eyes, translated directly for MacArthur's aides.

Kate canceled her Saturday botanical classes, aware that they could be picked up later, as new military nursing recruits were requisitioned. With more freedom, Kate was more relaxed and focused on her work. The downside was that there was more time for her own loneliness to set in.

Patrick remained busy with the medical research for the U.S. Army. She presumed he had backed off temporarily with his candid admission of interest. And Tim was "sowing his wild oats" in his spare time. Kate understood this as a part of the grieving process with a widower at the young age of 25. She longed for their days in Melbourne, and her naïve assumptions that the four of them were best friends and "family" when they were together. But she accepted the state of affairs and worked to move on in her new position in Brisbane.

Even at Nyrambla, where they started fresh in building their clandestine group, the complex chain of command was difficult, if not impossible to follow. As with Monterey and Moorabbin, almost none of the women who reported there even knew what the message they held in their hand meant, as they were not part of the intercepts or the end-decoding. As soon as Kate had arrived at Monterey in Melbourne, she had memorized the hierarchy of command for the Navy Security Groups so she could learn about the order of intelligence work.

Sean traveled to Brisbane in early March for Sigint Meetings with MacArthur's team. Kate was relieved to know that MacArthur was winning the battle for adding Sean's expertise to his team of advisors, and he soon would be arriving in Brisbane permanently. Once more, Kate asked her husband for details about the chain of command she was dealing with after her move to Brisbane.

An amused Sean conveyed to her, "It may have been a combination of your innate curiosity or your job in D.C., but you are not content to work only one part of the system. And frankly, I follow that sentiment as well."

As they rested with a spot of tea on the small sofa in her apartment late one evening, Kate asked Sean for details on the Pacific Intelligence Groups. Leaning her head against his chest contentedly, she questioned, "I don't see why none of us are allowed to understand the scope of our work. It's like being in a play and only seeing your small part. You don't have a clue what's happening in the other scenes because you're backstage and prepping only for your lines."

Sean moved her aside to stand up, heading to the chalkboard Kate had set up on the wall for drafting her teaching syllabus. He lifted his satchel up to pull out a detailed map and some tape. Placing it on the chalkboard, he gave her a strict warning, "You need to commit what I'm about to tell you to memory. I can't put it on paper for protective measures. He then placed dots with a marker on the primary Pacific islands— Hawaii… Philippines… from Australia up to Japan.

"The work on Japanese Navy codes is carried out by the Navy Security Group— technically a combined unit of both Australian and U.S. Naval Intelligence Groups. The small stations where the Japanese intercepts are managed are called Fleet Radio Units and Ned's station in Manila was an FRU, as you know." He placed a small "x" on all of the primary FRU stations.

"The command station in the Pacific at Pearl Harbor was under the code name of HYPO. Station HYPO is the cryptanalyst station that broke the codes for the Midway battle. It is commanded by Joe Rochefort and his lead cryptanalyst, Thomas Dyer. Both are absolutely brilliant, and men I would greatly like to know. You may still hear that HYPO term from time to time, but they are now called FRUPAC. This group primarily advises Admiral Nimitz, Commander in Chief, Pacific Fleet." He drew the connections on the map for Kate to visualize.

"Just so you know, Nimitz is fairly well on the same level as MacArthur, but as "5 stars" go between the U.S. Army and Navy, MacArthur has slightly more seniority. Nimitz is a submariner. I very much respect the man for his knowledge of sub designs and warfare, and we have a fair rapport. The same with 'Bull" Halsey." He smiled at Kate as he turned to emphasize his admiration for the man.

"Back to the lesson…the primary FRU station in the far West Pacific was the Philippines station…which was moved to Corregidor shortly after December 7th. At Corregidor, it was called the CAST Station, under Rudy Fabian— your new boss here in Brisbane. When the Japanese were advancing to Corregidor, this group was evacuated to Melbourne under the name FRUMEL. The main headquarters for FRUMEL is OP-20-G in Washington, D.C. This is where all of the critical messages are sent for analysis and for eventual reporting directly to Roosevelt's staff." He placed a star on the map near Washington, D.C. and smaller stars in Melbourne and Brisbane.

Pointing to Melbourne, he added further, "This was Melbourne… the Monterey Unit. It is now called the joint RAN/USN Fleet Radio Unit, Melbourne (FRUMEL), and is _one_ of two Allied Sigint organizations in the SW Pacific Area. FRUMEL is subordinate to the commander of the new USN 7th Fleet, Admiral Thomas C. Kinkaid, who reports directly to Nimitz. The other Allied Sigint unit is Central Bureau. This is YOU, Kate— Central Bureau here in Brisbane…Nyrambla… the Research and Control Centre for the interception and cryptanalysis of Japanese intelligence. Central Bureau reports to the HQ of the Allied Commander of the SWPA—the SW Pacific Area— Douglas MacArthur." He placed another map on the wall to depict the theaters of the war:

"FLEET RADIO UNIT Melbourne (FRUMEL) and the other U.S. Navy units also provide Signals intelligence information to Admiral Nimitz as CIC- Pacific, MacArthur, as commander of the SWPA, and Admirals Somerville and Fraser of the British Far Eastern and Pacific Fleets."

He waited as she absorbed this information. "It's arguably more detail than you need, but it will prove useful in your work and as the war continues, it will be more essential that key personnel understand this hierarchy."

"Finally, 'Sigint' is a code name for Signals Intelligence. That's me. And as far as you know, I don't even exist. Sigint operations are so secret that we were given our special 'Ultra Secret' classification. We manage the interception and decoding of Japanese military and naval messages. Our work goes straight to D.C. Even MacArthur is supposed to have limited access. He gets around that— crusty old mastermind that he is!" Sean sat back down on the sofa to continue the conversation. Kate prepared another cup of tea as he continued.

"Remember that Patrick worked at FRUMEL before he joined MacArthur's medical group. FRUMEL was the 75-man unit based in the Monterey Apartments Station in Melbourne, occupying the entire second floor. The primary intercept site for FRUMEL was located at Moorabbin, where Newman's girls worked in decoding. That's where your work with Jack Newman came into play."

"Well, what was the connection between Moorabbin and Monterey?" Kate questioned. "I was part of that work and never knew what was in my hands."

"Well, you do now," the dark eyebrows raised as she smiled at the suggestive innuendo.

"Australian couriers deliver all the traffic from Moorabbin to Monterey by motorcycle every two hours. About 90% of the Australian staff at Moorabbin are women. We refer to them in our private circles as 'Jack's girls'. You compiled their reports and made a final daily report to Jack. Jack's report was compiled, along with his own top-secret work and translations, in a document that still goes directly to Washington D.C."

"Your new boss, Lieutenant Fabian, is a U.S. Naval man, and his 75-man unit of FRUMEL was based at Monterey. Just before the move to Brisbane, he also took over for Jack Newman. And by the way, you asked before why we couldn't come up with a better name for our collective group. 'Central Bureau' literally *is* the most boring, nondescript name the Allied Forces could come up with. We're just another boring, mundane government entity to the outsider looking in. No one is supposed to even *suspect* that we're committing espionage or decoding critical information."

Kate responded to his explanation by adding, "Just so you know, I really enjoyed working for the Aussie. Jack was relaxed and mild-mannered. Fabian rarely makes an appearance here. He is a bit temperamental and more commanding, which gives us a bad reputation. Perhaps that trickles down from MacArthur. Neither of them is exactly known for being calm and collected. But… both are brilliant, and that *almost* makes up for the arrogant behavior."

Sean smiled. "That's the consensus from everyone who knows the two men. Before coming to Australia, Fabian and his U.S. Navy code breakers were stationed in Cavite Naval Station in Manila, then commandeered to a tunnel on Corregidor. When we knew Corregidor was going to be captured, his unit and over 1.5 tons of their equipment were transported out by submarines."

Kate looked away, reminded of that last day in Manila. Sean continued, "So Fabian's knowledge of Japanese is partially what got Newman pushed out of his position. That the two men had little use for each other is also an underlying reason. With Fabian, exceptions are made for his temper and cockiness. He is a very intelligent man."

Seeing that Kate was getting tired, he said, "As far as the two of us are concerned, my work in Brisbane is this: parts of Fleet Radio Unit, Melbourne—FRUMEL, headquartered at Monterey, which has been the primary source in unraveling Japanese *naval* signals, will remain in Monterey. The smaller unit I am commanding now will work directly in concert with MacArthur's staff here. The work from FRUMEL Monterey will come up the command channels to Central Bureau, here in Brisbane, which is responsible for Japanese *army* and *air force* codes. So, as it stands, between the two Lawrences here, we have just about every angle covered."

Kate asked softly, "And where, pray tell, do I stand with you, Commander Lawrence?"

"You report directly underneath me!" Sean teased. "And that's a position I relish, *Mrs.* Lawrence. Come here!" he mock-commanded with a wide grin. His smiling wife took his hand and joined him on the sofa, resting her head on his chest contentedly. Sean turned on the radio, letting the soft music of Harry James and his Orchestra's hit *I Don't Want to Walk Without You* lull the two of them into a peaceful sleep.

CHAPTER FORTY-SEVEN

OPERATION VENGEANCE

While waiting for Sean's move from Melbourne, Kate focused on establishing herself at Nyrambla, concentrating on various ways to enhance her work, including Japanese code breaking. The JN-25 Japanese codebook that Kate had started studying at Monterey in Melbourne was a complex code of numbers rather than characters. The Japanese used a massive codebook that contained over 30,000 five-digit groups.

These were used to compile signals and ciphers with a five-digit "additive" at the beginning of each message. As they encoded a single notification, they would find the 5-digit code that represented each specific word, syllable, or punctuation. This process was repeated until the entire message was completed. They used a mathematical technique called "non carrying," where there was no carrying of digits.

So, 8 + 6 would equal 4, 8 + 8 would equal 6, and so on. If the code group for "invasion" was 13563 and the additive they used was 24968, the resulting group would be 37421.

13563
<u>24968</u>
37421

The *37421* was the end product that would be radioed. The Allied codebreakers would have to determine the "additive" to deduce the original code group and word. Finally, they had to ascertain what the original code group actually stood for. Kate had to learn this system to understand the communiqués that were reported to her, and subsequently to Rudy Fabian. Since he remained in Melbourne much of the time, she had more time to study. For Kate, and everyone else involved in Nyrambla, the process was labor intensive, and took many months to analyze. And the American codebreakers

in Hawaii and Australia frequently disagreed with their Washington counterparts on the various code deciphers.

Despite this, Kate loved her work, and it was invigorating for her, even with the intensity of the analytics. By March, her routine was down to a fine science and her organizational skills were greatly useful to Fabian's group of cryptanalysts. Her memory was such that she could pick up a communiqué and remember previous messages containing similar repetitive codes, indicating that a key message or a plan was being repeated for emphasis. She would locate them in her locked filing system for review, to determine the date of the last "related" communication. Shorter time frames between repetitive messages meant the Japanese were on the move.

Her daily reports at Monterey had been managed in a hierarchy of sequences. They indicated the ranking of the most critical materials for the day from the women at Moorabbin. She managed the same at Central Bureau, Nyrambla. It was more often than not, tedious and boring work. Except for when it wasn't.

In early April at Nyrambla, Kate was working in the office when Central Bureau decrypted a Japanese Army Air Service intercept signal. The signal contained Admiral Isoroku Yamamoto's itinerary for his planned trip to Rabaul, east of Papua New Guinea, and NW of the island of Bougainville. The original intercept was discovered by No. 51 Wireless Section at Darwin and by Port Moresby, in Papua New Guinea— Yarran and Danilo's group.

Immediately recognizing the critical status of the message, Keith Falconer, Australia's most experienced interceptor, forwarded the direct message to Nyrambla. It was given the rating of a maximum reliability category for his confidence in his own rendition of the actual signals. Nyrambla decoded the message and then forwarded it to the Sigint Cryptography Unit in Monterey.

From there, a U.S. Navy linguist tidied up the decryption. It was returned to Central Bureau in Brisbane, using required hierarchy protocols, sent as a "highly classified" directive straight to Admiral Nimitz and Hawaii— FRUPAC. In essence, they were confident that Yamamoto was on the move, inspecting Japanese air bases in the South Pacific.

The Americans in Washington had received similar messages, including the exact plane model and the times of Yamamoto's tour of the Japanese bases on Rabaul. Since Bougainville was in Nimitz's territory, Nimitz and the White House famously made the decision to assassinate the principal architect of the Pearl Harbor attack.

On April 18, 1943, Yamamoto's plane was intercepted and shot down off of Bougainville by U.S. P-38 Lightning Fighters. The death of the commander-in-chief of Japan's naval fleet would be celebrated by Allied Forces around the world. Whenever, that is, it was finally safe to make the announcement. When General Douglas MacArthur heard the news, he famously wrote, "One could almost hear the rising crescendo of sound from the thousands of glistening white skeletons at the bottom of Pearl Harbor."

Despite this glaring success, the group at Nyrambla did not rest on any laurels. There was work to be done. Code groups still had to be sorted painstakingly by hand as the IBM tabulators were being calibrated. After that, there was much more work to be done, indeed.

Kate knew of the secrecy of the Yamamoto message, as there was a hushed flurry at 21 Henry Street, Nyrambla, when the message was received. She knew only of its actual contents when Sean arrived soon for a visit and a meeting with MacArthur and Admiral Bull Halsey. Sean was secretive, which taxed Kate's curiosity to the utmost, but she knew better than to ask. They met in the apartment established for Sean two blocks away, in MacArthur's GHQ Building. Kate often brought food for her husband, being far too obsessed with his work to leave the building.

Near midnight one evening, he sat at his table to eat a small bite of food and Kate asked, "Is there anything that you can convey to me? And more importantly, is there anything I can help you with?"

Sean smiled, saying, "I can confirm what your group already suspects. Yamamoto is dead. At this point, we are working on damage control. If the Japanese even *remotely* suspect that we've collectively broken JN-25 by having knowledge of his planned itinerary, the codes will be changed. The damage will be catastrophic, regarding loss of lives and loss of battles. So, it's not officially out for public consumption. I reckon it won't be until his death is announced in Japan."

"How is the damage control being handled? And *can* it be controlled?" Kate asked.

Sean replied gravely, "Our double agents are working to establish a credible rumor that coastwatchers near Rabaul had seen the planes in the area and through sheer luck, our P-38s in the area shot them down. They only knew it was a high-ranking official, per the story being concocted. We'll know if it's working in a week or so. If the codes change, we'll know the Japanese have wind of the itinerary leak. And there'll be hell to pay, most likely starting with our POWs in the Pacific."

"Alright, next question: 'Cartwheel.' What does that word mean to you? You called out in your sleep last night. Several times."

Sean smiled— a tightly controlled smile that showed that it was a most unintentional leak.

"Signals Intelligence work. Highly classified. It involves Yarran and Danilo as well, but on the periphery of one portion of the plans. It's best that you don't know more than what I've just said."

He walked across the room to switch the light off at the table. Turning to his wife, he grinned widely, saying, "Good thing I'm not sleeping with the enemy. There'd be hell to pay there too!" They both headed off to bed. Kate hoped that sleep would find her weary husband, and she vowed to keep him relaxed to every extent possible.

The worry lines on his forehead, the strain in his voice, and the intensity in his face frightened her.

CHAPTER FORTY-EIGHT

INNOVATIVE MEDICAL MEASURES

During the lull in the few weeks before Sean's final move, Kate was thoroughly occupied with a second medical project. She was pressed by the Red Cross to engage in classes for new medical advancements in surgical procedures. After a briefing concerning the medical developments, she decided to open a conversation with Tim about the slight estrangement she sensed was growing between them. Under normal circumstances, she would wait until this had a chance to rectify itself. Right now, though, it interfered with the pressing work she now knew was ahead of them.

She invited him for breakfast early one morning before she headed for Nyrambla. Tim came from med school. He was finalizing his fellowship classes in thoracic surgery, as part of his impending contract assignment in the army mobile surgical encampments. The young surgeon arrived at the café looking refreshed, tanned, and handsome… much the product of time spent in the hot Brisbane sun. Sitting in front of Kate, he seemed the spirited, confident college boy she remembered when he and Kerri got married. After they ordered, she approached the subject somewhat tentatively.

"Tim, I wanted to bring you here to discuss a few personal things. I have been sensing some alienation from you lately and I need to share my concerns." She stirred her coffee, looking up as her blue eyes searched his hazel ones intensively.

"I'm afraid this is going to sound selfish on my part, but there is a great fear of us drifting apart due to lack of communication about the directions we're both taking relative to the loss of Kerri. You have every right to replace her, and I know you will, and should. But that is something I have to face… and a challenge I have to manage when you do. So let me take ownership of that problem."

The food arrived just as Kate worked to overcome the intense emotions that welled up suddenly. They both refilled their coffees so they could continue without further interruption.

"I'm aware that you've been out 'sowing your wild oats,' so to speak." Tim's eyebrows raised at that overt remark. "I certainly understand," Kate continued, "but I do worry that you might be hurt. Not the *least* of which is by some errant Aussie hothead soldier who discovers his flirtatious young girlfriend in the arms of a handsome American doctor," she smiled mischievously at that vision.

"And let me add my final thoughts first, then you can butt in with whatever comments you want to add," she finished, as his hand raised in protest. "I don't want you harmed, and I sure don't want you replacing my beautiful sister with someone unworthy of your love and affection. You are a helluva guy, Tim. A wonderful man, a gifted surgeon, and an incredible person. And you deserve only the best in life. That's all. Now— your turn." She abruptly ended her little oration.

Tim placed his fork and napkin down, setting the tone of the conversation in a more serious manner. "Kate, darling. I think we both need this chat badly, so I'm going to divide my comments into three elements: first, the loss of your sister and how that has affected me; second, a reflection on the effects of the war and my personal plans; and third, how we both are managing handling an enormous void in our lives in the future." He took a sip of his coffee as he processed his thoughts.

"Let's start with this: There will *never* be another Kerri. I will grieve that loss for the rest of my life. And it's probably to the detriment of *our* relationship that I have not conveyed my opinions on that aspect to *you*. Our pain is at the same depth… and yet different in many ways. And if we are being entirely open with each other, some of that loss is assuaged by being near you. I see so many elements of her personality and looks standing before my eyes when you are near."

Tim hesitated, a slight flush covering his face.

"I'm attracted to you. Not only as Kerri's twin but as someone about as close to my perfect wife in personality and demeanor as I can ever possibly have. I am smart enough to recognize that for what it is. A replacement package, and a highly valuable one at that. So, I have been avoiding you, unfairly to you, I might admit."

Kate gave him a look of sympathetic encouragement as he continued.

"Over the past weeks of this move to Brisbane, as we've helped each other acclimate to the intensifying training and war efforts, I have been tempted to act on that. With Sean away so often, it was easy to fantasize that we're together and I'm back again as a happily married man, albeit in a non-physical relationship, at that. No— please hear me out, Kate!" he said as she opened her mouth to comment.

"Whether you realize it or not, you're an easy person to fall in love with, just as your sister was. You aren't putting yourself out there, so don't dare blame yourself. Just know that it's not 'against the law' to have these impulses, as long as I don't act upon them. So, here's where the 'sowing the oats' factors in. I'm erasing the *pain* of losing Kerri, not her memory. And in the process, I'm putting you into your proper perspective so our relationship can continue and strengthen. If we're not honest about all of this, it will tear us apart and we'll never be able to repair that rift."

"Secondly, I am toying with big decisions these days… the first being that I want to make this stay in Australia permanent. I have nothing to tie me to the States. Having said that, I also recognize that I am far too dependent on you and Sean and Patrick. We are family, and that means a great deal to me. But truth be told, I need to forge my own way and guide the medical work here into my ambitious career path. The decisions involving all these factors are significant, and I'm evaluating them one at a time." Tim studied Kate's face carefully as he finished with his last remarks.

Sighing resolutely, he said, "This brings me to another thought I have been fostering. I may never marry again, Kate. There are times when I recognize that as grief taking over my brain, but the truth is, Kerri is almost impossible to replace. I have set that bar so high that no one can jump over that monumental hurdle. So, until and unless they do, my career is my life and you all are my family. I am also aware that if I never marry, you may have pressure to continue to add me to your family endeavors and events.

That's a big 'ask.' So, my comments here affect both of our future family plans in many ways. That's all there is to this confession. And that's an awful lot to digest, sister Kate." His eyes brimmed with tears as he watched a small trickle flow down Kate's cheek. He reached across the table affectionately and wiped it away. Kate placed her hand on his and smiled.

"Tim, my darling brother… first, I will stand by whatever career path you take and, frankly, I'm overjoyed that you may plan to stay here. I am selfish enough to really *really* need you in my life and to hope that our paths remain forever intertwined. I cannot take losing you, after the loss of my sister. So, I'm relieved to hear of that decision and of a potential career path here in Australia. We can both take your dating— and mating decisions one day at a time. Because of your standards, I'm certain I will welcome whomever it is that might change your heart on that matter! And for the record, I'm selfish enough to really relish the attentiveness, and protectiveness, and the affection you lavish on me now. So that will be a cross for me to bear whenever this worthy gal finds her way into your life."

With that, she added, "I said my reasons for broaching this conversation and this meeting were selfish. Actually, they are altruistic, truth be told. MacArthur is interested in setting up a team of U.S. surgeons to manage some highly complicated surgical cases that we are seeing. Advanced weaponry is changing the level of battlefield wounds in this war. MacArthur's Chief of Surgery here is friends with Dr. Norman Kirk, who happens to be the U.S. Army's Surgeon General. MacArthur has requisitioned a teaching staff from Dr. Kirk's facility in Michigan, to lead us in these endeavors. Patrick is slated for this team. Your services have been requested as well. Apparently, MacArthur's relationship with Patrick's family keeps Patrick smack in the middle of these medical initiatives, so Patrick enjoys sharing the wealth of assignments with you, obviously!"

Tim offered information from his own research. "Kirk is advancing operating microscopes to reduce mortality rates in complicated vascular surgeries. He is also vastly improving the recovery process for amputated limbs by preserving residual limb and bone functioning for newer prosthetic devices. And his O.R. protocols are achieving a high success in army recovery centers back home. So yes, I'd be highly interested in joining the team. It's a fantastic learning opportunity."

Kate smiled, and said, "I thought as much. And for some reason, MacArthur cannot let go of his connections with me in Manila, so I'm on this team as an O.R. nursing advisor as well. I can't have either of us being tentative about working with another teammate. So, I hope we're together on this key assignment. Kate paused, then asked, "So, are we?" Tim nodded in agreement.

Kate added one final comment: "I need to make you aware that this is planned as a top-secret field operation. But I know these surgical advancements *will* be in use in a combat zone. I suspect that announcement will be soon, Tim. It's to be a major offensive, wherever it is."

Tim digested the implication of those words.

"Well then…our food is getting cold, so let's eat and chat about the work ahead of us."

Satisfied with the discussion, he recognized that he had a newfound respect for his astute sister-in-law. She never failed to forge lasting relationships, work and otherwise.

⎯⎯ele⎯⎯

TWO WEEKS LATER, Sean arrived permanently. The apartment reserved at the MacArthur HQ was set up efficiently as a convenient workspace. For a brief period, Sean rarely left the premises of the building. Kate remained focused on Nyrambla for the moment, until the elite surgical teams could be assimilated. Grateful just to have her husband nearby once again, she made a determined effort not to question him about his work.

Once more, he learned to value her devotion, and her decision to support the war efforts at the cost of private time with him. For now, they accepted the secrets they were both forbidden to share.

CHAPTER FORTY-NINE

A MAN NAMED "CHICK"

Their exhaustive schedules continued unabated as each of the four friends sought to manage their own obligations under increasingly intense deadlines. Shortly after dawn one early morning in May, Sean was awakened by a messenger from the MacArthur GHQ, with a request for a private meeting with MacArthur. He dressed quickly and hurried to the headquarters. As Douglas offered a handshake and pointed to a nearby chair, he turned toward the door and nodded as a handsome, dark-haired man entered the room. The general introduced the young Australian, using Sean's recent promotion and rank to clarify his significance to the project.

"Commander Sean Lawrence, I'd like to introduce you to Commander Charles Parsons. Most people know him by 'Chick'!"

Sean stood, intrigued by the introduction of Chick as more of a friend than an Armed Forces colleague. After a few pleasantries, the three soon sat down for a conversation that would have a critical impact on each of them in the room, and a profound effect on the war in the Pacific as well.

Looking somber, MacArthur stated solemnly, "What we are about to discuss is highly classified. And if any word reaches any of the upper military echelons… U.S. or Australian… it will be flatly denied by me. And, of course, you could be subject to court-martial, but I already know those measures will never be necessary or you would not be sitting here."

In a move that once again broke the chain-of-command for the U.S. Military, General MacArthur told the two men before him, "You have both been officially recruited into a strategic group known as the 'Allied Intelligence Bureau.' You will be reporting directly to me and no one else. Not even my closest aides know of this mission you are about to embark upon, and it will remain that way."

Turning to Sean, he stated, "Chick has volunteered— and I don't use that term lightly— for return missions to the Philippines. He'll be organizing a series of submarine voyages equipped with food supplies, radio equipment, information, personnel, and details of intelligence operatives. These will be supplied to the guerrillas on the islands to prepare them for landings being coordinated as we speak. For a return to the Philippines."

Seconds passed as Sean absorbed this impactful statement. Directing a comment to Chick, Sean asked quizzically, "Would you be the same Chick Parsons who operated the *Luzon Stevedoring Company*? If so, we met briefly at one or two functions in Manila," Sean stated.

Facing MacArthur again, he added, "I don't know how much you may have been briefed on this, if any, but the manganese and chrome mines under Chick's purview had been monitored regularly by Allied Intelligence prior to the invasions by Japan. The mineral resources and processing facilities were studied extensively by our expatriates on the island to determine the facilities' maximum output. And under confiscation by the enemy, *if* and *how* they could be sabotaged to minimize the availability of the mineral ores to Japan."

Parsons smiled, knowingly. "I'm the one that provided the regular data for the plans and the key elements to sabotage the equipment. We switched the mining sites months before the Japanese attacks. An elaborate and costly maneuver, I will add, but well worth the effort. I believe the current output is almost exactly half of the former annual exports under my purview, despite the best efforts by the Japanese to…shall we say, *encourage* better results by the workers."

"Well then," Sean added, "Your information was exceptionally accurate and useful, I might add. Credible sources tell us that the grade of ores being mined and transported to Japan has been compromised considerably. It appears that the Japanese neglected to do their homework, as far as mineral canvassing goes. The mineralogical composition is much lower. And the less productive stratigraphic position of their current host rocks was manipulated rather brilliantly."

Douglas MacArthur smiled at the exchange. "I think I should manage some fairly lucrative export businesses if I hang around the likes of you two after the war!" Both men sitting across from him smiled back.

Returning to the conversation at hand, MacArthur stated, "By combining several existing Australian groups into a single organization, my GHQ here has designed a two-fold mission: to obtain and report information on the enemy and to weaken the enemy by sabotage. This is aided most capably by the local resistance." Pausing to take a drag off of a cigarette, he returned to the briefing.

"To fulfill its mission, the AIB will use a combination of long-range patrols and isolated observation posts behind enemy lines. And by behind, I mean hundreds or even thousands of miles behind Japanese lines. Chick has managed one trip already, but Sean, we need your expertise in hiding these subs by use of the radar from the Signals Intelligence from Port Moresby. It has to be unbreakable. Strictly Aboriginal codes."

Continuing, he said, "Both of you will report your findings and your progress directly to me, as stated. But there are thousands of others who will be assisting. Organized sections for subversion and sabotage, surveillance behind enemy lines, coast watching, and written and verbal propaganda— by radio."

Finally, satisfied that the two men were on board with the current agenda, if not yet their upcoming assignments, the general ended the briefing with an admonition.

"Let me make it abundantly clear that neither of you are to do *anything* that would jeopardize your life or get you into the destructive hands of the enemy. You are too valuable to the operations. You will receive further instructions within the next two weeks or so. Good luck and Godspeed to both of you."

Within the next month, Parsons commandeered a second sub for a journey bound for Mindanao. More importantly, he offered an early sign that MacArthur would make good on the vow he had issued after retreating from the Philippines. The general was still in his headquarters in Brisbane, Australia, over 3,000 miles away. Still, to the ragtag, information-starved men immersed in guerrilla warfare, the presence of Chick's personal messengers were both profound and provocative. They whispered MacArthur's promise across the vast jungle settlements and villagers:

I shall return.

The effect upon the commandos and the civilians was nothing short of miraculous, exactly as MacArthur intended it to be.

CHAPTER FIFTY

SAVING CRITICAL LIVES

Within a scant few weeks of the inauguration of Sean's secretive project, Kate was also summoned to MacArthur's HQ. Mystified over the summons, Kate immediately complied. When she was escorted into his offices, she found Red Cross Field Supervisor Irving Williams deep in discussion with General MacArthur. She shook hands, and as signaled, took the chair offered to her, waiting for their chat to end. Douglas MacArthur turned to Kate, initiating the meeting. "Kate, I, along with Director Williams, am requesting your services in a long-term medical project that involves strategic planning for a return to the Philippines." Kate sat up sharply, waiting silently for him to continue.

After almost a year of work, the Hospitalization Division and the ETO Office of the Chief of Engineers in England have completed an expeditionary tented/hutted hospital prototype. It has been designed to house enough wounded soldiers as a 1,000-bed general hospital, or a 750-bed outpost station hospital. Right now, the structures are comprised of tents on concrete bases. They are based on the premise that the site in which they are constructed will be improved upon with paved roads, coinciding with water, sewer, and power lines." MacArthur simultaneously signed a stack of papers on his desk as he spoke, a habit in some of his personal meetings.

"The details are not forthcoming yet, but each tent has space beside it for a parallel hut with extensive medical equipment and doctor's stations. We know from previous briefings that too many lives were lost as critical patients were transported from one surgical station to various recovery tents when they were too unstable to be moved. This medical test station prototype in Wales was unveiled and operational from the early tented stage to complete roofing…designed to accommodate its full capacity of patients at each stage. They're to be under tarp and canvas until full roofs go on." He nodded to Director Williams for him to continue the discussion.

Irving complied with further details: "The 12th Evac Hospital was constructed in Carmarthen, Wales, to erect an expeditionary 750-bed station hospital serving troops in that area. The site was deliberately chosen due to its unsuitability, where rain, snow, land obstructions, and poorly drained marshy ground gave rise to a host of delays and seemingly insurmountable odds to a successful achievement. So far, it exceeded all expectations regarding the delivery of the final product. They were staffed and fully operational to progress to the European front as they became functional as a full-fledged mobile hospital."

"This is where you come in, Kate," he added, watching her face as she digested the details.

MacArthur interjected, "This is classified information, but we— the Allied Expeditionary Forces—are working on a return to the Philippines. The date, location, and timeframe will be announced at a later period. This will be a US-led expeditionary force, but we need Australian support teams, and you work well with the Red Cross and medical staff here in Brisbane."

MacArthur paused reflectively and then continued with the discussions, "Suffice it to say I have ample experience witnessing your skills at Sternberg Hospital, and Director Williams has attested to your surgical prowess during the journey of the *Mactan*. We are comfortable assigning you to help organize the training of the medics on the beach landings as well as to participate as a Senior Nurses Corps Officer in a planning committee for the hospital station. These plans will be overseen by my Medical Chief of Staff. You report directly to him."

Irving added gravely, "We cannot reach the scale of a Carmarthen 750 to 1000-bed experiment, but we expect over 70,000 civilians and POWs in the Philippines to be under horrific medical conditions when they are rescued. This hospital will be charged with their care and recovery. It is a monumental task of critical importance. Any questions, Kate?"

"Yes sir," Kate weighed her following statement carefully. "Except for my post-surgical teaching classes at the Red Cross, I am working almost full time at Nyrambla, as you may be aware. I will need assistance in managing whatever explanations you deem allowable to excuse me from my duties there. I believe the work there is abundantly important. Nevertheless, I'm honored and prepared to serve you both," Kate responded.

She paused reflectively. "You've always known me to be blunt, and I'm not going to hesitate here. By giving this assignment to a naval nurse of my ranking, we would bypass the usual chain of medical command. How will I direct information to the Army Corps of Engineers and the Red Cross Medical Chiefs who oversee the landings, since I hold a naval rank and this is primarily an army-based operative?"

With that, MacArthur nodded expectantly.

"With your usual forthrightness, you've posed some interesting questions," he said with a brief smile. "And we have a solution for that. The American Red Cross serves as the traditional reserve and recruitment service for the Army and Navy Nurse Corps. You're already an official Red Cross employee. That said, you have effectively been promoted to Lt. Commander status in the Red Cross, which corresponds with Army *and* Navy Nurses Corps rankings. We expect some extraordinary efforts from you and I'm sure you will exceed these expectations, Kate," He nodded to Director Williams, thanking him for attending the meeting. Irving exchanged final pleasantries and exited the room.

"Kate, please continue sitting. I have a few personal matters I would like to discuss with you." MacArthur stated frankly. "I'm aware of your work at Nyrambla and of your importance there. I will have my aides check in with your senior officers. As needed, you will likely be drawn in to assist with the code breaking work. I'm also well aware that your strong preference is to continue your work there, but we need your expertise in this project.

"As an aside," he smiled somewhat ruefully, "I would like to congratulate you on your marriage. Your presence at Sean's apartment has not gone unnoticed, but your husband informed me of his chief desire to assuage any besmirching of your reputation." He grinned broadly over the frank conversation with Sean shortly after his move to Brisbane.

"Your marriage is under the protection of my knowledge and acceptance. Further, if you receive any pushback, feel free to have my staff intervene. We can't have women convened to the kitchens when there's a war going on. That is all, young lady." He smiled again, as Kate thanked him for his understanding. She was greatly relieved that she and Sean could expect the same acceptance as any other married couple would have.

As the arduous work weeks continued, the days stretched into the cooler wintry month of a Brisbane July. Kate and Sean remained isolated in the pressing work they were handling. Kate worked in the Red Cross building, reviewing topography maps, intricate construction plans and medical data for their planned mobile hospitals, and the new hospital. And Sean, housed in the MacArthur GHQ building, was equally obsessed with managing his work with Chick Parsons.

As was his usual way, other than the inaugural meetings and directives, Douglas MacArthur left the various military teams that surrounded him to their own devices. He had enough on his hands continually waging battle with

Washington, the naval command at Pearl, and the Australian Canberra government over strategic military management.

MacArthur left for a July meeting with Roosevelt, Chester Nimitz, and Roosevelt's Chief of Staff William Leahy, in Hawaii. This conference was not well-received by the general, given that he was not told who he would be meeting with, likely a preventative measure for protection against a potential "Yamamoto" assassination incident.

Despite his strong misgivings, the July Pacific Strategy Conference event proved fruitful. Roosevelt remained as neutral as possible in the ensuing discussions. Admiral Nimitz, who favored a Taiwan landing for the Pacific invasion target, presented his organized, formal plans, and MacArthur presented the plans for the invasion of the Philippines. Roosevelt carefully studied both. Upon the general's return to Brisbane, MacArthur received a call from Roosevelt on August 8, stating that the Philippines target was approved and Leyte would be the landing zone. Nimitz was to provide the accompanying sea coverage for the invasion in the Gulf of Leyte.

Plans were called into action immediately, keeping both Kate and Sean all but overwhelmed with the flurry of activity to set this invasion into motion. They were often consumed up until the wee hours of the morning and seldom had much time for each other, but both knew the greater good of the people around the world was at stake and there were more important things to handle than their marriage at the moment.

In a subsequent meeting with MacArthur, Sean, and Chick Parsons, discussions surrounded every aspect of the work ahead of this planned invasion. As MacArthur mentioned to both men, "The Leyte Operation is to be the most crucial battle of the war in the Pacific. The fate of the Philippines will depend on our victory, as well as the future successful action regarding the war against Japan. My forces will converge with the Central Pacific Forces of Admiral Nimitz in a massive assault."

More forcefully, he continued his little soliloquy, "With Leyte under Allied control, the other islands will be within effective striking distance of land, sea, and air forces. Leyte is the springboard for the conquest of Luzon… and the final attack against Japan itself. We are committed to employing the maximum resources at our command."

All three men knew that a Japanese defeat would turn the tide of the near-invincibility of the Empire of Japan. But the Japanese battle fleet would undoubtedly expend its full efforts to thwart all invasion efforts. As Douglas MacArthur wrapped up the meeting, he stated, "The ultimate strength of both military forces will meet in this one location. For the Allies, a strategic win in the Philippines means land air bases could be used for their Pacific Theater of

Operations. We will achieve this goal with God on our side and the mighty strength of our formidable Allied Forces. And the likes of heroes such as the two of you."

In one of his most brilliant strategic moves, MacArthur had painstakingly covered every aspect of this impending battle: the crucial land invasion, the ensuing sea battle, and the strength of the planned medical bases to keep his forces healthy. Tantamount in each of these was the critical morale of the beleaguered resistance movement in the Philippines. He left absolutely no stone unturned. Sean and Chick knew that to fail in this endeavor would mean the death of thousands of POWs and civilians on the islands. The pressure was immense, but both men were up to the challenge.

CHAPTER FIFTY-ONE

ANNIHILATING THE "OTHER" FOE

With innumerable war projects underway, the various teams were now well into September, buried in their tasks. Up to now, Kate had little time to wonder about the work being undertaken by both Tim and Patrick. In another medical briefing, Kate was informed by MacArthur's staff that the Australian medical malarial experiments in Cairns had stepped up under the purview of MacArthur's Chief Medical Group. As the Red Cross liaison, she was asked to ensure that American doctors actively participated in the experimentation. This would allow for the direct messaging of any immediate breakthroughs to both the Red Cross and the American medical groups. Kate felt that task important enough to requisition Tim and Patrick for their participation, which meant a likely three-month stint in Cairns for both.

To this end, she invited them to dinner one night, so she could convey the "ask" from MacArthur's offices. The dinner was lively. The four friends were together again, enjoying the group conversations and interactions. Sean had decided to bring up the Cairns discussions first, primarily from an "operative" perspective. He could not discuss his missions with Chick; he could, however, explain the position of the battle-weary men on the Pacific Islands.

"From reports based out of the Philippines, the average soldier serving in the Pacific Theater Operation against the Japanese faces tremendous challenges that we can only begin to imagine," Sean conveyed. "Malaria isn't typically fatal to an infected soldier, but it's taking them out of action for a prolonged period— almost as long as being wounded in battle does. We're encountering two types of the disease in the PTO: benign, which causes violent chills, fever, and weakness…and malignant, a form much more likely to cause death. Both turn ready soldiers into deathly ill, bedridden patients in a short period of time."

Kate segued the talks to a medical perspective, adding, "In early 1942, Dr. Neil Fairley, the acting Director of Medicine for the Australian army, traveled with a team of scientists to England and the U.S. to highlight the risk posed by malaria in the Pacific. This trip led to key discussions among MacArthur's staff about the urgency to reduce malarial infection in the Pacific region. You both were involved in the initial MacArthur meetings, where he took the time to address the medical teams in the room regarding this endeavor. With that said, in early June, the Land Headquarters Medical Research Unit was established at the Australian Camp Hospital in Cairns, Queensland." She paused for them to absorb this information.

"The unit's first research experiments were under the directorship of an entomologist named Major Mabel Josephine Mackerras. They involved collecting mosquito pupae of the Anopheles punctulatus group in PNG and flying them to Cairns. They are growing the larvae to maturity in specially built laboratories. Right now, servicemen already carrying P. falciparum or P. vivax gametocytes have been exposed to the adult mosquitoes, which were then used to infect malaria-free volunteers from across Australia. Testing of a new antimalarial drug, atebrine, will be conducted under diverse physical conditions to simulate the war conditions in the jungles, including extremes of temperature and intense physical activity. Thus far, the limited test results have definitively shown during readings of blood smears that atebrine prevented malaria under the most extreme conditions."

Patrick and Tim were already serving as American advisors for the malaria clinics along the Brisbane River. Kate knew they were aware of some of the research work, if not most of the current clinical applications to prevent the spread. As Sean explained MacArthur's request to have American physicians that could report back to him on the findings, both men readily agreed to take the three-month stint in Cairns to serve as MacArthur's liaisons. It was also MacArthur's take that, as surgeons, they could assess and participate in determining the efficacy of atebrine on malaria-afflicted patients undergoing critical surgical procedures. Already serving on the surgical team under Dr. Kirk's staff, both also viewed it as an opportunity to expand their knowledge base further.

❧

KATE AND SEAN accompanied Tim and Patrick for the trek up north. The train ride toward Cairns was slow and almost unbearably stifling, even for August. Filled with thousands of U.S. soldiers soon headed for the front lines in the Pacific jungles, the arduous journey took them first to Townsville, where most of the soldiers were to disembark. Kate meandered up and down the cars, speaking with as many as possible. She made friends with the conductor, whose small daughter Maureen chatted animatedly in the aisles with the men in uniform, often dancing to Shirley Temple tunes on a handheld radio.

Kate watched as the conductor turned to wipe away the tears in his eyes. Both knew what most were thinking as the train passed miles of stark wilderness on their journey north; many of these soldiers were heading on a hellish destination to island battles for which they would never return.

The four guests stayed with Sean's sister, Lilibeth, her husband, Glen, and their two children, five-year-old Molly and three-year-old Max. The home was charming, located directly on the oceanfront in Cairns. There was a long flight of stairs leading to a second floor apartment area which they often sublet to U.S. officers in the area. The downstairs rooms were reserved for the family's use. The upper veranda and porch below were cool and refreshing, situated to invite the tropical ocean breezes to course through the comfortable sitting areas at night.

Lilibeth and Glen were perfect hosts. Their lively children were excited about their uncle and new aunt, giving their pregnant mum some respite from their energetic antics. As a virologist himself, Glen was already involved in the Cairns malaria experiments, and he provided a thorough update to Tim and Patrick on the highlights of the new drug. His introductions to the staff the next morning helped to pave the way for the two surgeons' acceptance on the Australian-based medical teams. Kate and Sean settled in for the next two days, with a slight respite from their routine by way of a diving expedition in the Great Barrier Reef.

A dream dive of Kate's dad Cary was a trek to the famously intricate offshore system of complex reefs, so Kate was anxious to manage a dive in honor of her dad. On the second morning, Kate and Sean rose at dawn, opting to make this impromptu dive in the famous icon with several local divers. A vast system of over 3,000 reefs and hundreds of islands stretching more than 1,250 miles along Australia's northeast coast, the area was richly abundant with life. Green sea turtles, seasonal humpback whales, great schools of dolphins, and a plethora of thousands of colorful fish were juxtaposed amongst the distinctive soft corals endemic to this giant reef system.

The waters off of their chosen dive spot of Green Island were calm and inviting on that morning dive. As they maneuvered themselves with a backward roll into the clear waters, Kate immediately spotted several sizable green sea turtles loitering near them. They dove with their guides, following the turtles for several minutes as they explored the vast coral and sea grasses. Close enough to watch their enormous eyes open and close as they peered at their visitors, the divers marveled at the beauty of their lustrous, green shells and graceful turns and dives.

Kate pointed upward to the sun's rays shining into the depths of the ocean. Just seconds later, she excitedly pulled one of Sean's flippers to point out a humpback whale and calf swimming in the waters ahead of them.

They watched, mesmerized, as the mama and calf rolled together gracefully and then headed for the surface through the surrounding coral reefs.

Their guide pointed out a giant Maori wrasse, fully 6 feet long. The fish seemed content to follow them around playfully in the swift currents for a few minutes. Its vibrant blue-green color flashed brightly against the sun as it swam close by the fascinated divers, displaying its distinct forehead hump as a prominent and distinguishing feature.

The hours spent in the life-giving waters were much too short, and they both reluctantly surfaced for lunch and a breather from the exertion of their undersea exploration. Kate sat on the boat's edge, reflecting on how much her dad would have relished this exploratory dive. Sean watched her as she silently mourned the loss of her father once again. After a quick hug, he left her to her own devices, and she soon joined him again, quiet but not morosely so.

They returned to the coastal home invigorated by their brief respite from their work in Brisbane. On an evening walk with their small niece and nephew, they crossed over an intricate arched covered bridge, spotting two imposing crocodiles as they meandered down the short embankment right next to their path. They held their tiny companions tightly as the gargantuan reptiles plodded into the deep creek several feet below. As Kate conveyed to Lillibeth on their return, her first view of crocodiles was a success only because all four hapless walkers returned unscathed.

The conversation at dinnertime was lively, and Kate found that Sean's sister shared similar personality traits with her mother, Madeleine. Kate was enamored with her new family, and grateful for the consistent welcome into their fold. Later, the adults chatted on the back porch, watching the waves roll in languidly onto the pristine shoreline. Kate contentedly rocked little Max to sleep. As an idyllic moon rose over the ocean, the conversation finally waned. Nearing midnight, the contented couple fell fast asleep in each other's arms, exhausted from their extended but productive day.

The next morning, they visited the Land Headquarters Medical Research Unit to meet Major Mackerras and tour the laboratories. With Glen's connections, the introduction of Patrick and Tim to Mabel was successful. The major was delighted by the attention to her research, especially at the request of the famous American general. The party from Brisbane was unanimously impressed with her dedication and competent research work. The young Lawrences left early that afternoon, satisfied that the extensive malaria research would protect hundreds of thousands of lives and countless soldiers.

The trip home was tediously long, but Sean had secured the small private car reserved for military leaders for their return trip. They finally had some time to talk, for once uninterrupted by their busy careers and the continual, omnipresent talk of the war efforts. Kate enjoyed the variety of the Queensland countryside and the luxury of the small dining car. Their long journey back to Brisbane was relatively peaceful. They both knew the break was the last one for many months.

CHAPTER FIFTY-TWO

MIDNIGHT IN MINDANAO

The young couple arrived home much elated by the successful trip to Cairns. However, within two days of the respite came Sean's summons yet again to MacArthur's chambers to meet with Chick Parsons. After the initial submarine missions that brought Parsons to Mindanao, submarine supply operations had become a regular occupation for both Sean and Chick. Sean worked tirelessly with Danilo and Yarran's radio team in Papua New Guinea to ensure that Aboriginal signals were utilized as the sole form of communication with the subs.

For Sean, who had managed at least one week-long underwater passage to the Philippines, this was hazardous work. Once safely ensconced in the jungles, Chick was, as he pointed out to Sean, on relatively safe ground— and in his home territory. A master of disguises, he famously moved in and out of the villages with confidence and ease. Sometimes, within plain sight of the Japanese. But the hidden allied submarine waiting for his subsequent return was in a constant life-and-death battle to avoid Japanese subs, enemy mines, and strafing Zeros.

Once the U.S. Navy received word of the triumph of the coastwatcher stations set up by Parsons and his team, as well as the rejuvenated spirits of the ragtag guerrilla teams deep within the jungles, they were happy to provide additional submarines for the guerrilla supply runs. Thus, two of the most modern of the fleet of submarines in the Navy, the *USS Narwhal* and *USS Nautilus*, began regular missions to the Philippines. The priceless supplies of generators, tons of ammunition, medical supplies, clothing, and food were received, stored away from enemy discovery, and distributed to emotionally and physically exhausted guerrilla teams.

As the months passed, these clandestine trips became more legendary among the coastal radiomen who relayed the success stories, the Allied Forces promoted Sean to the rank of commander in the Allied Armed Forces and captain in his Australian Navy for his celebrated reef scouting and various sub maneuvering measures. Sean made a tremendous effort to guarantee successful code transmissions by transposing a codebook of the most easily audible Wurundjeri words.

This vastly decreased the possibility of a garbled message causing a critical signal to be missed.

Principal among the valued supply distributions was the dispersal of wildcat radios to areas unoccupied by Japanese Forces. The jungles between these tiny outposts and Filipino barrios carried word at lightning speed; the thought of hearing General Douglas MacArthur's voice transmitted them even faster.

MacArthur's teams of Comms specialists had the foresight to know that the building of the strongest radio broadcasting network ever put to use by U.S. technology would be put to greater use as a promise to return and avenge the people of the Philippines was broadcasted. From the crackling airwaves thousands of miles away in Brisbane, the radios in tiny villages all over the islands carried the robust and booming voice of the Supreme Commander, saying, "*I shall return! I have not forgotten!*"

Almost more brilliant than the brief speech, though, was the playing of the Philippine National Anthem before the resounding dialogue from Australia. As a result, mountain tents, coastwatchers huts, and hidden basements all reveled in these propitious moments like no Filipino holiday celebration ever commemorated before.

Unfortunately, the subsequent summons of Commander Lawrence to MacArthur's Chambers was the preamble to highly vocal discord between the Lawrences.

Sean returned from a day of meetings just as Kate returned home from work with the mobile hospital planning unit. She knew from his face that he was summoned again for more ultra-secret work. That he was unwilling even to speak of the meetings was enough for her to realize that the assignment would be perilous.

The following week was tense. Sean mentioned as he stopped by briefly at Kate's apartment one evening that he would be heading to Canberra for another critical "Signals meeting" with Curtain and MacArthur's top military aides. Troubled by his avoidance of what she considered routine questions about the trip, she headed off to sleep, finding that the growing unease between them was causing a separation that she found both unacceptable and unavoidable.

The next evening, Sean decided to stay overnight at Kate's apartment and take a breather from his late-night work. Curious about his willingness to leave his quarters where most of his work was handled, she nonetheless planned a private dinner catered by the Lennon Hotel staff, making an effort to work through the barrier between them.

After dinner, they managed a brief stroll through the Brisbane Botanic Gardens, but the conversation was constrained. Kate was more than a little disturbed about their inability to work through the silence. They returned to a bottle of chilled wine, and she moved to the sofa to pour the Pinot Grigio that her husband uncorked. Sean turned to the corner window to raise it, inviting in the crisp night breezes from the river. Kate bridged the conversation first.

"Would you care to talk about *us*, Sean? We've been so distant lately, and I want to find out how we can work through that distance. Neither of us seems to know how to make things right between us at this point."

Sean turned and approached his wife, unbuttoning his shirt as he moved toward her, his sharp eyes penetrating hers and daring her to stop him.

"No, I wouldn't, Kate. At this point, it seems that lately, our best form of communication is by making love, and I feel like communicating *that* way."

He surprised her with his approach… in equal turns demanding and yet almost suppliant. Moving to the sofa, his hard body was suddenly on top of hers, his arms holding most of his weight above her body. Kate sensed he was also taking cues from her… ready to stop if he met any resistance. He met none. She was just as willing to see how far he would go to repair the rift, and this was a new approach for her, captivating in the intensity and the boldness.

It took seconds for them to be fully naked and intertwined, and the passion between them was raw. As his mouth explored, his hands slid purposely up her arms and he reached her wrists, pinning them beside her shoulders as she moved to let him enter her. He was almost primal in his need. She met his force with an equal force of her own. The air in the room was brisk, but their bodies glistened as they continued their lovemaking. Moments later, they both collapsed, satiated and replete. He rolled to move her on top, and Kate's head rested on his chest, neither moving after their vigorous coupling.

Sean reached out to stroke her hair affectionately, and after a few minutes of a contented silence, he whispered softly, "I love you, Kate Lawrence. The moments like this between us are pure magic, and they take away every ounce of anger and frustration. You possess my soul, just as you own my heart. Nothing can come between that kind of love." She answered in kind, "My anger never lasts beyond that first incredible kiss. I wish we could always stay this way." Curling up against him, they fell asleep thus, and the world was right once again.

After a day of fairly industrious intimacy, he left for his meetings in Canberra. The next morning, Kate took a small gift to his apartment for his return home, regretting her initial frustration over his secrecy. She entered his flat to find an envelope under the door. Thinking it might have been intended for the trip, she opened it.

The words were terse and ominous. "New orders. Mindanao at midnight. Second drop. Tacloban site. Parsons." Along with the note was an Australian naval compensation form labeled *Hazard Compensation— Next of Kin.* Attached to the paper was a reminder that said, "Required prior to next mission."

Kate sat down, knees shaking so hard that her legs could not support her.

TEN DAYS LATER, Sean returned to Brisbane near midnight on a Saturday evening. Exhausted, he slept hard for the next seven hours. Finishing some critical reporting for the next day, in the early evening he finally walked the scant few blocks to the Lennon Hotel. There was no sign of Kate there and no sign that her apartment had been occupied in the last few days. Mystified by her absence, he ambled down to the Red Cross building and found that she had left work early that day. When he asked where she was, one of the nurses responded, "You might want to try her friends' apartment. She's staying there while they're out of town. Patrick, right? Or is it Tim?"

Sean located a staff car for the drive to Patrick and Tim's apartment in nearby New Farm. He knocked sharply, only to find a surprised and subdued Kate standing at the door, clad in a sheer gown and robe. Surprised, he commented dryly, "Have you grown tired of the two places we have to ourselves? Looking for a change of pace, eh?"

She let him in— fists clenched, but unwilling to start an argument at that moment. There was no greeting or requisite kiss.

"Hmmm. What's behind the cold shoulder? I'm unsure why I'm being greeted by a puckish wife as if I got home late for the requisite evening meal. Whatever's on your mind, Kate?" he offered as an opener to the conversation.

She moved backward slightly, turning to seat herself on a nearby chair. Responding in a slightly caustic tone, she said softly, "I think I made it abundantly clear that we should be as open and honest as possible in our marriage. So can you tell me where you have been the past 10 days?"

Seeing the resolve on her face, he moved to stand next to the small fireplace, eyeing her closely. He turned to watch her reaction when he finally found the words to open the conversation. A few moments passed and the tension in the room was palpable. Finally, Sean entered the small kitchen area and poured water into a tea kettle, lighting the stove as he spoke.

As he worked in the kitchen, he responded in an even tone, "Do you mind starting out with any questions you might have? I have all night. And from the looks of it," pointing at her attire, "it appears you plan on staying here as well. I just need to know what is bothering you."

Kate picked up her medical satchel on a corner chair, removing an envelope. Silently, she passed it on to Sean, moving to the sofa to wait for him as he read it. He folded it and placed it in his pocket.

"Where did you get this, Kate? It was for my eyes only." His eyes flashed something she didn't understand, and their intensity frightened her.

She paused for a second, curling her legs underneath her, then answered in a measured tone, "I went to your apartment to place a gift on the table for when you returned. This was under the door, along with another form." She pulled out another piece of paper and he perused it silently.

"Again. As I said, it was marked for me, Kate. The contents were highly sensitive. I understand your curiosity, but I never thought you'd open my military documents!" He chose his words carefully, working to keep Kate's temper in check.

"There's no military seal on the documents. So, what you are telling me is that I had no right to read a piece of paper under the door of our shared apartment? You've always said, 'What's mine is yours! I have no secrets!' Where does that leave me, Sean?"

After a lengthy spate of silence, he spoke. The controlled response belied the frustration as he sought to control the damage of her knowing the intent behind the document's contents. He replied in an even, calm tone, "I cannot tell you where I was. I wish I could, but if you knew, I could bloody well be court-martialed, as it goes against MacArthur's expressed commands. It's for your own good that you know less than nothing about my current missions. Believe me, more harm than good will follow."

He let the words soak in and then waited to see if she would respond. Deliberately, she uncurled her body and placed both legs on the floor. Her words were careful and intentional:

"Sean, obviously, this was a hazardous mission you undertook. Where and why, I have no earthly idea, but I am honestly terrified right now. I wish I could make you understand the kind of fear a woman deals with at times like these. Think about it. You decide *not* to tell your wife that you are leaving on a mission for which you might never return. You just expect her to get down on her knees and pray faithfully every night, not even knowing in which direction she *needs* to pray, because she has no clue where on this bloody planet you might be heading. Do you know how difficult it is to watch you walk out the door, believing innocuously that you're on some cockamamie retreat with government officials? And then I find out you're possibly getting shot at, probably captured, then certainly tortured, and finally meeting with a violent, painful death?"

He paused to reflect on her words before responding. "Kate, darling. Millions of soldiers embark on even more dangerous missions, and their wives haven't known a bloody thing about their part in this war for *months* on end. It is what it is. It is the absolute *hell* of war. All I can tell you is that what I am doing will help expedite the end of this damnable war. I'm being careful. And I'm protected about as much as any officer can ever possibly be while they're managing their duties. I can arrange a signal from Yarran or Danilo, or Commander Parsons, to let you know I'm safe. But I cannot— and will not— be able to tell you what I'm doing or where I'm going. That's all I can say."

He moved into the kitchen again, finishing the chamomile tea he had started for both of them. Bringing the tea and some scones as a sort of burnt offering, they sat in silence as they drank, both recovering from the intensity of their marital discussion.

Exhausted, Kate announced in a determined tone, "I would greatly like for you to give me some credit for all of my prior discretion and tolerance about your work, Sean. I have never complained before now. I've been doing my best to provide space and leniency as you manage your work. But you *are* obsessed— to the great detriment of our marriage at this point."

She let those words hang in the thickness of the tension in the room. Standing up, she headed toward one of the bedrooms. In an air of finality on the subject, she spoke as she turned toward her husband:

"I'm going to bed. You are welcome to stay," she said resignedly, "but I'm asking that you take Patrick's room on that side of the apartment and I'll sleep in Tim's room. Good night. We'll talk later when our heads are better cleared."

The next morning found them amiable enough, but both were still immersed in their thoughts. Their silence, and the tremendous stress both were enduring continued to take its toll on the marriage.

⸙

AS THEY CROSSED into September, Kate had made it clear that she understood his reasoning, but she asked only that he not "volunteer" for any suicidal missions. They were not estranged, yet they were not a typical couple either. For any other marriage, this discord would have been a significant barrier. But these were far from ordinary times for thousands of couples worldwide. Hoping for the best after this epic battle in the Pacific, they concentrated as never before on making every detail of their work count.

At the final joint meeting in early October of all medical and military officers, they were informed that they were on a top-secret mission.

Accompanying naval fleets would set sail from the far corners of the South and Central Pacific. The blackboard in the "War Room" in Brisbane set the expectations of the mission, and simultaneously, the destination:

October 20th, 1944. A-Day for the Pacific invasion:

Leyte, Philippines

The mood was somber, expectant, and engrossing for the personnel absorbing the words. Every person to a man— and woman— was eager for the invasion to commence. They were ecstatic, even. If this invasion was successful, the end of the war was nearing. On October 10th, Kate and the entourage of medical and military teams responsible for the Allied Expeditionary Hospital flew to Manus, in northern Papua New Guinea. They boarded the *USS Nashville* and a sister ship, along with MacArthur and his support staff, on October 16th.

On that same day, Commander Chick Parsons was flown to Leyte by a long-range "Black Cat" PBY. Commander Sean Lawrence accompanied him on the mission. They were tasked by MacArthur himself to scout the invasion landing areas, to make contact with local guerrillas in the vicinity, and finally, to protect civilians near the planned bombardment areas. All of this had to be accomplished without revealing details of the imminent invasion.

A daunting mission, to be sure. But both were well-primed for their tasks.

Every effort was to be expended by millions of military personnel to ensure that this Leyte operation would succeed. To fail would be unthinkable. Too many innocent lives depended on the assembled strength of the Allied Forces. And thousands of vulnerable POWs were dependent on the grace of an Almighty God they each prayed fervently to every night… for protection and for triumph over a heretofore indomitable foe.

The largest and most multidimensional invasion ever to embark upon this earth sailed from multiple ports to converge as a "perfect storm" against the Imperial Japanese Navy. When they hit their knees, every man and woman in the invasion operative was thinking just the same: hoping that the grace and mercy of an Almighty God would prevail upon them as well.

The calm seas before them were a strong and reassuring omen.

CHAPTER FIFTY-THREE

I HAVE RETURNED!

U.S. Army official photo

The heavens proved to be on the side of the approaching Allied fleet. Thankfully, the task force met near-perfect weather and sea conditions during the voyage. Leyte's deep-water gulf and sandy beaches proved to be clear paths for tank-infantry operations. Tacloban Airfield was attested as a highly suitable choice for the airfield and hospital construction, a monumental task which was initiated immediately after the successful clearing of the beaches. The only challenge anticipated during this late landing was projected seasonal monsoon rains. Thus far, though, even the seasonal rains had held off.

The island's population consisted of over 900,000 people. Mostly rural villagers and fishermen, they would assist the American invasion from within. It *was* the absolute perfect storm.

By 1400 hours on A-Day, the beaches at Leyte were secured and triage tents were forming at the edge of the dunes. The nearby palms provided shade to those needing medical attention. By sunset, the Sixth Army had already advanced one-mile deep and over five miles wide. The 24th Infantry Division had taken the high ground commanding the beachheads as the supplies were unloaded onto the shore. With Tacloban Airfield secure to the north, more supplies for the troops could be offloaded via planes from the naval ships as well. The X Corps, composed of the 1st Cavalry and the 24th Infantry Divisions, had landed on Leyte carrying 30 days of medical supplies.

With light enemy opposition now, the unloading was almost uninterrupted, and the massive efforts of the undertaking were proving to be organized, and efficient. Tim and Patrick would be landing within the next hour. Both thoracic surgeons were charged with managing one sector of the intricate mobile surgical tents, as they had been trained to do extensively in Australia under MacArthur's specific request.

Kate watched as one of the senior officers from the XXIV Corps ordered the setting of the temporary medical tents directly behind a row of palms, closer to the interior swampland. She moved to his side to quickly suggest a change of venue.

"Sir, if I may say so, you do not want the surgical units to be that close to the interior swamps and stagnant water. You'll be inundated with mosquitos by setting up camp so close to their breeding ground. Get as close to the seawater as possible, preferably this side of the beach," she said, pointing to the palms nearest the surf.

"I have some useful oils I've packed in one of the medical shipments that will help in keeping those pests away. Trust me, mosquitos will rapidly become your worst enemy once you get settled in!" Kate smiled as she spoke, seeing his somewhat skeptical initial reaction morph into a look of curiosity by the end of her dialogue.

The XXIV Corps, which had trained in Hawaii in preparation for the assault, had advanced from the Hawaiian Islands on September 15, 1944 to their newly acquired Philippines target. Equipment for the corps had been palletized to permit easy handling and loading into smaller crafts. Once on the beach, runners with sleds advanced them quickly to their initial location near the newly constructed surgical tents. The pallets were waterproofed to facilitate unloading through the surf.

These improvements were gleaned from the D-Day landings and implemented in the invasion here. The beaches were now organized into a smooth, efficient operation. At Tacloban, more supplies for the assault troops could be offloaded via planes from the naval ships.

As hundreds of medical support teams were setting up surgical units, Kate's forward medical team was to scour the jungles for wounded and to evaluate the immediate medical needs of the casualties they located. Information was key to assessing the type of topography they were encountering, the injuries relative to the terrain, the enemy resistance, and where their forward medical patrols could temporarily encamp.

As Kate rested for a brief moment, she and two of her corpsmen watched from a short distance as MacArthur and the few selected media corps waded through the waters off of Red Beach and onto the shore. There was no rehearsal or multiple takes to get the best shot. Turns out, the best image was the first one… a gruff MacArthur wading through the water because the advanced floating supply piers were not yet set up for his landing craft to dock. It was a great media moment in history, rehearsed or not. The set lips and determined expression – all were perfect manifestations of a man who virtually made well-recorded history wherever he went.

Three other medics sat down on the fallen palm beside her, watching the scene before them in awe.

"We are watching history here," one of them said. "I guess this media moment has been staged to get it right for all the folks back home!" As the reporters buzzed around MacArthur and his officers, Kate responded, "There's no staging going on here. He's bloody pissed. I know the man well. For once, I don't think he gives a tinker's damn about the photographers!"

As all of her companions turned in surprise, the younger of the medics said incredulously, "You have met the man?"

Kate responded calmly, "I was responsible for the care of his young son, Arthur, in Manila in '41. I was part of a military mission there all the way to Corregidor." She smiled as she rose, hoisting her rucksack onto her shoulder and walking away, leaving mouths gaping in surprise. Somewhat grudgingly, the men had a new admiration for the lone female medic on the beach. With the efforts on the beachhead well under progress, Kate turned to study the swampy areas further away from the dunes, thinking silent thoughts of Sean and his work with Commander Parsons.

By evening, the landing zones were one long, massive supply depot with a well-orchestrated series of mobile hospital tents underway. Any wounded were triaged, and the dead were removed to transports several hundred yards beyond the beach. Kate's team rested up again before the evening's work. Now approaching dusk, their squad was ordered to work with recon patrols to search the areas further into the jungles and swamplands.

Replenishing her rucksack with supplies, Kate headed off with her patrol. As the sun fell, the impenetrable darkness of the jungle left them forming a tighter unit to keep watch over each other as they surveyed the surrounding areas west of the hills and into the swamps beyond. The group was silent as they managed this dangerous task, without assurances that the jungles on this path were fully cleared of enemy scouts and stray soldiers. They returned successfully an hour later, recovering two dead bodies and delivering several lightly wounded and fatigued young soldiers to the triage tents.

Removing her helmet and cap, Kate rested briefly to study her maps. She and three of her corpsmen watched from a short distance as the media corps moved around Red Beach, scouring the shorelines for propitious photo opportunities. Long after nightfall, following several hours setting up the medical tents, Kate found a resting spot under a palm tree, with several other medics. Digging into the soft sand to make an indentation for her hips, she moved to find a comfortable position, resting her weary head on her rucksack. With the waves lapping gently onto the shore some yards away and the distant sound of the medical tents still being readied, she fell into a hard sleep.

At dawn, Kate was awakened by the whirring motors of another wave of supply boats landing on the beach. Tim and Patrick had landed, with the secondary wave of medical teams and the subsequent waves of engineers. Both thoracic surgeons were assigned to initiate mobile surgical units, under MacArthur's express request. After their responsibilities here on the beach were completed, both of the men and Kate would take up positions in the newly established permanent hospital at Tacloban Airfield. As a part of MacArthur's selected advance team, the three of them knew what most on the beach were unaware of; the anticipated naval battle would begin soon. Depending on the heaviness of the sea battle, casualties could begin arriving simultaneously from both the jungles and the seas. They were preparing for the worst and would need all medical experts on hand.

Volunteering to lead the final medical patrols at dusk, Kate busied herself during the morning and afternoon administering some of her insecticide oils to the mosquito netting outside the tent walls. Grateful for Tim and Patrick's arrival, the three friends worked tirelessly, stopping only for a few minutes' rest and for requisite rations. By 1700 hours, the area looked well organized, coordinated, and ready for the expected casualties.

An hour before sunset, now wearing medical armbands to identify them to U.S. infantry, Kate joined a patrol team, setting out together to respond to radio calls for medical support nearby. Taking the westernmost trail, over an hour later they reached a small hill on a sandy, wooded path. As they stopped to rest, in the dark recesses of the jungle they heard a branch snap above. All ten in the small patrol unit crouched, listening intently for any further movement that would identify the source.

Deadly silence penetrated the surrounding jungle. In the darkness, a beam of moonlight glimmered fleetingly through a branch, illuminating the white areas on Kate's armband. She moved quickly toward the shadows. As she moved, sharp staccato blasts rang from above, and bullets whizzed beside her. Kate twisted and felt the sickening thud of a bullet hitting flesh.

Almost simultaneously, another grazed her temple as the first bullet passed through her right side, nicking the outer portion of the lowest rib. The pain was searing. A third bullet hit the gun in her waistband and glanced off as she lunged away from the light again. The returning fire around her instantly took the Japanese sniper down from the tree. He was dead before he hit the ground.

Adrenaline still flowing, the team circled tensely, watching for further movement. As they moved cautiously, a second sniper leaped from a nearby palm, jumping onto the end of a fallen log where Kate was staunching her wound. With lightning speed, the Bowie knife from her fatigues was in her right hand. This time, the moonlight was in her favor, and she stabbed the Japanese soldier forcefully, aiming under the ribs and toward the heart.

He fell onto her right side, and bullets from friendly fire whizzed above her as she toppled backward. As she fell, the last thoughts before unconsciousness mercifully overcame her were of her sister's face— her beautiful twin beside her in the jungle, pushing her to the safety of the ground. Kate could see Kerri's face perfectly, her eyes set in a determined, protective expression. Then Kate's head smashed hard against a broken branch, and the blackest of nights set in.

WHEN SHE AWOKE, her mind groggy from anesthesia and blood loss, she turned her head sluggishly as Tim filled a syringe and injected her with the vial's contents. "Just a little morphine, Kate. It'll help you sleep." He moved over to assess her chart and carefully examined her surgical wounds.

"Where am I? My unit . . . they need me…"

Tim sat down beside her. "I don't think you're going anywhere soon, Kate. You have a lot of healing to manage. You were shot. Do you remember any of that?"

"My unit . . . the patrols . . ." she mumbled. Her anxiety was rising as she fought to recover from her groggy state.

"I need to . . . go back." She began struggling to sit up. Tim gently covered her with a blanket, hoping the morphine would take effect soon.

"Sean . . . I want Sean…" She drifted off again.

EARLY THE NEXT MORNING, Kate was awakened by a medical team entering the recovery tent. She recognized Patrick, who was introducing himself to the new staff nurse attending her, along with Tim. Patrick pulled up a chair next to her cot, smiling, "You've had *quite* an ordeal here, Kate. How's your pain management?"

Evading the question, weakly, she called out, "Sean . . . he's out there. And my unit— I need to be there."

Patrick smiled. "Your unit's long gone, Kate. You've been out cold for a couple of days now. Healing comes first and then you'll be assessed for service. I highly doubt you'll be allowed back into the jungles. But we'll see."

She tried to sit up, struggling with Patrick until two staff members helped to lie her back down. Still struggling to remove his grip, Kate finally turned her head, defeated. Her mind began to falter again, her eyesight blurring rapidly with the effects of the morphine. She watched vaguely as Tim moved to open the flap to the tent across the room.

"You can see her now. She's weak and won't remember much of your little reunion here, but she'll know that you're here when she wakes up next," Tim instructed.

～ell～

CAPTAIN SEAN LAWRENCE entered the medical tent. His tall visage dwarfed the structure and he had to duck as his head glanced the canvas roof. Kneeling low to Kate, he kissed her gently, saying in a voice strangely pinched and strained, "I'm here, darling. I'm with you, Kate. You need to get some rest. I'll be back for you later. I promise." Kate sighed. The tears flowed freely as his warm hands clasped her cool, clammy ones. She finally slipped further into oblivion.

EPILOGUE

THIS DAMNABLE WAR!

When Sean returned later, Kate was stirring again.

As a nearby nurse checked her vital signs, Tim's voice echoed from outside the tent flap. Sean could hear every word as Tim spoke to Patrick outside:

"We're getting the orders written up. Kate's about ten weeks pregnant. She's heading back to Australia as soon as she can travel. We need to protect this baby and the pregnancy."

Sean exited the tent, joining the two men talking outside. His anxiety and surprise registered as he confronted his two friends for more details. "Does she know? And are you certain she's pregnant? She's had false alarms before," Sean said apprehensively.

"We don't think she knows and, yes, we're certain. She's been examined, and all signs are present," Patrick said as Sean turned directly to him for further answers.

Tim responded next. "I don't think Kate would ever remotely risk losing a baby. If she even suspected it, though, she likely didn't want to find out until after she returned to Brisbane. She came for you, Sean. Nothing could have stopped her from being here to find you."

From inside the tent, the nurse called out urgently, "Dr. Taylor! Dr. Danforth!"

Tim and Patrick reentered the tent, with Tim blocking Sean's entry to prevent him from interfering with the medical staff. Kate was thrashing in pain as the young nurse attempted to hold her down. Examining her, Patrick said urgently, "Her stitches are reopening with all of this activity. We need to get her back into surgery. I'll prepare the surgical team."

Tim sat beside Kate on the bed. As the staff surrounded Kate to prep her, he held her down gently, remembering sharply that he had managed the same for his own wife, Kerri, on her last day of life. A needle jabbed into Kate's arm, and she began to lose consciousness again.

"I won't let you die, Kate. Not on my watch!" Sean murmured as he stood at the tent's entrance, remembering the last time he'd whispered those agonizing words.

HOURS LATER, SHE STIRRED, recognizing groggily that someone was holding her hand. A low, soft voice said, "Good morning, sleepyhead. How are you feeling?"

It was music to her ears. Eyes still closed with the heaviness of the effects of the drugs, her head turned toward Sean's voice and she replied weakly, "I must be hallucinating that you're here, Sean Douglas. It's a rather bewitching dream." She smiled and nodded off once again, still reeling from the effects of the anesthesia.

When Kate awoke again, she was able to sit up, grateful that most of the anesthesia had finally worn off. Holding her stomach, she grimly said, "I'm a little nauseous. I am guessing the anesthesia disagrees with my innards." She smiled feebly. Sean took her hands in his, silent for a moment, his head bowed with strong emotions: fear, excitement, and wonder.

Finally, he raised his head and responded, "It's not the anesthesia, Kate. You're going to have a baby, my darling wife. *Our* baby. And I'm absurdly thrilled with the news." He gave her a wide grin and announced, "I'll take at least *half* of the blame for your condition."

Kate sat up gingerly, wide-eyed and alert from that blunt announcement. As she looked into his eyes, her own formed unshed tears. She looked down in awe at her slightly enhanced belly. "Twins, I'm hoping. To make up for the lost parenting time, Sean!"

The two of them were in their own world, chatting for a time, sharing their emotions and joy over the happy news.

A short time later, Tim, Patrick, and the army's chief medical officer entered the recovery tent. The officer, Kenneth Brannish, was the first to speak.

"Kate, were you aware that you are expecting?" The tone was questioning but relatively gentle. Kate responded emphatically, "No, I was not. I was so busy preparing for the medical work on the invasion that I assumed that stress was causing an imbalance in my body."

"We plan on sending you back to Brisbane to let you recover. It may be several weeks or so before you can journey. But we'll get you there. You need to be home recovering and preparing for a new family addition," Brannish said soberly.

With a sigh, Kate responded, "Well, you're wasting your breath with that little speech. I came here with a job to do and I'm going to manage it."

Before Sean could interrupt, she summoned her energy to continue resolutely, "I know all of the arguments you can produce. But the biggest one— that I need recovery time and decent maternity care— is a moot point. I won't break just because I'm pregnant. First, you literally have some of the best doctors on this island if I have *any* medical needs. And I'm being pampered far more than any pregnant woman caught up in this war. Second, I won't be coddled, and I won't be whisked away to safety because none of *them* have been given that privilege. Finally, I will be under far more stress by being thousands of miles away and worrying myself sick because I'm not here. You can tuck me away at the new Tacloban hospital, doing the job I'm charged with managing. That's all there is to it!"

Dr. Brannish looked at Kate's determined face and mustered up a response. "I will leave this decision to my superiors, and their decision will be final, but I will allow them to hear your arguments at least. You'll be under their orders, but I will at least consider your requests as a fellow medical officer of equal rank." With that, he exited the medical tent.

Kate insisted on changing into her officer's uniform to emphasize her position. Wincing painfully as the nurse helped her change, she rested afterward, preparing resolutely for the next battle. Two hours later, the same party reentered her recovery tent. As Kate studied their faces, the tent flap opened again. In walked none other than Douglas MacArthur, himself, with two aides. He greeted Kate warmly. With equal amounts of respect and affection, he stated directly to her, "I'm to understand that you are rejecting orders to return to Australia. I also am aware that Commander Lawrence has complicated this medical situation by putting one of my best medical officers in a family way!" He smiled and winked at Sean during that comment.

Continuing in a stern, commanding voice, he stated, "I agreed with your assessment, Kate, and thus I overrode the medical concerns. We need you in this operation. You were instrumental in many decisions, and your loss will cause delays in this new hospital build if you're *not* involved. Your condition will be assessed regularly by Dr. Brannish. Sean will be the deciding factor in your return home."

With that definitive statement, Kate's personal battle was over. There was a war to be fought, and she was supremely pleased that she was still in it. MacArthur faced the officers in the tent as one of his aides signaled for two photographers to enter the tent.

Turning back to Kate, he said, "to quote my one-time senior aide, Dwight D. Eisenhower, during his D-Day speeches,

"The eyes of the world are upon you. The hopes and prayers of liberty-loving people everywhere march with you."

As he spoke, he removed an object from a box handed to him by one of the aides, and pinned a Purple Heart on Kate's uniform. As Kate saluted him, the cameras flashed and, with a final salute to her, MacArthur smiled and stated as he exited the tent:

"Now, let's go and win this damnable war, shall we?"

Contemplating the book in Tasmania...

ABOUT THE AUTHOR...

Pamela Zdenek is passionate about history, travel, and especially, life with her family. The idea for her first historical fiction novel, *The Southern Cross,* was spawned while sitting at Douglas MacArthur's desk in Brisbane, Australia, where he conducted much of the war. Pam lived in Brisbane for almost two years, enjoying research for the book and relishing every moment in the inspiring scenery of this exquisite country. To quote her writing mantra, "The beauty of historical fiction is that with history as the ever-fascinating backdrop, fictional characters add the elements of natural human faults and foibles that greatly enhance the facts surrounding actual events."

Pam currently resides in Texas. In her spare time, her hobbies are pickleball, ethnic cooking, hiking trips, and adventure traveling to foreign countries, with her wonderful husband of over 42 years.

Together they have raised four children, who eventually "fled the homeland", scattering throughout Texas, Colorado and California. Hence, the vast travel.

Prior to writing novels, Pam worked in the energy field in regulatory and government affairs, serving on numerous committees in a variety of markets, and representing corporations in industry organizations. She now writes full time, and is working on her second novel, *The Southern Cross* sequel, **Cygnus**.

Find Pamela here:

Website: pamelazdenekbooks.com
Email: pamelazdenekbooks@gmail.com

Facebook Author Page:

Into each life, a little rain must fall.
~ Henry Wadsworth Longfellow

For my Daddy
June 8, 1992

All that I am or ever hope to be I owe to your dedication, and for giving me the most unfaltering love and special moments a child could ever know. I am eternally grateful to you for being there throughout the many bumps and bruises of early childhood. I hope I make you proud every single day when I look up at the Heavens and ask you to smile down so I can feel the warmth of the sunshine in your soul again. A part of my heart will always be dancing on your feet in Heaven. And as always, save the last dance for your special baby girl please… the youngest twin.

For my beautiful twin, Patricia Jeanne
January 21, 2000

As long as I sing your sweet, sweet song, as long as I remember the sound of your voice, and as long as the cherished memories ring deep into my soul… on the days when the loss hits hardest, the best part of you– not the deep sorrow I feel– will be the only part I carry openly in my heart. Half of me left with you when you gained your Heavenly Wings. I always felt that it was the "better half" and I'm doing my best to mirror your kind heart, your beautiful soul, and your compassion for others. I'll do my best to honor you and carry on. Until we can be together again… I pray every day that you keep sending me the signs, so I can feel your strength by my side once more.

For my precious niece, Jessica Marie ~ Pat's darling girl
June 22, 2014

Cancer beat the hell out of you, twice. But it never took away your heart or
your spirit. You taught us all to carry this pain with such dignity and grace,
and with every ounce of courage, through your incredible example. Thank
you for the honor of being your other mom after your own mommy left us. I
pray I never failed you in that bittersweet endeavor. Being there by your side
as you gave birth to your own daughter was one of the most memorable
moments of joy for me. Holding you as you left these Earthly bonds for ones
in Heaven was both the hardest and the most poignant moment in my life. I
will miss you forever, Jessica, but you are the stars that twinkle one last time
before the sun peeks out across the early morning sky.

For my beloved nephew Nathaniel Vincent ~
December 16, 2023

Thank you for the gift of being your other mom with Aunt Mary, along with
your wonderful and dedicated parents, Randy and Belinda. Between the 8
children we all raised together, you always knew you had the love,
encouragement, and the discipline of 6 parents when one of you misbehaved!
Now there are 7… and my heart aches with that life change. Those were
horrific days after the fire that took your life… waiting for news, and hoping
for that "miracle" that never came. So many strangers told us of your
wonderful, soulful heart, your dedication to your daughter, and your loyalty to
your many friends. You were always by their sides when they needed you, no
matter what! And now ALWAYS in everyone's hearts. We miss you so, Nate!

PROFESSIONAL ACKNOWLEDGEMENTS:

This book would not have been possible without the vast talents, the professionalism, and the monumental efforts of the following:

~ The cover design was performed by graphics art designer Gary Zdenek at GaryZDesigns. He also produced the back cover design and managed the ISBN details and publishing logo. The support between him and his lovely wife Diana was monumental. I cannot thank them enough for their help.

~ The initial interior layout was managed by the very talented Melissa Stevens of *The Illustrated Author*. I cannot thank her enough for designing a creative format that allowed me to envision the final product of the book.
(www.theillustratedauthor.com)

~ The final interior design and the creation of the end product for publishing was managed by the layout and interior design genius of Jen Houser of *Painted Wings Publishing*. An accomplished author, artist and designer, her many talents lent a professional polish to the end product of my dream novel.
(www.PaintedWingsPublishing.com)

~ And last but not least, my first reader (besides my dedicated hubby) and by far the best critic was Christine Schultz. Besides her vast marketing talents, finding ALL the right connections, and her website design genius, she is the greatest and the most dedicated supporter, and now, a beautiful friend. I am indebted to her forever.
(www.thedaxexpression.com)

www.ingramcontent.com/pod-product-compliance
Lightning Source LLC
Chambersburg PA
CBHW030922300726

48970CB00001B/273